FOUR-LEAF CLOVER

THE TRENT RIVERA MYSTERIES

BLAKE VALENTINE

Published by CRED PRODUCTIONS, 2024.

This is a work of fiction. Similarities to real people, places, or events are entirely coincidental.

FOUR-LEAF CLOVER

First edition. July 15, 2024.

Copyright © 2024 BLAKE VALENTINE.

Written by BLAKE VALENTINE.

PROLOGUE.

The man stood back, admiring the tableau through the gritted teeth of a grimace. He was dressed head-to-toe in black. The once grand barroom of The Diplomat Hotel was lit only by the ghostly shaft of moonlight that cut through its broken first-floor windows; they looked out upon the town of South Quay through sad, vacant eyes. Years before, the establishment had been *the* place to stay; *the* place to be seen; the jewel in the crown of the south coast. A holiday El Dorado for the superior set who wished to rattle their jewellery in the faces of all those they perceived as being beneath them.

But that was long ago. It stood now, abandoned and decrepit. Panels of wire fencing surrounded its site, replete with vivid images of snarling, non-existent guard dogs and hollow claims that tampering would activate alarms. Its ground floor casements were broken or boarded up. Half a century before, its gardens had drawn admirers from far and wide. They were now overgrown – a haven for wildlife that dwelled amongst the discarded detritus of a once affluent town which had lost its way.

Looking around, the man placed his gloves back on his hands. He straightened and nodded to himself.

Removing his phone from his pocket, he pressed a button. The screen illuminated. Its light cast his expressionless eyes in a ghostly glow, where they peered through the holes in his balaclava. One blue. One brown.

No messages.

No further orders.

He checked his watch.

It was time. He strode over to the dust-encrusted bar top and lifted down a jerry can. He was tall. Strong. The weight was easy for his thick arms to bear. His lips formed themselves into the hint of a smile as he upended the vessel. Liquid sloshed onto the carpet, splashing into its worn fabric.

'Stop!' a voice rang out.
He paused. Frowned.

* * *

Turning, the man placed the can on a bare patch of floorboards. The petrol fumes were overpowering. He wrinkled his nose slightly. 'What the fuck do you want?' he demanded. His tone wasn't aggressive – more perplexed.

He looked back at his handiwork: there were three of them. Two with mouths bound by duct tape. One without. All three were firmly tied to a long, cast iron radiator which ran the length of the wall. The eyes of the two wearing gags were wide; they'd grown wider still as the man began pouring the petrol – their eyes stood out in the moonlight like off-white marbles. The third captive had been less cooperative. So he'd been knocked out, smashed across the side of the head with an iron bar. In fact, the man had assumed he was dead, so hadn't gone to the effort of gagging him.

But he was still alive, and he was awake; he was tougher than the big man had imagined. *Much* tougher.

His boss had planned the whole set-up. She wanted the victims to be fully aware of their fate – to know what was coming before it came. To feel the ferocious heat of the flames charring their flesh and searing their eyes before they were consumed by them. Before they were turned to ash - along with the remains of the old hotel. But he hadn't expected the third man to wake up. He hadn't banked upon him being there at all. Despite looking only a little less derelict than the hotel, he'd put up quite a fight - even when faced with a SIG-Sauer P-226 pistol. For two minutes of fighting, he'd more than held his own, his lean frame disguising his resilience and skill. At one point, he'd even landed a punch that had given his much larger assailant pause for thought. But then he started coughing.

That had been the end of it.

The man in black frowned again and approached the radiator. The two gagged captives made frantic gurgling noises, wrenching at the ropes that restrained them. But they held firm. The man grinned a little, recalling how they'd entered the premises willingly. A little inebriated, they'd walked right into his trap. Just like his boss had told him they would. Once he'd produced the gun, they'd had no choice but to follow his orders.

By the time they understood their predicament, they realised it was too late to do anything about it. The man had taken his time – anticipation was something he revelled in.

'Problem?' he sneered. The ungagged figure looked up, his eye bloodied and swollen. His head lolled as if it was too heavy for his neck to support. He rested it against his shoulder for an instant before straightening it. He was thin; wiry. Strong – at least he had been, once upon a time.

'You won't get away with this, you know?' the man said. He spoke slowly, deliberately, pausing to spit a gobbet of blood from his mouth. 'People know I'm here.'

The dark figure smiled and shook his head. 'No one knows you're here, tramp. And nobody would give a shit even if they did.'

Glaring up at his captor with a look of icy contempt, the third captive opened his mouth. He enunciated his words clearly. 'Fuck you!'

* * *

Far off in the distance, a car horn sounded. It was followed by another. The Diplomat Hotel was an Eagle's Nest above the town. In the past, it had looked down. Imperious. Now it felt removed – a remnant; a symbol of the years of plenty preceding the town's pockets being slowly emptied. In its heyday, the great and good had flocked to the area's golden beaches, and frequented its dance halls, bars and discothèques. But that was before budget flights and the lure of the

Mediterranean. By the time the Chamber of Commerce realised the place was sliding, it had already plummeted.

'I think that knock on the head confused you,' the man said bluntly - his voice gravelly. He strode over and slammed his steel toe-capped boot into the side of the third man's chest. The captive shrieked in pain as the attacker brought his full weight to bear on his ribs.

They broke easily.

As the injured figure spewed a stream of expletives, the man removed his gloves and tore a strip of duct tape from a roll with his teeth. He stuck it roughly across the third man's mouth, silencing him.

'Better now?' he enquired, laughing. 'It's better for me – this way I don't have to listen to you whining like a little bitch.'

* * *

Ten minutes later, the man returned to inspect his prisoners once more. Since leaving them, he'd poured the contents of half a dozen jerry cans up and down the staircases, soaking what remained of the carpets and covering the exposed floorboards of rooms on all floors. For nearly three weeks, there had been hardly any rain. He knew that once the petrol sparked, it would take only moments before the place became an inferno.

The man pulled a low bar stool across the carpet and sank lazily onto it. It was one of the few pieces of furniture remaining in the bare room. Looking at the first two captives, he sneered once more. 'Miss Keane sends her regards.' He chuckled. 'I thought you might like to know that.' He paused, looking at the third man. 'You're different – you just pissed me off. You weren't even part of the plan. But three's a lucky number. So, the more the fucking merrier.' He looked around the room and slowly removed a cigarette from a packet, placing it in the corner of his mouth. Then he brought out a Zippo lighter.

'Oh!' His expression changed to one of mock alarm. 'Where are my manners?' He threw a cigarette towards each of the captives. 'You see,' he began. 'We have our own set of laws here in South Quay. You should know that – they're Leah Keane's laws.' He shrugged. 'You broke them... you pay.' The big man sighed. The gyrations of the bound figures were growing more violent; their gurgling more desperate. 'Me though – I obey the laws.' The man continued, grinning. 'That's why I'm going to step outside for my cigarette. You know – because of the smoking ban and all.' He laughed. 'Don't worry though, I'll chuck a light back in for you all.'

Yawning, the man rose from the stool. He walked slowly across the barroom and then exited the door, making his way down the grand staircase. As he did, the smell of fuel was overpowering. He opened the front door, glanced at the wasteland of brambles and nettles before him, and picked up the Molotov cocktail he'd prepared previously.

Stepping outside fully, he lit his cigarette, inhaling deeply. He wedged it in the corner of his mouth. Then, he touched the Zippo's flame to the petrol-soaked rag protruding from the bottle's neck. It ignited instantly, the flame roaring and hissing as it chewed at the fabric.

Holding the blazing bottle, the man took a last look around before tossing it almost playfully into the vestibule. It shattered, bursting in an explosion of flame. He nodded with approval as the petrol-sodden staircase followed suit almost immediately – twin paths of tangerine-hued sparks raced upwards, flaring.

The man yawned and flicked the butt of his cigarette through the open door. He then thrust his hands into his pockets and walked away.

PART ONE
Chapter 1.

TWO WEEKS EARLIER.

Trent Rivera sat down hard on the porch of the wooden holiday chalet, suddenly feeling a little more like his age. His job was simple – the chalet was no different to any of the others; they were flat pack creations from three decades previous. Perfectly serviceable, the dwellings were nevertheless tired-looking; they needed a facelift. That was where Rivera's work crew came in.

Two hundred chalets.

Two hundred facelifts.

Two months – give or take. At least that was the management's aim. That's why securing employment had been so straightforward.

Rivera looked around, scanning the huge field. It was tightly packed with box-like structures identical to the one behind him. It felt like a Levittown anchored outside of South Quay – Devon's once-upon-a-time approximation of the Côte d'Azur. Half of the chalets had weather-worn sidings in various stages of removal. The other half were freshly rendered and sparkling in the daylight. It was the end of spring. Three weeks before the holiday season began in earnest. The mornings were getting lighter; the evenings were growing longer, and – on good days – there was a smell of summer in the air.

Rivera looked up. The sun was high in the sky. The day was hot.

Too hot.

***

For more than a year, Rivera had lived a simple, almost puritanical life. He hadn't quit tobacco entirely, but he'd managed to limit himself to two hand-rolled cigarettes a day. Alcohol-wise, he wasn't teetotal, but he hardly drank, consuming two pints of beer a week at the very most. And he followed a mildly demanding exercise regime - he knew he was getting on a bit, but his body had served him well; it was important it continued to do so.

It was a lifestyle he'd ardently committed to. And he'd managed to keep his vows.

Until last night.

It had been a birthday party for one of his work crew – the drink had kept flowing, and before Rivera knew, he was three sheets to the wind. The innocuous phrase hid the hard truth. He wasn't twenty-one any more, but last night he'd drunk as if he was. Today he was paying the price. The wheels of his sobriety had well and truly come off, and he was reminded of how weak-willed he could be: his own worst enemy. Today his head was pounding like a jackhammer, and his morning thoughts had been filled with irrational fears and half-remembered recollections of things he'd said that he probably shouldn't have said. Then, there was the temperature: the day felt *far* hotter than he was. Slugging at a bottle of water, he poured some of it onto his forehead. He was shirtless and tanned; a shop-bought tattoo was inked onto his shoulder. It depicted the logo of Black Flag, the American hardcore band. They were one of his true passions, along with Fulham Football Club. Fulham's crest was etched onto his skin too, but that tattoo had been drawn by his brother – years before. He was no artist; he'd used India ink that had now bled into a blurred mess. If you didn't know what you were looking at, the design might have been anything.

Rivera squinted at the sunlight. He turned, picked up his claw hammer, and stepped back inside the chalet.

* * *

Rivera had been employed at The Golden Sands for a little over a month. The work suited him – it was physical enough to keep him fit, but not so taxing that he was exhausted at the end of the day. That meant his evenings were free for reading; since leaving the Army, he'd embarked on a course of self-improvement and had promised himself he'd read all the books people said he should read. His aim – once he'd done that – was to start reading all the books people said he *shouldn't* read. He was currently working his way through Thomas Hardy's novels; he'd picked a few of them up at a second-hand bookstore, and then a couple more at a book exchange. He found it was the best form of therapy: when he lost himself in a book, he freed himself from his military memories and the haunting spectres of his past.

'It's easy,' Derek Clarke – the foreman – had explained during his brief interview a few weeks before. 'You break them down, and then you build them back. Spruce them up. Make them look pretty.' He'd looked hard at Rivera. 'Like polishing a turd. Think you can handle that?'

He nodded. 'No problem.'

'Good. You seem like a bloke who's been working outside.' Clarke paused as he looked the newcomer up and down. 'Construction?'

Rivera nodded.

'Local?'

He shook his head. 'Spain.'

'Fancy!' The foreman raised his eyebrows and whistled. He then sneezed into a handkerchief and vigorously wiped at his nose. 'Seven o'clock Monday morning,' he announced bluntly. 'Don't be late, or I'll dock you the first hour.'

* * *

Spain already seemed like a distant memory. When Rivera arrived there, he'd been in a loving relationship with a woman called Betsy.

By the time he left, he wasn't. With her departure, he'd been at a loss. In the Army, it felt his every decision had been mandated: where to go; who to talk with; what to do. But, finally free of such control, he'd found himself oddly adrift.

Rivera's Army background had made him sharp and smart. He was good with strategy. Good with languages. And – if it came to it – trained to kill. As a soldier, he'd been on the front line. But when he wasn't in combat, the military had given him linguistic training; they'd then deployed him as a translator. He'd also worked as an investigator, chasing bad money through shell companies in myriad seedy places. It sometimes made him wonder if the ones wielding the money were even worse than those with the guns. For his first dozen years, Rivera was happily institutionalised. When it came to it, he didn't believe there were many orders he wouldn't follow. He'd assumed the Army would be his life.

But then things went wrong.

It hadn't happened overnight, but a cloud slowly descended after his last tour of Afghanistan. One evening, buoyed by the booze and barbiturates he'd been using to self-medicate his troubles away, he flipped. He hadn't hurt anyone; the victim had been the panel walls of the flat he shared with his then girlfriend. But the damage was done.

His violence had frightened him. But it had frightened her more.

She'd summoned the police who'd carted him off to the cells. The next day, two representatives from the military bailed him out and frogmarched him back to his flat. They proceeded to outline a choice that wasn't really a choice: walk, or be pushed. It had been a no-brainer. Rivera – now an ex-soldier - had signed the medical discharge papers they'd proffered. The liaison officers had been brusque but benevolent. They'd encouraged him to draw early on his military pension.

And so he had.

He'd bought Iris – his 1972 Volkswagen T2 Campervan – from a backstreet garage in Hammersmith. Her name came from the sprig of purple and yellow flowers painted on the driver's side door. He'd toyed with the idea of removing the decal, but he reasoned he was no longer in fatigues: a flowery van was about as un-militaristic as he could get. The vehicle had taken most of his money, but at least it meant he had somewhere to sleep. After that, he'd spent his days roaming the country.

Moving from campsite to campsite.

Healing.

He'd grown his hair and taken to wearing hippie jewellery. Inside, he may still have been a soldier, but outside he looked like any other turn-on-tune-in-drop-out traveller. Iris had come with a surprise guest too – a tabby cat he called Rosie. She'd announced her presence a short time after he'd driven the T2 through the streets of Hammersmith. At first, he'd thought about donating her to a cat shelter. But then he reasoned she was there first. She had squatters' rights; it felt like her vehicle.

And he respected that.

She'd stayed, and had travelled with him ever since. He kept her fed and watered, and she presented him with sacrificial mice, rats, and voles with an alarming regularity.

It had been a pleasant existence.

Iris.

Rosie.

Him.

* * *

As much as he tried to extract himself from the world, though, its darker side had a habit of drawing him back in. Betsy – the person with whom he thought he'd found happiness – had a theory. She told him he ended up in trouble because he was trying to right wrongs. To atone for past sins. He'd laughed, but deep down, he knew there was some truth in what she said. He'd seen things he kept shut away in the darkest recesses of his brain. Done things he kept buried in his subconscious. And when he saw bad things happening, he found it hard to walk away.

So, he very rarely did.

After a few months of them living in Spain, Betsy's father had fallen ill. She'd returned to the north of England to help her mother and, though Rivera had followed a short while later, things hadn't worked out. Being on a break in a relationship was something the ex-soldier associated more with sitcoms than real life. But it was the phrase she'd used, so he'd gone along with it. He just wished he knew what it really meant. Before being with her, fidelity hadn't been his strong suit. With her out of the way, he'd had various meaningless dalliances. That was nothing new. What *was* new was the sense of guilt that plagued him afterwards.

A fortnight after working his way aimlessly south, he'd wound up by the coast. The sign advertising a position at Golden Sands Holiday Camp was placed in the window of a coffee shop; a phone number was scrawled beneath it.

Rivera had called.

The same afternoon, the job was his.

Chapter 2.

'Hey Rivera!' The ex-soldier snapped out of his reverie. 'You're leaning on that broom pretty hard, don't you think?' Carrie Esposito spoke in a California accent utterly at odds with the environs of Golden Sands. She had a West Coast brashness and the exuberance of youth. Most people that crossed her path liked her immediately.

Rivera grinned. He paused, having swept away a pile of debris. It was mid-afternoon; he was lost for a moment, imagining the stodgy mass of carbohydrates he intended to consume that evening. It was a plan that had been percolating; an endeavour to put paid to the remnants of his hangover. He still had the brackish aftertaste of stale booze on his tongue, but his headache had subsided at least.

'Can't handle the pace any more, old man?' A row of perfect, pearl-white teeth beamed at him.

Rivera chuckled. 'I guess not,' he shrugged. 'I must be past my prime!'

Esposito grinned. 'The rest of us are heading to the clubhouse tonight.' she paused, dragging the cord of a drill from where it was trailing on the ground. 'Hair of the Dog. You in?'

'Absolutely fucking not!' The soldier's tone was indignant.

The woman laughed, walking away.

* * *

Carrie Esposito was very much the black sheep of Rivera's work crew. A glamorous, blonde college graduate – she was halfway through a round-the-world trip. When the ex-soldier first saw her, he'd assumed she was a model the holiday camp had brought in to photograph for an advertising brochure. When she'd opened her mouth, he was more confused – she looked like she'd be better suited to Sunset Boulevard than refitting prefabricated constructions in South

Devon. In truth, she *was* more suited to Sunset Boulevard, but she could hold her own on site just fine.

'What brings you here, then?' he'd asked shortly after meeting her.

She'd narrowed her eyes. 'If that's a seedy pickup line, then it's pretty poor – even by British standards.'

'It's not.'

'You sure?' She'd tilted her head slightly, unconvinced.

'I'm sure,' he'd nodded.

'Oh well, in that case it's the weather!' she'd smiled. It had been a day in late spring, which felt more like the depths of winter. The sky never really brightened, and venturing outside meant encountering a cold that seeped into the bones. 'When it clouds over, it's only a little brighter than creation's dark.' Esposito had paused. 'And then there's the food, of course. I'd hoped you guys would still have tripe on the menu, but so far - so bad.'

Rivera had frowned. 'I thought you Americans didn't get irony?'

Esposito had shrugged.

Over the next few weeks, Rivera had watched with amusement as his younger male co-workers made advances and were consistently rebuffed. They'd mistaken her Barbie-doll appearance and relentless positivity for vulnerability; cheerful smiles as a come-on.

They'd been wrong.

The ex-soldier hadn't had to intervene. Instead, he'd rounded the corner of a chalet one day and seen Esposito standing above one of the young men she'd been working with. He was nursing his jaw while she was brandishing a wrench. A couple of the youngster's co-workers looked on with a mix of horror and fascination.

'...the next time you say something like that to me, I'll knock your teeth out.' She'd spoken calmly; icily. 'All of them. One by one. Understand, asshole?'

'I don't see what the problem is,' the youngster had shrugged defensively. He raked his fingers over the ground. 'It's just banter.'

She'd glared at him.

'You should take it as a compliment – me hitting on you,' the man had continued. Having been floored by Esposito's punch, he was desperately trying to save face before his friends. To claw his way back to a position of respect. 'I'm a fucking catch!' he protested. 'Anyway,' he quipped. 'I like a woman who fights dirty.'

She'd sighed, and stood – her hands on her hips. 'Even if I liked boys... which I don't. Then I wouldn't like you.'

'What? Because I'm too much of a man for you?' the youngster had shot back, defiant. His eyes hardened as he began to stand.

'No... because you're a complete prick.'

Rivera had laughed.

The youngster – welcoming a distraction, and suspecting an easy target for his frustrations - had leapt fully to his feet. Teeth gritted, he glared at the ex-soldier. 'Oh – what? You want to make something of it, old man? You want a piece of me?'

Rivera had smiled thinly. 'People only talk like that in the movies, you know?' He'd turned to Esposito and shaken his head.

'Fucking come on then! What? Are you scared?' The youngster puffed out his chest and strode towards the ex-soldier; his arms were held out from his side – it was an attempt to give the impression of him having muscles that didn't exist. He swaggered, rolling his shoulders, grinding his teeth.

The young man was ten feet away from Rivera when he stopped dead.

It was as if he was frozen in time.

Before approaching the ex-soldier, he'd turned around, grinning wildly at his friends: he had youth on his side and nothing to fear. The older man was just that: old. His jaw was set. He needed to humiliate Rivera to save face: the senior contractor would pay for embarrassing him in public. Striding onwards, he'd whipped his head back around to regard his quarry once more. That was when the ex-soldier fixed him with his eyes.

Blue eyes.

Cold eyes.

Eyes filled with menace.

For all his bluster, the youngster was ill-prepared for what he faced. No words were spoken, but the glare boring through him was enough to provide a clear message: he was looking into the eyes of a killer.

Stuttering and stammering for a moment, he backed off and walked hastily away. 'Come on,' he announced to his friends. 'He's not fucking worth it – he'd only go whining to Bourse...'

* * *

'So how come you're in this line of work, then?' Rivera asked Esposito a few days later.

'Why shouldn't I be?' she frowned. 'Because I'm a woman, you mean?'

'No.' He shrugged. 'Just curious. You're from California, right?'

She nodded.

'And you know your stuff.'

'Most of it,' the American nodded.

'So what's the building trade like over there?'

'Pretty good, I guess. But I never worked construction back home. I'm from San Diego, although I spent summers with my Uncle Nelson out in Illinois. And when I graduated, I worked for his company. That's where I learned the trade properly.'

The ex-soldier nodded, then grinned. 'So... do they have lots of holiday chalets there then?'

Esposito laughed. 'No – he tended towards the higher end of things. He moved into working on enormous places. Lake Shore Drive, Chicago – billionaires' houses.'

'Yeah?'

'Yeah – but then it became fashionable for the super rich to have places outside of the city – rustic homes. So we ended up remodelling Dutch barns mainly. Stripping them down and building them up again so they were sparkly and shiny enough to feature on the pages of glossy magazines. Then, their owners would move in and decorate them with wildly expensive artefacts designed to make them look down-at-heel.'

'Authentic then?'

'Yeah – if authentic means a sanitised, Disneyworld version of the Midwest.' She chuckled. 'Most of them only spend a few weeks in them a year, anyway. They call them cabins even though they're way bigger than the homes most families live in. A lot of them employ Mexican gardeners whose only job is blowing leaves off of the lawns. It's all about appearances, right? That and making sure you don't pay any tax!'

The ex-soldier nodded.

'But...' she continued. 'If you've rebuilt a Dutch barn, then holiday chalets are child's play! I could do this stuff with my eyes closed – I'm doing the season here, and then I'm heading out to do Europe properly. I've done Asia and Africa already.'

'Nice!' Rivera nodded. 'Where are you headed first? After here – I mean?'

'Amsterdam,' she replied. 'I have another uncle there. He lives on a houseboat – he's great! He's called Jesus.'

Rivera paused. 'Jesus was a sailor when he...'

'...walked upon the water.' She grinned at the light of recognition that sparkled in his eyes. 'Don't go getting all Leonard Cohen on me now – it'll make me morose. Either that or homesick. Maybe a bit of both!'

The ex-soldier laughed.

Chapter 3.

Leah Keane sat at the bar of The George and Dragon; the pub was located a few roads back from South Quay's promenade. It had a flat roof and blacked-out windows. A chalkboard outside advertised upcoming football fixtures, along with the presence of pool tables and dart boards. The business had been built three decades before, after a former guest house had been razed, and The George - as it was known by the locals - had filled the void. Back when civic organisations created floral displays to welcome visitors to the town, the area where the pub was situated had been brimming with bed-and-breakfast establishments, small hotels, and rooming houses. Now, though, the grand old redbrick townhouses that remained had been subdivided into cramped flats frequently sub-let by unscrupulous landlords. What had once been a proud area had now become decidedly ragged round the edges; the council housed drug addicts; abused wives, and the second and third generation unemployed in the streets surrounding the pub. Much of the local population was washed up and burnt out before it even reached middle age – it was filled with the kind of people Keane could manipulate, dominate, and exploit; the kind of people who couldn't call the police if they had a problem.

Her kind of people. Once upon a time, she'd been one of them. A latchkey kid who was supposed to amount to nothing. The kind of child that truant officers didn't even bother with. She should have been in jail. Pregnant at fourteen. Dead.

But she wasn't.

Keane had done time, but by then she knew who she was. And what she was. Other people did, too. There were few chinks in her armour. Nothing vulnerable.

Once upon a time was a long time ago.

The George and Dragon was now one of the few fully functioning businesses in what had become yesterday's beach town. It was in the midst of an area known as Limetown, and it was at the centre of Keane's operations. She didn't own the pub. But, sitting at the bar on a high stool, there was no doubt who controlled the place. Her stool had line of sight with the door; it was she who gave the nod about whether any newcomers were welcome or not. The landlord – Danny – was only too happy to let her operate as she wished – he feared the consequences otherwise. Keane had a bar tab. It was unpaid – Danny didn't expect it ever *would* be paid. But the relationship won him certain favours. Not least, a reduction in the fees he – along with all the other owners of businesses in the area – paid the Keane organisation for protection.

Danny nodded at Keane as he handed her a fresh gin and tonic. The drinker took the glass without acknowledgement and lit up a cigarette. Though signs reminding people that smoking indoors had been illegal since 2007 were pasted on various walls in The George, they didn't apply to Keane. Nothing ever applied to Keane – not unless she wanted it to. The darkened windows meant she wasn't visible; the police were paid off anyway and gave the place a wide berth. There were few people who'd be brave enough – or sufficiently stupid - to summon law enforcement officers against the woman seated at the bar.

Certainly not in South Quay.

Leah Keane had a reputation. Most of the crime in the locality was orchestrated by her. Since jail, she'd refined her approaches, becoming a master manipulator. It meant she was never in the frame for anything. Ever.

People may have suspected she was behind things.

Sometimes they even knew she was.

But they could never find any proof. And even if they had, they'd have had immense difficulty fitting her up for anything. She wasn't conventionally beautiful by any means, but she carried herself with a certain glamour. Her clothes were immaculate. The teeth and nails were perfect. Had anyone seen her for the first time, they might have thought her an off-duty lawyer; the boss of a start-up. But, had anyone tried to chat her up, they'd likely have found themselves in a dumpster out back.

Possibly conscious. Probably not.

* * *

A tall, thickset man walked through the door. As he approached Keane, Danny swiftly delivered him a beer. Once he'd handed it over, he made himself scarce.

'Well?' Keane asked, as the man sat on an adjacent bar stool, sipping at his pint. She looked up from filing her nails.

'All good, boss.'

'Yeah?' Keane nodded. 'How much?'

'Less than we thought,' the man smiled. He looked at Keane, his eyes twinkling. One blue. One brown.

'And the vans?'

'All paid up for now,' he replied. 'Should be a good summer!'

Keane nodded as her phone screen lit up. The handset began vibrating on the bar. 'You see, that's what I like about you, Bullseye,' she announced. 'You might have a brain no bigger than an amoeba's bollock, but you're like a ray of fucking sunshine when you need to be.' As she rose, she patted the man on the shoulder, and then smoothed her dress, her heels clicking as she walked across the floor. As always, she was immaculately attired, and utterly incongruous with The George. Speaking into the phone, she raised the manicured nails of her free hand to acknowledge a pair of drinkers sat in the corner. They raised their glasses in appreciation, delighted to be able to bask – if only momentarily – in the glory of her shadow.

***

Leah Keane had many business interests – none of which she was directly involved with. These days, she thought of herself as an air traffic controller. From her control tower of health spas and wine bars, she directed the flight paths of other people. Front and centre was still her ice cream concern. She'd taken it over shortly after she'd been released from jail; it started with two vans. The ice cream trade had been profitable, but it hadn't been 99 Flakes and sugar cones that interested her – it was the opportunities the vans offered as a front to deliver a different kind of produce. In prison, Keane had heard about how similar operations had been run in bigger cities up north; she'd decided to bring the same to South Quay – *The Iceman*.

The thinking was simple: who would blink if an ice cream van was sat in the middle of a housing estate? The only oddity would be the looks of desperation in the long lines of customers in front of it. Of course, trade would diminish in the winter, but she could always venture into other areas to cover the shortfall. Her problem had been getting suppliers to take her seriously. In spirit, she was more man than most men. Tough. Unforgiving. Ruthless. But she was still a diminutive blonde with deep blue eyes who was decked out in business attire. When compared to the kind of hulks who dominated much of the drug business, it wasn't a look that screamed threat or intimidation.

Keane's way in had been a stroke of luck. She didn't believe in any kind of fate, but the discovery she'd made shortly after her release certainly felt like divine providence. Securing regular employment with her record had been difficult, so she and Bullseye had started a removals company.

As a child, Bullseye hadn't been popular. Growing up where he did was a waiting game: the bigger he got, the higher up the pecking order he climbed. Keane had been with him from the start – when he climbed, she climbed. And he remained completely committed to her – a forever faithful lapdog.

What the removals company meant in practice was that she gave the orders, and he did the work. To many in South Quay, he represented a resident evil, but when it came to his boss, he simply gazed lovingly and longingly with doe-eyes, willing to follow all instructions without question. To term the enterprise a removals company was a bit of a misnomer: Keane took the calls, and Bullseye loaded up a van with whatever goods he was given. He then fly-tipped the refuse at various locations in South Devon. Usually, the jobs were small – refrigerators; washing machines; tumble driers. Sometimes, though, the company was asked to do clearances.

It was on one such occasion that gold was struck.

The warehouse in Barton Cott was sizeable. Bullseye had simply been told that the contents needed to be disposed of. But he hadn't been told what the contents were. Usually, he followed Keane's instructions blindly, but – on this occasion – he'd called her for clarification.

It was just as well.

He'd uncovered a golden goose.

Blankenburg-Haan was a pharmaceutical company based outside Rotterdam. Before the use of synthetic opioids in the United States became an epidemic, they'd been tasked with developing an equivalent of fentanyl for the European market. Testing had been conducted and production had commenced. Pills were even shipped in blister packs to storage facilities ready for distribution. But then the press had reacted. That was the first problem – the opioid crisis was suddenly big news. Anything associated with it became toxic. And the European Commission, aware of how granting approval for the drug would look under such circumstances, withdrew their support.

So the opioids languished in a warehouse. Blankenburg-Haan declared bankruptcy, and successive corporations under whose umbrella it fell did likewise. Inventories were lost through mergers and acquisitions, and the facility in Barton Cott was effectively forgotten. It was only when the rent ran out that the owner of the storage yard had it cleared. The merchandise had been there nearly a decade when Bullseye stumbled upon it. But once his boss realised what it was, she knew that an opportunity was knocking which would allow any of her would-be competitors to be undercut.

Her first summer had been a success, and she'd bought two more vans. It was after that when the push-back started. Her biggest competitor was *South Quay Ices*. The Clements family had been in the trade since the early 1960s. But, where Keane mainly used her business as a front for other, more lucrative endeavours, their company was legitimate. However, despite the beaming face of the cartoon figure painted on the side of their vehicles, South Quay Ices were fiercely protective of their trade. They weren't willing to roll over and let a Johnny-come-lately organisation tread on their toes.

What began with posturing and arguments quickly deteriorated into an all-out turf war. The established company had drawn first blood – one of Keane's vans ended up in the sea, half covered by the tide. It was a marker – a literal line in the sand. A reminder to the woman about who was *really* in charge.

But Keane had other ideas.

She wasn't a street fighter. She certainly wasn't about to try to out-muscle the Clements family – she had Bullseye for that. There were certain things in her favour, though: first and foremost was the fact she was utterly devoid of compassion. The tit-for-tat approach suited her. In such instances, the victor is almost always the party willing to go lowest. Whatever their opponent does, they must be prepared to do worse.

And Keane was the kind of predator who would sink to the foot of the Mariana Trench and keep digging if it suited her. As a woman on the fringes of an underworld of men, she'd always had to fight twice as hard to prove herself. Being pretty and dainty meant she had to fight twice as hard again. Had she been butch and manly, she might have been taken more seriously. But she played the hand she'd been dealt. Her approach was simple: if there was anything in her way, she would steamroller it. No weakness. No mercy.

The Clements family didn't stand a chance.

That the fire which engulfed the family's apartment was arson had never been proven. It killed the patriarch and his wife, though. And, three days later, the Clements' eldest son and a nephew had disappeared. They were both involved in the business. The police suggested they'd taken the leftover money and fled to Ireland, but nothing had ever been confirmed. No bodies had ever been found. But everyone knew who now had the keys to the kingdom.

Three weeks after their disappearance, the remaining members of the Clements family had sold *South Quay Ices* to Keane at a vastly reduced rate. The deal hadn't been done through banks. The exchange had taken place in a parking lot on the edge of town, with the parties involved looking more like the James-Younger Gang than ice cream vendors.

From then on, there was only one name in town.

The Iceman ruled the roost.

Chapter 4.

The sun beat down on the Golden Sands resort. The sounds of hammering and sawing emanated from all corners. Clarke – the recently promoted foreman – had told his work force they would all receive a completion bonus equivalent to half a week's salary if all the work was finished before the opening day of the season. It was enough of an incentive to create a culture where the fitters worked hard and played hard.

Clarke had been drafted in not long before Rivera arrived; the previous foreman had left hastily – details were scant, but it was clear he didn't see eye-to-eye with the management. That morning, Rivera had been working on refurbishing a chalet close to the entrance when the post arrived. Due to a cement truck blocking the access road, the postal worker wasn't able to move his van through, so Rivera offered to take the mail up to the main office for her.

Walking up the path, the ex-soldier idly flicked through the stack of envelopes. Along with the usual mass of glossy circulars and flyers, there were a series of buff manila envelopes. They were all addressed to the same person: *AARON BOURSE ESQ.* He was – so Rivera had been informed in none too complementary terms by Clarke – the owner of the holiday park.

Bourse wasn't a man the ex-soldier had crossed paths with. All he knew of him was what he'd been told by others: he was wealthy and disagreeable, and he rarely paid wages on time. Bourse was also notoriously vain. His wig was thoroughly unconvincing - it didn't even deserve the more usual appellation toupée, and was often just seen as a rug. But he wore it all the same.

* * *

The opinions Clarke proffered about Bourse stopped just short of a character assassination. Carrie Esposito, meanwhile, rolled her eyes and recounted how the holiday camp owner had hit on her a couple of days after she'd first been given the job.

'Cringeworthy?' Rivera enquired, smiling wryly.

'You could say that!' she laughed. 'The usual kind of stuff – he said a girl that looked like me should be working inside. He could see to it that I had an easier time of things. And did I fancy dinner? Blah-blah-blah. I told him I wasn't just a day labourer – that I was a skilled tradesperson and had six people under me.'

The ex-soldier nodded. 'And what did he say?'

'Something along the lines of saying he wouldn't mind being under me. Or on top, if I preferred.' She shook her head. 'And then he tried to rub himself up against me. You get the picture...'

The ex-soldier grimaced. He liked Esposito; she was a good worker. A leader. He knew some of the male workers didn't care for a woman instructing them. But Rivera didn't think that way – in the Army, the most competent people he'd been led by were almost always female. He'd had to ask the American for carpentry advice on his first day of work; he later reasoned it wasn't something many of the male employees would have dreamed of doing. He quickly realised she knew far more about construction than he ever would, and so he'd bowed to her better judgement.

* * *

Esposito was also good with engines. Iris – Rivera's campervan – was parked alongside the workers' cabins. There was a small row of them, obscured by a high fence at the far end of the park. Workers were able to stay in the lodges for free. Rosie, though, had turned her nose up at the chalet and slept in Iris instead. She left neat lines of libations in the form of beheaded rodents along the front porch of his digs. Since arriving, the ex-soldier had worked around her, giving the Volkswagen a deep clean and polishing and waxing her paintwork. There was no doubting who the campervan really belonged to, though.

'She's beautiful!' Esposito announced when she'd seen Iris for the first time.

'Yeah,' Rivera nodded. 'But she's got some quirks – she gets a bit irritable at times.'

'Of course – she's an old lady! It's her prerogative,' she'd chuckled. 'What's the issue?'

'The brakes, mainly.' The ex-soldier shrugged.

Esposito disappeared beneath Iris. Her long, tanned legs stuck out from beneath the chassis. She emerged five minutes later, grinning, her hands coated in oil. 'Who last looked her over?' she asked.

'A mechanic in Spain,' Rivera replied. 'But then I had a tinker – so any issues might well be down to me. I know a bit about engines, but it's all trial and error – the kind of thing you could write down on the back of a bus ticket. Anything not in a Haynes manual is beyond me.' He paused, chewing his lip. 'Why?'

'Well... you said this was a 1972 model, right?'

The ex-soldier nodded. 'Yeah.'

'So, after 1970, disc brakes were used on the T2. Before that, you had drum brakes on all wheels.' Esposito wiped her oily hands on the material of her cut-off denims. 'Somewhere along the way, someone's switched your front discs for drums. It might have been all that was available when they did the work – they look old, though.'

'Yeah?'

'Yeah. They're perfectly serviceable,' she went on. 'But they have to be tweaked from time to time.' She paused. 'How's your motoring jargon?'

'OK, I guess,' Rivera shrugged. 'You might have to go slowly, though. Just imagine you're talking to a kid. And a dumb kid at that.'

She grinned. 'They have to be individually adjusted using a threaded tappet, which you move with a notched wheel. That needs doing – after that you should be good to go. It's kind of archaic really – I guess whoever looked at them for you wasn't so up to date with the campervan's history. Disc brakes are self-adjusting. They probably thought drums would be the same.'

'And can you fix them?'

'Easy,' she'd nodded. 'I'll need a few parts and a bit of time – but I'll talk you through it so you can do it yourself next time.'

Rivera grinned. 'Forgive the question, but where did you learn this stuff?' He paused. 'I mean, you know all about building and all about engines... I'm not being funny, but most girls – and boys – haven't got a clue.'

'My Uncle Jesus,' she'd smiled. 'Before he moved to Amsterdam, he had a workshop in Esmerelda Beach, San Diego. *So-Cal Cars*. It was on the corner of Graham and Burnette. It was a really cool place.' She paused for a moment, reminiscing. 'I haven't been under the hood of anything over here really – I just helped out Clarke's nephew one time.'

'I didn't know he had a nephew.'

'Yeah,' Esposito nodded. 'Kevin. He's got a Barbie-pink Volkswagen Beetle with eyelashes on the headlights.'

Rivera narrowed his eyes. 'You're winding me up, right?'

'Nope. Dead serious.'

Silence.

'Kind of... sounds like quite a feminine car, doesn't it?'

'Yeah,' the American nodded. 'That's kind of the idea. He's a sweetheart – it took me a moment to get my head around him being related to Clarke. They're like chalk and cheese. Kevin's a delicate little flower, and Clarke's about as subtle as a brick.'

Rivera laughed. 'So, does your uncle have a garage in Holland?'

'No. These days he uses his automotive knowledge to fix the engines of tour boats for Amsterdam's canals – when he's not comatose from smoking weed, that is. He loves it! Says it feels like being retired!'

'What – the weed or being on the water?'

'Both,' the American smiled.

* * *

Outside the main office, Rivera paused. Along with the official letters bearing the name of the GOLDEN SANDS HOLIDAY PARK, there were a number of other companies at the same address to which letters had been sent: GOLDEN SANDS HOLDINGS; GOLDEN HOLIDAYS LTD; THE SANDS CONSTRUCTION; GOLDEN CATERING; NIMROD CONSTRUCTION; NIMROD COURIER SERVICES; NIMROD SPORTS EQUIPMENT; SOUTH QUAY HOLDINGS; SOUTH STREET LIMITED.

The ex-soldier frowned. That Aaron Bourse had a hand in so many companies wasn't necessarily a surprise: he was a businessman. That's what businessmen did. But that he had so many companies with names that were variations on a theme set off the tiny pulse of an alarm deep in his brain.

In between bouts of combat and working as a military interpreter, Rivera had also been tasked with investigative work. Sometimes, it had been on the frontline – military cases. Often, it had been assisting the Military Police with tracking down AWOL troops. Then, there were murders and robberies. More often than not, though, Rivera chased the money. Financial investigating was where he'd begun to carve out a niche. Criminal enterprises, as he well knew, could hide people; they could hide goods and equipment, and they could mainly fly beneath the radar.

But it was far more difficult for them to hide money. No matter how well it was washed and wiped clean, the money invariably left a trail that could still be traced.

No matter who they were or how skilled their accountants, crooks still had to use banking systems. They were required to make money transfers. They needed to make transactions. And any movement of money created streams of numbers. There were always records, in spite of how hard people tried to eradicate them. And where there were records of money being moved, there was a trail. It was that which investigators followed. *Chase the money and you wind up with the man* – there was the mantra the ex-soldier's commanding officers had always sworn by. It was an approach that Rivera had adopted himself.

The ones who were good at hiding money were generally *very* good. Those who weren't tended to make similar mistakes. And, nine times out of ten, they used shell companies with a variety of names not too dissimilar from one another. It was a poor man's attempt at sheltering wealth - exactly the kind of thing that correspondence intended for the same recipient under a range of different guises at the same address tended to point to. The idea was that if someone remained one step ahead of the taxman and Companies House, they'd be able to avoid investigation. People knew how slowly the wheels of administrations turned. But it was sloppy. It was careless. It sent suspicions pinballing around the ex-soldier's brain.

Rivera sauntered back along the path to the chalet he was working on. Various thoughts now ran through his head. By far the most pressing concerned Aaron Bourse, and whether it might be worth looking into his operation a little more closely.

Chapter 5.

Keane was not the first person to hit on the idea of using children as drug mules. She simply took an existing system; adjusted it, and then applied it to South Quay. The logic was simple: the UK age of criminal responsibility was ten years old. Anyone caught with narcotics below that tender age couldn't be charged.

No comeback.

South Quay's estates were filled with feral children from broken homes. Once they grew bored with endless football matches on the hard surfaces of caged courts, they began to look for distraction elsewhere. With equal parts urban decline and faded seaside glamour, unemployment was extremely high; drug dependency was rife, and the area's social housing projects had turned into no-go areas for non-residents. They were – in effect – policed by the hood-wearing gangs of youths that hung around in stairwells and on pedestrian bridges overlooking their preserves. If they weren't dealers already, then they were dealers in training; friends of dealers; runners; lookouts.

Keane had simply recruited them. And used Bullseye to re-educate them.

It was a readymade structure she simply bent to her will. A few bribes here and there, and a selection of beatings dished out by Bullseye, meant most of her potential workforce was quickly onside. The only issue had been a man by the name of Tyrell Majors. It was his patch. He'd controlled the drug trade for years. He didn't take kindly to challengers.

One night, though, Majors disappeared.

The day after, Keane had moved in and explained how the new system would operate. After a week, a youngster named Romeo had tried to steal from her – he'd cut the supply Keane had provided and tried to sell it on at a profit for himself. It wasn't the worst thing he could have done. But it suggested he believed Keane was ripe for swindling.

And Keane was not.

Romeo had disappeared.

Keane didn't bother explaining what had happened. There was no need. She knew the imaginations of the estate hoodlums were capable of filling in the blanks. Rumours would suit her purposes very well. From that point onwards, people simply did as they were told.

* * *

Younger kids were runners. They were the only ones who ever really had drugs in their possession. Older ones were also on the payroll. Their role was to keep the peace – they made sure the mules never encountered any problems. They threatened and cajoled residents who were behind on payments. They were Keane's eyes and ears.

Within a couple of weeks, the operation was in full swing.

Majors' main problem, when he'd been running the operation, was drug transportation. He was a known figure. A marked man. The police managed to intercept several of his shipments before they'd even reached him. He was ineffective. Careless.

So Keane used her ice cream vans. *The Iceman* was a known business. If the vans were parked for long periods of time in the central concourse of one of the estates, they raised little suspicion. It was easy money – each van was staffed by two employees. The first dispensed 99 Flakes and ice lollies to the few customers naïve enough to ask for them. The second pressed packages into the hands of drug runners. Of course, each of them was given an ice cream too, so – to anybody looking on – the whole thing appeared entirely – if implausibly – legitimate.

Majors' other issue had been county lines organisations. Drug barons from big cities used vulnerable kids from the provinces to deal drugs on their behalf. A down-on-its-luck seaside town like

South Quay was a perfect target. It had a seemingly endless roster of youngsters who sought a lifestyle more glamorous than that which their environs could offer. During the tenure of Keane's predecessor, designer trainers and tracksuits had appeared, along with expensive watches. Keane's predecessor had been running scared from head honchos from Manchester, Croydon, and the Midlands. They had far more firepower than him, and could bring it to bear at any moment. The bribes he paid ate into his profits each month.

So, once Keane had taken over the turf, she'd set up a meeting. Through various prison connections, she'd managed to connect with the figure she saw as her chief rival. After to-ing and fro-ing for several weeks, they'd eventually set up a rendezvous in Birmingham.

She'd cut the woman a deal. Given the shabby hand-to-mouth existence of the street hustlers who did her bidding, the opulence of the woman's mansion in Edgbaston was a surprise – even to Keane. Her outward appearance was that of an enormously successful entrepreneur – she'd invested in a series of successful boutiques, and had reaped the rewards. Keane knew better than to be taken in by appearances, though; she was a case in point. Indeed, she was certain she'd perceived a flicker of surprise cross the woman's countenance – she'd clearly expected a swarthy jailbird coated in tattoos. To any onlookers, the women would have looked like venture capitalists discussing investments as they sat in the private room of a plush restaurant on Harborne High Street. They were cordial with one another – it resembled a scene from a boardroom. But they were wary, too. They both knew that nobody in the narcotics business attained lofty heights without being ruthless. And that once they were there, any newcomer was a potential rival – however well-dressed they were.

Throughout, Keane had been respectful. After all, the man her opposite number introduced as being her butler was one of the meanest characters she'd ever encountered - a hulking brute of a man with the stature of a wrestler. He was someone who might even have made Bullseye quake.

Over their expensive lunch – for which Keane footed the bill – the pair had hashed out an arrangement. They became partners. The woman from the Midlands would no longer be a supplier for South Quay. She would simply ensure that nobody else tried to muscle in. After that, the two of them would split the profits.

Keane's argument had been simple – she could provide the drugs, so the lady from the Midlands could sell her supply elsewhere. On top of that, she could reduce the level of risk. To all intents and purposes, her ice cream business was beyond suspicion – she bribed some key police figures to look the other way in any case. Not only that, but she could use under-tens where people outside of town could not. That way, even if they *did* get caught, the organisation could continue to operate as before. They'd soon recoup their losses. And fewer transactions would be scuppered. When this was weighed up, Keane's opposite number had eventually agreed. They'd shaken on the idea of a twelve-month trial.

As it was, the first year was so successful that neither of them ever looked back. Keane moved into property and loan-sharking as sidelines. She had fingers in many other pies too and continued the protection rackets she and Bullseye had been running on-and-off since their teens. She'd even taken a leading share in the Golden Sands Holiday Camp. As with most of her arrangements, she'd done so using a front. Very few of her business interests were in her name – it was a set-up that suited her fine.

* * *

These days, though, she wanted to move further into property development, and had her eye on a golf complex, as well as a number of hotels. It was all very well *looking* respectable; she now craved the social status and connections that could come with a legitimate profile. In the main, she only involved herself with the seedier sides of her enterprise when she and Bullseye were required to remind people where their loyalties lay. Now, such events were rarities, though. She had her sights set on the lifestyle the woman in Birmingham had displayed to her; her aim was to be entirely legitimate within three years.

So, a steady stream of opioids flooded into South Quay's many estates. Residents were hooked – they needed escapism from the pain and tedium of their mundane existences. Many were incapacitated; leaving their flats was difficult. But the infant runners made things easy with their door-to-door service. Their elder cousins were less cheerful when they visited, demanding settlement of debts. But mobile banking made it easy for them to clear out state credit payments and divert funds to Keane's various shell companies.

South Quay's addicted residents were scared of the hooded hoard that ran their estates. But they were scared of many other things too.

And a hit was a hit.

The sweet oblivion it offered temporarily numbed the pain. That had always been reason enough to turn blind eyes to clusters of youths on concrete concourses; to turn deaf ears to shouts, scuffles, and occasional shots in the night. Besides, under Keane's rule, things had settled down somewhat. The boss enjoyed her power. She liked having a reputation. But, more than anything, she worshipped money. The smoother her operation; the more money she made.

Chapter 6.

Rivera and Esposito sat on the porch of a half-finished chalet. A number of boards were leaned up against the balcony surrounding the deck. The pair were sharing one of the ex-soldier's hand-rolled cigarettes. Derek Clarke – the site foreman – approached. He was wearing a hard hat like all the rest of the crew, along with a high-visibility gilet over his shirt that flapped in the breeze. His beer gut protruded slightly.

'You got trouble?' Esposito enquired.

'Why? Something you've done?' Clarke asked, smiling a little. He shook his head.

'Are we still on schedule?' Rivera asked.

'We are – sort of,' the foreman replied, scratching at his arm. 'It's the electrics that are putting us behind, though.'

'Haven't you got that guy on it?' Rivera enquired. 'Dean?'

'Dave,' Clarke nodded. 'Yeah, but he's taking his sweet time.' He pursed his lips. 'I'm going to have to bring in my cousin.'

'Yeah?' Esposito said. 'So - you've got a solution then, right?' She frowned. 'That's OK, isn't it?'

Clarke shrugged. 'Well, it is, and it isn't.'

An uneasy silence descended. Something unspoken.

'Care to elaborate?' Esposito frowned. 'You sound pretty sketchy all of a sudden. This guy's not a liability, is he?'

'I didn't say anything!' Clarke protested.

'Exactly!' the American insisted.

The foreman sighed. 'Well... he kind of bears a grudge against this town and everyone in it. It's not his fault, though.'

'Why?' Rivera asked.

Clarke exhaled deeply. 'We're cousins on my mum's side. His dad's side is the Clements family.'

Esposito and Rivera looked at him blankly.

FOUR-LEAF CLOVER

* * *

'Well, you're a pair of bloody foreigners, aren't you?' Clarke sat down, shaking his head in mild annoyance. He turned to Rivera. 'Can I steal a ciggy off you?'

The ex-soldier nodded and handed over his pouch of tobacco. Clarke rolled his cigarette, and when he'd licked the paper, Rivera proffered a light. The foreman nodded in appreciation and then began his explanation. 'That's the issue with my cousin. He's one of the Clements family. If you knew your South Quay history, it'd make sense.'

'Yeah, you're going to have to throw us a bone here, Derek,' Esposito said. 'Neither of us are from round here. Remember? Whatever civil war you're talking about isn't something we're familiar with. You'll need to explain.'

'The ice cream wars,' Clarke announced bluntly.

Esposito laughed. She looked at Rivera, who shrugged, and then looked back at the foreman, frowning. 'Are you for real?' She paused. 'What the hell kind of backwater is this?' She scoffed, her Californian brogue becoming more pronounced. 'Disneyland on crack?'

Silence.

'I don't wish to sound naïve, but are you serious?' Esposito narrowed her eyes. 'What the hell were the ice cream wars? Did they pick up where Barbie and Ken left off or something?'

Clarke laughed drily. 'No. It was much more than that.' He paused. 'People fucking died.'

'What of - obesity and diabetes?' Esposito raised her eyebrows. 'Razor sharp sugar cones? You're shitting me!'

'No,' Clarke's face clouded. He shook his head sadly. 'It was much worse than that – *really* nasty stuff. There were always issues with pitches and the like. Back when this was a thriving seaside town, having an ice cream van was like having a licence to print money, so there was always competition. Fights. The usual.' He shrugged. 'It became a turf war kind of thing. When things went sour and the tourist trade went south, people started dealing drugs from the vans. Some people. It was good cover.' He paused and turned to Rivera. 'You must remember seeing stuff like this on the news, right?'

The ex-soldier pursed his lips and nodded. 'A little.'

'There you go then,' Clarke went on. 'Suddenly, the idea of this being a quaint coastal town with lots of well-heeled visitors was a thing of the past. And once the dealers moved in, you were talking about a *really* lucrative business with loads of outside interests. So, people fought to protect things.'

'What was it then – all out battles?' Esposito frowned.

'Something like that,' Clarke nodded. 'For a few years, at least. There were arson attacks; family members being threatened. All sorts. It was a right fucking mess.'

Silence.

'I read the papers,' Rivera announced. 'But the articles were all about Glasgow. I'm not sure I ever heard anything about this place.'

'You wouldn't have,' Clarke answered. 'It was hushed up as much as possible. The Chamber of Commerce still thought they could turn things around. They believed people would sack off the Costa del Sol eventually and come back here on holiday. Trade in castanets for croquet. Because of that, they did everything they could to keep things out of the press. Even the really juicy stuff.'

Rivera nodded. 'So where does your cousin fit into this?'

'Sid was one of the Clements family.' Clarke explained. '*Is* one of the Clements family. They used to rule the roost – in the ice cream world, at least. But then they were toppled. Of course, he's borne a grudge ever since, but there's nothing he's been able to do about it. And he's been *persona non grata* for bloody ages' He sighed. 'Everyone knows who pulls the puppet strings now, but they're untouchable.'

Esposito and Rivera caught one another's eye.

'Who?' Esposito asked.

'The new kids,' Clarke explained, a little uneasily. 'You know...'

'So, Sid's uncle was put out of business by the new kids in town?' Rivera asked.

The foreman nodded.

'And who are they exactly?' Esposito pressed. 'I mean, he's a sparky, right? So, what's the issue? He sorts plugs and wiring and that's it – it's hardly the stuff of vendettas.'

Clarke looked around shiftily and lowered his voice. 'Leah Keane,' he whispered. 'Don't go mentioning her name around town. Otherwise, she might consider you a challenge. Last time she thought someone was trying to muscle in on her business, her enforcer tied them to a workbench in a lock-up, and tightened their head in a vice until Keane had all the information she wanted. Then she cut their tongue out with a Stanley knife. That's how the rumour goes – and, knowing the woman, I wouldn't put it past her. Anyone that crosses her seems to vanish.'

'I still don't get the link with Sid,' Rivera frowned.

Clarke sighed. 'Have you taken a walk through South Quay recently?'

'Yes,' Rivera replied. 'Frequently. Beautiful place – quaint even. So long as you ignore the crappy veneer and the crowds of ne'er-do-wells.'

'Well, there you go then... it's all boarded-up storefronts; pawn shops; charity shops; betting shops. There's no work here unless you're working at the Golden Sands. At least nothing permanent.'

'But this is owned by Aaron Bourse,' Esposito frowned. 'Isn't it? I mean – that's what you told me. I'm sure it's his name on my contract.'

Clarke scoffed. 'Don't believe everything you read, young lady. Keane's bloody everywhere around here. She's calling all the shots in this town. Has been for years. You can't sneeze around here without her knowing about it. So, when Sid had been out of work for a couple of years, he had no choice but to go to her begging for a job, cap in hand. He'd burned all his other bridges.'

'And she employed him?' Rivera asked. 'Why? I thought they were rivals?'

'To humiliate him,' Clarke replied. 'Any time she needs something backbreaking or downright disgusting doing, then it's Sid who gets tasked with it. *Every* time. Sewage. Drainage ditches. That kind of thing. It's like a constant reminder of who has the power. He's spent more time shovelling shit underground than a coprophiliac mole.'

'Can't he move away?' Esposito enquired, frowning.

Clarke shook his head. 'His world is here. Always has been. Anyway, where would he go? He doesn't know any different.' He paused. 'The problem is that I can't really bring him here to help out long term. It would put him on a collision course with a few people he shouldn't be colliding with. But I need him to sort the electrics, otherwise we're never going to make the deadline. He's good at that. Competent. But if word leaks back, then Keane will flip her lid.'

'And there's no one else you can ask?' Rivera enquired.

'Why, are you any good with electrics?' Clarke asked, hopefully.

'No.'

'You?' He turned to Esposito.

The American shook her head.

'There we go then. I can't really ask anyone outside of her organisation,' Clarke replied. 'And if Bourse or Keane think we're running behind, then bang goes the chance of a bonus.'

'Sounds fun,' the American nodded.

'Yeah,' Clarke replied. 'Like squaring a fucking circle.'

Chapter 7.

Over time, Keane's business interests grew. The ice cream industry bloomed and blossomed until *The Iceman* was the only vendor in town. Her racketeering continued apace, but she began to feel like she'd hit a ceiling; she was wealthy and respected, but still not by those who sat at the head table, so she'd begun to legitimise her assets by investing in property. That changed things. She loathed the lawyers and accountants she kept on hefty retainers; they represented everything she hated about the white-collar world. Everything she felt had been stacked against her when she was growing up. For every ten pounds she made, it felt like she was having to pay someone to clean it; someone to hide it, and someone else to put the frighteners on anyone else who wanted to blab about it. And then there were the bribes – suitcases filled with cash prompted questions otherwise.

But she did it, nonetheless. She'd always been determined – by any means necessary – to drag herself up and out of penury. To grow up poor is one thing. To grow up hungry is something else. But to grow up in a flat with a crack addict mother moonlighting as a hooker while a disabled brother was left dribbling and soiling himself in the corner was something else. And then there had been her father. Or, at least, the man her mother said was her father. When he wasn't comatose, he was beating her, or selling her to his friends for wraps of cocaine. Neither of Keane's parents were still alive. The house fire they'd perished in was a quiet little footnote far away from the front pages. It started the night after her brother – left unattended – choked to death. The flames conveniently cleared her and Bullseye of the deeds they'd done before the gas had been turned on.

Ever since, she'd been determined to change things. Any time she felt herself falter, it was the desperate image of her mother kneeling in the kitchen before another grotesque punter grunting and gurning that spurred her on.

It was an approach that had served her well.

But, being rich and staying rich – Leah Keane realised – cost a lot of money.

It was one of the reasons she'd moved into loan sharking. The beatings Bullseye doled out whenever she let him off the leash weren't the forever kind – more warnings to remind people where they stood in the pecking order. Any time anyone had ideas above their station, she initiated a programme of re-education.

Loan-sharking made her a lot of money; the interest charged was enormous. And with every repayment, a little more of her enterprise grew closer to respectability. She believed that if she went clean, she'd be able to put her past behind her forever.

There were always plenty of customers needing payday loans. South Quay was a town filled with desperate people who couldn't secure cash any other way. They were dangerous waters, but Keane was the apex predator. Her associates always had ears to the ground in any of the pubs in town where their trade was plied.

Touting for business was never very challenging.

The terms and conditions were always clear.

Always simple.

Pay when instructed.

Or expect a call.

Chapter 8.

'Heads or tails?' Rivera asked Esposito, flipping a coin. As it spiralled through the air, it glinted slightly.

'Tails.'

The ex-soldier glanced down at his palm. 'Tails it is.' He paused. 'You want to drive?'

Esposito shrugged and held her hand out for the keys. The truck was branded with the Golden Sands Holiday Park logo. Three insipid palm trees and a sunrise scrawled in egg yolk yellow. The truck also carried a picture of a grinning crocodile - it was a vehicle used for carting goods around the site or through the town as required.

Today was one such day.

The pair had been tasked with loading furniture. The tables, chairs and sofas with which the chalets were filled could best be described as utility furnishings. No frills. They bore the scars and scrapes of several years' service. Naturally, the glossy pictures in the advertising paraphernalia featured brand new décor akin to that of a five-star hotel. The reality, though, was significantly different.

The Diplomat Hotel – so the work crew had been told – was owned by an organisation friendly with the Sands. Its owner was doing Aaron Bourse a favour; the shell of the old establishment was still serviceable, and watertight at least. It was because of this that furniture had been stored there while the chalets were being serviced. Rivera and Esposito weren't there when it was filled, but they'd been given the job of transporting the furniture back. Enough chalets had been refurbished that it could be stored in the completed ones while the others were being finished. It was a tedious task – last in; first in line for the jobs no one else wanted. Clarke had been apologetic when he'd explained what they had to do, but there was no dressing up how onerous it was.

* * *

'It must have been magnificent back in the day,' Esposito remarked as she ground the truck's gears, moving it up the driveway towards the old building. The incline was significant, with the vehicle's engine protesting as she drew to a halt. Rivera unlocked the gate that barred the way – the property was surrounded by fencing on all sides.

'Yeah,' he replied as he jumped back into the cab. He followed her gaze. The once manicured lawns of the hotel were now a mess. Litter and fly-tipped refuse scarred the grounds. But the shell of the building remained resplendent. The huge structure possessed a prominent view over the town and down to the beaches. Rivera imagined that sunrise and sunset were breath-taking when viewed from such a promontory. The tiles of the roof – in need of repair –glimmered in the light, and the turrets and balustrades gave it a castle-like appearance. 'What are they going to do with it?' he asked.

'Beats me,' she replied. 'They could use it for a movie set – like *The Shining* or something. I reckon it's spooky enough!' She grinned. 'I heard there's some local statute on it or something though.'

'What – like a preservation order?' Rivera enquired.

'That's the one,' she nodded. 'So they can't knock it down, right?'

'Correct.' Rivera paused. 'I guess. You'd need a whole lot of planning permission even to spruce it up. Seems a shame.' His voice trailed off.

'Would there be any point, though?' Esposito asked. 'Doing it up - I mean. You've seen the town, right? It's hardly Santa Monica!'

'True enough,' the ex-soldier nodded. 'It's got a pier, though!'

Esposito laughed. 'Yeah – good luck building a new Hollywood any place close to here!'

As the truck drew to a halt, the pair spotted a homeless man sleeping on the veranda. His sleeping bag was placed upon an old bench, and an assortment of items were stacked neatly beside. He stirred as the truck's engine was switched off. At first, he looked as though he was gathering his belongings, but then he settled back, eyeing the new arrivals with mild intrigue. Esposito looked at Rivera, frowning. 'What do we do with him?'

'What do you mean?'

'Do we move him on or something?' the American asked. 'I mean...'

'...he's not doing any harm,' Rivera interrupted, shrugging. 'Besides, Bourse won't ever find out. I shouldn't think Clarke will care, either. I don't see there's any point telling them, otherwise they'll call in people to do an eviction. We just need him to keep his head down – he's not troubling anyone.'

'OK.' Esposito sighed. 'How's this? I won the coin toss, and I drove. So you can talk to the derelict.'

'Fair enough.'

* * *

The homeless man rose from his bed, stretched, yawned, and regarded the pair as they drew closer. He was lean; wiry. Though he bore the slightly emaciated frame of one who skipped too many meals, he didn't look entirely unhealthy. His skin was weather-beaten; tanned. The only thing hinting at malaise was a wracking cough. Loudly clearing his throat, the man spat. He leaned on his knees for a moment, recovering his breath.

Esposito looked at him, expressionless. The ex-soldier frowned, his eyes narrowing.

The man straightened himself and leaned hard against the rail that ran around the veranda. 'You going to give me one of your rollies then, Rivera?' he asked brusquely. 'Or are you just going to stand there gawking at me all morning?' He laughed, drily. 'It's not a peepshow, you know!'

Esposito turned to Rivera, frowning. 'Wait! You know this guy?'

The ex-soldier nodded. 'Kind of.' He turned back to the homeless man. 'It's been a while, Fraser. I thought you were moving on to better things?'

'Devon rhymes with heaven for a reason, chief.' He paused enigmatically. 'It's not all it might be, but it's a darn sight better than a lot of other places I've been to.' The homeless man grinned broadly. 'You haven't gone too far since the last time I saw you – not as the crow flies.'

* * *

The trio sat down, trailing their legs from the edge of the veranda. Rivera and Fraser smoked while Esposito sipped at a bottle of water.

'I'd have brought you some cans of cider had I known you'd be here,' Rivera chuckled. 'Is that still your tipple of choice?'

'No – I'm through with that stuff these days, chief.' Fraser shook his head. 'Clean body; clean mind. Well - cleaner...'

Silence.

'So...' Esposito began. 'What's the story with you two, anyway?'

'Fraser...?' Rivera began.

'...Mr Rivera needed my help a while ago,' Fraser announced. 'He needed eyes and ears.' The homeless man drew hard on his cigarette. 'He might not have mentioned it to you, but he investigates things from time to time. Like a private eye, I guess – at least a cut-price-less-the-Big-Sleep-and-more-a-sleepy-seaside-town version. A midrange detective.' He looked at the ex-soldier and smiled. 'Budget, maybe...'

Esposito cast a sideways glance at the ex-soldier, frowning.

'I see everything,' Fraser continued. 'But nobody sees me. It makes me useful.' He turned to Rivera. 'Where was it – Saltmarsh Cove?'

The ex-soldier nodded.

'Good times,' Fraser wheezed. He yawned and stretched once more before grinding his cigarette out against the railing. 'Anyway,' he announced. 'I have a question for you.'

'Shoot,' Esposito said.

'Well, since you look all official with your truck and everything, I'm assuming you have a key to this hotel, right?'

Rivera nodded.

'So, how about you turn a blind eye and let an old homeless man sleep inside for a night?' Fraser asked. 'I might even avail myself of some of the facilities – if it's alright with you, I mean? I bet the water's still connected.' He paused. 'There are foxes out here – they make a hell of a racket and disturb my beauty sleep, you see.' He grinned. 'I don't look this good just by acting naturally, you know? I'll leave no trace, anyway.'

'Yeah, fine by me,' the ex-soldier nodded. 'Just keep it quiet and duck and cover if anyone arrives here who isn't us.'

'I won't tell if you won't tell,' Esposito shrugged. 'Makes no difference to me.'

'My lips are sealed, young lady,' Fraser smiled. 'If anyone asks, I'll say I'm a night-watchman.' He looked hard at the woman. 'San Diego?'

Esposito frowned. 'How did you guess?'

'I'm good with accents,' the homeless man smiled. 'And I've been around - a long time ago.'

'Yeah? Where?' the American asked.

'Oh, you know – here and there,' Fraser replied, shrugging. 'I've been most places once. And some places twice.'

'You're full of it, Fraser!' Rivera shook his head.

The homeless man winked. 'That's why you love me!' he chuckled. 'Now, let's get the doors open, shall we? That way I can move in properly.'

Chapter 9.

'Is this really necessary, Leah?'

Keane frowned. 'That's Miss Keane to you.'

The man asking the question laughed bitterly. He was shackled to a workbench in the basement beneath Keane's lock-up on the Church Moor Industrial Estate. He had a purple welt beneath one eye. The man had come because Keane had called him to a meeting; she'd wondered if he'd arrive with back up.

He hadn't. It was down to his own stupidity, she reflected. Dressed like she was, there was no way she was about to unload goods. But Curly had thought with his belt – he'd simply watched her bend over to reach into a crate. From that point onwards, he'd been hypnotised; he'd even wondered if the summons might end in a romantic entanglement. He was still pondering the possibility when Keane rose from the crate and smashed him across the face with a wrench.

He crumpled.

***

When the fallen man regained consciousness, he saw Keane had taken out a Heckler & Koch P7 and was pointing it at him. Any sense of bonhomie which might have existed before had evaporated. Curly found himself staring down the barrel where, moments before, he'd been trying to stare down the woman's top. She smiled, knowing there would be no cavalry arriving to bail Curly out. He knew it too.

'You going to risk firing that fucking thing here?' The man scoffed eventually. 'The bang will bring people running.'

Keane had smiled. 'Two things you should know, Curly,' she announced. 'Number one. With this baby, you get enough bang for your buck to blow a man's brains out, but you don't get so much of a report that it'll attract much attention. And number two, we're on an industrial estate.' She paused. 'Plenty of bangs and crashes.' She laughed. 'Besides – who's going to want to grass *me* up?'

Curly had shrugged. 'What now then?' He gritted his teeth. 'You always were a prick tease – so they say.'

Silence.

'See that hatch?' Keane nodded towards a hole in the floor. 'There's a flight of stairs leading down.'

'So?'

'Lead the way.' Her tone was cold. Emotionless.

The man frowned. 'I didn't know you had a basement here...'

'Nor does anyone else.' She paused. 'At least no one that matters.'

* * *

Curly stumbled his way down the steps, knocking into the rough walls. He squinted painfully at the glare of the naked bulb, his head pounding; he obeyed her order to handcuff himself to the bench. The man remained groggy from the blow as Keane snapped a second pair of cuffs onto his other hand. He was still seeing double when Keane had moved on to manacles, affixing his legs to the bench.

'What, then? Are we waiting until Bullseye gets here?' Curly demanded from the workbench, eventually. 'Do you have any aspirin? My head's killing!'

'No,' Keane shook her head as she removed the man's shoes and socks. 'And it's all me today. Sometimes it's good to keep your eye in. Don't you think?' She turned her nose up in distaste, draping her jacket over a nearby chair. 'Your feet fucking stink!'

Silence.

'Now then,' Keane said. 'The word is you've been fucking around with my operation.'

'I don't know what you're talking about,' Curly said tonelessly.

'Yeah, well, I'm not sure I believe that. You see, there's a whole load of kids who've shown up in South Quay wielding Baikals.' She paused. 'And that doesn't make me very happy.'

'What's a Baikal?' Curly's expression was one of innocence.

Keane sighed. 'Don't act all fucking innocent. You're not in a position to bullshit me.' She sighed. 'A Baikal is a Soviet-era handgun. Cheap. Fairly reliable. Reasonably easy to get hold of. But these are air pistols. Powerful enough to lose someone an eye or leave them lying in the gutter in need of medical attention if you catch them right. And *definitely* scary enough to frighten the hell out of someone. But not so deadly they'll leave people dead.' She paused. 'Not unless you're unlucky enough to hit someone on the temple.'

'So fucking what?' Curly demanded.

'So, these Baikals have been screwing things up for me. You give a load of kids guns, and they strut around thinking they're at the OK Corral. I need my supply to meet demand. No kinks in the chain.' She shook her head. 'You give a scally a gun and they think they can take the law into their own hands. And I think you've given a whole lot of scallies a whole load of guns.'

'Can we drop all this theatre?' Curly replied. 'I don't see what the fuck this has to do with me. I didn't do it, so fuck you.'

'You sure about that?' Keane raised her eyebrows. 'Only every kid we've spoken to claims the guns came from you.'

'Piss off,' the shackled man grimaced.

Keane walked over to the side of the basement and calmly picked up a blowtorch. She fired up the flame and then adjusted it until it produced a long, thin blue blade of light. 'Last chance,' she said.

Silence.

Keane approached the bench and held the flame close to the sole of Curly's left foot. The bound man tensed, winced, and ground his teeth as the acrid smell of burning flesh permeated. He began to heave at his restraints, rattling them desperately. A guttural scream started deep within him, emanating slowly.

'Stop!' he wailed. 'Please! I'll tell you what you want to know.'

'Disappointing.' Keane shook her head and slowly lowered the blowtorch, switching off the flame. 'I always thought you were a pussy, but I didn't think you were ever going to roll over as easily as that.'

'You burned half my fucking feet off!' Curly whimpered.

Keane laughed. 'I hadn't even started. Not properly, I mean. I'd have de-knackered you and flayed your fucking skin. And I'd only have been halfway there.'

'I'll fucking kill you,' the man spat.

'Yeah – good luck with that! From where you're lying, you've hardly got me quaking in my boots.'

'I mean it, bitch!' Curly snarled. 'When I get out of here, I'm going to bring a fucking army.'

Silence.

Keane tutted. 'You know that phrase about people in glass houses?'

Curly said nothing. Instead, he writhed in pain against his restraints. 'Fuck you!' The chains rattled.

Keane sighed. 'You know, we're not that different, you and I,' she explained. 'We're both in business. We both harm people if they fuck up.' She paused. 'That's how it works, doesn't it? Someone crosses you and you take care of them, right?'

The bound man said nothing. Instead, he emitted a roar of irritation as he grimaced and pulled in vain at his shackles.

'But there's a difference,' Keane continued calmly. 'You threaten people and then let them get away with things.' She paused. 'I don't.'

'What – so you're going to whack me now? Is that it?' Curly laughed. 'This is South Quay – not South fucking Central. What the fuck's the matter with you? You think you're an assassin now or something, is that it?'

Keane raised an eyebrow. 'Now there's a thought,' she replied playfully.

Curly laughed bitterly. 'You'll never get away with it.' His voice rose. 'People talk, you know. Bodies aren't that easy to fucking bury. They come back and bite you in the arse.'

Silence.

'Did you look around when you walked down here?' Keane asked, a look of amusement crossing her face. 'This basement doesn't exist – not on any records. Hardly anyone knows about it. Certainly not anyone who'll blab. Nobody even knows it's my place. It's down on record as a kitchen grouting warehouse – a place so boring that even painters and decorators give it a wide berth.'

Curly cleared his throat and spat across the room.

'Mind your manners now!' Keane cautioned, tutting. 'Anyway, what was I saying? Oh, yes - this whole place was *way* bigger when it was first hollowed out.' She grinned. 'But, these days, it's a magic room – it keeps on shrinking.'

Silence.

Keane took out a vanity mirror and examined her teeth, talking on as if absent-mindedly. 'Any time a corpse needs to vanish, it gets walled up and concreted over. So the room gets a little smaller each time.' She cast her eyes around. 'Clever, no?'

'Bollocks.' Curly's voice was uncertain now. 'This isn't the London bloody Dungeons.'

Keane ignored him. 'Remember Andy Hobson?' She waited for the name to sink in. 'He was your mate, wasn't he?'

The man on the workbench nodded.

'Yeah – well, I always thought he was a jumped up little prick.'

'So?'

'So when he was down on his luck and just out of rehab, I paid him to dig this out. The whole place.' She looked down at Curly. 'Where is he now, anyway - Hobbo?'

'Australia,' Curly replied. 'That's what I heard. We're not in touch.'

'Yeah,' Keane nodded, pocketing the vanity mirror. 'Australia. That's what people say.' She paused. 'But what I just asked you was a rhetorical question.'

'What the fuck are you talking about?' Curly's voice rose in pitch.

'See, when I was in jail, I did a lot of reading,' Keane explained. 'There wasn't much else to do. So, let me enlighten you... a rhetorical question is a grammatical device. It's when I ask you something, but I already know the answer.'

'So?'

'So, I asked you where Hobson was?' She paused. 'But I already know.'

Silence.

'When he was done digging,' Keane continued, 'he became part of the structure itself. Poetic really, don't you think? From builder to building. From digger to... oh – never fucking mind.'

Curly's eyes bulged manically. He kicked violently at his restraints, rattling the workbench as the truth dawned on him. The bench's legs, though, didn't budge from where they were securely bolted to the floor. The bound man's protests were suddenly sliced through by the whirring sound of a handheld power drill.

Keane walked up to the workbench and held the drill to the man's face. She dangled the revolving bit close to his eye. Curly jerked his head away automatically, swearing above the noise.

'So long then, Curly,' Keane announced tonelessly. She paused. The screaming of the mechanism mingled with the captive's roars as Keane pressed the drill bit to the side of the man's head. For a moment, the tip simply rested, whirring impossibly fast, sending flakes of skin and wisps of hair spiralling through the air. Then, the carbide cutting edge of the masonry drill penetrated the captive's flesh. From a small hole just above the man's ear, blood poured and started to splatter the surface of the bench. Keane grinned and increased the pressure.

Chapter 10.

The sky clouded over as Rivera walked back through the town. It didn't smell like rain, but the temperature had dropped considerably. Anxious tourists glanced suspiciously upwards as the clouds rolled in. As the ex-soldier strode along the promenade, he saw the beach was empty save for a few dog walkers. Limp, blackened strands of seaweed littered the sand, and plastic detritus marked the line of high tide. His gait was leisurely; lolloping even. But it still bore the unmistakable bent of the barracks parade ground.

He walked on.

South Quay in the sunshine reminded people why legions flocked to it once upon a time. Looking out across the bay when the sunlight was glittering on the water and small boats bobbed up and down lazily on the waves, it was almost possible to buy into the belief it was just like the Mediterranean. In such weather, dodgems and funfairs, Punch and Judy shows and roller discos became quaint. Kitsch.

The town shorn of sunshine, however, was a distinctly different prospect. Tacky tourist souvenir stands, which had a certain charm in better weather, suddenly seemed tragic; it was as if they too were desperately clinging to memories of the past. Cigarette smoke smelled acrid rather than beguiling, and the sweaty stench of yesterday's alcohol wafting from the arcades and their two-penny slots clung to passers-by. South Quay in the shade was a place long past its sell-by-date.

Rivera opted for the scenic route. From the seafront, he glanced up, observing The Diplomat Hotel looking down upon him from its commanding perch. The walk back to Golden Sands would take him about an hour. In lieu of a lunch break, he'd decided to travel on foot while Esposito had driven the laden truck back to the holiday camp. It was so full that the final pieces of furniture had only fitted on the passenger seat – he'd shared a cigarette with Fraser and then departed.

The ex-soldier scanned the shore.

Rivera's passion – other than literature – was birds. He'd liberated a sniper scope from the military upon returning from one of his tours of duty overseas. It hadn't been a conscious decision; he'd simply failed to inventory it. And so, when he'd walked off base one day, it had come with him. He found it worked extremely well in re-purposed form: rather than sighting targets through its crosshairs, he used its magnified lens to observe wildlife. South Quay harbour wasn't the most exotic of ornithological environments, but on a quiet day, there were cormorants aplenty.

It was these he was hoping to spot.

But, following ten minutes of leaning against the concrete sea wall as the tide lapped with increasing strength at its foundations, Rivera pressed on. The bird watching hadn't been massively successful. He decided to cut back inland for the rest of his walk – the wind was suddenly whipping up – and cold sea spray was being flung at the ex-soldier. Not for the first time, he considered the ludicrousness of palm trees being planted in the town. When the clouds came, they summed up the tragedy of the place - their fronds waving helplessly as they were buffeted by the breeze. Trees from the tropics standing like homesick refugees from Caribbean climes.

* * *

Walking the streets, the ex-soldier watched the world through his peripheral vision. It was something he'd grown accustomed to over the years.

Rivera knew what bad neighbourhoods looked like. The signs were sometimes subtle. He'd been in enough warzones and difficult situations to understand what to look for. Sometimes, picking up on almost invisible cues was the only thing that could keep someone from death or serious injury. That had certainly been the case with IEDs in Afghanistan and Iraq. The ex-soldier still bore scars. They'd healed, but the memories attached to them still surfaced from time to time. Raw. Sometimes he still dreamed of vicious tripwires twinkling in the sun across the sun-scarred scorched earth of hostile hamlets.

When he'd been redeployed, the Army provided intensive training in Pashto and Dari. Rivera's mentor had been a man named Mitchell Tyler. He was a rogue; a loose cannon. The ex-soldier always felt that – had he been in any other walk of life – he'd have been sectioned; condemned to life in a secure facility. Straitjacketed even. Being a translator in Afghanistan, though, meant his off-kilter mindset was perfect. He trod a line pitched exactly halfway between court martial and medals. As a result, the Top Brass tolerated him. They knew he'd slip up, but they also knew that in the battle for hearts and minds, there were few better people to have on board. The tribal elders took to him – that was reason enough for him to keep his position.

The experienced translator had taken the newcomer under his wing. They'd been together in Helmand just short of six months. Each day it felt like Rivera learned something new. But, every time, it seemed his mentor had known it before.

Then Tyler died.

A roadside IED exploded, destroying the truck he'd been travelling in. A firefight had ensued. But the insurgents had melted away into the hillside as the wounded troops awaited air support. Night fell, and another wave of enemy fighters targeted the stricken party. It was first light before they were finally evacuated.

The man's body had never been recovered.

By then, Rivera had already begun suspecting he wanted out of the military. Tyler's death only confirmed his decision. The whispers in his head were growing louder.

* * *

After news had come through of his friend's demise, Rivera felt like he was living on borrowed time. The next bullet – he believed – would have his name on it. He saw himself being buried alive; tortured; butchered. And, through it all, Tyler's voice rang in his ears; a rasping, wheezing, comical accompaniment to the show reel that plagued him.

There were occasions when Rivera swore he even saw the other man on the street.

Over time, Tyler's presence had diminished. But there were still occasions that he sensed him – it was when his senses were on high alert. At such times, Rivera imagined his mentor's voice once more. When he did, he stepped extra carefully, surveying his surroundings ever more sharply.

Was that child a lookout?

Was that woman carrying a weapon?

Those men by the café – did they have an explosive device rigged up?

That phone – was it being used to summon a hit?

When he'd first come home, the questions had been constant. A barrage. They haunted Rivera until they almost got the better of him. It had only been after a long period of travel in Iris with only Rosie for company, that he'd stopped regarding the rest of the world like a warzone. Before he ceased to imagine the green grass of British fields would explode in brilliant shell bursts of red, yellow and orange at any moment. Before he put an end to studying the faces of strangers for signs they were out to kill him.

It worked.

Eventually.

* * *

Today, though, his old feelings were back. Tyler's tones weren't as loud as they had been when he'd first been demobilised, but they were there nonetheless. There was – Rivera reasoned – something simply not right about South Quay. Huddled groups of poorly clothed people hung around on street corners, regarding the world with furtive glances. They looked haunted, desperate, as they scratched involuntarily at their sleeves. Some were clearly homeless. Others looked soon set to join their ranks. They drew hard on the stubs of cigarettes picked up from the ground and spoke in a curious mishmash of reedy accents with timbres borne of too many inhalations of synthetic smoke.

After the third group of such people, the pattern was clear. Rivera didn't believe in coincidences – these were stops on a drug route; a South Quay Silk Road. He thought back to what Clarke had told him about the gang using ice cream vans for cover. This was proof positive that there was substance to the foreman's suggestion. He wasn't just a prejudiced tabloid reader – the town was clearly in hock to something.

Or someone.

Chapter 11.

'Dammit!' Esposito hissed.

'Problem?' Rivera enquired. The pair had almost finished unloading the furniture into a number of the completed chalets. Chairs and tables were stuffed inside, reaching up to the ceilings.

'There were two big boxes of leads for the TVs,' the woman announced.

'Yeah?'

'Yeah – and they won't work without them.'

Rivera nodded over to the rows of television sets that covered the floor of the chalet they were standing outside. 'I'm not sure anyone's going to be watching them today. Not given the fact they're all set out facing each other.' He paused. 'And these blocks don't have any guests in them yet.'

'I know,' Esposito nodded. 'But Clarke said he wants everything back here today. Apparently he needs to inventory it or something – Bourse's orders.'

The ex-soldier sighed. 'What difference does it make if we do it today or tomorrow? I mean - is it really that urgent?'

'I guess not,' the American replied. 'But he was talking about PAT testing them or something. Apparently Bourse was on his case about it. When I saw him earlier, he was really riding the poor guy. I guess it must be important.'

Rivera nodded. 'Looking at these TV sets, I'd say most of them are about ten years out of date. I don't think you need a PAT test to tell you that. Half of them will be almost kaput – any money! It'd be like watching a snowstorm and wiggling around the aerial – like TV used to be...'

'Agreed,' Esposito nodded. 'But I can't be bothered getting into another argument with him.' She puffed. 'I'll walk back and get it.'

'Can't you take the truck?' Rivera frowned.

'No – maintenance needed it back half an hour ago,' she sighed.

'Don't worry, I'll go,' the ex-soldier announced. 'I'll take Iris.'

'No. It's my screw-up,' Esposito insisted.

'Coin toss?' Rivera raised his eyebrows.

The American frowned. 'You keep making offers like that and I'll start thinking you're one of the good guys.' She paused. 'Haven't you got anything better to do?'

'Not really. No.' He shrugged. 'You get to my age and an evening in with a book is a luxury – not like you crazy kids who go out and paint the town.'

Esposito grinned at the deliberate anachronism and removed a coin from her pocket. 'Heads, you go. Tails it's me. Fair?'

'Fine by me,' Rivera nodded. 'I can have a word with Fraser, anyway.' She flipped the coin.

'Heads it is. Just remember that I haven't finished with those brakes yet.'

* * *

Iris complained about the steep gradient leading up to The Diplomat Hotel. Rivera had changed down through the gears until there were no others left to choose from. Unlocking the security gate and sliding the fencing aside, he noticed a new stack of white goods had been fly-tipped just out of sight of the road. The ex-soldier frowned – he didn't think he and Esposito had been gone long enough for that to happen. And he reasoned someone must have been feeling pretty confident to ditch the stuff in broad daylight.

Shrugging, he climbed back inside the cab of the campervan and drove up the driveway to the hotel entrance. It was quiet. Walking up to the front door, he found it unlocked from where he'd given Fraser the key earlier. From the front porch, the sounds of the town were oddly distorted as they floated up the incline.

Inside, the hallway was dark. Rivera stepped into the gloom.

The homeless man appeared at the top of the stairs. 'Greetings, chief!' he announced loudly. 'Back so soon?'

'Yeah, I forgot something,' the ex-soldier explained.

Fraser laughed. 'That's what they all say, squire. You just couldn't wait to see me again. I know what you're like!'

Rivera laughed. 'You going to give me a hand or what?' he asked. 'I need to shift a few more boxes.'

'Can do,' the homeless man nodded. 'You can check out my digs if you like? Cold running water. Threadbare carpets. I've only got an inch or two of dust on any given surface... it's paradise! I've set myself up with a suite. Lap of luxury here, let me tell you!' As he descended the staircase, he had another coughing fit. 'I reckon I'm on the mend now – this indoor living's a right treat!'

* * *

'I'd forgotten how much of a beauty this old girl is,' Fraser marvelled, running his hand lovingly over the painted sprig of purple and yellow flowers on Iris' door. The two men loaded the boxes of TV cables into the back of the Volkswagen. 'I always wanted a T2.' He looked at the other man and grinned. 'I had to settle for a Ferrari, though. You know – needs must and all that.'

'You up to much today then?' Rivera enquired.

'Living like Lord Muck was my first plan,' Fraser replied. 'And then after that, who knows? I reckoned there might be a few ladies interested in me now I've got a period property with a view.'

'And in future – after your harem's visited?'

'I'm a rolling stone, chief. You know that...'

Rivera chewed his lip and eyed the other man for a moment. 'Look, I know you're not just some derelict. I know you're smart and I know there's a whole lot of history you don't want to talk about. My guess is military – maybe you'll tell me one day...'

'Yeah, one day. Maybe,' Fraser shrugged.

'But sleeping rough isn't doing you any favours,' Rivera said, a tone of concern creeping into his voice. 'England's cold. Wet. Miserable. And this place – South Quay... when I saw you last time – in Saltmarsh Cove – you said you were thinking about following the sun.'

'Yeah?'

'So why not?' Rivera shrugged.

The homeless man smiled a little. 'It's not that easy, you know? It's never that easy. It's not like I've got a villa in the south of France. And... it's not like I'm swimming in money exactly. We were so poor growing up that my mother sold all the curtains from the house – imagine that! My inheritance wasn't ever going to be up to much. Despite what it might look like.' He laughed hoarsely and then began coughing. 'So, once I hit sixteen, I left home. It's fine – I made my choices. Good... and bad.'

'Listen,' Rivera pressed. 'It's none of my business, but you're not sounding too healthy these days.'

Fraser scoffed.

The ex-soldier sighed. 'I'm working at the Golden Sands. You know – the holiday camp. I could probably swing you a job there if you liked?'

'Not really my kind of scene, chief. Still too chilly.' He grinned. 'You know how the song goes – *I'm going where the weather suits my clothes*?'

Silence.

'I know some construction workers in Spain,' the ex-soldier continued. 'Friends of mine. They'll employ you – I'm sure of it. Wall-to-wall sunshine. I'll sub you if you want to head down there. Sort your travel. You know, clean up your act. Fresh start – stuff like that?' Rivera paused. 'It'll do you good – working with your hands; working with the sun on your back.'

Fraser sniffed and looked down for a moment, examining his fingernails. 'You know,' he replied eventually, looking up. 'A while ago, I'd have punched your lights out for having the audacity to make a suggestion like that. I never did take too kindly to do-gooders.'

Rivera raised his eyebrows.

Silence.

'You'd do that, though?' Fraser asked quietly, disbelieving.

'Of course.' Rivera nodded, grinning.

'And there'd be a job when I arrived? Because I wouldn't want to get down to the Costa del Crime and find out you'd left me in the lurch.'

'Definitely – I'll call ahead,' the ex-soldier insisted.

Fraser leaned back against Iris and looked back up at the imposing façade of The Diplomat Hotel. 'It might surprise you, but years ago I stayed in places like this all the time.' He paused, a faraway look in his eye. 'They weren't derelict mind.' He shook his head. 'It's funny how things turn out.'

Silence.

'Give me a couple of days,' Fraser continued. 'Then I'll take you up on the offer. There are a few things I need to do here first, though.'

'Yeah? Like what?'

'Tie up a few loose ends.' The homeless man shrugged. 'See a couple of people. Locate my passport. The usual.'

'And then?'

'And then, I guess I'll get going. Old Fraser needs a change of scenery from time to time. I reckon a fresh start might do me some good.'

The ex-soldier held out his hand for the homeless man to shake.

'You're a good man, Rivera,' Fraser announced. 'The homeless encounter three types of people in this life: the do-nothings who walk on by like we're invisible; the do-nothing do-gooders who come and talk to us to make themselves feel better but don't leave with their pockets any lighter. They're real pricks.' He paused. 'And then there are people like you. There's precious few around.' He nodded for a moment, grateful.

'Don't go getting all sentimental on me now!' Rivera chuckled. 'I don't really do emotions.'

'No danger of that, chief!' Fraser began hacking again.

Rivera climbed into Iris' cab and started the engine. As he pulled away, Fraser banged on the side of the campervan enthusiastically.

'I'll see you soon!' he called out.

Chapter 12.

'It's business,' Keane announced. Even when dressed down in distressed jeans and a white top, she was glamorously immaculate. A thin silver chain hung around her neck; her shoulders were gym-toned and fake-tanned, and her hair had the lustrous sheen of several layers of product. Her eyes, though, were cold. Mean. To anyone looking on, she would have looked every inch the multi-millionaire. What wouldn't have been apparent was the illicit means through which the money had been made.

The boss enjoyed her wealth, but she did so elsewhere. Lavish holidays abroad. Fast cars. Scuba diving. Fine dining. Nobody really knew about her love life – nobody had the courage to ask. Not even Bullseye. That was an aspect of her life she left behind on the Turks and Caicos Islands; in Dubai; on beaches in the Maldives.

When it came to South Quay, though, she was all business.

* * *

Bullseye stood alongside Keane in front of the boss' abode. It was a double-fronted detached house on a well-established street. When her neighbours asked about what she did, she always said she was in risk management. It was true, she mused to herself – she managed whoever was at risk of a reminder from Bullseye about how to behave; whoever needed a kicking; who needed a forever kind of justice. The lie came easily, but it kept people at arm's length. Keane was confident none of those living in the surrounding streets would voice their suspicions about contributions she wasn't making to the Inland Revenue. But, all the same, she did her best to blend in. She'd even attended drinks events and street parties on occasion, marvelling at how tedious the lives of others truly were.

As Bullseye intoned, Keane absent-mindedly inspected a drainpipe and then began picking at a patch of moss growing on her pebble-dashed front wall. The driveway was made of bricks that were carefully laid in a herringbone design. A Range Rover was parked on it. The space was walled, with wrought-iron railings rising to a height of about ten feet. There were coniferous plants. Flowers. The house's front windows were double-glazed in a lattice design. It was no different from any of the other houses on the street, which screamed of aspiration and upward mobility. The only thing which looked incongruous was the enormous Rottweiler that stood with its paws on the windowsill, eyeing the male visitor with ill-disguised contempt.

'You sure about this, though?' Bullseye asked. He towered over Keane as he spoke. And yet, he was the one who looked uncomfortable; hesitant. There was no doubting the balance of power on the driveway.

'Of course I fucking am,' Keane shrugged. 'We've done it before. You've stashed the jerry cans there already, right?'

'Yeah.'

'And you remember how to strike a match?'

Bullseye nodded.

'Well then,' Keane frowned. 'What's the fucking problem?'

The man looked around nervously. 'The two... you know? You said you wanted them gone, right?' He paused. 'You mean *really* gone, yeah?'

Keane sighed.

'You know that thing we mentioned before?' Keane raised her eyebrows.

Bullseye looked at her blankly.

'Harris and the other fucking joker?' Keane continued.

The man nodded, his mouth hanging open a little. He narrowed his eyes slightly as the wheels revolved in his brain.

Keane looked hard at him. 'Invite them along.'

'What?' Bullseye frowned.

'You heard! Do I actually have to fucking spell it out for you?' Keane demanded, turning away from the drainpipe and giving the visitor her full attention for the first time. 'Pick them up. Tell them we want to talk things through. Take them out for lunch. Do something nice. But make sure you're carrying.'

'Why?' The big man frowned once more.

Keane sighed. 'Because when you've buttered them up and fed them caviar and they're half-cut on champagne, they'll think you're their friend again. And then you're going to use the piece on them.'

'What – shoot them?'

'No, you daft twat!' Keane shook her head. 'Save yourself a job. Take them to The Diplomat.'

'But the...' Realisation suddenly dawned on Bullseye's face.

'There you go!' Keane nodded. 'You got there in the end – I swear I sometimes wonder whether all those blows to the head busted your brain somewhere along the way.' She paused. 'Let the fire do its thing. It'll just be a tragic accident. And with us contracted for the rebuild, we can make sure anything that's found there gets hushed up, can't we? Just tie them up so they can't get away and then get the hell out of there before anyone sees.'

Bullseye nodded. 'What about the chairs?'

'What?' Keane frowned, narrowing her eyes in disbelief at the question. 'What about the fucking chairs? What the fuck are you talking about?'

The big man scratched at his neck, uncomfortable. 'I was there a couple of days ago – ditching some more stuff in the grounds.'

'And?'

'There's loads of furniture in the ballroom. I looked through the window.'

Keane nodded, pursing her lips. 'Yeah. That's bloody Bourse, isn't it? I said he could keep the stuff there while they're doing up those chalets. Thought I'd keep him sweet.' She paused. 'Don't worry – I'll give him a call and tell him to shake a leg. We've stripped everything else out of there we can sell already, so once that stuff's out of the way, you're good to go.'

Bullseye nodded. He stood, immobile, watching the woman.

'What?'

'What do you mean?' The big man looked mystified.

'What are you waiting for?' Keane demanded impatiently. 'Get yourself over to The Diplomat and let me know if it's clear!' Her voice took on a rasping tone as her frustration grew. 'I don't pay you to stand there gawking. Move!'

'I just thought that...' Bullseye began.

'...well don't think,' Keane interrupted. 'Leave the thinking to me.' She shook her head and glared at the man with disdain. 'Sometimes I wonder how you even remember to breathe. Go on – get the fuck out of here.'

Chapter 13.

Rivera sipped at a bottle of mineral water and tucked a worn paperback into his back pocket. He removed a rolled cigarette from where it had been wedged behind his ear. The mid-afternoon break was only ever brief. Workers simply sat out on the porches of whichever properties they were refitting and took a few minutes to catch their breath. The ex-soldier lit up.

Esposito was sitting cross-legged on the decking. Before her, a pack of cards was spread out, lined up in columns as she played Patience. Rivera, smoking, looked up at the sky. The earlier rain clouds had dissipated; the weather had remained dry as the heavy squalls of cloud had rolled away, leaving a blue-tinged canvas in their wake. Up above, the sun was shining unenthusiastically.

The ex-soldier watched, mildly interested, as Clarke walked towards them. He was speaking animatedly to another man in a grey suit, pointing and gesticulating. The dynamic was clear: the be-suited man was in charge, but he seemed rather uncomfortable in the face of Clarke's admonishment.

'That's Bourse,' Esposito announced softly, looking up from the deck. 'Get a load of that shiny suit – he looks like he should be selling timeshare properties and fleecing old ladies.' She shook her head and returned her gaze to the cards as the pair came into earshot.

'I don't fucking care!' Clarke said gruffly. 'My staff are no business of yours.'

'They're *my* staff!' the other man insisted. 'I pay their bloody wages. Don't go forgetting that, Clarke.'

The foreman turned, regarding the other man with disdain. 'You *can* go off a bloke, Bourse – remember that.'

'And you can be demoted to a lowlier position. Bear *that* in mind.'

Silence.

Clarke sighed. 'What then?' he demanded. 'What do you want me to do? Out with it – or have you just come down here to waggle your finger?'

'Check!' the boss ordered, bluntly. 'Like I said.'

Clarke sighed again and led the man over to the cabin where Esposito and Rivera were situated.

'This is Aaron Bourse,' Clarke announced through gritted teeth.

The ex-soldier nodded, eyeing the other man.

'He's the owner of the Golden Sands,' Esposito announced from the floor without looking up.

Rivera nodded again. He then looked at the foreman and raised his eyebrows, waiting expectantly.

Clarke cleared his throat. 'Mr Bourse wants to ask you something,' he explained. He turned and shook his head at the man beside him. 'Although why the hell he needs to ask you *now* is beyond me.' The foreman spat onto the ground beside him and rubbed the sole of his boot into the dirt.

'The fact it's beyond you is of no concern to me,' the owner said, adopting a supercilious tone. 'When you're given an instruction, Clarke, I expect you to follow it.'

'But why the urgency?' the foreman shrugged. 'Can't you just let the pair of them have their tea break like everyone else?'

'This afternoon break is unofficial, you know?' Bourse sniffed.

Clarke narrowed his eyes. 'Do you want to get everyone together so you can tell them that?'

Bourse looked hard at Rivera, ignoring his foreman's complaints. 'You were at The Diplomat Hotel today, correct?'

Rivera nodded. 'I was.'

'And is it clear?' Bourse went on.

The ex-soldier frowned. 'Clear of what?'

'All the furniture we've been storing there.' The owner held Rivera's gaze as he spoke.

'Yes,' Rivera replied. 'We brought the last of it back today. It's clear. Not clean, necessarily, but definitely clear. Why?'

'Good,' Bourse nodded, ignoring the question.

'Happy now, your majesty?' Clarke sighed, looking at the other man contemptuously. 'I told you they'd done a decent job. And...'

Bourse had already turned and had begun walking away.

'Sorry about that,' the foreman shrugged. 'It beats me why he's suddenly become so het up about this. He's never usually interested in anything.' He paused and lowered his voice. 'You two can take an extra five minutes.'

The pair nodded.

As Clarke walked away, Esposito turned to look at Rivera. 'What was all that about, do you think?'

The ex-soldier shrugged. 'No clue. Handbags at dawn – something like that, maybe?'

'Weird...' she shrugged, turning her attention back to the cards.

* * *

'Shit!' Esposito stood up and kicked at the wood of the chalet balcony in irritation.

'What?' Rivera frowned.

'I left my plane at the hotel,' she sighed.

The ex-soldier narrowed his eyes a little. 'Is this the time I'm supposed to make a hilarious joke about why you drove there this morning if you could have flown?'

The American gave Rivera a cold look. 'Very bloody funny. It's a good one.'

'What – the joke?'

'Piss off.'

'I'll ask Fraser to grab it tomorrow,' the ex-soldier shrugged. 'You should break a match – that'll be three times we've had to head up there today. It's beginning to feel unlucky. I mean – it's pretty and all, but not *that* pretty.'

'Break a match?' Esposito asked quizzically, a lopsided grin temporarily distorting her fine features.

Rivera sighed. 'Trying to make me feel older than I am? My folks used to say that bad luck came in threes, and to stop the trouble we needed to break a match,' he explained. 'Anyway - why not leave it until tomorrow? That way...'

'...no.' She shook her head. 'I'm going now – it's a good plane. I told you.'

Rivera frowned. 'Forgive my ignorance, but how good can a bloody plane be?'

'It's a family heirloom,' she explained. 'My Uncle Nelson gave it to me as a birthday gift a couple of years back. It's stamped 1902. There's a patent plate and everything. It's been passed down through the generations. The story goes that my great grandfather had it when he was restoring furniture in rural Maine. Some of the pieces he worked on dated back to the War of Independence. A few of them are in the Smithsonian now. And then my grandfather used it building homes in Topanga Canyon after the war for returning vets.' She paused. 'It's a violin maker's plane – there's no way I'm leaving it.' She paused. 'No fucking way.'

The ex-soldier sighed. 'You're not angling for another coin toss, are you? I'm going to wear holes in my bloody boots walking up and down that hill at this rate.' He shook his head. 'I've lost every time as it is.'

Esposito smiled. 'No! Don't worry. I'll go.' She began to stand up. 'Hey - they're screening *Citizen Kane* at the Central tonight.'

'Yeah?'

'Yeah.'

'Any good?'

'What – the film or the movie theatre?'

Rivera shrugged. 'Both – I guess.'

'Well, one's a classic. And one isn't.' She paused. 'I'll leave you to figure out which is which. You've heard of Orson Welles, right?'

'Wasn't he the guy who did the radio thing – *War of the Worlds*?'

'Yeah – very good. Top marks.' The American nodded. 'Well, he co-wrote it. And directed it. He even starred in it as the main character. So – a Jack-of-all-trades, and a master of... all.'

Rivera nodded. 'I thought all you young guns were out tripping the light fantastic, though? That's the scuttlebutt.'

'Yeah,' Esposito shrugged. 'Some of them are - the crew here are all out in town for Billy's birthday.' She paused. 'So - fancy coming along?'

'Where? The cinema or Billy's birthday?'

'The cinema – obviously! That sleazy fucker Stu is out with the rest of them. I don't want to be anywhere near that asshole.' She raised her eyebrows. 'So how about it – you, me and Orson Welles?'

The ex-soldier nodded. 'Why not?'

Esposito chuckled. 'Steady on – that enthusiasm of yours will get the better of you otherwise!'

Rivera grinned.

Chapter 14.

The foyer of South Quay Central Cinema was quiet. It usually was. Unless there was a new release of a franchise featuring fast cars being raced by felons, then the local population wasn't interested. A bored-looking student with multiple piercings, an array of tattoos on her forearms, and a sullen expression had sold Rivera two tickets. The booth in which she sat was laden with flyers and glossy leaflets, and the wall behind her was decorated with posters. She was leafing through Ian Hunter's autobiography. For a moment, the ex-soldier considered making conversation about Mott the Hoople, but then he thought better of it.

'Quiet tonight?' he'd muttered in an attempt to be civil.

The girl shrugged. 'We're an arts cinema in an artistic desert,' she explained. 'With a film like this, we'll be lucky to cover our costs. That's why we've started showing blockbusters at weekends. Otherwise, we'll go bust. Have you seen this town?'

Rivera nodded.

'Then what do you fucking expect?'

The ex-soldier frowned. 'Interesting way to address a customer...'

The girl looked up. 'Sorry. What do you fucking expect – sir?'

Rivera shrugged and backed away. In the past, he hadn't been fussy about where he'd sought gratification. He'd been out with a few students since his break-up with Betsy, but even he had to draw a line somewhere. The girl behind the counter was a bridge too far.

Waiting for his colleague, he idly thumbed through a few leaflets. Beyond the glass of the grandiose doors, he saw a security guard. The man had an earpiece wired to a radio, and above his black jacket, he wore a high-visibility gilet. Frowning, the ex-soldier regarded the man. He'd been in plenty of tough places before, but couldn't recall ever having seen a security guard outside a movie theatre.

He stepped outside.

'Alright?' the guard nodded, looking up from his phone.

'Evening,' Rivera nodded. 'Busy?'

The man shrugged. 'The usual. This place shits out wrong 'uns pretty regularly; you stick around and stuff will get spicy.'

'Forgive me for asking,' the ex-soldier began, 'but... this is a cinema.' He paused. 'Why the security?'

The other man sniffed. 'You've seen this town, right?'

Rivera nodded. 'Yeah – you're not the first person to ask me that.'

'Well, then... Losers. Wasters. Junkies. If you're not careful, they'll come into a premises like this to try to find somewhere to sleep. They'll steal. Clutter up the entranceway. Shoot up in the toilets. Same as everywhere else.'

'Yeah?'

'Yeah,' the man nodded. 'Weekdays I do security for the public library at the bottom of the hill. It's exactly the same story down there.'

'You're shitting me!' the ex-soldier exclaimed.

'Dead serious, my friend,' the security guard sighed. 'I've lived in this town my whole life. In the last ten years, I've seen it go downhill and then downhill some more. I thought it might have hit rock bottom already, but it just keeps right on fucking falling.' The man held up a hand as the screen of his phone lit up with an incoming call. He tapped at his earpiece and listened intently.

Rivera smiled politely and stepped back inside the vestibule.

* * *

'You OK?' Rivera enquired. Esposito looked drawn and pensive as she entered the cinema. She was still dressed in her work clothes.

'Sort of,' she nodded. 'I guess.'

'Problem?' Rivera frowned.

The American paused for a moment, weighing her words. 'Not exactly. Just something weird.'

'Weird – like how?'

Esposito frowned. 'Well, I got to The Diplomat, and Bourse was there.'

'So?' the ex-soldier shrugged. 'He stored his furniture there, right? He must be well in with whoever owns it.'

'It wasn't so much him,' Esposito explained. 'He was there with a woman.'

Rivera raised his eyebrows. 'Hardly a crime, is it? I mean – it seems a crime that any woman would consider him worth spending time with, but there's no accounting for taste – especially when you're talking about a guy like that. He's got money behind him, after all.' Rivera grinned. 'How else do you think he affords those shiny suits?'

The American grinned. 'Yeah, but something about it wasn't right. They looked too shifty.'

'Maybe they're having an affair?'

'No,' the American shook her head. 'It wasn't like that.'

Silence.

'What did you say to them?' the ex-soldier enquired.

'Nothing.'

'No?'

'Damn right! Last time I was alone with Bourse, he tried to jump me. And when I told him I liked girls, he told me he could show me what I'd been missing out on. It made me feel sick.' She shuddered a little. 'He gives me the creeps, even with someone else there.'

Rivera nodded. 'Did you get the plane?'

'I did.' Esposito nodded and held up the tool. It glinted a little in the overhead lighting. She looked hard at the other man, frowning. 'You think I'm over-reacting, don't you?'

'I don't know. It's just...'

'I know,' she shrugged. 'I probably am, but I swear there was something going on – more than just Bourse getting it on with someone. Besides, the chick he was with was *way* out of his league. More my type than his,' she smiled.

'And what was Fraser doing?' Rivera enquired.

'I didn't see him.'

'No?' Rivera chewed his lip pensively. He turned to regard Esposito. 'I'm going to head up there after the film – check things out. Speak with Fraser again. If Bourse is hanging around there, then I need to warn him off. Fraser's going to be leaving town soon – the last thing he needs is Bourse bunging him in jail and letting him fester in a cell.'

Esposito nodded, slowly. 'I'll come with you – I'll be curious to see if they're still hanging around.'

Chapter 15.

Keane was sitting in her usual place at the bar of The George as Bullseye walked in. Her day had featured a health spa, a massage, and a business lunch with three Oxbridge-educated investors. She'd more than held her own with them, but it was here she felt at home. This was her preserve. She raised her eyebrows.

The big man gave a subtle nod.

'You're not completely fucking useless then!' the boss chuckled.

'Piss off!' Bullseye smirked, revelling in the recognition. The establishment was only sparsely populated with other drinkers. It was a place where everyone knew everyone. And where all those present knew the importance of keeping their mouths shut. Either of the pair at the bar could have shot someone at point blank range right in front of any of them, and they would have denied all knowledge. The powerful aroma of smoke clinging to the big man, therefore, wouldn't even register in their memories.

'That smell,' Keane began. 'Reminds me of the kind of things we got up to back in the day.' For a moment, neither of them said anything. The shared recollection flickered in their memories.

'You'd reek of bloody petrol too!' Bullseye grinned, eventually.

'Thirsty work, was it?' the boss enquired.

'Fucking right!'

'Danny!' The boss' voice rang out. 'Get this man a nice cold beer.' Keane turned around to indicate the other drinkers present. 'Get them all a fucking beer.' She grinned at the barman as a few cheers rose from the establishment's various tables. 'Stick them all on my tab.'

The barman nodded, his eyelid twitching slightly.

***

A couple of drinks later, Keane leaned across the bar, lowering her voice as she addressed Bullseye. 'So – did you get rid of them? The two – I mean?'

Bullseye nodded.

'Any issues?'

'Not really.' The big man shook his head. 'I found a tramp, though.'

'What?' Keane's eyes widened. She tilted her head a little, uncertain for once. 'And... what the fuck? Don't tell me you let him go – he might blab. He might...'

'No.' Bullseye couldn't recall interrupting his boss many times before. It gave him a curious feeling. 'He knew too much. He talked about two people visiting earlier.' Bullseye chuckled. 'He was pretty angry at them for leaving the doors open.'

'And?'

Bullseye shrugged. 'And I tied him to a radiator like the others.'

Keane nodded, calmer now. 'Good – it'll have been me and Bourse he saw.'

Bullseye frowned. 'Why were you there again?' the other man asked.

'Insurance.'

Bullseye frowned. 'What? Already?'

'No, you fucking dope!' Keane shook her head. 'In case anything goes wrong. Remember, we can pin it on him – I left the CCTV running. And I made sure he had his phone on him. They'll be able to use mobile data to place him there. If we need it doing, I mean.' She paused. 'If...' She looked hard at the big man. 'Witnesses?'

'No – it was dead quiet. No one around.'

Keane nodded.

'Are we done then, boss? Can I get rat-arsed?' Bullseye asked, hopefully.

Keane produced a vanity mirror and touched up her make-up. 'Not just yet,' she replied.

'Why?' the big man frowned.

'There's a girl I want.'

'Yeah?' Bullseye's face lit up. 'What, like...?' He tilted his head a little, his eyes widening. 'Is she fit?'

Keane's countenance tightened. She glared at the other man. 'That's none of your fucking business,' she hissed. 'Anyway, it's not for that.' She shook her head. 'Whatever it might be that's going on in that pretty-dumb-even-for-nursery-school brain of yours. She works at the Golden Sands. Bourse told me.'

Bullseye nodded, then frowned. 'So, what do you want her for then?'

The boss pursed her lips. 'I went back over the CCTV. I showed it all to Bourse in the office – I wanted him to know that I could pin the fire on him if he decided to roll over. You know – standard kind of stuff.'

'And?'

'And she was bloody there. Sneaking around. She came in around the back. I nearly missed her – I was showing it to him on fast forward, but she kind of flitted into shot like a shadow.'

The big man nodded. 'Did she see you?'

'Possibly.' She paused. 'Probably. I told Bourse there was no way she'd have seen either of us. But when I went back over the film, I reckon there was a fair chance.'

Bullseye nodded. 'Why was she there?'

'Who knows?' Keane shrugged. 'Nosy. Unlucky. Who cares? But she needs taking care of.'

The big man's face clouded. 'You mean...?'

'Yeah.'

Silence.

'So...' Bullseye nodded. 'Where?'

Keane lowered her voice still further. 'She's staying in one of the chalets at the holiday park. Number 12 – that's what Bourse told me. There's a whole load of crusties living there – folk who're working on the refurbishment. With any luck, the police'll pin it on them. Especially if we give them a bit of encouragement. Know what I mean?'

'Won't there be people around though?' Bullseye frowned. He drew the back of his hand across his mouth to wipe away the froth from his freshly-poured pint that had gathered on his upper lip.

'No, apparently not – they're all out at some party. It's sorted. Bourse has had some lad chatting her up. He's been laying it on thick – pestering her, so she won't be going anywhere near. The rest of them will, though.'

The big man nodded. 'So, she's not going?'

'Clearly.' Keane rolled her eyes. 'Shouldn't be, anyway.' She frowned. 'Do you need me to draw you a diagram? Act it out with hand puppets?'

Silence.

The boss spoke again. 'There's a bloke she's been hanging around with, though. He's not one of the regular crowd. The foreman there really rates him – he reckons the sun shines out of his arse.'

'Yeah?'

Keane nodded. 'He's older. Looks like he could handle himself – that's according to Bourse, anyway.'

'Like he'd know!' Bullseye scoffed. 'He's a pussy at the best of times.'

The woman smiled, nodding. 'Yeah – that's what I thought. He's probably well past it.'

'What do you want doing with him then?' the big man pressed.

'The same,' Keane ordered bluntly. 'If he's there.'

Bullseye nodded. 'You sure?'

'Of course, I'm fucking sure!' the boss frowned. 'And if not, then there's no need to worry.' She peered down at her phone as it pinged, capturing her interest. She lifted it and looked at it intently. Raising her glance, she looked back to Bullseye, frowning as she did so. 'You still here?' she demanded.

The big man skulked away.

Chapter 16.

After the film, the foyer was deserted. Heading for the cinema entrance, Rivera and Esposito glanced at each other and then looked outside. The formerly disinterested girl from behind the counter was now standing on the pavement, talking quite animatedly. She was positioned next to the security guard. Both were standing a good distance away from the building, alternatively looking upwards and then turning to talk excitedly to one another.

Stepping outside, the smell of burning hit the pair immediately. The sound of sirens floated on the breeze; the light from streetlamps was a little wispy where occasional plumes of smoke wafted past.

The ex-soldier stepped away from the entrance and then walked out from under the awning. He approached the security guard and then looked up to catch a first look at the blazing hulk of The Diplomat Hotel; it burned like a beacon above the town, its flames shooting hundreds of feet into the night sky. Esposito stood beside him. People in the street stopped and stared at the spectacle above them. It burned with a yellow-orange glow, the shadowy skeleton of its frame darkly visible. Ghoulish. Macabre.

'Shit!' hissed Esposito.

Rivera stared, frowning. 'You weren't smoking when you were up there, were you?' he asked.

'I was not.' She shook her head. 'You don't think Fraser would have been, do you?'

'Doubt it.' The ex-soldier shook his head. 'He's usually pretty careful.'

The pair stepped back away from the curb as a police car raced past, its blue lights flashing. A drunken group of twenty-somethings emerged from a nearby pub rowdily singing. They fell strangely silent once they set eyes upon the spectacle high above them, staring solemnly like everyone else.

'How long's it been burning?' Rivera called over to the security guard.

'Not long,' the other man shrugged. 'It went up like a fucking volcano. One minute there was a spark, and the next it was Armageddon. The place must've been a bloody tinderbox.'

* * *

'And you say Bourse was there earlier?' Rivera turned to address his colleague.

Esposito nodded. 'Yep. And the woman – the one I told you about.' She turned to Rivera and squinted. 'Why? You think it's a coincidence?'

The ex-soldier kicked at a dislodged strip of cement that was coming away from the edge of a paving slab and shrugged. 'It's just... he seemed very keen on checking that none of the furniture was left there earlier.'

'Might have nothing to do with it?' the American shrugged.

'Maybe,' Rivera replied. 'But if it's a coincidence like you say...' He paused. 'Well - I don't tend to believe in them.' He chewed his lip. 'It's the furniture that bothers me. Why today of all days? He's never asked before, has he?'

Esposito shook her head. She stood back and regarded him quizzically.

'And that furniture was old. Knackered. There wasn't any need to move it all. Unless there *was* a need.'

The American frowned. 'Fraser said you'd been an investigator.' She paused. 'So, this is where that part of you takes over, right?'

Rivera said nothing. He simply turned to stare at the burning building once more.

'You don't think...' Esposito began.

'...he's a tough old goat,' Rivera cut in. 'He's been around. I have a feeling he's been through much worse things than this.' He paused. 'Anyway, you said he wasn't there earlier on, right?'

The American nodded.

The ex-soldier shrugged. 'He might have gone to ground. He wouldn't have wanted to draw attention to himself. If he didn't want to be found, then my guess is that he probably wouldn't have been found. He'll pop up. A guy like him... well, he could be anywhere.'

'Yeah, I guess we won't know.'

'I'm going up there to take a look,' Rivera announced.

'But they won't let you anywhere near!' Esposito was indignant. 'They'll have a cordon around it by now. Police and all sorts. You won't get within a country mile of the place.'

'It's alright,' Rivera said, deliberately calmly. 'It's not like I'm going in. I just want to take a look. If he's OK, he'll be hanging out and watching it – I bet.' He paused. 'Let's just say I want to satisfy my curiosity – check up on him.'

The American narrowed her eyes. 'Why are you *really* going there?' she demanded.

Silence.

'Fraser can look after himself,' she pressed. 'You said that yourself. So what's your reason?'

'It's because I don't believe it,' Rivera shrugged. 'Bourse asking about the place. You seeing him there. It doesn't add up. It's too convenient – places don't just catch fire. Not like that.' He paused. 'I mean – they do. But...'

'What? And you're just going to ride in like the sheriff, are you?' The American shook her head, incredulous.

'No,' he replied. 'But I want to talk with Fraser. He'll know what happened. I guarantee it. Then we might get a sense of what Bourse is really up to. There's something about that guy that doesn't ring true.'

'I think that's ridiculous,' Esposito replied. 'You playing policeman, I mean.' She sighed with indignation. 'I'm going home.' Rivera nodded. 'I'll see you later.' He crossed the road and - without looking back at his companion - began trudging up the hill. Esposito watched him walk away, then determinedly walked in the opposite direction, bringing to mind another English idiom: the one with a wild goose.

Chapter 17.

The heat emanating from The Diplomat Hotel was searing, even from the police cordon. As Rivera stood, he stared at the flaming remnants of the building. The upper floors had collapsed; the fire service trained their hoses on the centre of the inferno. They'd given up trying to save it. The structure would disappear – that much was clear. It was now just a case of bringing the blaze under control.

Police officers wearing high visibility jackets and troubled expressions patrolled the perimeter. A gaggle of excited youths had gathered, a couple of them sitting atop BMXs and idly kicking at the ground as they spoke to their friends. A girl shrieked and swore loudly, secretly delighted by the attention she was receiving. Most of the group were intermittently filming the blaze, broadcasting it on whichever social media channels would gain them the most views.

Rivera thought about sneaking through and crossing the cordon, but realised it would be fruitless – nobody would be able to get close to the fire without protective clothing. Anyone without it would fry. He wondered where Fraser would likely have holed up.

'Can I help you, sir?' a policeman enquired, wandering over to confront the spectator. His tone was brusque, but not unfriendly.

Rivera shook his head.

'Mind moving on, then?' The man was solid; serious. He'd evidently dealt with similar situations many times before.

The ex-soldier frowned and looked at the officer's badge: *MALONE*. 'But...' He gestured at the crowd of youths.

'They're just kids,' the officer explained. 'Don't take this the wrong way, but you look old enough to know better than to hang around rubber-necking.'

Rivera sighed and looked hard at the other man. He appeared to be around fifty. He carried himself with a calm authority. Where his colleagues were barking theatrically at the assembled crowd, Malone was calmly observing, only acting when he needed to. 'Any casualties?' Rivera demanded.

'Well, now,' the policeman replied officiously. 'That would be a police matter and...'

'There was a homeless man sleeping at the hotel,' Rivera announced bluntly.

Malone narrowed his eyes. 'Friend of yours?'

'An acquaintance, really,' the ex-soldier shrugged. 'I used to give him a few quid from time to time.' He paused. 'I walked up here to see if he was alright.'

Malone frowned. 'Has he got a name? This – er - acquaintance of yours?' The officer removed a notepad from his pocket.

'Fraser,' Rivera replied.

'First name?'

'That's all I've got.'

'Age?'

'Somewhere between forty and sixty, I'd assume. But with the sleeping outdoors and hard living, it's hard to tell.'

Malone nodded, knowingly. 'Rough paper round, huh?'

'You could say that,' Rivera nodded.

'Can you describe him – this man?'

The ex-soldier chewed his lip for a moment. 'Average height. Strong build – at least stronger than you'd expect someone to be after years on a cider diet.' He paused. 'Longish hair – brown. Green eyes.'

'That it?' the policeman asked. 'Any other known acquaintances? Haunts we might check out?'

'None that I know of. He was planning to leave town soon, and...'

'...well, there you go then!' Malone interrupted. 'Probably just wanted to get a head start, no?' He looked up a little too eagerly; he clearly didn't want to have to investigate further – Rivera's suggestion was like a get-out clause.

'I doubt it.' The ex-soldier shook his head. 'I was going to sub him the money for a ticket. He had a job offer he was intending to take.' He paused. 'This isn't just some derelict we're talking about here – it's someone you *need* to track down.'

The policeman sighed, nodding. He frowned once more. 'Very well. Can I take your name, sir?'

'Rivera. Trent Rivera.'

'You local?'

'I'm working at the Golden Sands – the holiday camp. You can reach me there.'

The policeman nodded. 'The Sands is a big place, you know?'

'I drive a 1972 Silverfish campervan,' the ex-soldier replied. 'It's parked outside my chalet – you can't miss it. It has purple and yellow flowers painted on the side.'

'Right you are, sir,' Malone nodded. 'No known casualties as yet in answer to your earlier question, but we're not going to know until the fire crews bring the flames under control.' He paused. 'Anyone else staying here with him?'

'Negative.' The ex-soldier sighed. 'Look – I was tasked with shifting the last of the furniture down from The Diplomat today. It was being stored there during the Golden Sands refurbishment. I knew he was sleeping there, but I reckoned it wasn't doing anyone any harm.'

'So, what were you – some kind of slum landlord?' The officer raised his eyebrows. 'You weren't taking money from him for rent or anything, were you?'

Rivera shook his head. 'The place was clear other than him – I can promise you that. And no – I wasn't taking any money from him. The building was pretty much derelict. What – you think people were using it as an Airbnb or something?'

Malone ignored the question. 'Anyone that can confirm that for me? The fact you weren't on the make, I mean.'

'Carrie Esposito.'

'Pretty glamorous name for these parts.' The policeman sniffed a little. 'She's American. We work together. She's my boss – well, kind of.' He paused. 'Anyway, Fraser was there – I knew him vaguely. And when he asked if he could sleep in the hotel for the night, I thought I'd turn a blind eye. She didn't have a problem with it – so that was that.'

The officer nodded and looked over as a shout arose from the group of youths. A large beam had crashed into the flames, sending sparks roaring into the night sky. A few of the spectators cheered. 'Bloody kids!' he grumbled.

'Not too much else for them to do round here, right?'

'True enough,' Malone nodded. 'He ever strike you as an arsonist, this Fraser?' the policeman pressed, turning back to Rivera.

'No – he was leaving town. I told you. I'm sure he had crosses to bear, but he had no problem with The Diplomat. And he certainly had no reason to burn it down. He's not that kind of guy. He's pretty much happy-go-lucky. Harmless. There's no way he'd have torched it.'

'Not even as a parting gift?'

'Doubtful.'

'Why?'

'Wasn't his style.'

The policeman frowned. 'What makes you so sure? You said you didn't know him well.'

'Call it a hunch,' Rivera shrugged.

The officer narrowed his eyes and then sighed. 'I've never really believed in hunches. I go for good police work and leaving no stone unturned.' He looked hard at the other man. 'I appreciate you telling me this, though. It'll help our investigation – no doubt. You've probably just given us a whole stack of extra work to be honest... so it goes.'

We're going to need to ask you a few more questions to follow up. You realise that?'

'Fine by me.'

'You see,' the policeman went on, 'you're now what we like to call a person of interest.'

'I know what that means.' Rivera's tone was dismissive.

'Oh – danced this tango before, have we?' The policeman raised his eyebrows, snapping his notebook shut. He studied the ex-soldier's face. 'Anything I should know?'

'No,' the ex-soldier shook his head. 'And yes, I have – from your side of the fence.'

'Metropolitan?'

'Military.'

The officer frowned for a moment. 'Very well, Rivera. I'll be in touch.' He reached into a pocket on his stab vest and pulled out a card. 'This is my direct line. You hear from your friend Fraser, you call me. Understand?'

'Roger that,' Rivera replied.

Chapter 18.

Bullseye was dressed in work clothes – decked out like a uniformed delivery driver. It was a disguise he'd used before. A liveried baseball cap was pulled down low on his forehead. He carried a clipboard and a box with an address label. His bulk made the brown and beige uniform strain at the seams.

The drive to the Golden Sands had been quiet. And once he'd entered the site, there had been no traffic. For many people, a deserted holiday camp would have been unsettling. Its eeriness second only, perhaps, to a deserted fairground with vagabond clowns. But Bullseye wasn't most people. He didn't think deeply enough for things to scare him; he simply did what Keane told him.

He'd seen no one.

A few rows of chalets away from where the staff were lodged, he switched off the engine and climbed out of the cab of his van. His boots crunched a little on the sandy track. Listening hard, he heard nothing other than the wind blowing in from the coast and rippling the leaves of the trees. Further away, the noise of sirens drifted down from The Diplomat.

Bullseye made his way towards Esposito's chalet. In spite of the fairly warm temperature, he wore gloves. In the box, he carried the heavy gas tank for a bolt gun. The idea for the weapon had come from one of his favourite films. He loved how much its use puzzled investigators when it was used as a weapon on screen. And what made it even better was that its use was equally difficult to trace in real life.

When Keane questioned him about it, he argued that it was designed for slaughtering cattle. Quickly. Painlessly. Putting them out of their misery. Most of the time that's what he used it for too – he just switched cows for people.

His boss regarded him quizzically, and then shrugged. 'Whatever works,' she'd sniffed.

* * *

Looking around, Bullseye noted that only Esposito's chalet had a light on inside. The rest of the lodgings were clearly deserted. The big man listened. There was a sound of low voices within the room. He pressed his ear to the door and paused. Television. Sitting on the edge of the decking, he calmly fitted plastic overshoes to his boots.

Then he lifted his contraption out of the box and knocked lightly on the door. As he did, he raised the bolt gun to eye-level.

'Hold on,' came a voice from inside.

Esposito's back was turned as the door opened. 'Find anything?' she enquired from over her shoulder. She held a glass of red wine in one hand and smiled broadly as she turned to face her visitor.

It took her a moment to register that the man beneath the baseball cap was not Rivera.

By then, Bullseye had aimed the nozzle and pressed the trigger. The device hissed and then clicked as the bolt retracted from just above the woman's left eyebrow.

For an instant, the American stood still, as if stunned. Then a thin spout of blood began running down her face from the wound.

Bullseye stepped into the room, his overshoes making a crinkling noise on the bare boards of the floor. He pressed the trigger again.

As the bolt retracted for a second time, Esposito slumped to the floor, her eyes lifeless. Dark blood pooled around her head. The visitor held his hand to her jugular and felt for a pulse.

Little. Less. Nothing.

The body would be found soon enough – the killer knew that. But Keane had ordered Bourse to turn off all CCTV on site for the evening. There was no way of hiding the murder, but there was a good chance of hiding the murderer. No witnesses meant no leads. Bullseye knew that. But he also knew that he needed to vanish. Fast.

The big man walked over to the television set and, using a gloved hand, flicked off the lights, plunging the room into darkness. From outside, he thought he heard something.

Looking around quickly, he stepped away from the chalet and hastily made his way back towards his van.

Chapter 19.

As he walked back down the hill to the Golden Sands, Rivera still heard distant sirens and the occasional shout. The fire was beginning to burn out – instead of the bright orange glow of the flames, a thick pall of smoke blanketed the buildings nearest the scene. It draped itself over terraces in an acrid stench, wrapping itself around the streetlamps, deadening sounds and making the place oddly resemble Dickensian London.

Trudging, Rivera pondered what he'd told Malone. That he'd put himself forward would doubtless have consequences. But he believed it was necessary. First impressions, as he knew, could be deceptive, but the officer had struck him as being an old-fashioned policeman. A little slow and ponderous, maybe. But honest. His kind of copper. Sometimes – Rivera reasoned – the old ways got results every bit as effectively as their new-fangled variants. The ex-soldier knew further questions would come his way, but he'd rather they came from someone like Malone than someone who had him pegged as a prime suspect.

He was a drifter, after all. That was never something the police looked kindly upon. Rivera liked to imagine the days of fit-up jobs and corruption were long gone. But he knew the truth was far from that. A crime scene needed culprits, and some culprits were more convenient than others.

The ex-soldier thought about the approach he would take were he in their place. They'd look into his military record to begin with. That way, they'd confirm he wasn't simply a derelict. And they'd verify Esposito had been at The Diplomat with him. That would be one of their first steps. But they'd still be suspicious. He knew he'd put his head above the parapet by heading towards the fire; by speaking to Malone.

But he needed to find out about Fraser.

He was sure the homeless man would be alright. He was a strange figure, but he was clearly a survivor. The not knowing was troubling him, though.

It was a hell of a fire, Rivera mused.

* * *

Before reaching the Golden Sands, the smoke suddenly cleared. The ex-soldier called into an all-night garage to replenish his stock of rolling tobacco. Afterwards, strolling familiar pathways, the resort seemed eerie and utterly silent. The freshly painted chalets looked almost luminescent in the darkness. Since there were no residents, none of the lights designed to guide guests were switched on. So, picking his way through familiar twists and turns, Rivera felt like a panther that had vanished in the night. It brought back memories from hostile lands far away – bad memories. It was only when he drew close to the staff quarters that there was any illumination. Even then, it was only a couple of parking lights secured to posts sunk into the earth.

Reaching the staff cabins, Rivera saw no signs of life. He strolled over to Esposito's chalet and knocked on the door. Their parting hadn't been unfriendly – more a difference of opinion. But he wanted to clear the air, nonetheless.

No answer.

The ex-soldier frowned for a moment and then reasoned she might have opted to join Billy's birthday revelries after all. The fire had clearly shaken her. Maybe she just fancied a drink to calm her nerves. He smiled to himself – at the American's age, the lure of a good time was always liable to make someone a little fickle, even if the festivities were for a lecherous braggart with few functioning brain cells. Rivera checked his watch, paused for a moment, but then thought better of it.

No matter – he told himself. He'd bring her up to speed in the morning.

Rivera walked over to Iris. The T2 stood glinting a little in the darkness, her headlamps two sad eyes. From within, he heard Rosie mewing. Sliding open the door, he stepped in and the cat approached. The tabby rubbed herself against his calves. He opened a pouch of food and forked it out into a bowl, mashing it slightly. Rivera then refilled her water using a fresh bottle he kept on the campervan's sideboard. 'You eat better than I do,' he cooed. 'And fresh water, no less!' The cat tilted her head, blinked her eyes, and looked at him blankly.

Yawning, he walked over to the door and paused at the threshold. He turned to face Rosie.

'You coming with me?' he enquired.

In response, the cat arched her back, stretched, and settled herself on the fold-down sofa. She tucked her paws beneath her body and narrowed her eyes, imperious. Rivera shrugged, checked the rear window was propped open for ventilation or escape, and then slid the door closed.

Then he walked across the rough ground towards his chalet. Opening the door, he yawned again, and wondered how many pages of Hardy's prose he'd manage prior to falling asleep.

Chapter 20.

Superintendent Cobb was a portly man of fifty-four. A wisp of hair was combed over his bald pate, which made him resemble an early-Seventies Bobby Charlton. Ordinarily, at eleven o'clock on a weeknight, he'd have been at Pier Bingo. He and his wife had been regulars there for the best part of thirty years. Same table. Same drinks. Same jokes, and the same innuendos being bawled out by the caller. They even sat with the same group of acquaintances that masqueraded as firm friends.

But tonight was different. Tonight, The Diplomat Hotel had decided to self-combust.

Cobb sighed. The usually sleepy station was a hive of activity – extra staff had been recalled and they were liaising with the fire and ambulance services. Usually, the night shift just saw a parade of drunks, addicts, and ladies of the night protesting their way to the cells. Tonight, though, was not a normal night. It felt, instead, like the scene of a crime drama. Younger officers found it hard to conceal gleeful expressions; this – after all – was an incident that classed as *proper* police work.

Luckily, the hotel was abandoned. Being deserted meant there would be no casualties. There would be no need to look for any, either.

No probable cause.

No paperwork.

The Superintendent looked up to see the figure of Malone standing in his doorway. He sighed. The other man was a career beat officer. For almost as long as Cobb had been on the force, his visitor had been pounding the pavements of the town; helping old ladies across the street; talking to kids about bicycle theft and attending summer fêtes where he manned desks beneath temporary gazebos and handed out leaflets about crime prevention. He was a good man. An honest man. Perhaps a little *too* honest.

While Cobb had climbed the greasy pole and played politics, Malone had kept his feet firmly on the ground.

He was a man with no ambition. But he was thorough. He never let anything go. And that made him an irritant. Especially to a pragmatist like Cobb.

'Jackie...' Malone began, his voice gruff.

'Dammit Jimmy, it's Superintendent. It has been for five years. How many times do I have to fucking remind you? We're not recruits at a passing out parade any more.' He paused. 'Respect the rank. Please.'

Malone nodded. 'I've just written a report... sir. About The Diplomat. I've submitted a search request.'

'No need,' Cobb announced brusquely. 'It's an open and shut case – there won't be fuck all left there tomorrow morning but smouldering ruins. And it was deserted. Confirmed.'

'Yeah – about that.' The Constable adjusted his collar.

'About what?'

'I was talking to a bloke by the cordon.'

'And?' Cobb pressed impatiently.

'He reckoned there was a homeless man sleeping at the hotel.' He cleared his throat. 'It wasn't just a rumour either, and this bloke wasn't a time waster. He gave me a name. So we'll need forensics to go through the ruins.'

The Superintendent looked hard at the other man, scratching at the stubble of his five o'clock shadow. 'I think you're mistaken, Malone,' he said tersely. 'There was nobody there.'

'But we can't be sure of that. And...'

'...do you really want me to send you up there tomorrow with a shovel?' Cobb sighed, cutting in. 'I'll have to put you in charge of it. You'll get your uniform all grubby.' A hint of a smile crossed his face.

'You wouldn't want to go pissing your missus off, would you? She's got enough on her plate as it is, what with...'

'...if that's what it takes... sir, then yes,' Malone interrupted.

Cobb shook his head. 'There are hundreds of fucking tramps in this town, Jackie. We don't know who any of them are.' He paused. 'Are you a hundred per cent on this? We'll never trace them anyway – even if we *do* dig someone up. And you know why?'

Silence.

'It's because no one gives a fuck,' the Superintendent explained, heavily.

'I have a name,' Malone insisted.

'Well, there's still no need to get hasty though, is there?' the Superintendent blustered. 'We'll have to give forensics a little time. No need to pull the trigger on that report of yours just yet.'

'I've already submitted it,' the Constable shrugged.

Silence.

Cobb pursed his lips and nodded slowly. He leaned back in his chair, sighing. 'Well, there we have it. Will that be all, Constable?'

'Yes, it will.' Malone paused on the threshold. 'Take care Jackie.'

Chapter 21.

Rivera woke with a start. The early morning sun streamed through the un-curtained windows of his chalet. His book lay open on the floor next to where his hand had trailed down onto the linoleum. In his head, he spooled through the events of the previous night. They came back to him with crystal clarity. All except for what he'd read – he couldn't recall anything Hardy had written.

The ex-soldier yawned, stretched, and watched as a line of ants trooped from beneath the kitchen sink cupboard to the fridge. He'd been waging an ongoing campaign against them for the last three weeks. He suspected that the ground beneath the Golden Sands was more ant farm than earth – the insects were everywhere, and no amount of spray or powder, whether eco-friendly or not, seemed to dissuade them. The ex-soldier was fastidious about keeping his surroundings clean.

The ants seemed indifferent. His latest weapon of mass destruction was washing up liquid. The results were mixed.

Rivera walked out to Iris, where he fed Rosie again and then smoked his first cigarette of the day. Turning to walk back to his chalet, he noticed that the curtains of Esposito's lodgings were still closed. He looked down at the tabby cat who was demolishing a morning pouch of chicken and turkey. 'She must have overdone it, don't you think?' he chuckled to the cat. 'They'll have been doing shots – any money.'

Rosie ignored him, concentrating instead on wolfing down her breakfast. She looked up furtively, as if regarding her owner as an irritant. Rivera left Iris' door open and headed off.

Chapter 22.

When Rivera reached the site of what had formerly been The Diplomat, the previous night's crowd was absent. Discarded energy drink cans had been left in the gutter close to the perimeter fence, and cigarette butts had been trodden into the pavement. The asphalt bore the shining outlines of places where gobbets of spit had dried and stained the ground. Inside the compound, various members of the emergency services stood looking at the remnants of the hotel. There was an atmosphere of fatigue; of uncertainty. It was as if the hill hadn't quite adjusted to its new, minimalist appearance. The smoking ruin looked raw. Angry.

A trio of ambulances was backed up close to the rubble of the ruins. The charred ends of a few beams stuck up through the collapsed brickwork in places, but there was little more to suggest what had stood there only hours before. Fire officers were still dousing the far section of the building; it was remarkable – Rivera thought – how empty the place looked. It was almost as if a tooth had been pulled from the gums of the town.

The ex-soldier studied the scene. He loved the early morning – particularly in summer. The time before other people were awake felt like a time he had all to himself. A time when the fresh face of a new day was yet to be tarnished by the rust of reality; a moment when almost anything was still possible. When he wasn't working, he would frequently stroll the town at sunrise and then retire to his campervan for a siesta later in the day. A daytime snooze remained the greatest perk of no longer having every khaki minute dictated by others above him in the pecking order. He usually spent such times people-watching. And pondering. He knew that every person who walked past him had a story. One of his penchants was trying to second guess what those stories were.

But those were everyday people going about their everyday lives.

This? This was something different.

Rivera had been around enough crime scenes to know what he was looking at. The aftermath of a fire shouldn't have been like the scene playing out before him. Once the fire was out and the site had been made safe, a sense of stasis would ordinarily settle on proceedings. Fire officers would make their investigations into the cause of the fire, and then a couple of Special Constables would be deployed to keep away overly inquisitive members of the public for their own safety. Usually a perimeter fence would be erected and then it was just a case of waiting for a decision to be made about the land. Later, the blitzed out bombshell would be bulldozed and something else would arise phoenix-like from the ashes. That was what happened when there were no casualties. And if a building was deserted, then even less attention was paid to security.

This, though, felt different.

The police cordon was still prominent. And it was being patrolled by regular officers. Then there were the ambulances. Paramedics would be sent as a cautionary measure, but once a site was declared clear, they'd be sent away. Rivera felt the first prickling sensations of ill-ease.

Peering through the fence, Rivera couldn't make out what the three parked ambulances were doing. All he knew was that they had to be there for a reason.

And it couldn't be for anything good.

***

'Help you, sir?' The policeman on the other side of the perimeter fence squinted in the early morning light, regarding the ex-soldier with suspicion.

'I just wondered if there'd been any casualties, officer?' The ex-soldier spoke confidently, cheerily almost.

'I'm not at liberty to say, sir.' The policeman shook his head. He had Sergeant's stripes. His lanyard bore the name DeFreitas. It glinted a little in the sunlight. His countenance was that of someone who'd already formed a clear opinion of the person they were talking to.

'But there are ambulances,' Rivera pointed.

'Standard procedure,' the other man shrugged, walking away.

The ex-soldier chewed his lip and looked over at the vehicles. One of the ambulance's sliding doors was shut noisily.

'You won't get much out of him,' a voice announced from behind him a few moments later.

Rivera turned and saw Malone approaching on his side of the fence. 'Good morning.' The ex-soldier nodded in recognition.

'Good morning yourself,' the officer replied. 'Up bright and early, aren't we? Nosing around again, is it?' He paused. 'If you're not careful, you'll end up pissing someone off with all this rooting around.'

Rivera sighed. 'I know what I'm looking at here...'

'What do you mean?' the policeman frowned.

'I was enquiring after my friend, remember?' He sighed. 'Ambulances with live casualties don't tend to hang around. This feels like something different.'

'What, exactly?' Malone pressed, his brow furrowing.

'Well, the fire's out. It was supposedly an empty building.' He paused. 'Under normal circumstances, it's game over. A couple of plods left to keep the peace, and that's it.'

'What's your point?'

'Three ambulances,' the ex-soldier said bluntly. 'They're not being used to carry salvaged bricks away. I know that much.'

Malone nodded. 'Worried about – er – Fuller, huh?'

'Fraser.' Rivera nodded. 'But even if he was in there, you wouldn't need three ambulances, would you?'

Silence.

'Three corpses,' Malone said quietly. 'It's not common knowledge, and you *definitely* didn't hear it from me. I've been posted here to shoo journalists away for when the word gets out. So, if anyone asks you anything, you keep your mouth shut. Got it?'

'So, why tell me?' the ex-soldier frowned.

'Because,' Malone sighed, 'if it wasn't for you, we wouldn't have gone digging for any corpses at all.'

Rivera nodded grimly. 'Any indication about whether Fraser was one of them?'

The policeman shook his head. 'It'll come down to dental records, I'm afraid.' He paused. 'And in the case of your friend, that could take a while. But if he was in there... it was a hell of a fire. It's melted the PVC window frames on some of the houses across the street. Anyone in the building wouldn't have stood a chance.'

Silence.

'Was it arson?' the ex-soldier enquired.

'Maybe,' Malone shrugged. 'Listen – I meant what I said; we wouldn't have thought anything of it if you hadn't told me.' He paused. 'Things like this happen. Buildings burn down. But nobody throws up too many roadblocks if they're empty. And nobody tends to look too hard for stiffs either. Not when there's no reason. So you've done a good deed here. We don't know who any of the bodies are for definite, but at least we know they were there. A good deed,' he repeated. 'Definitely.'

'It doesn't feel too much like that from where I'm standing,' Rivera muttered. 'Especially if Fraser *is* one of them.' He cleared his throat. 'You reckon it'll take a while, then?'

'It'll be a few days at least...'

'Malone!' The shout that came was laced with venom. DeFreitas strode towards the pair, an angry expression on his face. 'Is this gentleman causing problems?'

The Constable glanced at Rivera and then looked back at the Sergeant. 'No sir,' he replied. 'He was just asking for directions.'

'Directions?' DeFreitas' tone was incredulous. 'He doesn't need any bloody directions! He was sniffing around for bloody scoops earlier. I think he's press in disguise.' The man turned to Rivera. 'I warned you before, sir. This is a crime scene. It's a police matter and you have no business being here, so kindly leave.' His last words were delivered through gritted teeth.

'I'm a construction worker.' The ex-soldier held up his hands as if in surrender.

The Sergeant turned to Malone. 'Simple job, constable. You keep the perimeter clear. That means safe from prying eyes and definitely free from nosy journalists like him.' He pointed at Rivera. 'Understand?'

Malone nodded.

'Well, get bloody patrolling then!' the Sergeant barked.

The Constable began to walk away along the perimeter fence.

DeFreitas turned to look at Rivera, eyeing him coldly. 'And you... sir... if I see you again on this site, then I'll book you for being in breach of the peace. I'm not sure why this is such a difficult concept for you to grasp, but if I see you here again, I'll nick you. Got it?'

Rivera frowned and opened his mouth to speak. He then closed it, turned, and began to walk away, the only exterior sign of his frustration, his tightly clenched fists.

* * *

After hurrying down the first part of the hill, Rivera looped around. Cutting down an overgrown access path between two houses, he joined another street that brought him onto a road snaking back up towards The Diplomat Hotel site. It was an area with large, detached houses that were sat back from the road. Reaching the junction at the end, the ex-soldier found himself opposite the perimeter fence. He pressed himself backwards into the shadow of an overhanging chestnut tree and waited.

Two minutes later, just as expected, he spotted Malone's unhurried gait. As the officer passed by on the other side of the street, Rivera gave a low whistle. The policeman glanced back over his shoulder and then crossed the road. Constable James Malone's many years on the beat had given him a sixth sense for people. Though he'd never be recognised for it, he was part of the town's pulmonary. He'd known many of the town's hardened criminals when they were nothing but errant youths. He'd prevented more crime by being in the right place at the right time than anyone would ever know. It was a quality that couldn't be quantified. When most officers walked the streets of South Quay, they were shoulder-barged and spat on. When Malone walked past them, people stood aside. He knew them by name. He couldn't always prevent them going to the dark side, but he could show them a glimmer of light if they were willing to listen. It was because of this sixth sense that he'd decided to trust Rivera. He suspected the ex-soldier would seek him out in a manner just like this.

'Don't mind DeFreitas,' Malone said, glancing back over his shoulder once more. 'He's got a lot on his plate.'

'Yeah,' Rivera nodded. 'Three corpses. No kidding!'

The policeman looked around again, furtively, lowering his voice further. 'All three of them were found directly next to a massive cast-iron radiator.'

The ex-soldier nodded gravely. 'Well, that sets off alarm bells, doesn't it?'

'Yeah,' the Constable nodded. 'But not as much as the fact they were all roped to it.'

'What?' The ex-soldier narrowed his eyes in disbelief. 'So, this was a hit?'

Malone nodded. 'Looks that way, doesn't it? Those poor bastards weren't just sleeping in there. Put it that way. But whoever did it screwed up – they used fireproof rope. Imagine! I never even knew there was such a thing. But it's not much use if you're trying to hide your tracks. Not if it's shackling radial bones to radiators – bit of a giveaway, don't you think?'

Rivera nodded. 'So – this is a murder investigation now?'

'It is.'

Chapter 23.

Arriving back at the Golden Sands, Rivera walked over to Esposito's door and knocked loudly.

After a brief pause, he knocked again.

No answer.

He turned as Clarke's angry voice cut through the morning quiet. 'Where the fuck is everyone?' The foreman stomped towards him, hands in pockets and shoulders rolling. He was furiously chewing a wad of gum.

'Search me, boss,' Rivera shrugged.

'They've all been out fucking drinking,' he growled, vitriolic. 'They'll all still be half-cut. I don't even want to think about what time they'd have got back in. They'll be seeing double.' He shook his head and turned to the other man. 'Whose fucking party was it?'

'I – er...'

'Oh, come on! Don't give me any of that honour among thieves bullshit – It was Prescott's birthday, wasn't it? I'm going to dock that little bastard a day's pay.'

'Well,' the ex-soldier shrugged, 'don't tell him I said this, but it might do him good to be dragged down a peg or two.'

'Two?' Clarke spat, incredulous. 'Two hundred, more like! He's an arrogant shit at the best of times.' He paused. 'And this is *not* the best of times. At least it's not going to be for him at any rate.'

'Have you seen Esposito?' Rivera enquired.

'Of course not!' the foreman blazed. 'I haven't seen her or any of that useless shower.' He paused. 'Here.' He held out a giant bunch of keys. 'Get over to the tool shed and get cracking.'

The ex-soldier frowned. 'What do you want me to do?'

'Open it – I'll be there in five.'

'And you - what are you going to do?'

'Bloody wake them up,' Clarke shrugged. 'If they're feeling rough now, they're going to feel like death warmed up by the time I'm done with them.'

Walking towards the toolshed, Rivera smiled wryly. He heard Clarke's angry voice and the staccato machine gun hammering of his knocking as he worked his way along the row of chalet doors.

Chapter 24.

'What?' Keane rubbed her sleep-bleary eyes as she answered the phone. She blinked a few times. Her bedroom had double-aspect windows and a thick cream carpet. Tasteful vases and paintings adorned the room, and the furniture was bespoke, made with exotic woods sourced from far and wide. Potted ferns were tastefully arranged, and silhouettes of exotic butterflies were etched on the wall. As a child, Keane had always been the first to rise in her household. Having two drug-addict parents meant exiting their presence as early as possible was a prerequisite. Once they emerged, bleary-eyed from their stupor, they began screaming at each other, combing the cushions and carpets for loose change. Anything in the way of their early morning fix was an obstacle – their daughter included.

Keane had gravitated to Bullseye. Everyone she'd done business with since becoming a success had talked of their sessions with therapists. So, not wanting to miss out, she'd followed suit. After two sessions, she'd called a halt to proceedings – she'd been informed that she had issues. It was hardly news; she'd never trusted anyone. Only Bullseye. After she'd instructed him to cave in the skull of one of her randy cousins with the blunt edge of an axe, she hadn't seen much reason to trust anyone else. Once her parents were gone, she'd begun to rise later. These days, she made a habit of sleeping in until mid-morning, reasoning that – if there was nobody to order her to get up – she wouldn't.

'I'm sorry to disturb you so early.' The voice was troubled. 'But...'

'...what time is it?' Keane frowned.

'Seven-thirty.'

'Jesus! What the fuck's the matter with you?'

'It's Cobb, ma'am.'

'Yeah, I know who you bloody are. But why the hell are you calling me this early? It's practically the middle of the fucking night!'

Silence.

'Well?' Keane pressed.

'Er – slight problem,' Cobb replied.

Keane sighed impatiently. 'No – the witness isn't a problem. She's been taken care of.'

'What?' The Superintendent's voice was shocked. 'What do you mean?'

'What do you mean – what do I mean?' Keane snarled. 'What the hell are you talking about?' She paused. 'No witness – no problem. That's how we roll, right?'

'I'm not talking about witnesses,' Cobb announced. 'I didn't think there were any. At least - we haven't heard from any.'

'Then what the fuck *are* you talking about?' She was out of bed and pacing angrily at this point, her bare feet sinking into the deep tread of the cream-coloured carpet.

'We found three bodies.'

Keane's tone was incredulous. 'Why the hell were you looking? I told you to keep it quiet. It was a deserted hotel – why was anyone digging through the ashes?' Keane thumped at a mirror in frustration. It shook violently, distorting her reflection. 'I told you to cover it up! I *paid* you to keep things quiet and...'

'...we had a tip-off,' Cobb said apologetically.

'So?'

'So – it was on the system before I could dampen it down. I had no choice – if something's made official, then it has to be investigated. It's out of my hands.'

'Who?'

'Excuse me?'

'Who was the tip off from?' Keane paused. 'Nobody should have known.'

'Some bystander.'

'But how did they know?' Keane pressed in an icy tone. 'I don't understand.'

'They knew a homeless man was sleeping there,' Cobb replied. 'That's what I've been told – the other two... well, the three of them were together. Once we found one, we couldn't really avoid finding the others. Know what I mean?' He paused. 'Look... there were only supposed to be two. That's what you told me. We didn't talk about a third. It's screwed everything up.'

Silence.

'Who was it?' Keane pressed. 'The informant?'

'I'm not sure yet – I'm looking into it.'

'I want a fucking name,' Keane announced through gritted teeth. As she spoke, she ran her finger along the windowsill and noticed a faint rime of dust. Her cleaner would experience her ire for that, she vowed.

'Why? What are you going to do?' Cobb continued.

Silence.

'How much do I pay you?' the boss asked, distractedly.

'I – er – I...' the Superintendent faltered.

'...too bloody much!' Keane thundered. 'I pay you to make problems go away. Fat lot of fucking good that seems to do.' She sighed. 'Since you're not up to the task, here's how things'll go: there's a problem – I'm going to make it disappear. And you...' a tone of menace entered her voice, 'are going to help me by doing exactly what I say. Understand?'

'Yes, ma'am.'

Chapter 25.

'Have you seen Esposito?' Rivera asked as Clarke entered the tool shed. He wore a slightly smug expression; he'd evidently taken a sadistic pleasure in worsening the hangovers of his disgraced workforce.

'No.' The foreman shook his head. 'She's going to get a right bollocking when she gets here. They all are – they can forget about their fucking bonus. If we go any further behind, then we'll never finish on time.' He shook his head. 'I didn't see any of them, to be honest – just heard groans when I hammered on the doors. Serves them bloody right.'

Rivera nodded. 'You heard about the fire?'

'Yeah,' the foreman replied. 'Crying shame – someone could have done something good with that place. It used to be quite something. There was a hell of a dancefloor up there back in the day. They could have filmed *Strictly* there if they'd done it up. Mind you, it had a preservation order on it.' He paused. 'It's not the first time something like that's happened in South Quay. Nor anywhere else, I should think.'

'What do you mean?'

The foreman sighed. 'Long story – I'll tell you later. In the meantime, we've got a lot to do.' He paused. 'And the way it looks right now, it's me and thee.'

'So what is it today, then?' Rivera asked. 'More of the same?'

'For the rest of them – yes. And I'm going to have them breaking rocks like they're on a fucking chain gang. They deserve that. But we've got something else to do, you and me.'

'Yeah? What?'

'Don't ask – it's almost too ridiculous. Bourse's bloody orders. I've got a quad bike and trailer outside – we're going to load it up.'

Rivera nodded. 'You want any of these boxes?' He pointed to a laden pallet in the middle of the floor.

'No.' Clarke shook his head. 'They're full of branded bloody beach balls.'

'You're serious?'

'Yeah.' The other man sighed. 'Good for nothing. It's one of Bourse's bright ideas. Branding, he calls it. There's five thousand giant inflatable crocodiles in there, too. For the kids, I suppose.' Clarke shook his head, warming to his subject. 'And look at these!' He placed a branded cardboard spiral hat on his head. 'If you didn't look like a twat before, then you'll definitely look like one after!'

* * *

Twenty minutes later, Rivera and Clarke were standing on an open patch of ground between banks of chalets. Both men had their hands on their hips, and both of them were regarding the foundations with incredulity. The foreman's outrage was contagious.

'I'm not sure I see how it'll work,' Rivera shrugged. 'It's stupid.'

'I told you,' Clarke insisted, nodded earnestly. 'Bourse is a fucking imbecile.'

The structure in question was an abseiling wall. It was positioned close to the staff quarters and would be clearly visible from the road. The holiday camp side would be used for climbing, while the other would bear a giant billboard extolling the virtues of vacationing there to any passing traffic.

Clarke was incredulous. 'Back in the day, our target audience was fat couples who wanted to get pissed all day and then play bingo all night – while getting more pissed. Dinner-for-Fives we used to call them. But this – I don't get it. They're marketing it like some sort of outward bound thing.' He shook his head. 'I mean, who the hell's going to come to South Quay to get fit? It's insane! They come here for fried eggs, fried bread, and burger meat. Not for tofu and bloody spinach! The demographic hasn't changed. You stick some of those lard-arses up there, and they'll snap the ropes. Or break the fucking planks!' He passed Rivera a sheet of paper on which the building plan was outlined.

He scrutinised it, frowning. 'It looks like a bloody gallows.'

'Yeah,' the foreman chuckled.

'I mean it – it's like the scaffold they used at Mankato for the mass hanging of the Dakota tribe. This bit especially.' Rivera jabbed a finger at a section of the plan.

Clarke looked at him blankly. 'Yeah. Listen, I haven't got a clue about what you just said, but whatever it looks like, the boss is dead set on it. I've tried to talk him out of it, but he's all in.' He picked up a packaged coil of thick climbing cord. 'The rope alone has cost thousands.' He paused. 'He told me it's so strong it could lift up that campervan of yours.'

'Yeah?'

'Uh-huh. Waterproof.' He squinted, reading the label. 'Fireproof too, apparently.'

The ex-soldier narrowed his eyes, keeping his voice flat and level. 'Really?'

'Yeah, so it says.' Clarke looked around, sighing. 'But if you believe that, you'll believe anything.' He ground his teeth. 'This really would have been easier with a couple of other blokes,' he huffed. 'Anyway, first thing we need to do is set these uprights.' He looked at the other man. 'You've poured concrete before, right?'

Rivera nodded.

'Good – because you're going to be doing a lot of it today. Loads.' Clarke lowered his voice, conspiratorially. 'Don't tell the others this, but – since it's just the two of us and the rest of those drunks have deserted us – I'm sticking you on double time today, son.'

'Son?' The ex-soldier frowned.

'Yeah – sorry. Force of habit. You are a bit long in the tooth, come to think of it!'

'Thanks very much.'

'You're very welcome,' Clarke grinned. 'Anyway, it's not that much of a favour. It's not like I'll be out of pocket – I'm docking wages for the rest of them, so I'm quids in. Did you bring the spirit level?'

Rivera nodded.

'Right then. Let's get on with it.'

Chapter 26.

'All good?' Bullseye enquired. The pair were standing at the side of a disused quarry. It was a location they'd used before – a place they'd never known anyone else to frequent. Unless it was someone they'd brought with them. Far below, the rusting hulks of fridges and washing machines lay like a cemetery monument to the pair's previous fly-tipping exploits.

'Not good. Not exactly.' Keane shook her head. 'The Yank you sorted. How did you do it?'

'Bolt gun,' the big man replied proudly.

'Witnesses?'

'None.'

'You're sure?' Keane pressed.

'Positive. Why?'

The woman sighed. 'They've found the bodies up on the hill. The ones in the hotel.'

'How come?' Bullseye frowned. 'I thought that...'

'...tip off,' Keane interrupted.

'Who?'

'Some bloke called Rivera.' Keane paused for a moment. Seeing no glimmer of recognition cross the big man's features, she continued. 'Cobb just called me back. Rivera was the name mentioned in a report that was filed. Apparently, he knew some homeless guy was sleeping there.'

'Bollocks!' Bullseye hissed angrily.

'Anyway,' Keane continued. 'What's done is done. But someone was up there asking questions this morning – the wrong kind of questions. That's what I've heard on the grapevine.'

'What do you mean?' The big man's expression was blank. 'What kind of questions?'

'The kind of questions people ask if they know about things – police procedures. Investigations. Stuff like that.'

Bullseye nodded. 'So?'

'Cobb's pretty confident he can keep a lid on things. But he's got a couple of blokes who are bit too geeky for their own good. Jobsworths and the like. They're low-ranking, so they're nothing to worry about. But this other bloke sniffing around definitely isn't the kind of thing we need.'

'So, what do you want me to do, boss?'

'Keep your phone on,' Keane ordered. 'I'll be in touch.'

Chapter 27.

After lunch, a couple of additional workers were drafted in to assist Clarke and Rivera. The foreman ignored their apologies and hadn't budged on his decision to dock their pay. They'd worked on sullenly. The rest of the work crew had been deployed on chalet refurbishment.

The foreman worked hard; he was a man who led by example. He'd advised the ex-soldier against what he saw as errors, but had then taken the time to instruct him on how to improve. Rivera appreciated that. What he didn't appreciate was the lack of Esposito. Not showing up for work was pretty out of character for her. She was young enough to burn the candle at both ends, so he dreaded to think how much she'd probably drunk the previous night. He also worried on her behalf about how nuclear Clarke's reaction would be when he finally encountered her.

At the end of the day, Clarke held out his hand. 'You did well today... son.' He winked, chuckling. 'You've earned yourself a beer.'

'Are you buying, boss?' one of the younger workers enquired, his tone hopeful.

The foreman turned, glaring at the youngster. 'No. And if I even hear that you've been within spitting distance of beer on a school night again, then I'll be giving you your marching orders. It's not fucking good enough – what happened this morning. Got it?'

The youngster nodded, despondent.

* * *

As Rivera and Clarke rounded the corner, they slowed. An ambulance was parked outside the bank of chalets. A small crowd of workers milled around, some of them looking at the ground. Others smoked, talking to one another in huddled groups. They looked up as the pair approached. An air of tension had descended on the place.

'What's going on?' Clarke demanded. He cast his eyes around. 'And why the hell's Bourse here?'

The owner of the holiday park strode over to the pair. His lips were pursed. He wore a pained expression. 'I'm sorry,' he announced.

'Why?' the foreman demanded.

Bourse sighed. He worried his hands, rubbing them together in a tight clasp.

'Who?' Clarke asked.

'Esposito – the American girl,' the owner replied.

Rivera froze.

'What's wrong with her?' the foreman pressed.

Bourse shook his head slowly. 'The police have been searching her room,' he explained. 'She's dead.'

Silence.

The assembled group watched as the woman's body was wheeled out on a gurney. A blanket had been pulled up over her. Its edges were tucked beneath the thin mattress.

Rivera frowned and watched in numbed disbelief as Esposito was loaded into the rear of the ambulance. He barely even registered Clarke's touch as the foreman rested a fatherly arm on his shoulder.

The solemn moment was disrupted by the razor-cut wail of a siren. Two patrol cars rounded the corner closest to the cabins; they threw up clouds of dust and skidded to a halt by the bank of chalets. Four officers emerged from each car. Where those members of the force posted to The Diplomat had been relaxed – sluggish even – these officers were fast-moving; filled with adrenalin.

'Him!' announced Cobb angrily, as he pointed at Rivera. 'He's the one who was nosing around this morning. Nick him.' He breathed heavily as he spoke, fired up.

'Wait a minute!' Clarke protested. 'What the fuck are you talking about? He's...'

'...you stay out of this, sir,' Cobb interrupted. 'This is a police matter now.' He nodded to a pair of officers who had exited his car. 'He's coming in for questioning.'

'On what charge?' Rivera frowned, stepping towards Cobb. 'She was my friend.'

'Suspicion of murder... sir,' the Superintendent replied, his expression stony.

'That's ridiculous!' Clarke protested. 'He's been working with me all day. What the fuck are you talking about? You've got the wrong man.'

'This happened last night,' Cobb explained.

'Bollocks!' the foreman spat.

Rivera had enough experience with the legal system to know nothing could be done to avoid arrest in such circumstances. Things would move at their own pace; it would only be after a series of steps had been completed that he'd be set free. Any arguing would simply be wasted energy. Instead, he stared with cold hostility at Cobb.

Clarke, though, moved into the path of the Superintendent as he approached the ex-soldier. As he did, police colleagues took one of Rivera's arms each. He struggled a little, but it began to dawn on him that this wasn't a battle he could really fight.

Malone – who had been travelling in the other car – stepped over. 'I guess you know how this works, right?' he said quietly. 'Due process and all. Got to go through the motions for now.'

Rivera nodded.

'Mind if I put the cuffs on you?' the Constable asked. Clarke was noisily remonstrating with the officers who were trying to shepherd him out of the way. His protests were now vocal rather than physical.

'You may,' Rivera replied. 'I might not have been quite so compliant if your Super had been trying to put the cuffs on. But since it's you...'

'Appreciate it,' Malone continued. 'I'm sure this'll all work out. I tried to explain things to Cobb – how you'd come forward and all. But it's all a bit of a mess. They're flailing around and pointing fingers.'

'Understood.'

Malone fitted the handcuffs and ushered Rivera towards the waiting police car.

Chapter 28.

Bullseye was sitting in the kitchen of Keane's house. The boss' huge Rottweiler eyed him suspiciously – it was crouched beside his bar stool at the counter, its teeth bared. Its eyes were fixed upon the big man. Keane handed the visitor an energy drink while she nursed a cup of herbal tea. The stash of fluorescent cans in the fridge was kept there purely for when her enforcer visited. Keane's kitchen was fitted with surfaces of granite; the fronts of cupboards were all shining steel. Above a central island, expensive, copper-bottomed pans hung down from a rack. The room looked out onto a terracotta slate patio and an AstroTurf lawn. There was expensive all-weather furniture on both surfaces and landscaped plants and flowers. The garden was walled, but it looked like any other garden on the street, save for the broken glass set in cement at the top of the brickwork. Keane took great pains to preserve the veneer of privileged domesticity.

'I have the full name,' the boss announced bluntly.

Bullseye nodded. 'For the busybody, you mean?'

'Yeah – the informant. The fucker who's been sticking his nose in.'

A silence followed – it wrapped itself around the island, clinging to the seated figures. The big man held his breath; he knew it was better not to interrupt his boss when she was holding court.

'Trent Rivera.'

'Still never heard of him,' Bullseye replied.

'Yeah, that's just it,' Keane shrugged. 'He's not from round here.' She paused, sipping at her tea. 'Cobb called me again.'

'And?'

'This bloke was in the military. He's worked on and off as an investigator. He's good – so Cobb says. People talk about him being a bit of a hard man. But he's getting on a bit.'

Bullseye scoffed. But his grin swiftly vanished when he caught sight of his boss' continued seriousness.

'He's just the kind of man who'll cause problems,' Keane explained. 'The American is out of the picture, so they've got no witnesses from The Diplomat.' She paused. 'Problem is – if this bloke starts digging, then he might start fucking things up.'

'Why not put him in the frame for killing the girl?' Bullseye enquired.

Keane frowned. 'You know what? For you, that's almost an intelligent suggestion.'

The big man grinned, both surprised and delighted. He placed his can on the granite surface and leaned back, beaming, puffing his chest out with pride.

'It won't work,' Keane said bluntly.

'Why?' Bullseye was instantly deflated.

'I'd thought of the same thing – straight away. But then I spoke to Cobb. This Rivera is out of the picture for the murder. They're going to hold him twenty-four hours for questioning, but he's got a couple of cast-iron alibis. There's definite proof he wasn't at the Golden Sands when she was killed, so we can't go down that road. And this whole thing has blown up too big to have him whacked in his cell – South Quay is big bloody news all of a sudden.'

Bullseye frowned. 'How can they know he wasn't there? They can't be that Pacific, can they?'

'The word's *specific*, Einstein,' Keane corrected him. 'And... maybe. Especially if you screwed up on something. All they need's a time stamp.'

'But I was careful, and...'

'...you're a useless prick,' the woman interrupted. 'We both know that.'

Bullseye bridled.

'It's not rude,' Keane went on. 'It's a statement of fact. You've got muscles and you get the job done, but it's like giving a kid scissors – I never quite know what else you're going to damage. You're guaranteed to have fucked something up somewhere along the way. That's not surprising – the only mystery comes when we start trying to work out what it was.'

'So what do you want me to do?' Bullseye looked hurt.

'Nothing yet.'

'Why? Come on – I can take care of things.'

Keane smiled thinly. 'Because it would look too suspicious – especially now.' The boss paused, swilling the leaves in the bottom of her china cup. 'We'll warn him off.'

'You want me to do that?'

'No. Not yet,' Keane shook her head. 'You keep your powder dry. Get Matty Austin's boys to do it. They owe us. Let's get them to do the heavy lifting here and then we can follow up if need be.'

Bullseye narrowed his eyes and then nodded. 'You think they're up to it?' The big man crushed his can and threw it towards the refuse bin in the corner. It missed and bounced off the wall. The Rottweiler, snarling, pounced on it, and began to chew it viciously. The big man looked towards his boss, horrified.

Keane stared at him, ice in her eyes. Eventually, she sighed and spoke through pursed lips. 'I suppose we'll have to wait and see, won't we?'

Bullseye nodded. 'So, what's the plan?'

The boss poured the remnants of her herbal tea into the sink. 'Once he's let out of the nick, set up a welcoming committee.'

'Where?'

'At the Sands. I'll get Bourse to organise a condolences dinner for all his work force. Make it compulsory for them to attend,' Keane explained. 'For the Yank, I mean. And I'll get Cobb to release this Rivera at the same time that everyone else is out of the way. I'll make sure the CCTV goes dead, too. Then Austin and his boys can go to work.' She paused. 'When you talk to them, make sure they know they're not killing the bloke – he just needs beating up badly enough that he'll leave town. Once he's out of the picture, then I can't see him causing us any problems. Got it?'

Bullseye nodded.

Chapter 29.

'Do I get a solicitor?' Rivera enquired.

'Is that a sign you're guilty?' Cobb asked, barely suppressing a smirk. The interview room was nondescript. Gouges and divots had been scraped into the Formica surface of the table; the green carpet tiles were stained and worn – some were sat atop one another like imperfect jigsaw puzzle pieces.

'No, Superintendent,' the ex-soldier replied wearily. 'It's a sign that I know my rights. I know how the law works. And I know I'm not guilty.' He paused, eyeing the other man coldly. 'Why am I here exactly?'

'We want to ask you some questions.'

Rivera sat back and picked at a scab on his elbow.

Cobb leaned forward. 'You can ignore me all you want, son. But the fact is – I'm holding all the cards here.' As he switched on the recording equipment, he made the usual announcements about time, date, and persons present.

'So, did you do it?' Cobb asked bluntly. 'Did you kill Carrie Esposito?'

Rivera sighed. 'I asked *you* a question, Superintendent. What am I here for?'

The Superintendent narrowed his eyes. 'We want to ask you some questions with regard to the murder that occurred at the Golden Sands Holiday Park last night. And...'

'...without an official charge, you cannot keep me in police custody for more than twenty-four hours,' the ex-soldier interrupted. 'And you are obliged to provide me with a lawyer appointed by the state.'

'Did you do it?' Cobb pressed, ignoring his arguments.

'No.' Rivera shook his head. 'And unless you're going to charge me, and provide me with said lawyer, then I shall answer no further questions on the matter. I gave you my whereabouts at the suspected time of death. I provided you with my movements, and I categorically deny seeing Carrie Esposito after we parted company following the screening of *Citizen Kane* at the Central Cinema.' He cleared his throat. Rivera wasn't a man given to shows of emotion, but he noticed how a slight quiver had come to his voice.

The Superintendent frowned. 'Why did you go to The Diplomat Hotel?'

Silence.

'What time did you leave The Diplomat?'

Silence. Rivera sat back in his chair.

'How long are you intending to spend in South Quay?'

Silence. The ex-soldier folded his arms and stared back with contempt.

Cobb leaned forward and pressed a button to cease recording. He stood up wearily. 'Watch yourself, Rivera,' he cautioned. 'You're walking a fucking tightrope here. And you're still the last person to see Carrie Esposito alive. Juries find little details like that *extremely* interesting.'

The Superintendent left the room, and a lower-ranking officer entered to escort the ex-soldier back to the cells.

Chapter 30.

Rivera's cell could have been any cell, anywhere in the world. Plaster had been scraped but remained unrepaired; obscenities had been scrawled on the walls. There was an aroma of bleach, urine, and unwashed feet. He sat down at the foot of the narrow bed and started thinking. Whenever bad things happened, he tried to think back to when he'd experienced worse. Sometimes it helped. Other times it didn't.

The ex-soldier was no stranger to death. But he knew that there had to be means, motive, and opportunity to explain any murder outside of a warzone. It was this which was troubling him: the opportunity was obvious – there hadn't been anyone else at the Golden Sands when the crime occurred. The means was cloudier – he didn't have any information about how the killing had happened. But it was the motive that was troubling him the most.

Why would anyone kill Esposito? She was an innocent – like Jane Fonda's character in *Barbarella*. The world should have formed a Mathmos-like protective bubble to cocoon her, but instead, she was gone.

He racked his brains, but could think of no answer. And so, he did what he always did – looked for anomalies. If something didn't fit, then it was usually a good starting point.

And the only anomaly he could think of was Esposito going to The Diplomat and seeing Bourse and the woman. Other than that, the day of her death seemed like a regular day. Unremarkable. The American told Rivera she hadn't been seen, but could she have been wrong? Might they have considered her a threat?

It seemed unlikely, but to go to such extremes meant someone had something significant to protect. And if that was the case, people grew edgy. They made mistakes. Something wasn't adding up, but he couldn't work out what.

The ex-soldier vowed to keep digging. But he couldn't mine information from where he was. So, instead, he opted to close his eyes.

Sleep when you can. Eat when you can. It was advice from the military which had stuck with him.

* * *

Rivera was jerked into wakefulness by the grille of his cell door sliding back. He blinked for a moment against the harsh brightness of the strip lights overhead.

'Food,' a low voice announced: Malone.

The ex-soldier moved over to the hatch and crouched down.

'Any word, Constable?' he enquired.

'You're safe as houses,' Malone whispered. 'I know it may not look like it right now, but it's true. Safe as milk.'

'A Captain Beefheart fan then, are we?' the ex-soldier chuckled drily.

'Kind of,' Malone replied.

'Anyway – what gives?' Rivera demanded.

'You have alibis, so Cobb can't hold you any longer than twenty-four hours,' Malone whispered. 'Number one – I recorded the time you spoke to me. And number two, they've got you on CCTV at an all-night garage buying ciggies. You're golden.'

The ex-soldier nodded. 'They must have pin-pointed time of death, then?'

'Yeah. Whoever did the hit was a bit of a cowboy, it would seem. Either that or they were disturbed. Your girl was in the midst of a phone call. They reckon she must have put her phone down to answer the door and that was when it happened. Whoever it was didn't notice – and whoever it was she was talking to in the States called it in. There was a bit of to-ing and fro-ing between police departments, but they got there eventually.' Malone paused. 'Anyway, the time corresponded with when you were out and about. The CCTV was time-stamped.'

Chapter 31.

The Yardbird Clover estate was one of the most notorious in South Quay. It was a place to which ambulances rarely ventured without a police escort. Before Keane had taken over running its various operations, it had been like the Wild West. Refuse lay uncollected, and undertakers demanded danger money to remove the dead. Matty Austin and his many cousins ruled the concrete canyons and walkways with an iron fist. The Austin clan had assumed control three generations before and hadn't relinquished it since. They ranged in age from mid-twenties to mid-thirties. All of them were big – their brawn topped up by regular steroid-fuelled gym sessions. Looked upon from a distance, they were almost like carbon copies of a master version, distinguished only by their choices of tattoo. All were heavily inked, and all sported an array of piercings.

A task like the one Keane had set them was music to their ears. It allowed them to sate their bloodlust, while also serving as a reminder to people in the locale not to go against them. Not to cross them. Their nefarious deeds were circulated on various encrypted networks – they were like calling cards. As long as people continued to fear them, they were satisfied they were doing the right thing.

The call came through late in the morning. By mid-afternoon, they were in position. Bourse had booked his workforce a meal in a restaurant located in the town centre. Once the taxis bearing the workers had departed, the five men moved into the area surrounding the workers' chalets. They checked nobody was around and then settled down, passing the time by smoking, scrolling on their phones, and proffering homophobic insults to one another.

Until their target arrived, there was nothing to do but wait.

* * *

Cobb dropped Rivera off a little way into the holiday park.

'Wow! Door-to-door service here. No expense spared,' Rivera scoffed.

'Watch your tone,' Cobb growled. 'You can fucking handle things from here.'

The ex-soldier nodded and climbed out of the car. Walking away, though, he hesitated for a moment, pondering. Cobb had been perfectly happy to drive his patrol car all the way up to the chalets on the previous day. Rivera shrugged and then walked away.

As he walked, he began considering Malone's warning.

So, he wasn't entirely surprised when, approaching the chalet, he saw an assembly of hard men arranged to greet him. Rivera was of the mind that there were two kinds of people: those who ran from trouble, and those who ran towards it. The ex-soldier was of the latter persuasion, but he didn't run on this occasion – he sauntered towards it, whistling. His mind ran a series of very swift calculations. This wasn't a hit – it was too public. But, whatever it was, it clearly had a link to Esposito. And, whoever they were, they were clearly in cahoots with Cobb. The Superintendent had delivered him right into a trap.

Rivera walked towards his chalet, showing no fear. As he did, he noticed that one of the men was filming him on a phone. That gave him pause for thought – he reasoned it was probably for use in reporting back what they were doing to whoever was paying them.

It made little difference to the ex-soldier.

As he approached, he sized up each of his potential adversaries. They were all bigger than him. And probably stronger, too. They carried themselves with the slouching self-assuredness of men who knew their place in the pecking order extremely well. They were alpha males. Whichever gutter they were living in, they'd clearly settled themselves down into a comfortable rut. Rivera studied them with his peripheral vision. They were – he believed – the kind of people who'd rarely strayed beyond a two-mile radius of their front door. That meant they'd be good at a South Quay style of fighting. How they'd fare when faced with more exotic forms of combat was less certain.

'Afternoon,' Rivera called out cheerfully.

Five sets of expressionless eyes stared back at him, unblinking.

The ex-soldier made his way over to Iris. A plan was forming in his mind. At least, the beginnings of a plan. Once things started happening, he knew he'd have to improvise. But it would help if he could at least wrong-foot the opposition. In such instances, a partial plan was better than no plan at all. He was loath to risk damaging the campervan, but if he was in front of it, it would force his assailants to pivot round and change their positions.

And they couldn't get behind him; Iris was joining the fight. He smiled inwardly – he hoped the sprig of purple and yellow flora on her side was offending their anabolic sense of masculinity.

As he approached the T2, Rosie emerged. She pawed at the ground by the front wheel on the driver's side. Rivera bent down to stroke her. As he did, he cradled her and reached slightly under the chassis. His fingers felt behind the wheel until the tips came into contact with the end of a lug wrench. A few days earlier, when Esposito had adjusted Iris' brakes, she'd emerged triumphantly from beneath her just before the work crews set off for the day. Her chalet was locked, as was the campervan, so she'd simply slid the tool behind the wheel and said she'd collect it later. Until now, Rivera had forgotten about it. Reaching down, he firmly pushed the cat beneath the chassis.

'Pretty poncey picture you've got on the door there,' a hateful voice came from behind. 'I'm surprised you haven't got a rainbow flag flying. Faggot!'

Rivera's fingers closed around the handle of the wrench. He reasoned that, in such situations, it was better for a person to get their revenge in before their assailant attacked. Glancing at the reflection in the T2's side, he rose and twisted in the same fluid motion. The glinting wrench arced through the air, smashing into the side of the other man's head.

His challenger's knees buckled and he hit the ground with a thud. He might still have been alive. He might not.

It made little difference to Rivera.

The next two men approached him more warily. They clearly hadn't expected to lose one of their number so swiftly, and the lug wrench made them hesitant. In the distance, the man at the rear continued to film proceedings.

When Keane had called, he'd promised it would be easy – a pushover. The Yardbird Clover crew hadn't reckoned on weapons – Rivera's actions had thrown them, as had his apparent lack of fear. They were used to intimidation softening up their victims, but it just wasn't working here. As the pair approached the ex-soldier, they looked around for anything that might serve for armaments, but came up short.

Without speaking, the two men aligned themselves. Their plan – it seemed – was simple. They were aiming to charge their quarry from different directions. It was simplistic. But, doubtless, it would have worked in the many pub car parks the men had fought in before.

For Rivera, though, dealing with the attack was relatively easy. The men were big, which made them slow. He danced around to one side, which meant the man at the rear was no longer charging at the ex-soldier. Instead, he was charging towards the back of his friend.

The lead man was so busy watching the wrench dangling from Rivera's hand that he didn't see the reverse roundhouse kick the ex-soldier unleashed. One moment the man was watching the tool glint in the late afternoon sun, and the next, the whole force of Rivera's body weight had been brought to bear through the heel of his boot.

It was a crushing blow that hit him just below the temple. The attacker's head careered off to one side and a gobbet of blood sprayed from his mouth. It took a moment for his body to catch up with the head's momentum. He was unconscious long before he hit the ground. Whether he'd ever be able to do Sudokus again was a matter of debate. Rivera wasn't too bothered: he wasn't sure his would-be attacker would have had too much of a penchant for logic puzzles, anyway.

Following the despatch of the first attacker, the second man continued as if in a daze. He was seemingly unable to process what had happened to his friend. Clearly, in the past, he'd been a wingman. His friend had done the fighting; he'd simply done the posturing. So, he simply staggered blindly on, his arms in a fighting stance and his feet shuffling on the sandy ground. Rivera swung the wrench back the other way. This time, the tool struck the assailant just beneath the eye. Its impact opened up a huge cut across the man's cheek. He sank to his knees, clutching absent-mindedly at the injured area. The ex-soldier finished him off with a crunching kick to the jaw.

So far, the fight had lasted a little over ten seconds.

The fourth man was cannier than the others. He'd had a little longer to look for a weapon, and so lifted a lead pipe from where it had been leaning against the steps of one of the chalets. The oldest dwellings required updates to their plumbing as part of the refurbishment. The makeshift truncheon was a cast-off.

As the man began to approach, wielding the lead pipe, his friend at the rear continued to film. The fourth man was more tactical than his predecessors. He sized up the situation better and looked lighter on his feet. The two men tip-toed around each other, looking for potential weaknesses.

Rivera was mindful of the final adversary, too. He was conscious that – at any moment – he might join the fray. As it was, though, he seemed content to remain in the background.

'What's this all about?' Rivera enquired. 'Can't we just talk about it?'

The other man said nothing.

'Who were those guys anyway – your boyfriends?' the ex-soldier smirked.

Rivera watched as the other man's complexion changed. The jibe had filled him with hatred. His cheeks glowed red, and his eyes narrowed. He was grinding his teeth as he eyed his target.

'Is that what this is all about?' Rivera blew him a kiss. 'You fancy me? You should have said!'

The fourth man was unable to contain his rage any longer. He raced at Rivera, roaring, raising the lead pipe above his head like a centurion running into battle.

Pausing, the ex-soldier read the other man's intentions. They were not subtle – he wanted to knock the ex-soldier's head clear of his body. He wanted to knock it over the stands; clear out of the stadium. Rivera tensed, and then – as the other man approached – he launched himself, driving his back foot into the earth and then powering upward. The lug wrench smashed into the other man's wrist as it swung round, holding the pipe. The sound of a bone breaking was clearly audible.

The other man stepped back, dropping the pipe. He stared down at his useless hand. Rivera then smashed the wrench into the unguarded side of the man's head.

He hit the floor.

Rivera looked up expectantly.

The final man was still filming. It was only as Rivera began approaching that he lowered the phone. It was clearly a situation he hadn't planned for.

'What the hell is going on?' the ex-soldier asked, annoyed.

Silence.

'Who the fuck are you?' he pressed.

'Insurance,' the man said bluntly.

Rivera frowned. 'I'm not sure that quite works,' he announced. 'You saw what happened just now. So how are you going to make a difference?' He stepped forward. He was around twenty yards away from the other man, and closing with each slow step. 'Insurance means you mop up the mess when everyone else has failed,' he paused. 'But I can't see you doing that.'

The man laughed. 'You were in the forces, right?'

Rivera nodded.

'So, you'll know that a kind word and a gun gets you much further than just a kind word.' The other man grinned.

'Isn't that from *The Untouchables*?' Rivera frowned. 'Have you really got so little imagination that you can't think up your own cusses?'

Silence.

'I didn't hear too many kind words from your mates back there,' the ex-soldier continued, shrugging.

'Seen one of these before?' The man drew a pistol out of his pocket.

Rivera grinned.

'Something funny, fuckstick?' the man asked.

'That's a Colt Single Action Army Revolver. It's a bloody antique, mate!' The ex-soldier laughed. 'It's a cowboy weapon – probably over a century and a half old.'

'It'll still kill you,' the other man said defensively.

'Yeah, maybe. But the chances of hitting me are a thousand to one. At best.'

Silence.

'Well, come on then. Let's get this over with,' Rivera said impatiently. 'I need to feed my cat.' He started walking towards his chalet.

'Where the fuck are you going?' the armed man asked, annoyed.

FOUR-LEAF CLOVER

'I'm moving out of the way of the VW,' Rivera explained. 'I don't want your stray bullets chipping the paintwork.'

The man frowned. 'I never miss.' He raised the gun and fired.

Rivera shrugged. 'First time for everything.'

The man fired again.

'You see...' Rivera began. 'You've got one hundred and fifty years plus of wear and tear on a weapon like that. I said it was an antique – that was me being kind.'

The report of another shot rang out.

'It reduces accuracy, you see,' Rivera continued. 'If you get worn cylinder stops, it can lead to misalignment with the axis of the bore... you'd know that if you'd been trained.' He paused. 'But I guess that's not the case.'

The man fired again.

'Getting better!' Rivera chuckled. 'I swear I almost felt that one.' He paused, grinning. 'Now, where was I? Ah yes – if you haven't been cleaning it and maintaining it, then it can lead to problems in the throat and the barrel. And if you've been using corrosive primers, it'll diminish accuracy even further.'

The man pulled the trigger once more.

'You've got quite a short barrel, too,' the ex-soldier explained. 'But I suspect girls have told you that before.' He smiled. 'Anyway, the longer the distance between rear and front sight, then the better the sight radius.' He paused. 'You firing from that distance...' he shrugged. 'It's pot luck with a weapon like that.'

The man fired again.

Rivera grinned. 'And that's your lot.'

'What the fuck are you talking about?' the other man frowned.

'The Colt Single Action Army Revolver – also known as a six-shooter. Reason being – you get six shots. Someone must have been up all night wondering what to name it. Anyway, you just fired your sixth.' He smiled. 'Trouble counting?'

Panic clouded the man's countenance. He raised the pistol and pulled frantically at the trigger. He then dropped the gun and started running, still clutching his phone.

Chapter 32.

It didn't take long for Rivera to catch up with the remaining man. Even though his adversary was smaller than his accomplices, he was still built bulkily rather than being honed for speed. He raced away down the sand track between the rows of chalets with the ex-soldier in pursuit, closing the distance between them all the time.

The escapee was brought crashing to the ground with a sliding tackle beside the tool shed. The man's knees gave way, and his phone skidded across the ground. Both men hit the floor in a tangle of limbs, but the ex-soldier recovered fastest, rolling away from the escapee.

Rising, the fifth man threw a half-hearted punch. He'd evidently been given the job as camera man due to a reduced lack of fighting ability. Rivera smashed his fist into the man's face. He sat back dazed against a water butt, not being quite able to compute how he'd ended up in such a position.

The ex-soldier walked over to where the man's phone had fallen and picked it up. It was in the midst of a video call with a camera icon flashing red in one corner. The screen at the other end was blanked out, with the video and audio switched off. The only identifying mark was the letter 'K' in a green circle at the top right-hand corner.

Rivera glared at the screen. 'I don't know who you are,' he announced. 'Or what the fuck you're playing at. But the next time you send a gang after me, I'm not going to play as nice as I did today.' He ended the call and chewed his lip for a moment as he walked over to the water butt. Despite the lack of rain, it was almost full – Rivera suspected it had been topped up with leftover water from the sprinklers.

He dropped the phone into the water butt.

Turning, Rivera grabbed the fallen man by the collar. The would-be assailant feebly remonstrated, but the ex-soldier booted him in the ribs and then forced his head under the surface. It wasn't necessarily a vindictive action – he was simply taking the most direct route he could think of to secure the information he desired.

The other man kicked and bucked against Rivera's grasp. His arms flailed manically, but his head remained under the surface. He was stronger than the ex-soldier, but the smaller man had the element of surprise.

When he reasoned he'd been under the water long enough, Rivera hauled him back out. The sodden man gasped for a second, and then his head was thrust back under.

Sixty seconds later, the ex-soldier hauled the man's head back out into the air. As he stood, spluttering and gasping, he gripped his throat, feeling his thumb and forefinger almost touch behind the man's windpipe. 'Who sent you?' he demanded.

'Fuck you!' the other man wheezed.

Rivera forced the man's head back under the surface of the water once more. Again, the man flailed and kicked. Again, he stilled. He was only allowed out when the ex-soldier judged he'd had enough.

'Well?' he demanded. 'You either answer or I hold you under for twice as long. And, before you think I'm bluffing, remember – I have nothing to lose. You tried to shoot me, remember? The way I see it, I'm doing you a favour.'

Silence.

Rivera made to grab at him again.

'Wait!' the other man called helplessly. He coughed and spat out a mouthful of water.

'I'm waiting,' the ex-soldier pressed, reaching for the other man's throat once more.

'Leah Keane,' the man spluttered.

Chapter 33.

Cobb's face was almost puce with anger. His office phone had been ringing off the hook; he'd been inundated with requests from journalists trying to cover the story emerging from the Golden Sands Holiday Park. The murder had been bad enough, but the previous day's events were something he'd been totally unprepared for. Death was something he'd encountered before. The latest events, though, were not.

The local paper's front page had looked like a mock-up of a frontier town. The photograph resembled a Western wanted poster in a town like Tombstone. He, though – to his chagrin - had not been cast as a lawman in the Wyatt Earp mould.

'Problem Jackie?' Malone asked as he walked in. 'They said you wanted to see me.'

'Dammit, Constable! How many times? It's Superintendent. Or it's Sir.'

'Right you are,' Malone nodded. 'Anyway, what seems to be the problem?'

Cobb narrowed his eyes. 'You've not heard?'

'Heard what?'

The Superintendent sighed. He slid a copy of the local paper across the desk and waited for the Constable to take it in.

Malone whistled softly. Then he frowned. 'There's not a whole lot of detail here, Jackie. I mean – not really.'

Cobb drummed his fingers on the table for a moment. 'Five men from the Yardbird Clover Estate. All known to us. Bad to the fucking bone.' He paused. 'They were found at the Golden Sands Holiday Park yesterday evening.'

'What? Dead?'

'No. But not far off. They'd each received a beating. A proper pasting.'

'Well, it's all go round here, isn't it? We're only one step short of *Midsomer Murders* the rate we're going!'

'Yes,' Cobb nodded. 'And that's the bloody problem. There were five of the bastards lined up with nooses around their necks. The ropes were slung over the wood of the new abseiling structure. They had inflated beach balls placed beneath their feet to take their weight. If any of those had punctured...'

Silence.

'And that's not all of it,' Cobb continued.

'No?' Malone's eyes darted a little. He tilted his head to one side.

The Superintendent gritted his teeth. 'Each of them had a piece of card slung around their neck. It was like a mock execution. Something like you'd see on a bloody history documentary.'

'Anything written on them – the cards, I mean?' Malone enquired.

'Yes.'

'What?'

Cobb sighed. 'Who the hell's Leah Keane?'

'What?' Malone frowned. 'She's...'

'Yeah, I know who she bloody well is,' the Superintendent interrupted. He looked at the other man gravely. 'That's what was written on the cards. One word per card. One card per man.'

The constable chuckled. 'Ballsy!'

'It's no laughing matter, Malone,' Cobb insisted. 'Whoever did it sent photographs to the papers. It's a PR disaster. It's making it look like we can't control things here. We'll be plastered across the national dailies tomorrow.' He mopped at his brow. 'We're already all over their bloody news feeds as it is.' He shook his head. 'Keane's not going to like her name being taken in vain either.'

Silence.

Malone sighed. 'Look, we all know that Leah Keane is poison. And we all know that she runs most of the rackets and drugs in this town. Anytime something goes wrong, you can usually trace it back to her.' He paused. 'Maybe it's about time she was brought down a peg or two. No?'

'You just don't fucking get it, do you?' Cobb frowned. 'Part of our role here is to keep the peace.'

'What? And let criminals get away with things?' Malone frowned. 'You've changed Jackie.'

Cobb sighed. 'Listen Jimmy, you have to pick your battles sometimes. If we're not careful, it'll be like bloody Stalingrad here. If Keane takes umbrage, then she'll send her people out onto the streets. And if that happens, we'll have a fucking civil war on our hands.' He paused. 'What do we know about this bloke Rivera? The one we nicked. I mean – might this be his doing?'

'Why?' Malone frowned. 'What makes you think he's involved? It strikes me he's the only one who's been telling the truth so far. He came forward to volunteer information – remember that?'

Cobb nodded. 'But he's still a piece of the puzzle that doesn't fit.'

Malone frowned and then looked hard at the other man, choosing his words with deliberate care. 'Is that what you think, Jackie? Or what Keane thinks?'

The Superintendent stared at the other man, his teeth gritted. When he spoke, his tone was devoid of expression. 'Close the door on your way out, Constable. We're done here.'

Chapter 34.

'I want him dead,' Keane said thinly. Her eyes blazed for a moment before she reverted to being her usual self. Her tone wasn't hateful; it was simply matter-of-fact. The kind of tone one might employ to order something as mundane as a takeaway. She was sitting on her bar stool in The George and Dragon. Bullseye and his boss had the bar to themselves. Keane had switched her usual business attire for a designer tracksuit. It was clearly a clothing choice with considerable cost, but it was the first hint her usual, calm comportment had frayed a little.

The big man nodded, sipping at his beer. 'Can do.'

'I don't care who he is or what he's done. I want him gone,' the boss continued. 'He's a bloody liability. Killer's eyes. I saw them on the phone stream – he's a fucking lunatic. You get a guy like that nosing around and they're a loose cannon – there's no telling what they'll do.'

'So...?'

'So, fucking get on it,' Keane instructed. 'I'll speak to Cobb. Make sure Bourse is on board.' She paused. 'But take no chances this time – you saw what he did to Matty Austin's boys. He's no pushover.' She paused. 'He reminds me a bit of Terry Lyons. Remember him?'

The big man nodded. Terry Lyons had been an ex-Army enforcer for Tyrell Majors. Once his boss disappeared, he made a very brief play against the Keane organisation. He was tough; trained. The night he and Bullseye had confronted one another, even Keane had been a little concerned about the outcome. But that had been the night the big man had truly won his spurs. Lyons had insisted on a public place in front of a newsagent, assuming it would ensure fair play. As a result, he'd left his pistol in the glove box of his car.

Bullseye had shot him in the leg. Then - in full view of anyone who hadn't runaway – he pissed on him. As Lyons was in the throes of pleading for his life, Bullseye put a bullet through his head. What fixed his fame as a local legend, though, was the way that – after that – he calmly waited in line at the newsagents behind two half-deaf pensioners before buying a Twix.

'Guns then?' he asked, shaking himself free of the memory.

'Damn right!' Keane blazed. 'And when you're done, stick him in the crypt. No messing.' She shook her head. 'No one drags my name through the mud like that and gets away with it.' She sighed. 'South Quay's on all the bloody news channels. He's making us look like fools. It's going to cost me an arm and a fucking leg, hushing everything up. And if I *don't* manage to keep my name out on the papers, then who knows what'll happen? They'll have people here looking into all sorts of things. It's a bloody disaster.'

Bullseye nodded. 'So... when?'

'Soon as,' Keane nodded. 'You get rid of this Rivera bastard and you get rid of the problem. Simple.'

Chapter 35.

'Someone to see you,' Clarke announced to Rivera. He'd been wrestling with the side panelling of a chalet whose planks had rotted.

'Who?' the ex-soldier frowned.

'Police, mate. Sorry.' The foreman shrugged. 'They're over by your chalet.'

'Again?'

'Yeah – they must be desperate to pin something on someone.' Clarke sighed. 'I guess you're still in the firing line at the moment, old son.'

Rivera nodded and made his way over towards his lodgings. As he approached, he saw the figure of Malone sitting on the porch. The Constable was flicking back through the pages of his notebook.

* * *

'Lovely day.' The policeman raised a hand in greeting.

'Yeah,' Rivera nodded. 'So, what brings you to my humble abode?' He paused. 'If we start seeing much more of each other, people are going to start talking...'

'You travel pretty light, I'm guessing?' Malone said, ignoring the ex-soldier's words.

'I do. Me. My cat. And my campervan. Why?'

'I'm guessing that – if push came to shove – you could probably leave town at the drop of a hat, right? Fly by night.'

'Correct,' the ex-soldier shrugged, his brow furrowing. 'Why? Where are you going with this?'

The policeman sighed. 'What you did with the Yardbird Clover boys was outstanding! I mean – nobody has any proof it was you, but everyone has a pretty good idea.' He chuckled. 'That's what justice looks like. To my mind, anyway. It made me wish I could have joined in – the law hasn't been able to touch them for years, but you gave them the treatment they deserved.' He grinned. 'I only wish some of those beach balls had been less robust...'

Silence.

'What makes you think it was me?' Rivera demanded.

Malone smiled, but didn't answer. 'Here's the deal,' he said, heavily. 'Leah Keane will now want you dead. Not just injured. Not incapacitated. Dead. She's got the whole bloody police department in her pocket – other than me, that is. Of course, I didn't tell you that, but I reckon you're savvy enough to figure it out. And your employer – Bourse. He's the same.' Malone sighed. 'Everyone knows where the corruption is around here, Rivera,' he continued. 'But nobody wants to do anything about it. Keane's aware of that. If you have a poor town, people can be bribed easily.'

'So?' the ex-soldier pressed.

'So, I'm asking you to do me a favour.'

'Go on,' Rivera frowned.

'Leave town.'

'Not how I operate,' the ex-soldier shook his head. 'I don't run from trouble.'

The policeman sighed. 'I knew you'd say that.' He paused. 'Look, you're an intelligent man, Rivera. Clearly. So you know when to attack and when not to. But do yourself a favour. Even Napoleon had to retreat sometimes.'

Rivera frowned.

'I'm not asking you to do this forever,' Malone explained. 'But think about it. Bourse will fire you. There are precious few jobs in town, and once he puts out the word, nobody else will hire you. Cobb's determined to make the murder charge stick. He's going to keep on pestering and hassling until he can either pin something on you, or you get so fed up you snap. Then there's Keane – she's a fucking terror. And she's lost face because of you. She wants you dead, and she'll stop at nothing to get what she wants.' Malone paused. 'She doesn't fuck about – but you know that already. You can't fight all of them off. Not forever. Things don't work like that. Not here. Not anywhere else either. And I can't protect you – I'm one of the few good apples in a rotten barrel. But I've got no power.'

'So, what do I do?' the ex-soldier enquired. 'I'm not liking the sound of this.'

Malone sighed heavily. 'Get out of here. Give me a few weeks. I'll find out what I can. We all know who the problem is here, but with things being hushed up by the force, there's no way of making anything stick. Not yet anyway. Once we've got an angle, I can bring you back in.'

'What are you going to do in the meantime, then?' Rivera pressed.

'I'll get the evidence – if there is any. But I can't do that right away. We've got to let things die down.' He paused. 'I know Derek – your foreman. We go way back. I'll get him to hold your job for you if I can. *If* he can. That way, when you return, you can slot right back in.' He paused. 'Look – with someone like Keane, you back her into a corner and she'll be hyper-alert. Like a rat. It's when she's relaxed and complacent we'll get opportunities. And that's not the case. Not right now.'

'How do we swing it? Because they're going to wonder – if I just vanish, I mean. They won't just forget.'

Malone shrugged. 'Your aunt in Inverness – she's fallen ill. You're going to take compassionate leave – look after her for a bit. If Derek tells Bourse, then you can be damn sure the word will get back to Keane. And it's far enough away they won't come after you. It's not how they work – their world is here.'

Rivera sighed. 'I don't like it.'

'What – the story?'

'No. Running away.'

'Look – I'm going completely against my oath here. I'm contravening the police code of conduct in every way. But this is war. Leah Keane's the enemy. You don't have to win every battle to win a war – remember that.' He shrugged. 'And you're not running away. Call it a tactical retreat. Whatever makes you feel better.'

Silence.

'You talked about justice before,' Rivera said. 'Here's what I think: The Diplomat fire was deliberate. Keane had something to do with it, and Esposito died because of it. Not only that, but Fraser burned to death as a result.' He paused. 'Justice is about balancing the books. And, right now, Keane's in debt. A lot of bloody debt. She owes a whole lot of people for a whole lot of pain. And it's come time to call in her accounts.'

'Agreed,' Malone nodded. 'And I can't think of a better bailiff. But we need to time it right. You do it wrong, and she'll stay free. I'll do what I can to help you. Everything I can. But you need to skip town for a while. Let Keane think she's in the clear. If she lowers her guard, there's more chance of me getting proof.'

'You're a good officer, Malone,' Rivera announced as he shook the other man's hand. 'Had it been anyone else asking, I'd have told them to piss off. I'm not convinced... but I'm going to humour you – for now.' He paused. 'But I won't forget. That's not how I roll. And forgiveness is a sign of weakness – I'm not going to be forgiving Keane anytime soon.'

The policeman laughed. 'I'll take you not lumping me in with her as a compliment.'

'Do.' The ex-soldier paused. 'And know this – you're talking about evidence and things like that... it makes it sound like a regular investigation.' Rivera looked hard at the other man. 'But I'm off the books. We're not doing the kinds of things that'll end up in the courts.' His countenance hardened. 'Once I've got proof, I'll act. And I don't care who that proof comes from – you or anyone else.'

The hint of a smile softened his features. 'Let's just say that when it comes to the roots of revenge, I'm agnostic.'

'Understood,' Malone nodded.

PART 2
Chapter 36.

6 WEEKS LATER

Rivera sometimes wondered if he simply wasn't cut out for domestic life. Leaving South Quay, he'd headed north to Castlethwaite to see Betsy. Since she'd left Spain to attend to her father, the pair had corresponded via text message and the occasional phone call. It had always been the ex-soldier's intention to patch things up; he hoped that visiting might rekindle the feelings she'd had for him previously. Either way, he knew he needed to put distance between himself and the south coast. It wasn't that he was scared. Rather that he was worried about what might have happened if he'd taken the law completely into his own hands. The sinister figures ruling the roost in South Quay appeared to have a long reach. Rivera realised that to avenge Esposito and Fraser, he'd need a proper strategy.

Numbers were against him. And if he put a foot wrong, he'd end up in jail and Keane would stay free.

At first, life in Castlethwaite had been pleasant. Betsy was happy to see him; her parents lived in a large house, and the pair had plenty of room to themselves. However, having her family in the background wasn't conducive to romance. Betsy and Rivera's time in Spain had felt like a honeymoon – it had been exotic.

Carefree.

Glamorous.

It was the everyday mundane nature of life they seemed to struggle with. And Castlethwaite's existence seemed more mundane than most places. The couple suffered as a result. They could coexist perfectly in the sunshine; it was the rain that seemed to be their kryptonite.

Rivera and Betsy had sat down one evening and talked things through. She was adamant she wanted to give their relationship another go. But, until her father was either placed in a home or made a recovery, she felt her role was supporting her mother with his care. The couple tip-toed around the subject. Neither had said that recovery wasn't likely – although he had occasional better days, he was ailing fast. And neither had voiced the idea he might continue to decline. Instead, Rivera had gamely accepted they'd try being a couple again at some undefined point in the future that might or might not arrive. The ex-soldier had reluctantly agreed, but – in doing so – he'd shifted back to his natural state: the tom cat feelings Betsy had suppressed had surfaced once more. He suddenly found his eyes snagging on women they shouldn't have. He knew there was only one way they'd progress if left unchecked.

* * *

Rosie, meanwhile, had settled back into life in the Lake District very quickly. Her daily kill tally had gone through the roof. It was because of this that Rivera had moved her out to sleep in Iris – that way the floor of the campervan bore the brunt of her stalking prowess, and he didn't have to continually clean the immaculate flooring of the house.

The ex-soldier had messaged Malone on a couple of occasions, but had simply been told that things were progressing. He'd accepted the Constable's suggestion before, but - in truth - he was itching to get back to the fray. Being in the Lake District was beginning to bore him. At the back of his mind were nagging thoughts of Keane and revenge.

He was restless.

Since leaving the Army, life on the road had made Rivera even more restless than usual - if he was confined in one place for too long, he became tetchy. Added to that, he felt powerless: powerless to mend his relationship; powerless to help Betsy's father, and powerless to bring the mysterious Leah Keane to justice. Not a day passed when he didn't think about the fire and its aftermath. The ex-soldier was convinced the deaths of his two friends were attributable to the woman who seemed to be untouchable.

So the phone call came at just the right time.

* * *

The number was unknown. Withheld.

Rivera suspected a marketing scam. He'd normally have let it go to voicemail, but something made him answer it, nonetheless.

'Hello.'

'Am I speaking to Trent Rivera?' The accent on the other end of the line was American – it had a slight drawl. The timbre was rasping; deep.

'Let me save you some time,' the ex-soldier announced bluntly. 'I don't care where you're calling from, and I don't care what you're selling... I'm not buying.'

'...The name's Larry Esposito,' the voice at the end of the line cut in. 'You knew my daughter.'

Silence.

'I'm truly sorry for your loss,' Rivera said heavily.

'Appreciate it.' The tone was calm. Measured. Clipped.

'How did you get my number?' the ex-soldier frowned.

'A police officer by the name of Malone,' Larry Esposito explained. 'I had to jump through a hell of a lot of hoops, but I reached you in the end. We held the funeral back here. Stateside. After that I started asking questions; I finally started making some headway.'

'Can I ask why you sought out Malone?' Rivera enquired, chewing his lip.

'I was in the NCIS – rank of Major.' He paused for a beat. 'Naval Criminal Investigative Service. Ask around if you like – there are plenty of people who'll vouch for me. No one really calls me Larry, though – I go by Lefty most of the time.' He paused. 'That's if you're asking around, I mean.'

'Alright – er – Lefty.' Rivera paused. 'So, how can I help you?'

'I'm coming in on the red-eye – I'll be at Heathrow Airport first thing tomorrow morning. I want to see things for myself. No offence, but I'm not sure I trust the police that worked on this very much.'

'I'm not the police,' Rivera announced bluntly. 'So, no offence taken.' He paused. 'And, with respect, I'm not sure I'll be able to do anything more than they're already done.'

'I know,' the voice at the other end of the line agreed. 'But the police there seem to think it was an open and shut case.' He paused, and then continued, bitterly. 'The hell it was – murder can't get swept under the carpet in the space of just over a month. They're missing something – for sure. And, according to Malone, you're one of the few people who might share my view.'

'Very well...' Rivera began.

'I'm coming to South Quay,' Lefty continued. 'Are you based there?'

'Negative,' the ex-soldier replied. 'But I can head down.' He hesitated. 'What did Malone say about me? I mean – other than me not believing the official verdict?'

'That you're quite the bloodhound,' the other man replied. 'He said that if I'm going to trust anyone, then I should trust you. And that in a tight spot, you know how to handle yourself.' He cleared his throat. 'I know this won't bring my daughter back, Mr Rivera. But I can't rest thinking someone's got away with killing her.' The voice paused as the speaker gathered his thoughts. 'I guess what I'm trying to say is that I'm going to do a little investigating myself. So, I wondered if you might like to help turn over a few stones?'

'Yeah – I'm in,' Rivera answered immediately.

'You sure?'

'Absolutely,' the ex-soldier nodded.

'Good. Malone said you had some information. Apparently there's more stuff that's come to light too. What say we carry this on face-to-face?' The other man paused. 'I should be in town around twelve hundred hours tomorrow. I'll text you the details of where I'm staying.'

'Roger that,' the ex-soldier replied.

The American hung up.

Chapter 37.

'So, what do we know?' Lefty wasted no time on pleasantries. He had the air of a man on a mission. He was slightly taller than Rivera. Trim. Toned. His black hair was greying slightly at the temples. His approach in all things was direct. Once he'd established he was talking to the right person, he launched straight into questioning – all niceties cast aside.

The Regency Hotel had recently had a facelift. It retained an old world Art Déco charm on the outside, but inside was all plastic and cheap photographic prints.

Rivera sighed at the question. 'Well, that's quite a long story.'

The American raised a hand. Once he had the waitress' attention, he pointed to his coffee pot and indicated that he wanted another of the same. The Regency was a significant step up from the type of places the ex-soldier was familiar with staying in. When Rivera arrived, the newcomer had already been in place, seated at a table with a notebook before him. A cleaner had been mopping the floor around his seat. 'I'm not here to mourn, Mr Rivera. I'm here to find a murderer. And then...' The ex-soldier met the American's steely glare. The two looked hard at each other for a moment. Then, a waitress arrived with fresh coffee.

'Let me get this straight,' Lefty continued as Rivera filled his cup from the pot. 'You were working here and then you skipped town, right?'

'Correct,' the ex-soldier replied heavily.

'Why?'

'Let's just say I was about to take the law into my own hands. I wanted rough justice – vigilante kind of stuff. I'm not working for anyone – I just kind of follow my own moral compass, I guess. So I started, and then I realised if I went any further, there'd be no turning back. And languishing in a jail cell isn't really too high on my bucket list. Malone – he's the beat policeman here – he warned me off. He said he'd help me gather evidence.'

'And you believed him?'

The ex-soldier sighed. 'I had no reason not to. He's the only straight officer in South Quay – as far as I can tell.'

Lefty pursed his lips. He nodded slowly. 'Alright. Paint a picture for me. So far, I'm having trouble piecing things together. I've got a killer on the loose, but everywhere I've seen so far looks like Fawlty-fucking-Towers.'

Rivera smiled. 'Carrie and I worked together – she was my boss. The holiday camp we were employed by is called the Golden Sands. We were doing a refurbishment of the chalets. Nothing fancy. The foreman there – a guy called Clarke - seems like a straight up kind of guy.' He sipped his coffee. 'Anyway, when The Diplomat Hotel burned down, we'd been there, moving furniture out of storage. Carrie left her plane there and went back. She said it had sentimental value.' The ex-soldier paused. 'Her going back is the only thing I can think of which seems out of place; the only possible thing that might have been out of the ordinary.'

'Why?'

'Because she saw Aaron Bourse there – the owner of the camp. She didn't like him – it's a long story which I'll fill you in on later. Bourse was there with a woman.'

'Did Carrie know her – this woman?'

'Negative. Anyway, we went to the movies together that evening, and when we came out, the hotel was burning. So I went up there and she went home.'

'Why?' The American frowned.

'Why what?'

'Why didn't you both go back to the holiday camp?'

Rivera grimaced, nodding. 'That's a question I've asked myself – many times. I can't help but think that if I hadn't gone, things might have worked out differently.' He sighed. 'There was a homeless man sleeping at the hotel – a guy called Fraser. I knew him, vaguely. I wanted to check he was OK. What with the fire and all.'

'And?'

'He was in there. One of the victims. There's been no official confirmation – according to Malone, he's like a phantom. He doesn't seem to exist on any records; he was ex-military, I believe. But Malone as good as gave me the nod: it was Fraser alright. Anyway, when I was at the scene that night, I got talking to Malone. The next day, he told me there'd been three bodies found in the wreckage. But whoever did it tied them to a cast iron radiator. They used fireproof rope.' He paused. 'I assumed Carrie had joined some of the other youngsters who were out on the town partying, and that's why she wasn't opening her door. It was only after work the next day that she was found.'

'Shot?'

'So, they tell me. I don't have any further details. They had me in the frame at first – until my various alibis were proven. It stank of a cover-up from the start. But if it was, then it was the kind of thing that goes deep. Not the kind of thing an outsider gets much of a look at.'

Lefty nodded. 'I don't like it. I know you've only given me the skeleton bones of this thing, but from where I'm sitting, it doesn't add up.' His hands squeezed at one of the packets of sugar that had been placed on his saucer. 'The post-mortem kind of looked hooky too, if you ask me. But – either way – I don't buy it; the verdict.'

'Roger that,' Rivera replied. 'Then there's the organised crime element.'

'Go on.'

The ex-soldier glanced around before speaking. 'The name I've heard bandied around is Leah Keane. She's a local gangster, but she looks more like a high flier. She's the kind of person who has friends in lofty places – seems to run a slick operation. Rackets. Drugs. The usual...'

Lefty nodded. 'What's her link?'

Rivera shrugged. 'No clue, I'm afraid. But – by all accounts – ne'er-do-wells don't so much as sneeze without her permission around here. Much less burn down hotels. Or beat people up. Or...' Rivera's voice trailed off.

'And you've had run-ins with her?'

'Not directly. I suspect the people I encountered were on the fringes of her organisation. You know the type. Hard men. Criminal records. Loyal. Never left South Quay. Get the picture?'

Lefty nodded. 'And could it have been her at the scene? This Leah Keane?'

'Maybe,' Rivera shrugged. 'No way of telling - at least not yet.'

'Anything else?' The American pursed his lips.

'No. That's about all I know.' Rivera scratched absent-mindedly at his arm and sighed. 'Look... sir, I know you've come a long way. And I know you want to find Carrie's killer. I'd like to help you. But it's not going to be easy – I'd hoped Malone was going to come through with something useful. That was my proviso when I left town.'

'But he hasn't?'

'No – truth be told, he's gone a little cold on the whole thing.'

'Tumbleweed?'

'Yeah, something like that.'

Silence.

'Are you working at the moment?' Lefty asked.

'What?' Rivera frowned.

'Do you have a job?'

'Well, I *did* have a job. I daresay I could ask Clarke to take me on again, but I have my suspicions that Bourse would put up a few barriers.' He paused. 'I'm good, though – I have a campervan. I still have a little cash in my pocket. So, I'll stick around for a week or two. See if I can help you out. I feel like I owe it to Carrie. And I've got an axe to grind with a few people around here – at least, that's how it feels.'

'Three hundred a day,' Lefty announced bluntly.

'What?' the ex-soldier frowned.

'Three hundred a day. Pounds sterling. That sound fair enough to you?' The American smiled a little. 'Plus expenses, of course.'

'Really?' Rivera chewed his lip. 'I mean – I can't make any promises that we'll solve this thing.'

'Yeah, really.' Lefty nodded. 'I don't do things by half measures, Mr Rivera. When I go in, I go *all* in. From what you've just told me, I'd say we've got plenty of leads to chase down. We'll start with them and see where we get to. Malone told me about your background, too.'

'He did?'

'Yeah. So, I guessed you'd be a good guy to have on my side.' He looked hard at the other man. 'You in?'

'I'm in,' Rivera replied. 'But, before we start this, let's just get one thing straight.'

'Go on.'

'We're pretty much on our own here. The way I see it, Keane's got most of the force in her pocket – most of the town. If we go into battle, it's just going to be the two of us against all of them.' Rivera paused. 'I think Malone's a good guy – at least he means well. But...'

'...we can't count on him when the shit hits the fan, right?' Lefty pursed his lips.

'Correct.'

'Did you ever seen *Butch Cassidy and the Sundance Kid*?'

'Yes,' the ex-soldier nodded.

'It was always my favourite movie,' the other man grinned.

Chapter 38.

'Who the hell are you?' The man who greeted Lefty and Rivera as they approached the staff quarters at the Golden Sands was around sixty. He had the weather-beaten complexion of someone who'd worked outside for most of his life. 'This is private property,' he announced, looking hard at both men. 'I can't let you onsite lads – not without some kind of official documentation, I'm afraid.'

'Rivera,' the ex-soldier announced. 'Why? Who the hell are you? I thought Clarke was calling the shots around here.'

The other man's mouth curled slightly into a grin. 'Rivera, huh? Derek's told me about you,' he nodded. 'Said you're alright.' He paused. 'I heard you'd left town, though? Sunshine not work out for you?'

'I've returned,' the ex-soldier replied, thinly.

'Yeah?' The other man raised his eyebrows. 'Better watch yourself – round here, there are daggers in men's smiles.'

'*Macbeth*?' Lefty enquired.

'Yeah. I know my Shakespeare. I've had plenty of time on the dole to read up on the Bard.' The man narrowed his eyes. 'And who might you be?'

'Captain Larry Esposito. US Navy retired.' He paused. 'You can call me Lefty.'

'Oh, I can, can I?' The other man raised his eyebrows. He then checked himself, frowning. 'Hang on – that was the girl's name, wasn't it... the...' His expression grew serious. 'I'm sorry.' He sighed. 'I heard about what happened.'

Silence.

'You weren't to know,' Lefty shrugged. 'Anyway, Rivera asked who *you* are.' He looked hard at the other man. 'Do you have a name?'

'Sid Clements. I'm the sparky. Derek brought me in here to help with some of this chalet rebuilding. They've had a couple of cowboys doing the wiring before me.'

'Is Clarke around anywhere?' Rivera asked.

The other man nodded. 'Come on. I'll take you over.'

* * *

'So what? Are you like a private investigator now or something?' Clarke chuckled after the ex-soldier had greeted him and introduced Esposito. 'I know you've been away for a bit, Rivera, but I didn't think you'd come back with a whole new career.' He frowned. 'Shouldn't you be in a trilby and a mackintosh or something?'

The ex-soldier shook his head and introduced the American. Over a mug of tea, Rivera further explained what he and Lefty were doing. Clarke filled him in on what had happened during his absence.

'So it's Agatha Christie-style now?' the foreman went on. 'Well, good luck. We all know the official story's rotten, but nobody's looking into it as far as I can tell.'

'Something like that,' the ex-soldier shrugged.

'So, are you going to be doing some digging, then?' the foreman asked.

'You've got that right,' Lefty nodded. 'Someone killed my daughter. And I'm damn well going to keep on digging until I find out who.'

'And then what?' Clements pressed.

'Vengeance,' Lefty shot back, his eyes blazing. 'I'm not fucking about here, buddy.'

The electrician nodded.

The four men were seated in a vacant chalet. A light patter of rain sounded on the roof. Rivera rolled a cigarette and stood up to step out onto the porch. The weather was warm – the chalet smelled of fresh pine. There weren't too many of the dwellings that needed completing now.

'You'll be going after Keane then,' Clements announced quietly.

'Looks that way,' the ex-soldier nodded.

'Well, good luck to you.' He turned to Lefty. 'Has your man here told you about how she put me out of business years back?'

The American nodded. 'A little. I've been hearing about all sorts of conflicts. Sounds like you've had a regular civil war going on in South Quay.'

'Yeah, well, take care of yourself. She's vicious.' Clements sighed. 'I mean it. Ruthless as they come - a proper bastard. I've only kept the wolf from the door through scraps of work she's thrown me ever since. Horrible stuff – humiliating. It's only recently she's thawed a little. There'll be a plan for it, for sure. Bourse is in her pocket – any money.' He paused. 'The fact I'm back here now means Keane must have given him the nod. And the only reason they're letting me anywhere near the place is that they've been running behind. That's why half these chalets are still unoccupied. She doesn't usually forget grudges – Keane.'

Silence.

'Anything you can tell us?' Lefty asked. 'To help us, I mean? A start?'

Clements shrugged. 'Have you had a word with that copper?'

'Who?' Clarke frowned, narrowing his eyes at the other man.

'You know - Malone,' the electrician replied.

'Oh – him.' The foreman turned to Rivera. 'Any news on that front?'

The ex-soldier shook his head. 'No – he's gone a little quiet all-in-all. I'm not sure he's going to shed as much light on things as I thought. I'd kind of hoped he'd be our inside man, but I suspect he's being hushed up. Either that or he's lost the stomach for it.'

'Writing cheques he can't cash, huh?' Clements chuckled.

Clarke nodded. 'Keane will be putting the dampers on anything he wants to go digging for.' He paused, looking hard at the new arrivals. 'You'll have to tread carefully, boys. She's got eyes and ears everywhere.'

A sudden wind whirled, whipping up loose sand on the path outside and flinging dust against the panes in the glass door. A few birds rose, screeching into the air from a nearby tree.

'Laramie Holdings,' Clements said bluntly.

'Excuse me?' Lefty frowned.

'Keane has a lock-up on the Church Moor Industrial Estate under that name,' the man continued.

'You know where it's at?' the American asked, looking at Rivera.

The ex-soldier nodded. 'I'm assuming not many people are aware of her operating from there, right?'

Clements sniffed, nodding slowly. 'Correct – don't go telling anyone either. South Quay's mistress and master has a habit of making people disappear if they go poking around. I can't imagine she'd enjoy having any of her secrets uncovered.' He paused. 'But that might be a place to start – I'm sure she's got other lock-ups. Especially now she's such a big shot. But she's pretty much had that one from the start.'

'So, how come you know about the industrial estate?' Rivera asked.

Clements turned to Clarke. 'Remember Hobson?'

'Who? Andy?' the foreman nodded.

'Yeah... well, he was in business with me. I mean – if you could call it that. When Keane put our ice cream vans out of commission, she still bore a grudge against me. I was someone she disliked intensely. But she *really* hated Hobson.' Clements scratched at his collar. 'He was like me, but worse off – he couldn't get any work at all unless Keane threw him a bone.' He sniffed. 'Problem was – he was still gambling. Christ knows what kind of debts he had, but he was pretty desperate. He was holding on by his fingernails, really.'

'Why didn't you leave, the pair of you?' Lefty enquired. 'Cut your losses? Start over?'

'I kind of wish we had,' Clements shrugged. 'Pride – I suppose. When you're younger, you think you'll bounce back. Especially if you've always lived in the same place. To be honest, I regret not going – there and then.' He paused. 'But hindsight's a wonderful thing.'

'Hobson *did* leave, though,' Clarke insisted. 'Australia.'

Silence.

'That's what everyone says,' Clements nodded. He lowered his voice conspiratorially. 'But if you believe that, you'll believe anything.' The electrician cleared his throat a little. 'I got given any bad jobs Keane couldn't get anyone else to do. But Hobson... like I said, he had it even worse than me. And he was tasked with digging out a basement below Keane's warehouse – by hand. She told him it was top secret and got that big fucking bloke of hers to lean on Andy. By that stage he was so skint he'd have gone along with anything.'

The other men in the room said nothing; they simply waited for the man to continue.

'One day he was sick. He couldn't make it, so I went in his place. He knew that if he missed a day, he'd never get paid. And I was at a loose end, so I went along. Did him a favour. He gave me the keys and the instructions and that was that. There was nobody else there.'

'What did Keane say?' Rivera asked.

'She never knew,' Clements replied. 'She was away somewhere. And she never *did* know. And then, a few weeks later, Hobson disappeared. Australia was what people said, but I know where that rumour came from...' His voice trailed off.

'How big was it – this basement?' Lefty asked.

'I'd say about the size of a four-car garage,' the man replied. 'Maybe more.'

Clarke gave a low whistle. 'Why did you never tell me this?'

'Why do you think?' Clements shot back. 'What you don't know can't hurt you. At least, it can't hurt you as much as what you *do* know. Anyway, anyone with a secret basement that big has big secrets to hide. And – given everything else we know about her – I'd say that'd be a good place to start looking. That bitch has been living high on the hog for too long now – I'll do anything I can to help put a nail in her coffin.' He sighed. 'But go easy boys – I mean it. And know this: if you go up against Keane, you're going to war. No ifs. No buts. And don't go expecting an armistice. It'll go on until there's only one man or woman standing.' Clements sighed again, more heavily. 'You boys are trained. You're tough. But you're no spring chickens. If you start this, then you're going to need to put her and the big man in the morgue. Otherwise, it'll be like you're dealing with the Hydra's fucking heads.'

Chapter 39.

Bullseye was laughing. It wasn't his usual cruel sneer. Instead, it was a guffaw imbued with childish glee. Keane – sat beside him – was filing her nails. Rather than paying any attention to what the big man was watching, she was reading the local newspaper that was balanced on her knee.

The pair were sitting in the back room of The George and Dragon where Danny had been instructed to set up a makeshift cinema. A screen had been rolled down, and on the wall, the source of Bullseye's amusement was projected. Before the films went live, she and her enforcer vetted them. In truth, the viewing was all done by him. She reasoned her target audience was equal parts unsophisticated and stupid; he therefore made a perfect test dummy.

Keane was feeling good. For a brief moment, it seemed as though the drifter might spoil her plans. The Yardbird Clover disaster had left her reeling. But a number of enormous bribes had been levied; the stranger had left town, and things had settled back down. She would make her money back soon enough – she always did. And, in the meantime, her new project was on track.

* * *

Keane liked humiliation. She always had. Her latest venture saw humiliation paired with desperation. And it linked straight to the kind of entertainment Bullseye found hilarious. She, herself, had no interest in what was filmed. But she knew a sure thing when she encountered one. Realising there was money to be made was reason enough to tolerate sitting through screenings.

It was a simple plan: Bullseye handpicked a number of customers in thrall to the trade plied by Keane's ice cream vans. They were all addicts. Hooked so badly, they'd do anything for a fix. So he made them box. It was them he was watching on screen – a pair of rough-sleeping junkies boxing like a pair of crazed pugilistic crack whores. It was bloody and brutal; unrefined and messy. In other words, it was exactly the kind of entertainment that people with strange fetishes and powerful broadband connections sought out.

The first such fight had resulted in a fatality. Of course, there were no medics on hand – the contests were held on the parking lot of a disused amusement park. A few crude floodlights had been rigged up; they cast ghostly shadows upon the rusting remnants of dodgems and ghost trains. A business acquaintance had suggested to Bullseye that he should film the events – the junkies attacked each other with such venom that it made for a spectacle which would surpass anything on regular television. The big man had gone to his boss with the idea.

So, Keane broadcast the next fight on pay-per-view. Profits spiralled with the fights that followed. She would – she reasoned – be raking in almost as much as she did through narcotics during the ninety minutes or so that the fighting was on air.

Bullseye settled back into his seat and laughed uproariously as one of the addicts repeatedly slammed a section of broken guard rail into the bloodied face of his unresponsive opponent. His eyes were crazed – it was doubtful that he even saw half of what was happening to him. It didn't matter, though. The damage was done.

Keane wasn't present at the fights. Her perception of herself as a refined businesswoman didn't fit. She delegated their organisation to her appointed overseers. The evening was run like a gladiators' tournament – combatants fought until there was only one participant remaining.

Bullseye laughed again, and sipped at his pint, content.

Leah Keane was back on track. She took a cut of all the money gambled on the fights – she always did.

Life was good.

Chapter 40.

Rivera and Lefty sat outside *The Filling Stop* - a sandwich shop close to the railway station. It was early evening. They watched as passengers from the London train spilled out of the station. The suit-wearing professionals stood out. South Quay was generally a ragged town – chic wasn't a word that readily applied; locals dressed cheaply, and plus-size tourists tended towards Day-Glo colours and an absence of taste. The two men silently regarded the anomalous group that passed them by. Housing in the town was cheap. Commuters would sleep and weekend there, but their lives and ambitions were elsewhere. It was the same brain drain that was being played out in provincial towns all over the country – there was nothing to hold them. If housing in big cities wasn't so expensive, they'd be nowhere near the place. As it was, though, they departed incredibly early each morning and – if they were lucky – made it home before dark. The train journeys were long; the carriages cramped. They were surrounded by fellow commuters, all of whom watched the outside world spool by as if on an unravelling film reel. Hermetically sealed, it sometimes felt as though they were simply observers of a life they weren't really living.

'So...' Rivera exhaled the last smoke from his hand-rolled cigarette before stubbing it out in the table's ashtray. 'What are you thinking?'

'Well,' Lefty began, as he watched the last of the commuters shuffle away. 'I've been looking at the postmortem.'

'Thoughts so far?' the ex-soldier pressed.

'No shell casings and no bullets.'

Rivera nodded.

The sandwich shop was almost deserted. The few commuters who'd stopped in had departed with paper cups and plastic packets bearing takeaways, their skin the pasty grey hue suggestive of a computer monitor tanning regimen.

'And yet the cause of death has been recorded as shots from a pistol,' the American said.

Rivera nodded. 'What are you thinking?'

'Well...' Lefty frowned. His eyes widened, and he struggled to hold back tears for a moment as he inhaled sharply. 'I have to disassociate here.' He grimaced, tapping distractedly on the table. 'Two shots and no exit wounds. That doesn't add up. I'm not saying your local cops are useless, but there's been no blood pattern analysis, so we can't make much of a judgement based on that. However...' his voice cracked for a moment. 'The tissue damage isn't consistent with a round from any handgun I've seen before.'

'So?'

'So, I'm thinking a captive bolt pistol. One of those fire extinguisher-like contraptions where the bolt retracts after it fires – the kind of thing they use in slaughterhouses.'

'That's a bit Coen brothers, isn't it?' Rivera narrowed his eyes.

'Maybe,' Lefty shrugged. 'But there were no bullets in the corpse. And it's not like the killer dug them out – that much was clear from the outset.'

Silence.

'Sounds like a proper hit then,' the ex-soldier continued.

'Agreed.'

Rivera sighed. 'I'm sorry.'

'You need to stop fucking apologising!' Lefty grumbled. 'You keep doing that and I'll get compassion fatigue – you'll start to sound insincere.' He sighed. 'The only way I can do this is by treating it like a case and keeping emotions out of it.' He paused. 'So stop fucking saying you're sorry.'

'It's a very British thing to do,' the ex-soldier protested. 'We talk about the weather and we apologise.'

The American shook his head, slowly. 'Yeah. And then you drink tea and crappy warm beer and carry on in quiet desperation, right?'

Silence.

'When she came back from The Diplomat, what did she say?' Esposito asked.

'That she'd got the plane. And also that she'd seen two people there. A man and a woman.'

'Security cameras?'

'The place was derelict,' Rivera replied. 'And the cameras were ancient - they probably weren't even working.'

'But they could have been switched back on?' Lefty pressed. 'And if she *was* on camera and they thought she'd seen the two of them, then it would potentially give them a motive for the hit. Right?'

Rivera nodded slowly.

'So... are we assuming the woman was Keane?'

'Possibly,' Rivera nodded. 'Probably. I've never seen her, but Clarke seemed to think Bourse is in her pocket. If that's the case, then her walking into The Diplomat wouldn't have been too surprising.'

The American nodded. 'What's the verdict on the cause of the fire?'

'We should know any day now,' Rivera replied. 'According to Malone at least – he said it was going to a panel of experts for review. That's the last I heard of it.'

Silence.

'What are the chances it was deliberate – the fire?' the American enquired.

'High – but I doubt the report will show that.'

'Yeah,' Lefty pursed his lips. 'Me neither.'

'You know there was a preservation order on the hotel, right?'

'Meaning what, exactly?'

'It means it's illegal to make any changes or modifications to the existing building.' Rivera paused. 'You're not allowed to tamper with the existing structure.'

Lefty frowned. 'So if someone wanted to knock it down and start over...'

'...they wouldn't be allowed.' Rivera finished his sentence.

'But if there's nothing on the site?'

'Then I guess there's no problem,' the ex-soldier replied.

'So... arson?'

The ex-soldier puffed out his cheeks and exhaled. 'Looks likely.'

Chapter 41.

'Rivera's back.' Bullseye's announcement was blunt. After satisfying himself that she wasn't going to throw something at him, he settled himself onto a bar stool next to his boss. It was shortly after nine o'clock in the morning, but the regulars at The George were already into their second or third pint of the day. The sweet, stale smell of last night's booze seamlessly shifted into being the sweet, stale smell of today's. A fug of cigarette smoke hung over a table at the rear, where three men were playing cards for a stack of banknotes.

'You what?' Keane narrowed her eyes. For a moment her tone was no longer that of an urban sophisticate – instead, it reverted to the tenement timbre of her childhood.

'Remember? The bloke who was sniffing around. Ex-military – he left town and...'

'...yeah – I know who he is,' Keane interrupted. 'What the fuck's he back here for? I thought he was yesterday's news.'

'Dunno.' The big man shrugged.

'Who told you?'

'Bourse – he said he'd seen him and some other bloke at the Sands.' He paused, catching Danny's eye and pointing at the lager pump. 'Maybe he wants his old job back or something?'

'Yeah?' Keane scoffed. 'Well, that's not going to bloody happen. Who was the other bloke?'

Bullseye shrugged again. 'Bourse said he'd never seen him before – said he was older.'

Keane puffed her cheeks out, sighing. 'Well, Rivera was hardly fresh-faced, was he? And if this bloke's older, then it's not like he's going to be back up, is it?'

Silence.

'You want me to take care of them?' the big man enquired.

'Maybe. But we need to go easy here. If we're not careful, people are going to start asking questions. The fuss about The Diplomat bodies hasn't fully blown over yet.'

'I thought Cobb was sorting it?'

'Yeah, he is. Superintendent-says-a-lot-but-does-fuck-all,' Keane nodded. 'He's a useless prick. I wouldn't put it past him to botch things up.' Danny delivered a fresh pint and a gin and tonic, setting them down in front of the pair. Keane gave an almost imperceptible nod of acknowledgement before the barman walked away. She tapped her nails against the glass distractedly.

The big man nodded. 'So?'

'So keep an eye on them. But keep things calm for now. Understand?'

'Yeah.'

'And if we hear that they're digging and things get too close to the bone, then we make them disappear. Clear?'

'Crystal,' Bullseye replied.

Chapter 42.

'Seen this?' Rivera enquired as Lefty climbed out of his rental car. He'd parked beside the ex-soldier's campsite pitch. He handed a copy of the local paper that he'd purchased on his early morning walk to the visitor. *The South Quay Herald Express* bore a picture of the burning Diplomat Hotel. Above it sat a bold-lettered headline:

HOTEL FIRE ACCIDENTAL.

The American scoffed. 'What's this – like a satirical paper?' He scanned the story and then turned onto the inside pages, where the editorial continued. 'There's no mention of any bodies.' He looked up at Rivera, his expression one of disbelief. 'What the hell's going on here?'

The ex-soldier shrugged. 'Smells like a cover-up. No?'

Lefty sighed, nodding. Then he looked behind Rivera and caught sight of Iris. 'Nice ride!' he exclaimed.

'Yeah – she's a little temperamental at times, but she's worth it.'

The American grinned. 'Takes me back – my brother's college buddy had one just like it. We did New York to Mean Old Frisco in five days in it once.' He folded the newspaper and tucked it beneath his arm. 'How are they treating you here anyway?' He cast his eye around the campsite. Rivera had opted to stay a couple of miles outside South Quay in Brushton, near the zoo. The site was busy – it was high season. But the ex-soldier thought it would allow him to stay under Keane's radar. Especially if Keane's organisation sent people out to snoop. Enforcers like hers would have well-worn patches; territories they'd patrol. And if they ventured outside them, they'd do so in numbers – easy to spot.

'It's alright,' Rivera shrugged. 'Little noisy with all the kids running around – my cat's never been so reclusive. She hasn't ventured out of the T2 during the daytime yet.' He looked at the shiny Ford hatchback the other man had arrived in. 'How are the new wheels treating you?'

Lefty nodded. 'Nice enough. I paid cash – hopefully the auto's unremarkable enough to fly under the radar.' He paused. 'You set?'

'Yeah.'

'Good. Let's roll. I have a few things I want to check out.'

* * *

'Is this the place?' Rivera asked. He narrowed his eyes slightly as he looked around.

'Yeah,' Lefty nodded, checking a dropped pin on his phone map. The rental car was parked high up on the coast road. 'Clarke said he had something for us. I guess he didn't want to see us at the Sands – worried about Bourse sniffing around, maybe?'

'You still don't trust Clarke?' Rivera asked.

'Do you?' the American shot back.

The ex-soldier shrugged. 'He always struck me as an alright guy.' He paused. 'Anyway – he called *you*, didn't he?'

'He did,' Lefty nodded. 'But we don't know if that was of his own volition or on someone else's orders.' He paused. 'I'm not saying he's with them. I'm just reserving my judgement. We can't prove he's beyond suspicion at the moment, can we?'

'True,' Rivera nodded.

Silence.

'That mark on your arm,' Rivera began.

'Albania. Ninety-seven,' Lefty answered quickly. 'It always galls me – I was in Bosnia; Iraq; Yemen. Hell, I even went to Sierra Leone – they were all hostile places, and I never got so much as a scratch. But Albania… it was a rescue mission. We were just offshore from Kavajë – evacuating US personnel from Tirana.'

'Shell blast?'

'Uh-huh. I was lucky, I guess. I only feel it in the cold.' Lefty paused. 'And you?'

'What about me?'

'Well... in the US, they don't tend to parachute people straight into investigative roles. Not until they've seen active service or they're whiz kids with computers.' He grinned. 'You don't wear thick glasses and you haven't got a side-parting.'

'Maybe I'm just bucking the stereotype?' Rivera shrugged.

'The hell you are!' the American smiled. 'You've served then? Combat?'

'Yeah – some.' The ex-soldier's voice trailed off. 'I'm not getting into comparing scars, though – things like that just turn into fishermen's tales.'

The American laughed. 'Roger that. The reason I ask is – I need to know if you still remember how to shoot?'

Rivera nodded. 'Think it'll come to that?'

Lefty pursed his lips. 'If I find out Keane's responsible for my daughter's death, then she dies.' He gritted his teeth. 'I might have been born in the Sixties, but all that peace and love passed me by – I was too young. Where I'm from, it's an eye-for-an-eye.' He looked hard at the other man. 'You get me?'

'Yeah. We're speaking the same language. People who are high enough up the pyramid think justice is a monetary thing – a penalty you have to pay if you're caught with your fingers in the cash register. I've always believed justice is about blood.' He sighed. 'I'm not a violent man, Lefty... but I believe in right and wrong.'

'You and me both,' the American nodded. 'So let's try to do some good here, shall we?'

Chapter 43.

Lefty's phone pinged.

The two men had been waiting in the rental car for almost half an hour. After talking a little more about military service, they'd both withdrawn into themselves. The coastal road commanded a huge vista, and the men gazed out across the bay, retreating into their thoughts. Clouds scudded across the sky and sunlight broke through periodically, glittering on the water. Far out on the horizon, a pair of huge cruise ships sat, immobile. The noise of the incoming text brought them both back to the present.

'Well I'll be damned!' Lefty exclaimed.

'Progress?' Rivera enquired.

'Yeah – a little.' The American lowered his phone. 'I tried submitting a public information request to find out who really owns The Diplomat. It was much easier than such things are in the States – filling in the form at least. The results... less so.'

Rivera nodded. 'Let me guess – blind alley?'

'What makes you say that?'

'A few niggling thoughts. But, before I left the job, I ran the mail over to the office at the Golden Sands one morning. A hell of a lot of different companies were listed, and Aaron Bourse seemed to be involved with all of them.' He paused. 'When I was investigating properly, I used to do a lot of financial work – it's an old trick; burying bad money beneath layer on layer of shell organisations. I guessed that's what he was doing, but I couldn't prove anything.'

'Yeah – that's pretty much the size of it,' Lefty nodded. 'I had no luck with public information, so I called in a favour – an old friend has access to the kind of databases they don't tend to grant civilians access to.'

'And?'

'And there's a hell of a web been spun to throw people off.' Lefty paused. 'South Bay. London. Zurich. Mexico City. The Philippines. The list goes on and on. Each time the company seems to be just an empty shell owned by something else. Or some*one* else.' He laughed in appreciation. 'Someone's worked damn hard to make all this seem legitimate! But my buddy has been able to put taps on some of the wire transfers.'

'So he's followed the money?' the ex-soldier nodded. 'Smart move.'

'Yeah. He knows what he's doing – I trained him!' The American laughed. 'Anyway, that's ancient history. But he's found the owner. They managed to hide most things, but they made a couple of errors. You need the kind of accountant that only oligarchs keep on retainers to be completely untraceable. The owner's not quite in that league.'

Rivera looked at the other man expectantly. 'Well, don't leave me hanging, Lefty – who?'

'Laramie Holdings. They don't have a proper address – it's just a PO Box registered to one of those huge office blocks in central London – that's what he told me. And that's where the trail goes dead. But...'

'...that's the name Clements mentioned,' Rivera interrupted.

'Exactly!' Lefty nodded. 'And if Laramie Holdings owns The Diplomat Hotel, then it proves Keane is pulling the strings. I mean, it proves it to *us*. I'm sure it'd be more difficult to make a link that would stand up in court, but it's a start, right?'

Rivera nodded. 'What do you reckon a site like that is worth?'

The American shrugged. 'Many millions, I should think. It's huge. You build something new and shiny on that patch of ground, and it could galvanise the whole town.'

'Yeah.' The ex-soldier paused. 'So I think we've got our motive.'

Chapter 44.

South Quay didn't have a business district as such. The closest it came was a series of steel and glass constructions on the edge of town with enormous parking lots attached. A cluster of fashionable coffee outlets had sprung up to keep the employees in caffeine; a couple of chain eateries dished up bland, inauthentic Mexican and Italian. There was also a van which visited regularly selling Texas barbecue fare. The top two floors of one of the structures were rented by a large telemarketing company; hordes of twenty-somethings trooped in each morning for ten hour working days. They were paid on commission only, and were expected to make up to 150 calls per shift, hard selling whichever products their overlords had sourced. The buildings were – so *The Herald Express* had suggested – like modern-day workhouses.

Keane didn't care about such newspaper stories. She'd taken a six-month lease on half a floor in the name of Evergreen Construction. The company had only recently been set up – its sole focus was selling the redevelopment of The Diplomat site. She'd had the office space decked out as a going concern – it included a glass-fronted room set aside for her as an office. Keane wasn't intending to spend any time there, but wasn't beyond taking a no-show salary all the same. She'd farmed out the hiring of employees to one of her underlings and kept them on a retainer. Today was the moment she would start putting her latest plan into action.

The boss had dressed – as usual - in expensive business wear and heels. It was a look that spoke of money; of promise. As she strolled across the carpeted room, she breathed in the air of newness: new desks; new computers; new phones; new fixtures and fittings throughout. Large potted plants were positioned tastefully, and next to the water cooler stood an expensive coffee machine. Keane didn't want her workers traipsing over the parking lot for mochas and lattes

– she wanted them to be focused and industrious. She'd employed a couple of acquaintances as managing directors and had left them to organise things. As a result, when she entered the room, she nodded in appreciation. The company's logo was emblazoned on the wall. There were posters, business cards, and branded stationery. The whole set-up looked entirely convincing.

A dozen newly hired employees sat before her. They were all university graduates – she'd insisted on that. She'd instructed her underlings to hire them based on the quality of their diction. All of them were wearing suits – not tailored affairs like hers, but they were suitably dressy, nevertheless. Six young men and six young women – all of them looking like they'd strolled off the set of *The Apprentice*.

Keane drew to a halt in front of the assembled group. She held an iPad in the crook of her elbow. 'Good morning.' She smiled courteously at those assembled. Her tone then changed to something more acerbic; she spoke a little impatiently. 'Cookie,' she called out. 'Show them the plans, will you?'

At this, the overhead lights were switched off, and an image was projected onto the wall.

'This,' Keane began, indicating a section on the screen with a laser pointer, 'is Gatsby Mansions.' She paused for a moment, letting her words sink in. 'It's a complex of two hundred and fifty apartments. They're going to rejuvenate South Quay and put it back on the map. And you're going to sell them,' she explained. 'One-bedroom apartments cost two hundred grand. Two beds are three hundred. Three beds are four hundred.' She cast her eye over her audience. 'Get the picture?'

Twelve heads nodded in confirmation.

'There will be a health spa; gym; swimming pools; secure parking; gardens; a nature walk; sea views – all the properties will have balconies, and there'll be a twenty-four-hour concierge. On each of your desks, you'll find a brochure and a script. Your job is simple.' She paused. 'This is a great opportunity. So sell the crap out of it.'

Twelve pairs of eyes stared back at the glamorous woman. She had a presence that captivated them. Each of the new recruits suddenly felt a strong desire to gain her trust; to win her praise.

'You get five hundred a week as basic pay,' she went on. 'Bonus equivalent to one per cent of the ticket price for every deal closed where you sell a place outright. Two per cent for any deposit on a ten-year payment plan.' She smiled. 'Interest's where we really clean up, see?'

A hand rose. 'Isn't this a little steep, ma'am?' a young man asked. He nodded towards the direct debit schedules that were outlined. 'Won't we be crippling them with payments in arrears here?'

Keane sighed. She looked around the room. As she did, an uncomfortable silence descended. She didn't so much glare at the speaker as look disappointed. Exasperated. Pitying.

'Do you hate money or something?' The boss frowned. She tilted her head slightly, frowning; uncomprehending. The young man squirmed in his seat.

'No, ma'am.'

'Are you a communist?'

The young man shook his head.

'Good. Because if you are, then you know where the door is. We like money around here. I'm offering you the chance to make a *lot* of it. Quickly. That's what we're about here.' She paused and looked into the eyes of each new employee. When she spoke again, it was with a quiet, calm voice. 'Some of you *may* know who I am. Some of you may not. It doesn't matter, but you should know that I only demand one thing: loyalty. I want you to prostitute yourselves for the highest price.' She shrugged. 'That's all – stick with me, and I'll make you rich.'

Silence.

'Good.' The boss smiled broadly, her bleached white teeth gleaming. 'Signs go up advertising the new apartments this afternoon. They'll be just like this one.' Keane indicated the wall behind her. 'These pictures will be posted around the site, and we've got billboards going up on the South Quay Expressway.' She grinned. 'Remember folks, this is free market economics. Capitalism is beautiful. It means we can sell people things they don't need for money they don't have, and have them believe we're doing them a favour.' She chuckled. 'There's one born every minute. They're out there, so hit the phones and bloody find them.'

The new employees nodded, a little uncertain.

Keane sensed their ill ease. 'Cookie here will talk you through the details,' she continued. 'And Emerson will answer any of your questions.' She paused again; tension flickered through the seated group. 'If you sell more than twenty properties by the end of the week, you'll get a thousand-pound bonus. Each. Cash.' The boss smiled a little, sensing excitement percolating. 'And there's a special one-off bonus here.' She reached into the pocket of her suit jacket and withdrew a wad of cash. 'There's two grand here,' she announced, absent-mindedly flicking through the banknotes like a croupier might fan a deck of cards. 'I'm going to leave it with Cookie. First person to make a sale... it's yours.'

Sensing the sudden enthusiasm, she smiled. 'Well – what are you waiting for then?'

Any other words were drowned out by the new employees racing over to their workstations.

Chapter 45.

Lefty started a little as Clarke tapped on the glass of the driver's side window. 'Fancy a drive?' the new arrival asked once the American had lowered the window. He grinned, the gap in his teeth making him resemble a Dickensian urchin. 'There's something you need to see.'

Lefty hesitated for a moment. He narrowed his eyes slightly as he looked at Rivera. Then he shrugged. 'Jump in.'

* * *

The rental car pulled to a stop beside the perimeter fence of what had once been The Diplomat Hotel. Yesterday, the site had been nothing more than rubble and scorched ground. The summer weather meant nature had been frantically clawing back what was hers, reclaiming the land with creepers and grasses. But, today, diggers and bulldozers were suddenly present.

'What the hell?' Lefty began.

'Yeah – told you I had news,' Clarke replied from the back seat. 'I guessed you'd probably want to see it for yourselves.' He sighed and looked out of the window. 'Some fucker's going to make a bloody killing here.' He caught himself and lowered his voice as he addressed Lefty. 'No offence.'

'So, how does this work then?' the American pressed, ignoring the man's previous words.

'You've seen the local paper, right?' the foreman enquired.

'We have,' Rivera answered.

'So... once the fire was deemed to be accidental, the preservation order became officially null and void. That's what I heard, anyway. It means that whoever owns the site gets to do what they want with it. And what you're seeing before you is the result.'

Lefty looked at Clarke through the rear-view mirror. 'Do you know who owns the site?'

'No.' Clarke shook his head. 'But I don't think that matters. I took a walk up here this morning. There are signs tacked up to the fencing for Evergreen Construction. If you find out who's behind that, then you find the root of the problem. Whoever it is can't hide everything, can they? Surely? Someone's got to pay wages for starters.'

'Agreed,' Lefty nodded. 'But surely things don't move this fast?' He frowned. 'The ruling on the cause of the fire was only made public this morning. What's the time frame on something like this usually?'

'Not this bloody quick,' Clarke replied.

'No. You'd have to put in for planning permission. The council would have to approve it. It can be a lengthy process...' Rivera explained.

'...but it's not this time, is it?' Clarke butted in. 'That's why I wanted to bring you up here. Whoever's behind this has got some serious clout. The council rubber-stamping this so quickly can only be because of two things.'

'What are they?' Lefty asked.

'Either they're very efficient,' Clarke replied. 'Or someone's crossing their palms with a whole load of silver.'

'Let me guess,' the American laughed drily. 'They're not usually models of efficiency?'

'No – it took us three fucking months to get permission to refurbish the chalets at the holiday park. And they were already there. *And* Aaron Bourse is pally with the Chamber of Commerce. If he can't move things...' the foreman's voice trailed off.

Silence.

'So, it took him that long for something that minor, but this thing – this *major* thing – has been done and dusted in three hours?' Rivera sighed. He turned to look at Lefty. 'I smell a rat.'

'Yeah,' the American nodded. 'I hear you. A pretty fucking big rat, too.' He looked back at Clarke in the rear-view mirror. 'Do you know anything about this – er – Evergreen Construction?'

'Not really.' He shook his head. 'Actually, no. There used to be a company called Evergreen Building, but that was a good few years back.'

Rivera turned to Lefty. 'It could be the same old shell company trick.'

'Yeah. And this one...' he turned to Clarke. 'Is it local?'

'Yeah,' the foreman nodded.

'How'd you find that out?' Rivera enquired, frowning.

'It's on all the signs,' Clarke shrugged, frowning. 'Phone number. Website. Postal address. Everything...'

Lefty chuckled. 'What say we take a closer look at one of these signs?'

The ex-soldier nodded.

'Thank you, Mr Clarke,' the American continued. 'I appreciate the information.' He looked hard at the other man. 'We might well be in touch again soon. That alright?'

'Yeah – I'm with you guys all the way,' the foreman nodded. 'Anything to help nail Little Miss Keane. Count me in.'

'She's little then?' Rivera enquired.

Clarke grinned. 'Yeah – I mean, she's not a midget, but I'd put her at no more than five foot four.' He paused. 'Hitler. Mussolini – most dictators are small, aren't they?'

The ex-soldier smiled.

'You alright to walk back from here?' Lefty enquired. 'I want to have a poke around the site – I don't wish to delay you.'

Clarke nodded. 'It's downhill – I'll be fine.'

Rivera turned to Lefty as the foreman walked off towards the Golden Sands. The two men crossed the road. 'You still think he's crooked?'

A hint of a smile crossed the American's face. 'I guess you could say I'm coming round to the guy somewhat. And he certainly seems to bear a grudge against Keane, so I reckon he'll be with us more than he'll be against us.' He paused. 'Let's hope it stays that way.'

Chapter 46.

Lefty parked the car in a public parking lot between the town library and a supermarket. As the pair exited an alley on foot, they passed an overflowing dustbin, and stepped over a bedraggled box hedge whose leaves and branches were tightly wound with sweet wrappers and crisp packets. An overweight street sweeper in fluorescent orange eyed them disdainfully; a long-handled grabber leaned against his leg as he smoked a cigarette.

'Remind me why we're here again,' the American said. 'The library – I mean.'

'Well, if we're lucky, they might have some paper information on Laramie Holdings,' Rivera replied. 'The internet hasn't told us much, but even secretive companies have to file information physically if they want developments like the one on the hill to happen.' He paused. 'It's one of those archaic rules – there still need to be physical signatures. Especially with something of that size.'

Lefty nodded. 'Won't there be a lag? I mean – in getting stuff printed? I thought these guys were disorganised, right?'

'Maybe,' Rivera shrugged. 'But sometimes places like this can be mines of information. If you're lucky, they can sometimes help you join up the dots.'

The American nodded. 'Most of our public libraries have been under-funded so much that they're barely open on weekdays.' Lefty stopped, frowned, and looked ahead. 'Is that what I think it is?'

'What?'

'A security guard.'

Rivera nodded.

'What? Are books such a precious commodity these days that they need to be guarded or something? Have they got first editions here?'

The ex-soldier chuckled. 'No – it's because half the town's in hock to Keane's dope. That's why there's so many homeless people here. The security guard's posted there to keep the peace – to stop junkies shooting up in the bathrooms or sleeping in the chairs. That kind of thing. Glamorous...'

'You're kidding!'

Rivera shook his head. 'No - and some evenings, he has the same gig at the town cinema.' As they approached, the security guard nodded at the two men. Then he peered at Rivera, recognition dawning.

'I remember you,' he said. 'The night of the fire, right?' He paused. 'So this is my day job.' He grinned. 'Pretty glamorous, hey?' He paused. 'Shame about The Diplomat – someone could have restored that to its former glory. It's a big piece of town history been lost there.'

'Yeah,' Rivera nodded. 'You're right about that.'

The two men entered the library.

* * *

Twenty minutes later, the two men left the mezzanine level where the archives and records were located. They'd drawn a blank. The clerk helped them as much as she could, but recommended trying the Chamber of Commerce in the town hall. It would – she assured them – have records which were more up to date than those which could be accessed in the reading room.

The walk to the town hall was short. Along the way, Rivera noticed the usual groups of huddled, sunken-eyed addicts waiting for their fix. He watched as a gaggle of them made a beeline for an ice cream van as it pulled over, desperation writ large upon their faces.

Lefty regarded the scene with interest. 'It's ingenious, isn't it?' he began. 'You've got to hand it to them. I mean – who'd suspect a fucking ice cream van, right?'

'I know,' the ex-soldier nodded. 'They've got things sewn up.'

'Mind you, look at the state of them...' The American's voice trailed off as he looked at the huddled, ragged mass waiting at the window of the van. 'It's hardly a victimless crime, is it?'

* * *

The next place the pair entered was an anteroom off the town hall. Its walls were made of dark-panels of wood and the spotlights set into them were bright; harsh. Lefty rang the bell on the counter.

'Welcome to the Public Records Office. I'm new here,' a young woman announced as she stepped through from a back room. She had an innocent, naïve positivity about her. Her hair was tied back, and she wore dark-framed glasses. The woman stood, a little nervously, behind the dark wooden counter. The walls of the waiting area had posters for various local events that were tacked above blue plastic chairs.

'OK...' Rivera began.

'Sorry.' She laughed with embarrassment. 'What I mean is that I've only been here a week. Today's the first day I've been left alone, so you might have to bear with me. I'm flying solo!' The woman blushed deeply.

The two men nodded.

'We're in no hurry,' Lefty smiled broadly and spoke in relaxed fashion. 'You take your time. This is the Public Records section, isn't it?'

'Yes – although it all comes under the Chamber of Commerce now. They've amalgamated some of the departments.' The woman eyed the pair a little nervously, hoping she was coming across as competent.

The American nodded.

'What was it you were looking for anyway?' the woman began.

'Information on a recently founded company,' Rivera replied. 'They're operating in South Quay. Might you be able to help?'

The woman frowned. 'I'm not sure...' she answered. 'I mean, I *might*. But I'm not sure of all the protocols, and...'

'...Captain Larry Esposito. Naval Criminal Investigative Service.' The American held up an identity card for the young woman to study. That the card was out of date was no matter – his demeanour was entirely convincing. The young lady glanced at the likeness and then nodded. 'What we're doing here is rather important,' Lefty continued before lowering his voice. 'Confirmation shouldn't take more than five minutes of your time. And what we're doing is rather hush-hush.' He paused, noting the effect his authoritative tone continued to have upon the young woman. 'If you don't – er – mention anything, then neither will we.'

'Alright then,' the woman nodded, satisfied. 'Come on through.' She indicated a large filing cabinet. 'Any companies operating in town are required to file paperwork fourteen days prior to that work commencing.' She pulled open a drawer. 'It's all here – I alphabetised it myself,' she added, a little proudly.

* * *

The drawer contained no information on Keane's operation. Laramie Holdings wasn't mentioned at all on any of the papers the woman withdrew.

'Anywhere else we might look?' Rivera asked, hopefully.

'Well...' the woman replied. 'That drawer is for the jobs that have received approval. This one here,' she indicated another cabinet, 'is for those which are pending.'

'Thanks,' Lefty said, moving towards the section that had been indicated.

Again, though, the search through the index cards drew a blank. The American drummed his fingers on the side of the filing cabinet in irritation.

'You've been very helpful, ma'am,' Lefty announced in a charming tone that belied his frustration. 'We won't keep you any longer.'

The young woman nodded eagerly. 'What was the company's name?' She frowned. 'You never know – someone might have mentioned it.'

'Laramie Holdings,' Rivera answered.

She frowned and chewed at the end of a pen. 'You know – I've seen that written somewhere. It rings a bell.' She frowned and then walked over to an in-tray and rifled through a sheaf of papers. 'Here!' she announced triumphantly, holding up a typed page. 'I knew I'd seen it.' She paused. 'I'm not sure why it was there, though.' She scrutinised the paperwork. 'It's been approved, so it should be...'

'...clerical error,' Rivera interrupted, smiling. 'It happens all the time. Your boss probably just wanted to hold it back to check some detail or other.'

Lefty nodded in agreement, catching the ex-soldier's eye. 'You should leave it where you found it – just in case.' He paused. 'Mind if we have a quick look, though? We just need some information about one of the directors. Then we'll leave you to it.' He sighed. 'Otherwise, there'll be all sorts of delays.' He let his words sink in.

'Of course,' the woman nodded brightly. 'I'm just making a cup of tea. Would you like one?'

'We're fine,' Rivera nodded pleasantly.

'Right you are,' the woman replied. 'I must say, this is quite exciting. It's usually very quiet here – this is the most drama I've seen since I've started.'

'You're doing a great job...' Lefty spoke sincerely.

'...Isla,' she beamed.

'A great job, Isla, definitely,' Rivera agreed, nodding. 'But we don't want to get in your way. We'll just take a look and then leave you to it. We only need a name – that's all.'

As Isla walked through a door at the rear of the office, Lefty read out the names of the directors. 'Chester Morganfield; McKinley Burnett; Bessie Alexander; Lucille Rainey.' He raised his eyebrows.

'They don't sound like spring chickens,' Rivera replied.

'You've got that right,' Lefty nodded. 'And none of them are Leah Keane.'

'Address?' the ex-soldier asked.

'Yeah – right here.' The American held up a printed page. He photographed it with his phone.

'Good,' Rivera replied. He chewed his lip for a moment. 'Let's just – er – remind this young lady of how it's probably best to keep schtum about us being here before we go, shall we?'

'Roger that,' Lefty replied. 'Don't worry – I know just how to phrase it.'

Chapter 47.

'You sure this is the place?' Rivera frowned. 'I know we said they sounded like old people's names, but this is ridiculous.' The rental car was parked on a narrow lane set back from the coastal road. Twenty minutes had passed since the pair departed the Public Records Office.

'Yes,' Lefty insisted, checking the sat nav on his phone. 'It says it's right here. We might be barking up the wrong tree, but we still need to check it out.'

Cliff View Retirement Village advertised itself as a comfortable location for seniors; it boasted great views and offered a relaxed pace of life. It was a large red brick house that, once upon a time, would have been the residence of a single family. Since then, though, it had been extended, and a huge glass-fronted balcony had been built around the part of the first floor that faced the shoreline. A few residents peered out – they were sitting in wheelchairs and had blankets upon their laps. A few white-coated orderlies could be seen attending to them.

The ex-soldier smiled faintly. 'The guys up there can't be members of the board – surely?'

Lefty shrugged. 'It seems unlikely, but we might as well ask.' He looked at the other man. 'Shall we?'

'Yeah – what's the cover story?'

'You still have that list of names?'

'Yeah.'

'Pick one.'

The ex-soldier scanned the list. 'Chester Morganfield.'

'Right,' Lefty nodded. 'Let me do the talking. We'll be Chester's nephews over from America. In a provincial place like this, they'll go for it – I reckon.'

'You think that'll work?'

'We won't know until we try. But I'm gambling on him not getting too many visitors,' the other man shrugged.

* * *

'Give it to me straight, Sheila,' Lefty demanded, looking hard at the woman. The two visitors stood in the vestibule of the Cliff View Retirement Village, opposite the woman who was in charge. Rivera noticed the drawl of the American's accent had become more pronounced in talking to her. 'How is he? I need to know.' He paused. '*We* need to know. We've just driven straight here from Heathrow.'

'Well,' Sheila replied, uncomfortably. 'It pains me to say it, but he's not exactly *compos mentis* these days. I mean – he has his moments, but he's not what he was.' She grimaced a little. 'I'm sorry to say, but I'm not sure he'll really recognise you.'

'Hmmmm,' Lefty nodded. 'He taught me how to fish, you know?'

'Oh! How lovely!' the woman exclaimed, affecting a light, breezy tone. 'Shall we go and see him then?' She began leading the two men down the corridor.

'He taught my brother Chuck here how to ride a bike.' He turned and looked at Rivera. 'That right Chuck?'

Rivera nodded, smiling sadly. He ran a finger beneath his eye as if wiping away a tear.

The warden narrowed her eyes, slowing her step as the trio made their way along the orange-striped carpet of the corridor. Polystyrene ceiling tiles were punctuated occasionally by lights and sprinkler outlets. 'This isn't about power of attorney, is it?'

'No ma'am,' Lefty replied. He frowned. 'Why do you say that?'

'Oh, it's nothing important, I'm sure,' the woman shrugged. 'Only, a couple of weeks ago, his grandson was in here with his lawyer, and he was setting things up so he could manage his affairs. I thought you'd have been informed – you know, as relatives.'

'Ah – yes,' Lefty nodded. 'My Uncle Dwight told me something about that.' He shook his head. 'Must be the jetlag kicking in! I remember now. Heart-breaking, but it seemed like the only thing to do, really. Especially now.'

'Quite so,' the warden nodded as they turned a corner into the residents' lounge. 'Anyway, I think it's so nice of you boys to visit Chester on his birthday – really I do!'

'His birthday?' The American frowned.

'Yes – of course,' the warden nodded. 'Isn't that why you're here?'

'Yes ma'am it is,' Rivera broke in, affecting an accent more befitting of John Wayne than middle America. 'That's why we're here, y'all.' As he spoke, Lefty regarded him with incredulity.

'Charming!' Sheila beamed. 'You sound like you've just stepped off a movie set.'

* * *

Chester Morganfield was seated in an armchair. His dull, lifeless eyes stared blankly at his two visitors. His dentures sat in a glass of water beside him and the puckered skin around his mouth gave him a wizened appearance like a past-its-sell-by-date crab-apple. On his head, care staff had placed a foil party hat. He wore a pale blue t-shirt with a cartoon birthday cake in rainbow colours. Emblazoned across the front, his name was written in block letters. The lounge was filled with high-backed chairs and low coffee tables. The TV played at an ear-splitting volume.

In the armchair beside Chester, a similarly attired man sat. His t-shirt read *McKINLEY*. Beside him were two old women suspended somewhere between sleep and wakefulness. Their t-shirts bore the names *BESSIE* and *LUCILLE*. All of them looked as irritable and bemused as Mr Morganfield.

'Well, it looks like we've found our members of the board,' Rivera announced once the warden was out of earshot. 'Lively bunch, aren't they?'

'Yeah,' Lefty nodded. 'I'm beginning to think smoking Keane out might be more challenging than I'd thought it would be – she's certainly putting up a few roadblocks. This is proper subterfuge. It's like a campaign of misinformation – clever stuff.'

'It is that,' Rivera nodded. 'Blind alleys and wrong turns all the way.'

'Any ideas?'

'A few. Maybe. But I definitely wasn't expecting this.'

Chapter 48.

Keane frowned at the screen of her phone. She then lowered it, placing it face down on the bar of The George and Dragon. She sighed and then looked at Bullseye, her face oddly calm: the eye of the storm.

'Problem?' the big man asked.

'Let's call it an irritation,' Keane replied. She scratched a little at the tattooed flesh of her wrist. The butterfly there had been inked on the day she'd dispatched her parents.

'You need something doing?'

The boss ignored the question. She reached into her pocket, drew out a cigarette, and lit it. She exhaled, and then idly dragged her finger through a wisp of smoke.

'You back on the tabs then?' Bullseye enquired.

Silence.

'That was Sheila Hendry,' Keane announced, exhaling smoke as she talked. 'You remember her?'

'Yeah – Bucket-crutch Hendry.' The big man smiled a little uncomfortably. 'That's what the lads used to call her. Where's she now?'

The boss sighed. 'You know... I'm not what they'd call a feminist warrior.' She paused. 'In fact, if I can make money out of someone, then I don't give a shit if they're man or woman.'

'What about trannies?' Bullseye enquired earnestly. 'They're...'

'...but not being a feminist warrior,' Keane interrupted, 'doesn't mean that I don't have sympathy with the sisterhood.' She frowned. 'This whole objectification of women – you talking about Sheila like that...'

'What about it?' Bullseye shrugged, bemused.

'You do know that women talk the same way about men, right?' the boss announced.

'Don't be daft!' Bullseye scoffed. 'They...'

'...just don't go shouting their mouths off like you and your mates,' Keane cut in. She raised her eyebrows and smiled at him. As she held his gaze, she blew a cloud of tobacco smoke into his face.

The big man frowned.

'So think about that – next time you're berating Sheila Hendry. Remember that one of your former conquests is probably laughing with her mates about the fact you're hung like a mosquito.' Keane chuckled. Bullseye opened his mouth to protest, but she raised a hand to silence him. 'Enough,' she ordered. 'I don't want to waste time talking about how you can't touch the sides of whichever desperately unfortunate girls you occasionally manage to persuade into bed.' She paused. 'Cliff View.'

'What?' The big man frowned.

'That's where Hendry is.'

'Yeah? So, what do you want with her?'

Keane ran her tongue around the back of her teeth distractedly, as if searching for an errant scrap of food. 'Remember the board of directors?' she asked, looking up at the big man as she flicked the ash from her cigarette.

Bullseye nodded. Then he frowned. 'What – is there a problem with them?' He paused. 'I thought Sheila was keeping an eye and...'

'...no – not them!' Keane shook her head in irritation. 'Those geriatrics won't cause anyone any fucking problems – not unless their bed pans need emptying.'

'What then?'

'Two men were sniffing around there today. Sheila said they were American.'

Bullseye nodded. 'Not Rivera then?'

Keane raised her eyebrows. 'You wouldn't make much of a fucking detective. Anyone ever tell you that?' She paused. 'You ever think people might put on accents?'

'Hmmm.' The big man nodded. 'Smart! Just shows, doesn't it?'

The boss frowned. 'What's not so smart is that I told you to keep an eye on Rivera. Work out where he's going – things like that.'

'Yeah,' Bullseye shrugged. 'He gave me the slip. He's a wily bastard that one – a bit tricksy.'

Silence.

'Here's what I think,' Keane began stubbing out her cigarette. 'I think Rivera's trying to do things by the book. And I reckon he's going to be digging for bloody clues. This other guy – American or not – I think Rivera's brought him in as back-up.'

'What, like muscle?'

'No – he doesn't need that. Remember what he did to the Yardbird Clover boys? But he's underestimated us all the same. He thinks he can strut around South Quay like he fucking owns the place. Probably thinks we're scared of him or something.' Keane paused. 'My guess is that he's trying to build a case against us.'

'Why?' Bullseye frowned.

'Well – remember how he told the coppers about the tramp in the hotel fire? He's by the book. Clean as a whistle. He thinks he's a rebel and a renegade, but he doesn't do things like we do. He's weak...'

'Really?' The big man was unconvinced. 'He didn't look too weak when he smacked the Yardbird Clovers.'

'Of course he is,' Keane insisted. 'He's trying to build a case - any money. Gather evidence. Shit like that. He probably thinks he can put us in the frame.'

'So...?' Bullseye frowned.

'So, keep an eye on him and let him keep digging. He won't find anything. And, if he does, then he'll end up going all round the houses. He'll be tied up in fucking knots. He'll manage to do approximately fuck-all. And then – when his back's turned – we'll take care of him.'

'What – so we don't need him gone?'

'Yeah, but not yet.'

Bullseye nodded. Then he narrowed his eyes. 'How come you think he's weak, boss? I mean – there were five blokes he put down back there...'

'Yeah,' Keane nodded. 'I know. He fucked them up. But they're all still with us. All still alive. They might be limping, but they're not in the ground. Understand?' He paused. 'And that's how we know he's weak. Get me?'

The big man pursed his lips and nodded.

Chapter 49.

Lefty parked the rental car beside the perimeter fence of The Diplomat site. He and Rivera looked out; bulldozers had been hard at work piling up earth and debris into great mounds, levelling a central area. Viewed from the pair's vantage point, it was immediately clear just how sizeable the property was. A small group of men in high-visibility jackets stood around a digger. The low din of their voices travelled a little on the breeze.

The new arrivals exited the car and walked over to where a huge hoarding had been tacked to the fence.

COMING SOON: GATSBY MANSIONS
A DEVELOPMENT OF 1, 2, AND 3 BED APARTMENTS.
LUXURY LIVING AT AFFORDABLE PRICES.

Computer-generated images were etched onto the sign, bringing architects' designs to life. The appearance was slick. Professional. The pictures showed bright interiors and well-tended, tree-lined walkways.

'Impressive!' Rivera remarked. 'This clearly wasn't just dreamed up overnight, was it?'

'No,' Lefty agreed. He pointed at the small print beneath the image which read *EVERGREEN CONSTRUCTION*. 'She moves quickly, doesn't she - Keane? Laramie Holdings begat Evergreen Construction. And tomorrow... who knows?'

'Yeah,' Rivera nodded. 'Another day; another company. I'm surprised she can keep up with herself.'

'Fucker.' Lefty thrust his hands into his pockets. As he stared out across the freshly flattened expanse, his eyes blazed. 'This'll be her undoing, though. She'll have used this tactic before – to bury things. And the more you do things like that, the more chance there is of screwing up – we hope.'

'So what do we do?' the ex-soldier enquired.

'We dig. Things can't stay buried if pesky investigators keep uncovering them, can they?' The American smiled slightly.

Chapter 50.

'So, what do we know?' Lefty asked. He and Rivera were seated in the lobby of the American's hotel. It was quiet. An elderly couple were waiting for a taxi, and a bored-looking receptionist was surreptitiously checking her phone. Both men had a glass of sparkling water on the table before them. The walls were adorned with sepia photographs of South Quay in its golden age. The display started with depictions of the Victorian era; moustachioed faces and demurely dressed women. It then progressed through the wars all the way up to the Seventies. Donkey rides; kiss-me-quick hats, and sun-burned, long-haired couples bleary-eyed from Watneys Party Sevens. The resort – depicted in its sun-drenched finery – was gloriously unaware of the fate awaiting it, and the soon-to-be burgeoning popularity of southern Spain.

'Well, I think we can safely say our suspicions have been confirmed,' the ex-soldier replied.

Lefty nodded. 'So, it's all about Gatsby mansions, right?'

'I guess so. The plans were all in place. But she couldn't build with the preservation order, so she burned The Diplomat down. Two of the bodies would have been people who'd wronged her, I presume. Either linked to that or for something else – I doubt she's particularly fussy. And, in that case, Fraser was just an unfortunate victim.'

'And Carrie?' Lefty's voice lowered in volume as he said his daughter's name.

'She could have placed Bourse and the woman at the scene. I think that was all. I'm guessing we can assume it was Keane who was there that night.'

'Agreed. And if not, it would have been her who ordered the death, anyway. That's where all roads seem to lead around here.'

Rivera nodded.

'You know… back when I was investigating, it always amazed me how cheap life seemed to be.' He paused. 'I never thought I'd be saying the same thing when it came to my own flesh and blood.'

Silence.

'Could we frame her?' Rivera asked. 'I mean – I can't see that it'd be easy, but there must be hundreds of skeletons in her closet.'

Lefty frowned. 'She seems to cover her tracks pretty well. And, to be honest, I'm not sure how much of a punishment prison would be for a woman like that, anyway.' He cleared his throat. 'My kind of vengeance is a little swifter.' He let the comment hang in the air.

'Yeah,' the ex-soldier nodded. 'She'd be the kind of crook who'd have enough contacts on the inside to make things bearable. Doubtless she'd get friendly with the screws pretty quickly. She's probably done time before – I wouldn't be surprised.'

Lefty nodded. 'Anyway, the way I see things, it's a moot point.' He paused. 'She's not going to fucking jail. It'd be too much of a let-off.'

'An eye-for-an-eye then, right?'

'Fuck yeah.'

Silence.

Lefty narrowed his eyes as he looked at the man opposite him. 'What are you looking at?'

The hint of a smile played across Rivera's face. 'I think I've just made the guy Keane's put on our tail.'

'Yeah?' The American tilted his head slightly, frowning.

The ex-soldier grinned, winked, and then laughed noisily, as if the man opposite had told him a joke. He lowered his voice. 'Did you ever do any training on losing trails when you were in the military?'

'I did,' Lefty nodded. 'But it's been a while.'

'Yeah – I don't think this guy will have been trained – let's just leave it at that.'

'How come?'

'Because he's tall. About six foot seven. And he's built like a brick shithouse. My guess is that he weighs around seventeen stone. He's got bowling balls for shoulders, and his face is so pock-marked it looks like he's been slicing scabs off with a pickaxe.'

'He sounds dreamy!' the American sighed. 'And instantly forgettable – an ideal guy to put undercover. Kind of sounds like a mark who'd just melt into a crowd!'

Rivera grinned. 'I thought Americans didn't do sarcasm?'

'Blame cable TV! We have British programmes now. It's all about satire Stateside these days. Your sarcasm's catching.' Lefty paused. 'What colour hair's he got?'

'Black. But he has a red baseball cap pulled down over it. One thing we can definitely say - he's not the mystery man from before the hotel fire. Carrie would have described him – you're not going to forget someone like that in a hurry.' Rivera paused. 'He's probably one of Keane's heavies.'

'You think he'll attack?' the American asked.

'No. I mean – maybe. But for now, he's pretending to read the news on his phone.' The ex-soldier sighed. 'That's if he *can* read.'

'What do you want to do about him, then?' Lefty asked.

'Ten quid says he can't keep a trail.' He paused. 'That's about twelve dollars seventy on today's exchange rate.'

'Feeling confident then?' The American smiled a little. 'I like those odds. So?'

'Shall we have some fun with him?' Rivera asked.

'You're on.'

* * *

Beneath the mezzanine level, South Quay Public Library had a viewing gallery that ran around the edge of three sides of the main room. It was an area where students worked, and where counsellors delivered occasional sessions to people on their caseloads that they were trying to reintegrate into society. Before being repurposed as a library, the building had been an auction house, and before that a corn exchange. Rivera and Lefty strolled noisily through the streets of South Quay towards their destination. As they climbed the library's stone steps, Rivera saw the security guard. The other man nodded, and – in the space of five seconds – the ex-soldier outlined his plan and slipped the man a twenty-pound note. The guard frowned, nodded, and then looked up as Bullseye approached.

The viewing gallery could be accessed by two sets of steps. One was to the left of the main entrance; the other was to the right. Lefty climbed the steps to the left of the door. He then made his way around the viewing gallery until he reached the halfway point.

Bullseye entered the library a moment later.

The big man was utterly out of place in a world of books. He'd never been to a public library before. As he cast his eye around the room, he had two burning questions: the first was why the hell was it so quiet? The second, was why would anyone ever come to such a place? It smelled old and musty, and there were hardly any women – at least not the kind of women he liaised with. Looking straight ahead, he spotted Rivera. His quarry was idly rotating a spindle of books. He approached him, uncertain. As the big man walked, he passed several other people perusing the shelves. Frowning, he decided he'd do the same thing to blend in. Absent-mindedly, he picked up a book. He then narrowed his eyes as a pair of high school girls started openly laughing at him. Glancing down at the cover, he slowly sounded out the words: *Coming Out – A Guide*.

Reddening, he slammed the book down on the shelf and then froze. The sound had drawn the attention of a dozen pairs of eyes. To draw attention away from himself, Bullseye pretended to look at the shelf. Then he looked up once more. Rivera was in the same place, but now his back was turned; he was leafing through what looked to be a heavy volume. The big man paused; he wondered whether to stick or twist. If Rivera hadn't noticed him, then he was in the clear. If he had, then might he not be walking into a trap?

Gritting his teeth, the big man began to approach the book spindle. The library suddenly felt very quiet, while the sound of his footfalls sounded extremely loud. In the silence, Bullseye tried to tread as softly as possible. He was conscious of the sound of his breath as he edged closer and closer to the other man. Rivera stood completely still, seemingly studying the pages before him intently.

The ex-soldier's sudden movement was so quick, it made Bullseye gasp. He whirled around, taking the big man utterly by surprise. 'Hold this, please,' he said, urgently, pressing the volume into the other man's hands.

Bullseye suddenly found himself standing and holding the book Rivera handed to him. As the ex-soldier brushed past him, he whipped the red baseball cap away and threw it like a Frisbee up to where Lefty was waiting, leaning over the rail. The American plucked it out of the air.

'Oh, sir!' Lefty called out, drawing the attention of all those in the building. 'Oh, sir!' he raised his voice further. 'I believe this is your hat.' From the viewing gallery, the American dangled the headgear.

Bullseye simply stood, perplexed.

'Why don't you come on up here and get it back?' Lefty continued.

The big man was so taken aback that he simply nodded. With the eyes of half the library on him, he would lose less face by going to fetch it. Or so he thought. He trudged off towards the foot of the stairs while the American appeared to make his way towards the top of them.

As Bullseye ascended the stairs, he was lost to sight. A few more of the library's visitors regarded the unfolding scene with interest. While the other man climbed the steps, Lefty doubled back. Emerging onto the viewing gallery, the big man frowned. The American was almost back at the point where he'd caught the hat. However, he was now leaning over a table occupied by a student, seemingly talking them through an algebraic equation.

Bullseye began walking. As he did, Lefty looked up. He waved his hand in encouragement while holding the red cap aloft with the other. The viewing gallery clung to three sides of the library's rectangular shape. It was only as the big man neared the first corner that the American turned and began to run.

Lefty may well have been too old for the military. But he was lithe, and light on his feet. He hurried away from the other man. His pursuer, meanwhile, was big, bulky, and slow on his feet. His brand of intimidation didn't involve running. It was all about puffing one's chest out and scowling. Cardio wasn't really on the menu. As Bullseye hurried, it was as if his arms and legs refused to coordinate. He bashed into tables and careered into walls.

Halfway round the gallery, the big man realised his error. He'd passed the point of no return – Lefty was too far ahead of him to catch up, but turning back wouldn't be any better. He slowed to a halt just as the American's head emerged at the foot of the staircase. The man turned and grinned upwards. Rivera joined him. Both men waved cheerily.

Rivera and Lefty then ducked out of Bullseye's line of sight. They disappeared from view between two rows of shelves and vanished beneath the angle of the viewing gallery floor. As the big man gripped the balcony rail, his knuckles whitened, and he ground his teeth in frustration. Meanwhile, the escapees stepped through the door, which the security guard then closed behind them as he sauntered off to retake his post at the front door. The pair made their way down a long corridor filled with re-shelving trolleys and stacks of withdrawn texts, and through a fire exit which opened onto a back alley.

'I enjoyed that!' Lefty announced, chuckling, as the two men stepped onto the bustling high street. 'It's been a while since I laughed at someone making a prick out of themselves like he did!'

'Me too,' Rivera grinned.

Chapter 51.

'You're a fucking liability!' Keane shook her head in annoyance. Bullseye rarely ventured to Keane's house without being summoned – but he'd thought it better to come clean and admit his failing straight away on this occasion. For a moment, he'd considered leaving town – such was the wrath he expected to be met with. As it was, he'd decided to own up; he lacked the imagination to make a proper getaway. 'He's made you look like a right tool,' the boss scoffed. 'They both have!'

The big man grimaced. 'So when do I go in shooting, boss?' His voice was hopeful. If nothing else, he reasoned that the promise of violence would appease her.

'Not just yet – you'll get your chance soon enough. But we need to play this one clever. Savvy.'

'I want that bastard dead,' Bullseye announced. Killing to him was a job. Usually. Now, though, it suddenly felt intensely personal.

'Yeah,' the woman nodded. 'Me too.' She paused. 'They were playing with you. Taking the piss. You know that, don't you?'

'But why?' Bullseye frowned.

'Because they can,' Keane shrugged. 'I sent you to keep an eye on them. Incognito. But you must have stuck out like a sore bloody thumb.' She paused. 'Besides – they'll be trained in things like this. Military and all that – they probably enjoyed it.'

'Yeah,' Bullseye's voice rose. 'And that's why I want them fucking dead.'

The woman nodded. Her voice was softer. Reassuring. 'They will be. I'll let you pull the trigger. Or you can fight them hand-to-hand if you like – I don't give a shit. The important thing is this: when you do it, we'll have a whole lot more money than we have now. And, it's money that makes the world go round – remember that. You just need to keep a lid on things for now and then we all get rich. But if you screw up or lose your head, you'll spook them. And that risks making the money stop working.'

'But I thought they'd tracked Sheila down?' The big man frowned, sipping at a can of energy drink.

'They did.' Keane nodded. 'And by now, they'll know that Evergreen is a sham company.'

'So?'

'So, it doesn't matter. I have a dozen other companies I can change the name to any time it's necessary. I've already pulled the plug on the one they've found. And each set-up has a board of directors in an old people's home in town. There's only two of them – they can't keep up with everything. At least not before we've done what we need to.'

'We keep on with what we're doing, then?'

Keane nodded, fidgeting idly with a stray strand of wicker at the edge of a fruit basket. 'Yeah – you'll get your revenge, but think about your Christmas bonus first. They're losers, but they're trained, so we've got to get things right. If this goes the way I want it to, I'll even throw in a duplex at Gatsby mansions. How does that sound?'

Bullseye's face brightened. 'Cor! Really?'

'Yeah – that'll beat living with your mum all these years, won't it?'

The big man nodded eagerly.

'I'll even throw one in for her if you like – get the old girl living in style for once!'

'Yeah?'

'Yeah. She probably deserves it – she's put up with you all these years, hasn't she? So... for now, you just need to keep a low profile. I'll use someone else to keep tabs on them – someone less obvious. You're out of commission as a sleuth, but it's no matter. Your skills lie elsewhere. And at least you've flushed out that they're working together and putting their fucking noses where they don't belong.'

Keane paused. 'We'll just keep laying a trail of breadcrumbs and then we'll have a bloody ending. It'll be like a mash-up of *Hansel and Gretel* and *The Big Bad Wolf.*' She grinned. 'Fucking brilliant!'

Bullseye frowned in incomprehension.

The boss smiled. 'And when you get that baseball cap of yours back, you can be Little Red Riding Hood!'

It slowly dawned on the big man that Keane was taking the piss. A smile gradually spread across his face – understanding that the joke was aimed at him was beyond his comprehension.

Chapter 52.

The Hob in the Well was a brightly lit pub off South Quay's high street. It had a rainbow flag outside of it. The barman serving Rivera and Lefty was wearing leather lederhosen and a dog collar. He looked at the two new arrivals with amusement. Behind him, a large print of Roy Lichtenstein's *Drowning Girl* was hung on the wall.

Lefty looked around as the barman poured the drinks. 'You didn't tell me this place was going to be full of dudes,' he announced in a low voice, frowning slightly.

Rivera shrugged. 'I didn't know. This was the place that Clarke said to meet.'

Suddenly, the jukebox sprang into life, playing loud, plastic pop music. 'Yeah!' the barman shouted from behind the bar. 'Come on, girls!' He gyrated to the Eurovision soundtrack as he handed over the drinks.

The two new arrivals smiled gamely, nodding a little.

'You think this is a wind up?' Lefty asked Rivera. 'I mean – Keane might have put him up to this?'

'Maybe,' the ex-soldier nodded. 'But...' He stopped, as Clarke and Clements walked in.

* * *

'I didn't peg this as your kind of place,' Rivera said as the four men sat around a table in a booth. The music was playing at ear-splitting volume.

'It's not,' Clarke replied. 'Not that there's anything wrong with it. I prefer football and ale myself, but what I like about here is that it definitely *isn't* Keane's kind of place. And the big man wouldn't be seen dead in here either.'

'That's right,' Clements nodded. 'Keane wouldn't come close – nor would any of her acolytes. This is pretty much the safest place in South Quay for you boys.' He smiled. 'So I hope you like the music!'

Lefty nodded. 'I've got to hand it to you - smart move.'

Rivera nodded in agreement, sipped at his beer, and then placed it back on the table. 'So, when I called you earlier, I mentioned flushing her out. Our lady's not exactly gone to ground, but we're not having much luck getting her out in the open either.'

Clements nodded. 'So what do you have in mind?'

'We're going to make a scene,' Rivera announced. 'Steal one of her vans. I reckon that'll get her going. And, after that, I have a few other ideas. I think we need to send out some kind of message – let her know we mean business.'

'I'm liking this!' the electrician chuckled, leaning forward in his seat.

'Who's the protection?' Lefty asked.

'That big bloke, Bullseye,' Clarke answered. 'At least most of the time.'

The American looked at Rivera. 'Sounds like our man from the library?'

The ex-soldier nodded. 'Yeah. I can't work out if his nickname is literary or just plain dumb. But like I said on the phone – if we get him out of the way, it might bring Keane out all guns blazing. It'll make her seem weak if not. Vulnerable. She can't have that. She'll have to go all in - otherwise she'll risk being shut down. And then we'll see what we can do.'

Clarke nodded. He stuck his hand up in the air and beckoned the barman over. 'This is Kev,' he announced. 'My nephew.'

The barman grinned awkwardly. 'Sorry if I laid it on a bit thick earlier – just needed to test your mettle. I don't generally wear the collar.' He winked. 'Usually.' The barman looked at the American. 'I'm so sorry about Carrie – I liked her.'

Lefty nodded.

'Kev's going to apply for a loan from the Keane organisation,' Clarke said abruptly.

'And you're sure it's safe?' Kev asked; his voice soft. 'I mean...'

'Don't worry, kid,' Clements assured him. 'This'll be an open and shut thing. We promise. You won't need to do anything other than meet with them – it'll be ten minutes tops.'

The barman nodded, uncertain.

'Keane approves each loan in person,' Clarke explained. 'And she takes Bullseye along with her for backup – always has done.' He paused. 'When Kev gets a time and a place, he'll let me know. That'll give you a window to do your business. We'll know for sure at that moment in time that the pair of them will be occupied. And after that...' He looked hard at the two men sitting opposite him. 'Make no mistake, boys, you're crossing a line here – once you do, there'll be consequences.' He cleared his throat. 'So you'd better be damn sure you want to do this. Because they'll come for you. And me. And Kev here – it'll be like bloody Armageddon if you fuck things up. You hear me?'

'Loud and clear,' Lefty nodded.

'Yeah,' Rivera added. 'This could work.' He frowned at Clements. 'I'm right in thinking that he ditched a van of yours in the sea once upon a time, yes?'

The electrician nodded. 'Yeah. Why?'

'Just thinking...' the ex-soldier replied. The hint of a smile played across his face.

'Anything good?' Lefty asked.

'Yeah – a couple of ideas. I'm reckoning on red rag to a bull...'

Chapter 53.

Keane looked up from her phone. 'Kevin Shaw?' she asked Bullseye.

'Who?' the big man frowned.

'Yeah, I've never heard of him either,' Keane replied. 'But he needs money. Quite a lot, too.'

'Want me to check him out?' Bullseye raised his eyebrows.

'I think so.' The woman sucked at her teeth.

'You sure? Who's vouching for him?' The big man stuck his finger into his nose and examined the prize he produced that now clung to the end of his fingernail.

Keane regarded him with disdain. 'No one – but we might make an exception in this case.'

'Why?' Bullseye frowned.

'Because he's asking for fifty large,' Keane shrugged.

The big man gave a whistle and turned to look hard at his boss.

'I know,' Keane continued. 'Think of the fucking interest on that.'

'You want me to come along like usual?'

'Yeah – I'll tell him to meet us out the back of Payday Loans at eleven tomorrow morning. We'll keep awake for this one, though – just in case. He's an unknown quantity.' She paused. 'He kind of sounded like a poof on the phone. So I can't see it being a problem, but we won't take any chances.'

'You sure we want to meet him then? What with him being ...fruity?' The big man's discomfort was obvious.

Keane regarded him with incredulity. 'Fifty large is fifty fucking large, dumbass. For that amount of money, you can set aside your prejudice.' She paused. 'Anyway – you're just scared he'll fancy you. Or that you'll fancy him...'

'Want me to bring my baseball bat?'

'Might as well,' Keane shrugged. 'Just in case...'

Chapter 54.

'So we're on?' Rivera asked. 'Yes... OK... Good.' He hung up the phone and turned to Lefty. 'Right then,' he began. 'Eleven o'clock. That's when Keane's meeting Kev. So that's when we get on it.' He looked at an app on his phone and then grinned. 'It's perfect – low tide. If this doesn't get her going, then she might be more of an ice queen than we thought.'

'Ice queen – Ice cream. You're like a bloody poet, you are.' He grinned. 'Happy with the plan, then?'

'Yeah – we'll head down the high street. I've walked it at that time before. That's when the ice cream vans make their rounds.'

'And then?' Lefty raised his eyebrows.

'Then we go the whole hog,' the ex-soldier grinned. 'Just like we talked about. Once we've got a way in, the rest of it should take care of itself.'

'They do have CCTV there, right?'

'Yeah – so bring that hat – the red one.'

'Why?' Lefty frowned.

'It suits you.' Rivera shrugged.

Chapter 55.

Keane parked her Range Rover behind the Payday Loans office. She then walked around to the front of the building. It wasn't located on the modern industrial estate on the edge of town. Instead, it was in an area of relics; strips of shops that had somehow clung onto life through successive recessions: garages; gyms; a butcher's shop; a cut-price supermarket, and Keane's establishment. Standing outside, she rang a buzzer on the door. The woman on the front desk immediately pressed a button to admit her. Keane nodded at her as she walked past, disinterested. The closing door chimed as it shut.

On the counter were various leaflets advertising the rates offered on loans, and the prices that would be paid for gold and jewellery. The business that took place at the front was legitimate; it was registered with the tax office and was all above board. The receptionist conducted her day-to-day duties from behind a Perspex screen. At any point, a button could be pressed that would bring steel shields crashing down. That would both lockdown the entire operation and, simultaneously, summon the police.

Keane, however, had little interest in the front of the house. The receptionist pressed another button and the door to the rear of the shop opened. It wasn't secretive like a speakeasy – it was simply not accessible to the public. The new arrival walked through the door and into a corridor. A series of offices were located there – it was out back where the *real* business of the Payday Loans organisation took place.

The woman nodded to a couple of employees as she passed the open doors of their offices. She then walked into the largest room, which was situated at the end of the corridor. Bullseye was already there. He was reclined in the chair behind the desk; his booted feet were on the table. He gazed down lovingly at the mottled Louisville

Slugger bat he cradled in his hands. 'You're bright and early,' Keane said. 'What – did you shit the bed or something?'

Bullseye didn't rise to the jibe. 'This is a big one, isn't it?' he shrugged.

Keane nodded. 'The interest on this one's going to pay off Fuller – he's been whining like a little bitch.'

Bullseye frowned. 'Who – Tyre and Exhaust Fuller?'

'No,' Keane shook her head. 'Fireman Fuller. Remember?'

'Oh, him.' The big man nodded. 'You still going to pay up, then?'

'I am – he delivered.' The boss paused. 'But I'm sick and fucking tired of hearing from him.'

Bullseye nodded once more.

Keane sat down on a vacant chair. The office was bare. A potted plant sat in one corner and a row of filing cabinets lined another wall. Behind the desk, a large canvas print of South Quay adorned the wall, along with a blank calendar. This was not a working office – contracts were drawn up by other employees who then processed loans. The office was purely a place of intimidation masquerading as a run-of-the-mill commercial location. It had no need for frills or finery.

* * *

The phone rang.

Keane picked it up. '...OK. Ten minutes.'

'Is he here?'

'Yeah – Kevin Shaw.'

'And?' Bullseye raised his eyebrows.

'He's wearing make-up and silver hot pants.'

'What?' Bullseye's tone was incredulous. 'But that means...' His voice trailed off.

'What?' Keane narrowed her eyes. 'Money's money. Anyway,' she grinned. 'He might be your type.'

'Right type to give a fucking kicking to more like,' the big man grumbled.

Keane shook her head. 'No.'

'But – we've got a reputation,' Bullseye protested. '*I've* got a reputation. If people think I've gone soft, then it'll fuck everything up. And...'

'...and this fruit wants to borrow fifty grand!' the woman said bluntly. 'I don't care if he's dressed in drag. Frankly, I don't care if he's dressed like the fairy on top of a fucking Christmas tree. With the money we'll make back off this loan, he could be stark bollock naked for all I care.'

Bullseye huffed, frowning. He shook his head, muttering.

'We'll let him stew for a while out front, though,' Keane announced. 'Remind him we work on *our* terms here.'

Chapter 56.

Rivera waited until the crowd in front of the *Iceman* vehicle had dispersed. He'd observed their usual practice: the vehicles didn't move straight on after dispensing their wares; they'd hang around, at least paying lip service to the idea they were legitimate. The van was parked at the front of a vacant lot. A boarded up building which had previously been a carpet showroom stood behind it. The ground was overgrown – summer weeds spouted, and the usual detritus of nights out and drunken behaviour was strewn about: empty cigarette packets; discarded bottles and cans; newspapers. Two rusting fridges also sat close to the wall. They'd been bashed and graffitied.

As the ex-soldier approached the hatch at the front, Lefty slipped around to the back of the van. Cones and cups were stacked up against the rear windows – he could look through to watch proceedings without being spotted. There were two men in the van. On the bodywork of the vehicle's side, a smiling proprietor was painted – he beamed as he held two enormous ice creams in his hands while dancing along the sands of the beach. The inhabitants of the van looked about as far from the artist's impression as was imaginable. Both were dressed in black t-shirts. One was hunkered over the cash register, counting money. As he leaned, his T-shirt rode up, revealing pale, blotchy skin with protruding boils. The other, who approached the window, had a scarred face. Two teardrops were tattooed beneath his left eye.

'Help you?' he enquired, unenthusiastically.

'Yes – I thought I might have a 99 flake,' Rivera replied.

The man frowned and hesitated. 'Are you serious?'

'Why yes,' the ex-soldier nodded, affecting a plummy, aristocratic tone. 'Lovely day for it, don't you think?'

The man at the hatch turned and elbowed his co-worker to get his attention. He then turned back to the customer. 'You *really* want an ice cream?' he asked. 'I mean – it's fine. But...'

'Yes, please!' Rivera answered eagerly.

The two men laughed. 'You're not from around here, are you, mister?' the man at the hatch said.

'No.' The ex-soldier shook his head. 'I'm here on holiday. Now... my ice cream.'

The man behind the counter leaned out a little way, regarding his customer with a disgruntled expression. 'Large cone or small cone then?' he began. 'I...' Then his words were cut off. Rivera reached up, grabbed him by the collar in a fluid motion, and wrenched him through the hatch. As he did, he pivoted and swung his arm, increasing the force with which the man impacted the ground. He landed on his shoulder with a thud that echoed from the front wall of the vacant building. The man groaned a little and tried feebly to raise his head. The ex-soldier smashed his fist into his face, exploding his nose. He lay still.

As he was dragged through the hatch, the man's feet had knocked pots, cones and boxes off the counter. The noise had distracted his co-worker; he'd turned to look at its source, so he didn't notice Lefty sliding open the rear door. The American climbed up into the cabin and punched the second man hard in the kidneys. It was a vicious blow - a punch containing all the hatred, suffering and sorrow the man had endured since being notified of his daughter's death. It was a punch borne of the desire for revenge. It was a punch that landed with the force of a sledgehammer. The ice cream vendor crumpled, his hands clawing uselessly for purchase on the counter as he began to slide down onto the vehicle's floor.

His eyes looked set to pop out of their sockets. The expression on his face was halfway between shock and anguish. As he sank towards the floor, Lefty reached up and drove his head into the metal top of the counter. The edge struck him right across the bridge of the nose. A moment later, he tipped the unconscious man out of the van, where he landed close to the wall.

Rivera, dragging the first man's motionless body around to the rear of the van, nodded. 'Shall we sit them up against the wall?' he enquired. 'People round here are used to seeing junkies who've overdosed. I can't imagine they're going to raise too many eyebrows.'

Lefty nodded. He swiftly went through the men's pockets, withdrawing a roll of banknotes from each. 'Charitable donation,' he announced, winking as he held up the spoils. 'Might come in handy.'

'Good stuff,' Rivera grinned. 'Shall we do this, then?'

* * *

Ordinarily, vehicle access to the pier was strictly prohibited. It was only the emergency services that were allowed to drive across the boards. Rivera pulled the *Iceman* ice cream truck to a halt beside a turnstile. It was here that a bespectacled youth was charging people fifty pence to pass through and onto the pier. He looked entirely disinterested with his position of employment. That suited the ex-soldier's purposes perfectly.

'What's your name, son?' Rivera enquired authoritatively.

'Adrian,' the youngster replied.

'Right – you need to let us onto the pier. New plan.'

'Not allowed.' The youngster whimpered a little, pointing at a sign that prohibited vehicular access. He didn't look much older than sixteen, and was evidently extremely nervous. Rivera had no intention of making his life a misery – he simply needed to get the van onto the pier to make his plan work.

'You local?' the ex-soldier pressed.

Adrian nodded.

'You know who Leah Keane is?'

The youngster bit his lip, quaking a little.

'Well,' Rivera continued. 'These are her orders. I'm only the messenger here.' He narrowed his eyes. 'You want to go and explain to her why you won't let us on?'

Adrian shook his head. 'But it's not allowed,' he repeated. 'It's only my second day. This is a holiday job, and...'

'Look, buddy,' Lefty broke in. He'd been counting the money from the ice cream van's cash register. He added the total to the rolls of banknotes he'd removed from the vendors' pockets. 'Here are three and a half thousand reasons why you need to do what we say.' He paused, holding up the wad of money. 'That's more than you'll make in a whole summer here, for sure.' He looked hard at the youngster. 'Now, open the gate. Take the money. And walk away.' The American cleared his throat. 'We're in something of a hurry, so give me those keys, too.' He indicated the bunch hanging from a nail behind the counter.

The youngster scratched at his acne-scarred cheek for a moment. Then he handed over the keys, took the money, and stepped out of the booth.

* * *

Few tourists batted an eyelid at the ice cream van making its way down to the end of the pier. Lefty had closed the hatch and hung a 'closed' sign on the window. As they edged along the boards, Rivera turned back from the driving seat. 'He gave you the key, right? For the gate, I mean,' he asked the other man.

'Uh-huh,' Lefty replied. 'So, provided there are no fishermen, we're all good.'

As the van drew to a halt, the two men stepped out. 'Smile for the camera,' Rivera urged, donning Bullseye's red cap. 'Let's make this as obvious as possible. Send a message.'

Lefty waved up to where a CCTV camera was positioned, capturing their every move. 'Go big or go home, right?' the American grinned.

'Something like that,' Rivera nodded. He lifted down several large tubs of ice cream and a scoop from the van. Lefty then emptied out two boxes worth of illicit narcotics. The blister packs of pills that kept South Quay in thrall to Keane's organisation were all neatly bagged. He spread them out across the slats of the pier.

Standing back, the two men admired their handiwork, grinning. Beneath the display of drugs paraphernalia, Rivera wrote a message in foot-high ice cream letters:

FREE DRUGS: HELP YOURSELVES!

Lefty then moved around to the front of the van. At the end of the pier, a gate opened onto a narrow gantry upon which fishing enthusiasts were allowed to stand as they cast off their lines. The gantry – at this hour – was empty. The American clambered down and checked the sand below for any people who might have been on the beach. There were none. Using the key he'd procured from the youngster in the booth, Lefty unlocked the gate and swung it open. He eyed the front of the van and then looked back at the gap.

'You think it's wide enough?' Rivera enquired.

'Sure!' the American replied. He shrugged. 'And there's only one way to find out anyway – I'm not about to climb down there with a tape measure. Either way, the van will be out of commission, right?'

Rivera nodded, then disengaged the handbrake and put the van in neutral. He then wound down the window, keeping a hand on the steering wheel. 'Feeling strong then?' he called out. 'This'll be a bit of a beast to get moving!' Lefty walked round to the back of the vehicle where he began to push.

Straining and heaving, the two men slowly began to move the vehicle towards the gate. 'I'm getting too old for this!' Lefty wheezed.

'You and me both!' Rivera replied.

As its wheels inched over the pier's slats, the vehicle gradually began to gain momentum. As its front wheels tipped through the gate, it hung for a moment, suspended, until gravity took over. Seconds later, and with an almighty crash, the van landed upside down on the sand below. The reverberations of its impact could be felt through the slats of the pier. A few shocked onlookers stood looking over the side of the pier in disbelief.

Lefty swung the gate closed and locked it behind him. 'I guess now's a good time to make ourselves scarce? Once the old bush telegraph swings into action, this place will be swarming.'

'Roger that,' Rivera nodded.

Chapter 57.

Keane frowned at Kevin Shaw, who was sitting cross-legged across the table from her. The visitor was ill-at-ease. It was unsurprising – Bullseye was staring at him hatefully. He didn't speak, but loudly chewed a wad of gum. If it is possible to carry out such an action disdainfully, he was succeeding. 'What's the problem?' Keane enquired.

'Those aren't the terms advertised at the front of the shop,' Shaw pouted. 'The interest rates are too high. I'll never be able to make those repayments.'

'Are you wasting our time?' Bullseye blazed as he broke his silence. He rose, filled with anger, but Keane placed a hand on his arm to prevent him from advancing.

'You'd make a good dancer,' Shaw announced to the big man, sniffing, absent-minded. 'You're light on your feet.' Physically, he knew any contest would result in him being crushed, so he opted for barbed words instead.

Bullseye's facial expression collapsed. He was simply incapable of processing what the visitor had said. On the one hand, it resembled a compliment, while on the other, it sounded accusatory. He frowned and shook his head, as if trying to regain some semblance of understanding.

'We're talking about fifty grand,' Keane announced. 'So the usual rates don't apply. Standard practice.'

'Well, that's not what it says out front,' Shaw huffed.

Silence.

'The interest would be five per cent. Per day.' Keane cleared her throat and looked hard at the visitor. 'Final offer – you need the cash; you accept the terms.'

Shaw frowned. 'So that's... two and a half thousand. You must be joking!'

Keane shook her head. 'You don't like it – go to one of the banks on the high street. I'm sure if you beg hard enough, they'll consider lending you a quarter of the amount you need. But you won't get any more.' She paused. 'That's why you ended up here in the first place – I'm your last resort. I'm your guardian fucking angel, sunshine.'

The visitor stood. 'I'm most disappointed,' he announced. 'Really – you should be done for false advertising or something. This is... this is... preposterous!' Before his departure, Clarke had briefed Shaw – his task was simple: don't start enough of an argument to risk a kneecapping, but be ornery enough to ruffle feathers. And certainly enough to cause talking points. Any delay caused by the loan sharks picking apart events was a good delay – it would buy Rivera and Lefty time.

'Close the door on your way out,' Keane announced, bored. She produced a file and began to work on her nails.

Shaw paused at the threshold and turned. 'Preposterous!'

'Get out!' snarled Bullseye, raising his baseball bat. The visitor hurriedly departed; Bullseye sat down heavily. 'Bloody queens!' he growled. 'Where do they get off coming to a respectable place like this?'

Keane laughed. 'Oh – I don't know. When you lend money, you can't be too fussy about who you lend it to. Besides,' she grinned. 'I think he liked you.'

The big man opened his mouth to speak and then closed it, gritting his teeth.

'He'll be back,' Keane continued. 'Give him half an hour to get over himself – we'll just sit here and wait. He'll sign.' She paused. 'The way I see it, he doesn't have a choice.'

Chapter 58.

By lunchtime, news feeds all over South Quay were lighting up with news that one of the *Iceman* ice cream vans had somehow fallen from the pier. Details about exactly how it had happened were scant, but the irrefutable proof that it *had* happened was clear for all to see. A press photographer had snapped a series of pictures of the vehicle lying broken on the sand. The progress of the incoming tide had been charted in a sequence of stills as waves slowly engulfed the van.

For most of the people that read the article, the event was a curiosity – a strange occurrence. Leah Keane, though, knew exactly what it meant. And for Clarke and Clements, it was revenge that had been a long time coming. It was a declaration of war – any attempts at diplomacy or opportunities for ultimata had been skipped. The van being in the water was a direct line to hostilities.

The Hob in the Well was closed. But Shaw poured a measure of tequila for each of the assembled group. He solemnly placed a shot glass on the high table around which the men were standing. Clarke raised his glass, and the others followed suit.

'Gentlemen,' he began. 'This morning went well, but I think we can probably consider ourselves at war as of now.'

The men drank their shots and placed them noisily back on the table.

A quiet filled the room; it was tinged at the edges with uneasiness – a sudden realisation that they were all committed to a course of action.

'These are burner phones,' Lefty announced, breaking the silence. He handed one to each of those assembled. 'The numbers of the people in this room have been programmed into them, but there aren't any others.' He paused. 'We use these for communication from this point onwards. The way I see it, we're moving towards our end game now. And that means each one of you – each one of *us* – is vulnerable. Any problems, holler.'

'So what's the plan?' Shaw enquired.

'Nothing for now,' Rivera replied. 'We wait. It's advantage us. It'll be up to Keane to make the next move. And then we'll react.'

'Another?' Shaw enquired, holding up the tequila bottle.

'One more. No more,' Clarke nodded.

Chapter 59.

The closed pub was quiet. Where before the group had been buoyant and combatant, fuelled by the adrenalin of a successful first stage of the plan, now they'd drifted into silent reflection. Lefty had lent his rental car to Rivera, who'd insisted he needed to feed Rosie. Though there was some good-natured ribbing, nobody tried to stop him. Before departing, he helped the American carry two holdalls from the trunk into the building.

Rivera returned from attending to his cat a little over half an hour later.

'What news?' Lefty asked.

The ex-soldier shrugged. 'The cat's not hungry any more. But if you're asking about Keane, then nada.'

'Maybe she won't call,' Clements volunteered.

'She'll call,' insisted Lefty, a dark tone creeping into his voice. 'We just have to hold our nerve and not get forced into any silly decisions.' He turned to Rivera. 'Where did you park the car?'

'A few streets over – I thought I'd leave it out of the way.'

Lefty nodded. 'Good call.'

Silence. The men cast eyes around the room, avoiding one another's glances.

Rivera's phone rang. 'Unknown number,' he announced, holding it up. The screen was bright in the murk of the barroom.

'Go ahead,' Lefty instructed. 'It's your phone, right?'

The ex-soldier nodded and pressed an icon to answer the call. 'Hello... yes... when?' He drummed his fingers on the table. 'OK.' He hung up.

'That her?' the American asked.

Rivera nodded.

'How did she know where to reach you?' Shaw frowned. 'We're in South Quay – she's not the bloody FBI!'

'Bourse,' Clarke replied. 'From when Rivera worked at the Sands. The gaffer doesn't break wind without Keane's permission, so he'll have had his HR department drop everything once she requested the number.'

Lefty nodded. 'Anyway, what did she say?'

'She wants to meet me. Peace talks.' Rivera replied. 'Or so she says. I never pegged her as an ambassador, though!'

'Are you going to go?' Clements enquired, raising his eyebrows.

'No,' Lefty announced. '*I* am. This is my party – for now.'

Chapter 60.

'You sure about this?' Rivera enquired as Lefty busied himself looking through the contents of the holdalls he'd brought from the car. 'I mean – I know this is personal, but it's not *too* personal, is it?'

'Sure I'm sure,' the American shot back, defiant. 'This is between me and her.' He paused. 'Carrie was my daughter.' He paused. 'Don't worry – my judgement is still sound.'

The ex-soldier nodded, grimly. He turned to the others. 'So, we're all happy thinking it was Bourse who sold us out to Keane with the number, then?'

Clarke nodded. 'Yeah – he's the source. He's linked to this somehow.' He grinned. 'Definitely not a man to be trusted.'

'Right,' Rivera replied. 'So him and Keane are both potential threats. And what about the big man – Bullseye?'

'He's never let go of Keane's coattails,' Clements scoffed. 'Never. He's a follower – a clinger. I remember he used to be just the same with his mother when he was a lad; he hung onto her apron strings too. Probably still fucking does.' He shook his head in disdain. 'Yeah – he'll be there too. You can bet your arse on that.'

'So...' Rivera asked. 'Plan?'

'Well, I guess we'll figure that out as we go along.' Lefty shrugged. He spoke over his shoulder, rifling through one of the holdalls that he'd now lifted onto the high table. He turned. 'For now, though, how's this: you three,' he eyed Clarke, Clements, and Shaw, 'do what Rivera tells you – and try to keep a low profile so far as far as possible. Don't go putting yourselves in any unnecessary danger.' He faced Rivera. 'You, sir - I have a few presents for you,' he said, his tone suddenly serious.

'I guess Christmas has come early?' the ex-soldier shrugged.

'This is a B360,' Lefty began, lifting a box out of his bag. 'It's an Asset Tracking Device.'

'Meaning what exactly?' Rivera asked. 'I don't really speak technology. I'm still stuck in the era of vinyl and cassettes, really.'

The American held a small graphite-coloured panel to Rivera's mobile phone. 'Meaning you can track my whereabouts. It's accurate to two metres. Although...'

'...I sense a but,' the ex-soldier said, waiting expectantly.

'Yeah – it's only going to be useful for as long as it remains hidden in my jacket pocket.' He slipped the small device into a paperback book with a hollowed-out section. 'So let's just hope they don't frisk me too thoroughly. If nothing else, you'll know my last whereabouts. We'll have a cut-off time – it'll give you a starting point.'

Rivera nodded. 'And what's this?' he asked, reaching into the bag and holding up another gadget.

'This is a military signal jammer,' the American explained. 'It's simple, really. One function and one function only. Here,' he indicated a button on the face of the gadget. 'You press this and it jams all electronic and radio signals in a radius of... maybe fifty metres barring too many buildings being in the way.'

'How long does it last?'

'Maybe thirty minutes,' Lefty replied. 'It's got super powered batteries, but they take a lot of juice. It has to work hard to chuck out an electromagnetic field of that size.'

Rivera nodded.

'I'll leave it up to you to pull the pin on it. You only get one shot. So use it wisely.'

'Right you are.'

'Keys?' the American raised his eyebrows.

'Here,' the ex-soldier handed them over. 'Well... I guess this is us then, no? You're the advance party, and I'll be the cavalry with these guys.'

'Simple!' Lefty's tone was one of forced jollity and inflated confidence. He shook hands solemnly with each of the men in the pub.

'See you on the other side,' he grinned, before stepping out of the door with a cheery wave.

Chapter 61.

The club room of The Golden Sands was busy. Lefty walked up to the main entrance. He was wearing a black denim jacket and dark blue jeans. He looked fit and trim – two qualities that instantly marked him out as being different to most of the clientele. Though the majority of them were younger than him, they wore their years in aprons of fat and triple chins. Two shaven-headed bouncers with curly-wired earpieces blocked his way. They regarded him, frowning. From inside, the sounds of a disco rang out, and glitterball lights made lurid patterns as they danced, spinning across the ceiling. The thumping bass line made the glass of the long windows shimmer and the wooden decking beneath the men's feet vibrate.

'Problem, guys?' the American enquired.

One of the bouncers put a hand up and held it in front of the American's chest. Lefty's ingrained reaction would have been to twist his arm until it ripped out of the socket. But he restrained himself, standing still as the doorman's shaven-headed clone whispered animatedly into his mouthpiece.

'Where's the soldier?' the man asked, looking up.

'Change of plan, Kojak,' Lefty announced. He met the other man's glare with an impassive expression. 'Now quit wasting my time and take me to Keane.' He sniffed. 'I've no time to talk to the staff,' he continued haughtily. 'I want to talk with someone who can actually make decisions. So, hurry up and do your job, will you?'

The bouncer's colleague gritted his teeth. He was about to advance on the American when his earpiece clearly conveyed a further utterance to him. He stopped dead. 'Right,' he announced through gritted teeth. 'Follow me.'

* * *

The Golden Sands' nightclub had its name emblazoned in huge, glittering letters: *GOLDS!* Heavily-paunched men sat in chairs, eyeing the world through angry inebriation. Their wives and partners sat beside them, uncommunicative. Many of them wore permed hair. Further out on the dance floor, younger men danced with their shirts open, punching the air, while scantily-clad younger women gyrated around their handbags, which were placed on the floor. In corners of the room, more amorous couples seemed surgically affixed to one another. Passing them all, the shaven-headed bouncer unclipped a rope barrier at the foot of a flight of stairs and indicated that the American should ascend.

He did so. At the top of the stairs was a set of double doors. Pushing through them, the pair entered a large room dominated by four snooker tables. The light above each was illuminated, but – other than that – the room was in darkness. It gave it an air of threat; of mystery. The smell of feet and burger meat from *GOLDS!* was replaced with the scent of stale tobacco fumes. The noise of the music was more muffled.

Three figures were sitting at the far side of the room.

Lefty approached. The bouncer remained stood by the closed door – the American felt his eyes boring into his back.

'Where's Rivera?' the woman enquired.

'Keane?' Lefty asked.

The woman nodded. 'Answer the fucking question,' she demanded.

'My daughter was Carrie Esposito.' The American looked hard at Keane; in the half light, he swore he saw a slight flicker cross her eyes, but it vanished almost instantly.

The woman laughed drily. 'Well, Mr Esposito, it's nice that we've got that sorted and out in the open. I was thinking we'd have to put the thumbscrews on you.' She raised his voice. 'Bullseye!'

Bullseye rose from where he was sitting. It was as if his whole body unfolded as he straightened his bulk upwards, towering over the nearest snooker table. He moved towards Lefty. 'Don't worry – he's not queering you up. He's just going to check you're not armed,' Keane explained.

'I'm not,' the American announced.

'Then you've got nothing to worry about. Have you?' The woman's tone was icy. 'Who knows? You might enjoy it. You *both* might.'

Bullseye patted Lefty down. His hand lingered over the man's jacket. He reached into the American's inside pocket and drew out a paperback novel. 'Look!' he exclaimed, laughing. 'A fucking book! What do you think this is?'

The American frowned. 'Is that a rhetorical question, or do you want an answer?' he enquired.

'Fuck you,' Bullseye replied.

'I'll lend it to you if you like.' Lefty raised his eyebrows. 'You never know, you might learn something.'

The big man stared back, incredulous. He scoffed and slammed the book hard into the other man's chest. Lefty took hold of it and replaced it in his inside pocket.

* * *

'So, what do you want, anyway?' Keane asked, irritated. 'I'm a busy person. I figured I'd give you five minutes.' She paused. 'But you're boring me.' She cast an arm around the room. 'You want a drink?'

'It's simple,' the American replied. 'What I actually want is you dead.'

'Charming!' Keane shrugged. 'Join the fucking queue.'

Lefty said nothing.

'Why?' Keane pressed, frowning.

'I know you were behind the death of my daughter,' the American answered, coldly. 'You might not have pulled the trigger.' His voice caught a little. 'But you may as well have.'

The boss laughed drily.

'Something funny?' Lefty demanded, tilting his head slightly.

'Yeah – you.' Keane smiled. Bourse and Bullseye laughed along with him. She paused. 'Sentimental type, aren't you?' She paused. 'I've never been to your side of the pond. I've got a record that your border guards wouldn't regard too kindly.' She yawned. 'Tell me - do you have apprentices over in the States?'

'That's quite a departure,' the American frowned. 'What the hell's that got to do with anything?'

'Answer the fucking question,' Keane pressed.

'Yes. We do.'

The woman nodded. 'Very well.'

'Why?'

'I thought I'd throw you a bone – give you a bit of context. You see, Bourse here is kind of like an apprentice. For the longest time, I thought of him as being my bitch. But now I'm giving him a little responsibility. You know – see if he might be able to grow a pair.'

Lefty said nothing. Bourse bridled a little.

'Well, go on then,' Keane urged Bourse, using the kind of tone one might employ to address a reticent child. 'Get on with it.'

Bourse, sweating profusely and looking uncomfortable, reached behind the low sofa he was sitting on, and withdrew a sawn-off James Purdey & Sons shotgun.

Lefty rolled his eyes. In the quiet that followed, a cheer rose from below. The DJ played the first few bars of *The Grease Medley* – it sounded distorted through the floorboards; the bass came through in bursts.

'You don't seem particularly freaked out,' Keane frowned. 'It's not a replica, you know?'

'Yeah – well, this isn't the first time I've had a gun pointed at me,' the American shrugged. 'And this guy doesn't look like he'd be able to shoot straight, anyway.'

'I could ask him to pull the trigger,' the woman suggested. 'See if that makes you any less cocky...'

'You *could*,' Lefty shrugged. 'But you'd mess up your snooker tables.'

Keane laughed. 'They're *his* snooker tables. Not mine. I wouldn't give a toss – not really. But it might be more useful to me if you're alive. For now, at any rate.' She paused. 'The only thing that's surprising is that you actually came to see me. You must have known it wasn't going to end well.' She narrowed her eyes. 'It's because I'm a woman, isn't it? You thought I'd be all compassionate.' She laughed, shaking her head. 'Men are so fucking stupid.'

Silence.

'Where's Rivera?' the woman demanded.

Lefty said nothing.

'Fine, have it your way,' Keane announced, standing. 'Come on then,' she sighed. 'We're going for a drive – you, me and Bourse.' She turned around to address Bullseye. 'Remember what we talked about earlier?'

The big man nodded.

'Good – go and have a word then. You get them onside and we'll get this whole thing sorted. They're the weak links. You can find out if they're as pussy as you think they are.' Keane turned back to see Bourse prodding Lefty towards the main door with the barrel of his shotgun. 'Woah!' he called out.

Bourse turned. 'What?'

'What do you fucking mean, what?' Keane widened her eyes. 'You're going to walk him out at gunpoint across the dance floor of *your* club?' She shook her head. 'I mean – I know South Quay's got a reputation, but we're not in fucking Compton! Are you really that fucking stupid?'

Bourse opened his mouth to speak, but then closed it.

'Fire escape,' Keane ordered. 'Now.'

Chapter 62.

'What's all this about then, Jackie?' Malone enquired. He stood in front of a local news bulletin board outside the staffroom of the police station. The overhead light was harsh and yellow. It gave the two men jaundiced complexions. It was late – a hubbub of voices sounded from the front desk, but the corridor was quiet.

'Let's just take a drive, shall we?' Superintendent Cobb replied impatiently.

'Fine,' Malone shrugged.

* * *

It was dark as the pair crossed the staff car park behind the police station. The sound of their footsteps echoed from the rear wall of the building.

'If you want a chat, we could just have it in your office, or in The Forresters' Arms, couldn't we?' Malone frowned. 'Why all the cloak and dagger bullshit? What's going on?'

'I don't know,' Cobb shrugged. 'Maybe I'm feeling nostalgic! You remember when Webster was here? We had to go off grid to talk about everything then.' He clicked his key fob. The lights of a silver BMW flashed on and off.

'Unmarked car!' Malone explained. 'You drafting me in for a stakeout or something? Jesus – this really will be like old times!'

Cobb chuckled. 'No – nothing like that. You're uniform through and through these days – remember? We just need to swing by The Diplomat site. There's something in the report I need you to explain to me.'

'Can't I just do it at the nick?' the Constable frowned. 'Draw you a picture or something? It'll save time. It wasn't like I used too many long words for you, was it?'

The Superintendent grimaced. 'I think it'd be better if we're at the scene, Jimmy. Just to avoid confusion – I need to be clear on a couple of things. That's all.'

'If you say so,' Malone shrugged. Cobb started the engine and pulled out of the parking space.

Five minutes later, the BMW turned off the coastal road. As it left the asphalt, its suspension bumped over the uneven ground of the track now being used as an access road to the Gatsby Mansions development. Other than the light cast by the vehicle's headlamps, the track was only dimly illuminated by a couple of orange bulbs affixed to the top of some of the fence posts; Cobb carefully drew the BMW to a halt.

'Feels a bit fucking spooky here, doesn't it just?' Malone began. 'You haven't been watching mob movies again, have you? A bloke might worry that someone wanted to take advantage of him...'

Cobb scoffed and undid his seatbelt.

'So, what's going on then, Jackie?' The constable narrowed his eyes, looking at the other man quizzically. 'I mean, really? You didn't bring me out here to talk about old times, did you?'

'I – er...'

Cobb was interrupted by the sound of the BMW's rear door opening. A large man slid onto the backseat and closed the door behind him. Before the vanity light dimmed, Malone reached up to the rear-view mirror; twisting it, he peered at the new arrival.

'Bullseye,' the Constable sighed. 'It's been a while.'

'I'm sorry Jimmy,' Cobb announced heavily. He then opened his door, stepped out of the car, and disappeared into the shadows. He was visible only by the glow of his lit cigarette.

* * *

'What's going on then, kid?' Malone asked. 'You think you're in a spy movie now or something, is that it? This is all very Cold War, isn't it?'

'What do you mean?'

Silence.

'How's your mother?' the Constable continued. 'She still living on Crofton?'

'Yeah,' the voice that came from the rear was quiet. Hoarse. The big man avoided the gaze of the eyes in the rear-view mirror.

'So, listen...' Malone began.

'No! You fucking listen!' Bullseye raised his voice.

'Oi!' the Constable shouted. As he raised his voice, he caught the big man's eye for a moment in the reflection. Bullseye looked away. 'Watch your tone when you're talking to me, son. Don't go forgetting who made sure you didn't starve when you were growing up.' He paused. 'It sure as hell wasn't that pathetic excuse you had as a father – whoever the fuck he was.'

Silence.

'This place here – this hotel...' Malone went on. 'People died here, Wesley. You know anything about that?'

'They don't call me that any more,' the voice from the back seat came back. It was hurt. 'Wesley, I mean.'

'No – I don't suppose they do,' the Constable sighed. 'Even your own mother thought twice about calling you by your birth name after a while. But that's what happens if a loser like your old man gives his son the same name.' Malone shook his head. 'I remember how you'd go scrabbling around on pub floors for pound coins that your dad's old associates would chuck down for you. That was your birthright. His legacy. Friends don't stay very loyal in the game you're in – you know that, right?' The Constable shook his head. 'And that includes Leah Keane – ever since you took up with her, you were fucked. You might not realise it yet, but it's true. You never were the sharpest tool in the shed. She'll be the death of you, though – she's a fucking banshee.'

'Yeah, I remember how you helped out, Uncle Jimmy.' Bullseye lit a cigarette, ignoring Malone's criticisms of Keane.

'So... Are you going to tell me about the fire?' the Constable pressed.

Silence.

'I'm not sure South Quay's Superintendent would take too kindly to you nicotining up his car,' Malone sighed.

'He's not in charge any more. You know that, don't you? We all know who runs this town.'

'Even so...'

'You want one?' the big man asked.

'Go on then,' Malone replied. 'It's been a while.' Bullseye passed the pack and a lighter. The Constable lit a cigarette and exhaled slowly. 'So...?'

'How's Jonas?' Bullseye enquired.

Silence.

'I asked you how...' the big man pressed.

'...I heard you,' Malone cut in. 'He's much the same. Can't walk. Can't talk. Can't control when he goes to the bathroom. Mind of a two-year-old. And Jeanie still sleeps in the same room as him every night so she can feed him; change him; comfort him when he has nightmares.' He paused. 'That what you wanted to hear?' He paused. 'He's my son.'

'I'm sorry, Jimmy,' Bullseye sighed. 'But this is business.'

'Business?' the policeman's tone was incredulous. 'What the hell do you know about business, you jumped-up fuck?' He slammed his hand angrily against the heavy plastic of the dashboard.

'I'm bringing you a message,' Bullseye began.

'Oh yeah?' Malone chuckled. 'This should be bloody priceless!'

'Yeah – well, it's not from me,' the big man muttered, suddenly uncomfortable. 'You know that, don't you?'

'Keane...' the Constable sighed. 'I never figured her out. I mean – is she your girlfriend, or what? Because I always thought...' His voice trailed off.

Silence.

Bullseye spoke softly. 'She's said that if you don't retract the stuff in the report about the fire that she'll...'

'She'll what?' Malone pressed, his voice terse.

'Jonas and Jeanie...'

The comment hung in the air for a moment, circling the cab of the car like the wisp of a smoke ring.

'She thinks she can come after them then, does she, Wesley?' Malone pursed his lips.

'Yeah, Jimmy. She does.' Bullseye paused. 'And she can. She *will*. You know that.'

'And what do *you* think, son?' the constable paused. 'I always hoped you'd have brain enough in that skull of yours to make your own decisions one day. To be your own man.' He drew hard on his cigarette. 'I remember when I taught you to ride a bike – you were never freer than on that day.' He shook his head. 'I look at you now and wonder where the hell everything went wrong. You had potential.'

'That was a long time ago, Jimmy,' Bullseye insisted.

Silence.

'It wasn't *that* long ago.' Malone shook his head.

'I mean it, Jimmy. You don't take back that report, and Keane's going to come for you – all guns fucking blazing.'

The Constable sighed. 'She won't just send anyone, though. She'll send *you* – you know that, right?'

'Yeah.'

'Think you're up to it?' Malone smirked. 'I've still got a few moves.'

The silence was only interrupted by the ticking of the car's radiator as it cooled.

'Please, Uncle Jimmy!' Bullseye's tone was suddenly plaintive. 'I don't want to – you know that.'

'So, she's got Cobb properly in her pocket these days, then? Right?' The policeman tried to change the subject.

'She's got everyone in town in her fucking pocket. You know that. Everyone who matters, anyway.'

'Except me. I'm incorruptible,' Malone laughed. 'Remember?'

'Think of Jonas.' Bullseye paused. 'Think of Jeanie.'

'Threatening me isn't going to do anything. You know that,' the Constable said. 'And you need to take a long, hard look at yourself. It's not too late for you to do something good.'

'She's not threatening *you*,' Bullseye protested. 'Not really. She's threatening *them*.'

'She'll be the death of you, you know.' Malone's voice took on a harsh tone. 'I always said that. She'll chew you up and spit you out. And you'll be left with nothing. That's if you're even alive.'

'She pays well, though,' Bullseye protested.

The Constable turned in his chair and looked directly back at the other man properly for the first time. 'Last thing I heard, you were still living with your mum. Is that what being paid well looks like these days?'

Silence.

'She's going to give me a flat here – in Gatsby Mansions. Free! She'll pay you, too, Jimmy.'

'I already have a job, thank you.'

'More than that. *Loads* more. A year's salary in a week.' He paused. 'How does that sound?'

Malone sighed. 'I ought to send you home with a flea in your ear. You know that? It's just a shame that, growing up, you didn't have a pot to piss in. Otherwise, you'd realise how piss pot poor the pay she's giving you really is.'

Bullseye sighed. 'What can I tell Keane, though?' The big man's tone grew more urgent. 'I need to tell her something. You know how these things work? Just something to get her off your back for now.'

'Tell her I'll think about it.'

'You mean that?'

'I told you, I'll fucking think about it,' Malone answered in irritation.

Bullseye nodded. 'Anything I can do. For now, I mean? You need money?'

'No. But grind your cigarette out on Cobb's leather upholstery. Make a right bloody mess – that should piss him off.'

'Right you are,' the big man replied, obliging. He paused. 'I'm sorry, Uncle Jimmy – you know I don't have a choice, right?'

'Yeah, I know, kid,' Malone sighed. 'I know.'

Chapter 63.

The kidnapping was expected.

Lefty and Rivera had only spoken about it in hushed whispers – for one, they didn't want to alarm the others who'd been roped into proceedings. The second reason was that Clarke, Clements and Shaw had no training; no military experience. The American felt they should be kept away from the front line for as long as possible.

Rivera agreed.

After descending the fire escape, Bourse – his shotgun trained on Lefty the whole way – had escorted the American to Keane's car. He'd then sat in the back seat with the sawn off pointed at him. Keane had driven. The American hadn't done anything to oppose his captors – by making himself a sacrificial lamb, he was hoping the next part of the plan could be brought into play.

'You should be careful with that crow-scarer,' Lefty had counselled.

'Shut up!' Bourse had replied.

'I hope she's paying you well for this,' the hostage had sighed, nodding at the front seat. 'A successful businessman like you – this is the kind of thing that could ruin you.' He paused. 'Those things are notorious for having a hair trigger. If you rest your finger just outside of the trigger guard, then it means any time we hit a bump in the road, you're less likely to accidentally discharge your weapon.'

'So?' the holiday camp owner had shrugged.

'So, you should think about that; it's not so easy to explain away a body. Or a bloodied-up car. Or even a shotgun blast that sounds like a thunderclap. Especially if it blows out a car's windows.'

'Shut the fuck up!' Bourse repeated. But he moved his finger slightly away from the trigger all the same. In the front seat, Keane chuckled softly to herself.

* * *

'This is a place we call the crypt,' Keane announced proudly as the group reached the bottom of the flight of steps that ran into the basement hollowed out beneath the lock-up. 'You want to know why?'

'I'm familiar with the etymology of the word,' the American shrugged. 'But I didn't come here for a history lesson. I came here to find out why you killed my daughter. And I came to kill you.'

'Yeah – good luck with that, Uncle Sam!' Keane scoffed.

'Thanks,' Lefty shrugged.

'Lie on the workbench,' Keane ordered, ignoring him.

'What?' the American frowned.

'You fucking heard.' The boss raised her Heckler & Koch P7. 'Now... Billy-big-balls-Bourse over here was never going to have the guts to shoot you.' He paused. The holiday camp owner bridled. 'But I will,' Keane continued. 'And I'll sleep like a baby after doing so. You see,' she went on. 'There are two types of people. It's quite simple, really. There are the ones who'll sit up biting their nails, knowing they're going to have to face the hangman at dawn. And then there are others. People like me. The ones who have to be woken up for their execution.' Her countenance darkened. 'Get on the bloody bench, Yank.' She paused. 'Chuck your jacket on the floor – I don't want it getting in the way while I'm carving you up.'

'No.' The American's face was devoid of expression.

Keane smiled. 'Alright. It's your choice.' She paused. 'Anyway, you know how I asked you about America before?'

Lefty nodded.

'Well, the truth is I know a little more about the old US of A than I was letting on. I mean – there's a lot I *don't* know. Plenty I couldn't give a shit about, too. And don't fucking get me started on baseball.' She cleared her throat. 'I *am* familiar with this, though.' She held up a thin, red stick. 'You ever encountered one?'

Lefty sighed as he looked at the implement. 'So you're going to resort to that kind of approach, are you?' He shook his head. 'Small world mentality.' He paused. 'I'm not saying people should duke things out in the town square, but stuff like this is the preserve of a Kommandant.'

Keane smiled thinly, nodding. 'So fucking what? I'm surprised me playing dirty was ever in doubt.' She shoved the cattle prod towards the American. Wedged as he was against the workbench, he had nowhere to escape to; the current jolted through him, throwing him to the floor.

'Right then, Bourse,' Keane grinned. 'Lift the fucker up and cuff him to the corners.'

The first time Bourse tried to manhandle Lefty onto the workbench, he got a punch in the mouth for his trouble. But after another jolt from the cattle prod, the captive couldn't help being more compliant. Instead, once he'd stopped shaking, his limbs hung limp.

'You haven't answered my question,' the prone man said, eventually. 'Why did you kill her?'

'Oh – so you're still talking?' Keane sighed. 'Well, it's obvious, isn't it? Because she might have seen things she shouldn't have seen.'

'*Might*?' Lefty's voice cracked a little.

'Yeah – no hard feelings, but I couldn't take the chance. You, though...' she began. 'You and that Rivera are a whole lot worse. You just don't know what's good for you. Don't worry, though,' she smiled. 'I'm going to teach you a lesson. You had a chance to walk away. Fair warning. But you blew it. And one of my fucking vans ended up in the drink.' Her expression darkened. 'That's unforgivable.'

Lefty smiled. Keane removed a belt from the nail in the wall it had been hanging on. She folded it and then snapped back the two ends. The leather made a slapping sound. She then let the heavy buckle dangle.

'Before I started in the ice cream business, I was in protection,' Keane announced. 'You know what that means?'

Silence.

'Alright then – if you want to remain quiet, I suppose I have no issue with that. Unless I want to make you talk, of course. And I *will* make you talk if I want to.' Keane lit a cigarette. 'I'm pretty well educated when it comes to dishing out pain.' She blew a cloud of smoke towards him.

'It's a filthy habit,' Lefty announced.

The woman stared hard at him for a moment. She then jolted him once more with the cattle prod. The American bucked and wrenched against his restraints before lying still.

'Fuck you!' Lefty spat. His tongue bled from where he'd bit it involuntarily.

'You are most welcome,' Keane smiled. As she waited for her captive to stop juddering, she stubbed her cigarette out on his arm. 'Now where was I?' she continued. 'Ah yes – protection. You see, in that line of business, you can't let anything go. Ever. I've simply carried on in that fashion ever since. Drugs. Property acquisition. And ice cream.' She paused. 'These days I wear thousand dollar outfits and the kind of jewellery that film stars have to scrimp and save for. It's amazing really – people think anyone dressed like me can't be a gangster.' Keane paused once more. 'But there's a saying in my old neighbourhood: once you've got a gun; you're a gangster. And, once you're a gangster; you're always a fucking gangster.'

The American said nothing. Like many self-made people, Keane delighted in discussing herself and her exploits. Lefty knew that, in his predicament, any delay was good for him.

'It was the ice cream trade that really made me,' Keane went on. 'That's what elevated me. Before, they'd never have let a lady like me onto the head table. They'd have thrown me a few scraps here and there. Crumbs. But nothing like now.' She paused. 'You know why?'

'I assume you're going to tell me,' Lefty replied, affecting a bored tone.

'Money. That's one thing your fellow countrymen seem to have nailed. It's money that makes the world go round. Once I realised that, I knew I simply had to make as much of it as I could, as quickly as possible.' She shrugged. 'So I did. You'd be amazed at what kind of doors it's opened.'

'Why *Carrie*?' Lefty demanded. 'You said she might have seen you. But she might not. What difference would it have made? You could have let her live.'

'Because I'm going legitimate.' Keane gave a quiet laugh. 'And I wouldn't want someone saying I've been underhand in my dealings now, would I? Especially when I'm doing them a favour and clearing the land of the eyesore that was there before.'

'We're talking about an innocent girl dying here!' the American shouted. He bucked against his restraints on the cold metal of the bench.

'Yeah, well - we're going to be talking about you dying soon,' Keane replied. 'So I don't give a shit.' She nodded at Bourse. 'Me and him. Jedi warrior and trainee.' She indicated Bourse.

'So why don't you get on with it, then?' Lefty snarled. 'Anything's better than listening to you talk.'

The boss smiled thinly. 'You remain useful to me,' she announced. Her tone was supercilious. She looked over at Bourse. 'Are you wearing a watch?'

The holiday camp owner nodded.

'Good. Buzz him every fifteen minutes.' She handed the cattle prod to the businessman. 'But until Rivera gets here, we keep him alive.'

'Really?' Bourse replied, frowning.

'Yeah, really,' Keane answered. She paused. 'It goes against my better judgement, but that's just how it is. There are three reasons I'm known in the trade as the Iceman. You know what they are?'

'Ice creams?' Bourse began.

'Correct. Although a babe-in-arms could have fucking figured that out.' The woman shook her head in disappointment. 'The other two are as follows: number one – I used to freeze bodies so nobody could determine the time of death. And, number two, I'm as cold as a frozen lake in Alaska when it comes to dealing with people.' She looked down at Lefty. 'You like that, fuckstick? Alaska – that was for your benefit.'

'Yeah? I'm just thinking of ways to thank you,' Lefty snarled.

'And what then?' Bourse asked. 'When Rivera arrives, I mean?'

'Then we kill him and the Yank,' Keane shrugged. 'But until then, we use the fucker as bait.'

Chapter 64.

Malone's phone buzzed. He paused, stepped to the side of the pavement, and then removed it from his pocket. He was near South Quay's only shopping mall. It was his usual type of drill – the kind of job he'd done for nearly thirty years: moving along congregations of youths; helping forgetful parkers to locate their cars; checking licences held by buskers and hawkers, and - occasionally – chasing pickpockets and petty thieves.

The Constable looked more closely at the phone.

He frowned, sighed and then dialled a number as he leaned against a brick wall. The mall was deserted. Bright lights illuminated the empty parking lot.

'What if I say no?' he asked, once the call had connected.

'Then you know what'll happen,' the voice at the other end replied.

'You can't fucking touch them,' the Constable said. Defiant. 'Don't be so bloody ridiculous.'

'We've already got them,' the voice said. 'And there's only one way you'll get them back.'

'But...' Malone spluttered.

The call disconnected.

Chapter 65.

'Right then, boys,' Rivera announced, his tone almost cheerful. 'We know where he is, at least.' He handed the tracking device to Clarke. 'We'd better get moving.'

'The crypt?' Clements enquired.

'Yeah – looks like it from what this screen is saying,' Clarke nodded, looking at the electronic readout before him.

'So, what's the plan, then?' Shaw enquired.

'You stay here,' Clarke instructed. 'You don't need to put yourself in the firing line. They'll recognise you, anyway. We're better off if they can't link us.'

'But...' Shaw protested. 'They'll recognise you, too – Leah Keane will know the beached ice cream van was a message.'

'He's right,' Rivera cut in. 'You're better off here, Kev. That way, you'll be surrounded by people. Witnesses. There's less chance of anything happening. I know they're a big organisation, but they're going to have priorities tonight. It's unlikely you'll be one of them.'

'What about these two?' the barman frowned.

'Well... I can't do it all on my own,' the ex-soldier shrugged. 'I'll need a little help. I'm going to try and keep them out of harm's way, though, as far as possible.'

'How?' Shaw pressed.

'By using them as a decoy. They won't need to do any fighting.'

Clarke and Clements both looked hard at Rivera with furrowed brows.

'You never mentioned that before,' Clarke said.

'It's because I've only just thought of it,' Rivera replied. 'You drive us up there to the industrial estate. I'll hop out of the car before you get there. You two then start talking to Keane about wanting to bury the hatchet – you want to get back into the ice cream trade. Something like that. But tell her you only want one pitch – something small. Say you're feeling your age – you want something a bit more sedentary to do. Distance yourself from what happened at the pier – pin it all on me.'

'You think she'll buy it?' Clements demanded.

'Possibly,' the ex-soldier answered. 'But that's not what's important – you just need to stall her. If you can do that, then I can carry out some reconnaissance. I can't imagine her defences are particularly sophisticated. But we don't know how many folks she'll have there.'

'She'll have the Yank tied up down in the basement, any money,' Clements insisted.

'What are her usual numbers like?' Rivera asked.

'Bullseye – it's all about him,' Clarke replied. 'He's cocky. They both are.'

'OK,' Rivera nodded. 'As long as we get there soon, Lefty will be OK. Hopefully.'

'What makes you say that?' Shaw asked.

'Keane wants me,' the ex-soldier said bluntly. 'She'll have seen the whole fandango on the pier. This isn't about revenge for an ice cream truck, though. This is about her saving face. That's all it's ever about with people like that. She wants to kill me. And Lefty. But definitely me.'

Silence.

'So...?' Clarke pressed, eventually.

'Well, we can't call the police,' Rivera replied. 'We know that much.'

'What about Malone?' Shaw asked.

'He's a good guy,' the ex-soldier nodded. 'But he has no clout on the force. And Cobb does – he'll shut the whole thing down, so we can forget about phoning it in. They're not going to be knights in shining armour. Not for us.'

'So?' Shaw pressed.

'So we have to do things for ourselves,' Rivera replied. 'That's it.' He turned to Clarke. 'Is your car nearby?'

The other man nodded.

'Well, let's get going then,' Rivera said. He picked up one of the bags Lefty had left. Clements shouldered the other.

'You sure we haven't left this too late?' Clarke frowned.

'No – she wants a grandstand finish,' the ex-soldier explained. 'She already has Lefty, so she'll be pumped full of confidence – she knows she's already halfway there. I wouldn't be surprised if she'll want to put my execution online. Lefty's too. That's why she'll want to hang on until she has both of us.' Rivera grinned. 'But she's not reckoned on you two rocking up and throwing a spanner in the works.'

'What if she decides she wants to bump us off too?' Clements enquired.

Rivera frowned. 'Either of you ever fired a gun before?' he asked as the trio approached Clarke's car. The ex-soldier clicked the key fob, and the lights blinked.

'Long time ago,' Clements nodded.

'An air pistol,' Clarke nodded. 'At the fair.'

'Fine,' the ex-soldier nodded. He laid Lefty's holdall on the edge of the car's trunk and rooted around in it for a moment. Glancing quickly up and down the pavement to check the men weren't being observed, he drew out two gleaming handguns.

'Where the hell did you get those?' Clements hissed, his eyes wide.

'No clue,' the ex-soldier shrugged. 'Lefty must have talked to a few unsavoury characters.' He paused. 'He'd have been spoiled for choice around here. Mind you, they're not so difficult to get hold of. These are called Baikals. They're cheap and cheerful. They won't do that much damage, but unless Keane gets up close, they'll look pretty convincing.'

'You want us to fire them?' Clarke asked, frowning.

'Not unless you absolutely have to,' the ex-soldier replied. 'This is just an attempt to delay things. She wants a stand-off. Like something from a Western. Her versus me – or versus her enforcer. The odds will be stacked, of course – so she can feel like a conquering hero.'

'What makes you so sure?' Clements asked.

'Because she's never been to war,' Rivera replied. 'She fancies himself as a warrior, but she thinks it's all about theatre. She wants Custer's Last Stand – any money. But that's not how these things work. Ever.'

'So, what's she going to do?' Clements enquired as the men climbed into the car.

'Nothing without me,' Rivera said. 'And it's the big guy – Bullseye – who'll do all the heavy lifting, anyway. He's the threat if it comes to a fight. Not Keane.'

'Which is a problem,' Clarke said, heavily.

'Why?' Clements asked.

'Because he's just walking into the pub.'

Rivera and Clements turned quickly to look back down the road towards The Hob in the Well. The large figure of Bullseye was silhouetted for a moment.

'You're sure?' Rivera asked.

'Yeah, that's him,' Clarke nodded.

Clements turned to the ex-soldier. 'So, how does this fit with the plan?' he asked.

Silence.

'The plan's changed,' Rivera answered eventually. 'He's still after me. He'll be heading to the industrial estate – he can't do anything without Keane's say so.'

'So?' Clements frowned.

'So, let's get going. We can head him off.'

'But what if he's shot Kev already?' Clarke demanded.

'Then it'll make no difference,' Rivera shrugged. 'We just need to tip the odds in our favour.'

'And how the fuck do we do that?' Clarke grumbled. 'She's got Lefty. She'll have Kev now, and she's got that bloody giant on her side. What have we got?'

'The element of surprise,' Rivera shrugged. 'Don't underestimate how important that can be.'

'If you say so,' Clarke frowned. 'But forgive me for feeling pretty bloody pessimistic.'

Chapter 66.

A fly buzzed around the flickering light that was slung from the basement ceiling. The holiday camp owner continued to brandish the sawn-off he'd been given – it cast long shadows on the rough cement of the basement wall.

'Still think she's going to be on your side after this is all over?' Lefty asked from his prone position. His lip was bleeding badly now from where he'd bitten it repeatedly during applications of the cattle prod.

Bourse said nothing.

'She's making a monkey of you, you know?' the American continued. 'She'll be up there right now smoking cigars and drinking brandy... people like her never get their hands dirty. It's patsies like you that do all the work. She's giving you the run-around – what are you? Blind?'

'What do you want?' Bourse asked eventually, pursing his lips.

'Did you know my daughter?' Lefty asked.

'Yes – a little. I mean – I knew who she was.'

'So – were you there when...'

'...no,' Bourse interrupted.

'But you knew about what was happening?'

'Not exactly. No.'

Lefty lay back and closed his eyes. 'Not exactly,' he laughed drily. 'Not exactly yes, or not exactly no?'

'Neither.'

The American opened his eyes; for a moment he focused on the buzzing fly. 'It's never neither.' He shook his head. 'You're in too deep, kid. You've bitten off more than you can chew here.'

Silence.

'I'm not a horrible person,' Bourse insisted. 'I mean it.'

'You don't have to be a horrible person to do horrible things,' the American said. 'You just have to do horrible things. Human history is littered with nice people who did nothing when they should have acted. The only thing necessary for the triumph of evil is for good men to do nothing – that's a quote which has been falsely attributed to Edmund Burke.' He paused. 'Are you going to release me?' He raised his eyebrows. 'Last chance. Because when it all kicks off here, you're going to get lumped in with the bad guys. And I'm not feeling particularly forgiving.'

The holiday camp owner grimaced.

'Well?' Lefty pressed.

Bourse looked at his watch. He raised the cattle prod and approached the workbench.

'It's your funeral, big man,' the American sighed. 'You can't say you weren't warned.'

Chapter 67.

The evening was darkening by the time Clarke's car approached his destination. It was a summer's night; ground level appeared black. But overhead, the clouds seemed to glow, luminescent. The charcoal outlines of pine trees that hemmed the ridge above the Church Moor Estate cut the sky in a jagged line. South Quay was busy, but – away from the tourist traps – there were few people on the streets.

Clements was familiar with the layout of the complex and gave directions. 'The gates are open,' he announced in a low voice. 'That means they're expecting someone – otherwise they lock the whole place up like Fort bloody Knox.'

'Bullseye?' Rivera asked.

'I should think so,' the other man nodded. 'If he's going any place with her, then it'll be here – away from watching eyes.'

Passing over a series of speed bumps, the car drew further onto the industrial estate. The fence around the complex's perimeter was topped with barbed wire. The site was deserted – light fell intermittently from the security lights positioned on corners of the access road.

'Here,' Clements said. 'Kill the headlights.'

Clarke did as he was asked. The vehicle was at a junction. In all directions, corrugated iron sheds and warehouses could be seen. Their surfaces glinted dully in the gloaming. A large sign advertised the whereabouts of tyre changing services; exhaust fitters; kitchen decorators; paint stores; bodywork shops, and builders' merchants.'

Clements peered out at the sign for a moment. A map was displayed beneath it. 'Number 27,' he announced.

Rivera looked at the sign. 'Kitchen grouting?' he frowned. 'Really?'

'Yeah,' Clements nodded. 'Perfect cover, isn't it? Who the hell's going to check out something like that? It's the most boring thing on there. Even people in the trade would be sent to sleep by it.' He paused. 'Maybe photograph the map on your phone or something – just in case?'

The ex-soldier nodded and then looked back. 'What's the set-up? I mean, I'm assuming she chose it because of where it is, right?'

'Maybe,' said Clements, 'but she's had it a long time. The good thing is that her warehouse is in a kind of cul-de-sac. There's only one way in and one way out. We'll park at the entrance and – if we can – leave the lights on so you can see what's going on. That way, Bullseye won't be able to get straight in and there'll doubtless be some kind of altercation when he demands that we move.'

'Good,' Rivera nodded. 'You think you can keep Keane talking?'

'Yeah,' Clements nodded. 'Clarkey here never shuts the fuck up. Not once he gets going – it's like turning on a tap. Anyway,' he sighed. 'If all else fails, I'll ask her about the crypt – tell her I covered for Hobson that day all those years back. That should keep her guessing – she won't think there's anyone who knows about it. It might give her pause for thought.'

'You really think she's going to keep the coppers out of the loop on this one?' Clarke asked. 'I mean – she could bring them in and get rid of us...'

'She won't do that.' Rivera shook his head. 'She wants a grandstand finish. Like I said - there's only so many things Cobb and company can turn a blind eye to. It doesn't matter what Keane's paying them – they're not going to sanction ritualistic murder and execution.' His voice trailed off. 'Any other back-up you can think of? Anyone she might call?'

Clarke shook his head. 'No – she's got Lefty. And she doesn't know Sid and I are coming. She'll imagine you'll be arriving alone, and she'll reckon Bullseye will be able to deal with you. The big man's never failed her before. He's like having a private Army. That's what she'll think – that's why she's risen to where she is.'

'Yeah,' the ex-soldier nodded. 'But she's started a war on two fronts now without knowing what she's getting into.' He paused. 'I'm going to be the blizzards twenty miles outside of Moscow.'

Clarke frowned. 'Yeah?'

'Yeah,' Rivera replied. 'But what about when Bullseye's out of the way? What then?'

'Switch on that jammer the Yank gave you,' Clements replied. 'Otherwise you can be sure that Keane will get on the phone and start snivelling that someone should come and rescue her.'

'Roger that,' Rivera nodded. He turned and looked at the other man. 'You sure you were never in the military? You seem like quite the strategist.'

Clements grinned. 'No, sir. But I've read a lot – so I got the whole Russian winter reference. And I saw active service in the ice cream wars – remember? That blooded me good and proper.' He paused. 'Know this, though: someone like Keane's always got plenty of people to call on. Even if you get Bullseye out of the way. This is a town full of ne'er-do-wells, and she pays well enough to take her pick. So don't give her the opportunity. If it all goes south, she might even try calling Cobb. And we know that's only going to go one way. Chopping down gangsters is one thing. But police...'

'True,' the ex-soldier nodded.

'Right then,' Clarke announced. 'Time for you to sod off, soldier boy.'

Rivera nodded, stepped out of the car, and closed the door quietly.

* * *

Once Clarke's car had departed, the industrial estate was silent. So quiet that Rivera was conscious of the echoes of his footfalls bouncing from the corrugated iron walls. The roads were roughly tarmacked, replete with uneven manhole covers, potholes, and speed bumps. Surfaces were designed for work vans and pickup trucks – not pedestrians.

Having studied the map, Rivera made a plan – it was simple. He knew that once the first fist was thrown, his strategy would likely go out of the window. But, until then, he'd hope for the best. He reasoned that if Clarke and Clements could block the cul-de-sac as they'd suggested, Bullseye would have to get out of the car to instruct them to move. The likelihood that Shaw would either be in the backseat or trussed up in the trunk would mean the vehicle causing the obstacle would have to move. He doubted the driver would want to carry the prisoner any further than he needed to.

Rivera, therefore, positioned himself in the narrow alleyway between two small workshops. He was about ten yards behind the place where Clarke's car was parked. The engine was switched off. The red taillights were still on, and he'd made sure the rear fog lights were on too – they seemed almost searing in the now full darkness. His hope was that – if he *did* have to step out – the glare would temporarily blind Bullseye.

That would distract him for a moment.

A moment would be all the ex-soldier required.

Bullseye and Keane – as he knew – would have secured their reputation through posturing. Through drama. They'd have engineered standoffs where their quarries would have been forced to very publicly back down. That was how things worked on the streets.

It was all about front.

It was all about face.

It was all about the pecking order. And piece-by-piece, Keane and her enforcer had clawed their way out of the gutter, until they'd risen right to the top. But they were big fish in a small pond. And, once their battles had been fought, Rivera reasoned, they'd have lost their sharpness. Slipped into complacency.

The ex-soldier, though, remained sharp. He was concerned with survival. If a fight could be shortened, then he'd shorten it. And move on. He knew that the longer Keane or his accomplice could stretch out an altercation, the more likely it was to go wrong.

He didn't plan on providing such an opportunity. Moving down the alley, he simply settled down in the shadows; a viper waiting to strike.

Rivera was tensed like a coiled spring by the time he heard the car engine approaching. The ex-soldier edged forward, steadying himself against the corrugated iron side of the building. A Walther P5 that Lefty had provided was tucked in his back pocket, but a hunting knife was clenched in his fist.

He'd opted for silence.

For surprise.

He closed his eyes for a moment as the headlights of the approaching car bounced and danced across the rough ground, hoping that avoiding the light would preserve some semblance of night vision for him.

The car horn blared out, splitting the silence.

No response.

The car horn sounded again, klaxon-like.

Ten seconds later, the car door was wrenched open and heavy feet stepped onto the gravelly surface. The driver clambering out of the vehicle was accompanied by a string of expletives. Narrowing his eyes, the big man squinted at the obstruction in front of him.

Rivera rushed forward.

Chapter 68.

After Shaw had departed, the boss had realised something didn't ring true about the loan request. The glamorous woman may not have had much schooling, but when it came to money, she was sharp as a tack. And when it came to someone trying to get one over on her, she was sharper still. She'd let Shaw leave the office, but it had always been her intention to follow up on what she saw as offensive behaviour. If word got out that her organisation would tolerate time wasters, she'd let herself in for all sorts of problems; there were always desperate people in South Quay who'd rob Peter to pay Paul for their daily fix. They were the root of much of her income. But she didn't want her business putting its head too far above the parapet. So, she'd opted for decisive action. She'd run all the angles and smelled a rat – something needed to be done.

The body count was going to be high enough, anyway. Keane had reconciled herself with that. Shaw would be just one more casualty – he could join the American and Rivera in the crypt. After that, the boss reckoned she'd be in the clear: respectable businesses; influence at the Chamber of Commerce. She'd told herself the same before, but this time she really meant it. Besides, the properties at Gatsby Mansions were selling like hot cakes. She was resentful that so many bonuses were being paid out to her budding telephone entrepreneurs, but she supposed it was simply the price of success. She'd visited the trading floor on a couple of occasions and was surprised by how refreshing it had felt to walk among those entrenched in polite society. A novelty.

Keane hadn't trusted Shaw, though. What she *did* trust were her gut feelings. She'd reasoned there was something not quite right about the loan application. It was too much. Too sudden. Too out-of-the-blue. So she'd sent Bullseye to fetch him. She was going to ask the man currently trussed up in the boot of the big man's BMW a few questions. Nicely. And if she didn't get a straight answer, then she'd unleash her accomplice. He wouldn't ask quite so nicely.

But she'd definitely get an answer.

* * *

The arrival of Clements and Clarke had wrong-footed Keane. She thought herself unflappable, but the car parked in the entrance of the cul-de-sac was confusing. There was no reason for it being there. Especially at that time of night.

She was even more confused to see her old nemesis emerging from the vehicle. She disliked Clarke intensely. But she *hated* Clements. She'd seen neither man for years. Not face-to-face. And she'd forgotten how much Clarke talked. She was about to order him to move the car, but she couldn't shut him up.

Once Clarke started talking, he couldn't stop. Keane was about to threaten him; she nearly took out her pistol, but then what he said grew interesting. Her former rivals – always so resentful - were suddenly begging for the opportunity to sell choc ices to pensioners from a pitch on her patch. She had no real issue with it – it wouldn't eat into her profits in a way that she'd notice. And, really and truly, it meant nothing to her if they *were* operating in her area. What amused her was their tone; their desperation. What Leah Keane loved more than anything was humiliation. And this was about as humiliating as anything she'd seen. So, she reasoned, it was worth a moment of her time.

Of course, she wouldn't let them back into the trade – years before she'd promised herself that she'd never make a decision that would place her in a position of weakness. Keane fancied herself as tougher than the rest. She knew the rest of the world saw her as being just that. And toughness meant never reneging on a decision.

She smiled. Her former rivals – the ones who'd warned her off when she'd first started ascending the hierarchy of the town may as well have been on their knees before her. She felt – she realised – like a demigod. As if, by the swoop of her mystical sword, she wielded the power of life and death over the mere mortals stood in front of her.

It was only when the horn of another car sounded that she looked up, and realised the route to her lock-up was blocked.

Clarke, meanwhile, was still talking.

'Oi! Clarke!' Keane hissed after hearing the car horn. 'Shut your fucking mouth for a minute, will you? Bullseye needs to get through...'

'Bullseye!' Clarke exclaimed, his eyes wide. 'What's he doing here?'

'Trying to get through, you useless prick.'

Clarke and Clements frowned and then looked stupidly back at the vehicle, as if unable to fathom what Keane was talking about.

'What?' Clements asked.

'You fuckers heard me,' the boss continued. 'Shift it – otherwise I won't even consider your offer, and the only work you'll get around here is cleaning the crappers on the seafront – and that'll only be if I feel sympathetic.'

'Oh!' Clements said – as if the penny had just dropped. 'Right you are, boss.'

* * *

Bullseye only made it two steps from the car before Rivera's knife severed his carotid artery.

Having made the decision to take the man down fast and permanently, the ex-soldier moved with lightning pace.

For a moment, the big man groped at his wound, uncomprehending. Then he sank slowly down against the side of the car. Rivera didn't waste time watching. There was no need. He knew there was no coming back from an injury like the one he'd dispensed. The ex-soldier knew how fragile life was: one click of the fingers; one well-placed slice of a knife, and a thing of flesh turned to a thing of dust. He raced around to the trunk. As he opened it, he saw the shape of Shaw, his hands and feet tied. The captive's eyes bulged in terror.

'Don't worry,' Rivera said softly, resting a comforting hand on the bound man's shoulder. The barman recognised him in the glow of the trunk light. He reached forward with the bloodied knife and sliced through the ties. Then, he helped the other man out of the car. 'Can you walk?' he enquired.

'Yeah,' Shaw muttered. 'Back at the bar, he put a gun in my mouth.'

'Right,' Rivera nodded. 'Well – you don't need to worry about him now.' He paused. 'Do me a favour, though, will you?'

'What?' the other man asked, nodding hurriedly.

'Get out of here – go and hide somewhere. But get going. There's enough of a casualty count already with this thing – I don't want to add any more.'

'Do you want me to call the police?' Shaw enquired.

'Absolutely not.' Rivera shook his head. 'Just keep the burner phone with you. I'll let you know when things are clear.'

Shaw nodded and began to move away, pausing only to help as Rivera heaved Bullseye's swiftly-becoming-lifeless bulk into the trunk of the car, dumping his corpse into the space the other man had vacated. The ex-soldier wondered if the barman might baulk at the task. But he remained stone-faced. Resolute. As Shaw jogged away, Rivera slammed the boot shut and stepped around to the driver's door, nodding at Clarke as the other man climbed into the vehicle parked in front of him. 'One down,' Rivera said softly. 'Just pull forward until you're as close as you can get. I'll follow.'

Clarke nodded. 'Switch on that signal jammer,' he instructed. 'Once she gets suspicious, she'll start calling for help otherwise.'

'Way ahead of you,' Rivera nodded.

The foreman put his car into gear and pulled forward. The wheels made a crunching sound on the uneven, gravelly surface, and the lights danced as the car advanced. Rivera followed suit, driving after the other vehicle in Bullseye's car. The lights picked out the figure of Keane sitting on a chair set upon the side of a loading dock. Beyond, the cavernous interior of the open warehouse door loomed darkly behind her. Clements stood at the foot of the dock, alternating his gaze between Keane and the cars that were advancing.

Bullseye's car had blacked-out windows. As it drew to a halt, Keane ignored the driver and leaped lithely down from the dock instead. She landed softly on the gravel and bared her teeth as she popped open the trunk, ready to inspect her latest offender.

Chapter 69.

Keane reeled back, a horror-stricken look upon her face. She couldn't believe what she was seeing. It was as if she'd suffered a hammer blow. Bullseye's dead visage stared back at her. As his corpse continued to bleed out, it was taking on the ghostly pallor of the newly dead – a look made worse by the light of the trunk.

'What the fuck?' She turned to face Rivera. Her expression was one of venomous hatred and complete disbelief combined.

'Switcheroo,' the ex-soldier shrugged.

Keane looked towards the decking.

'Guess the tables have turned now, no?' Clarke grinned.

'Yeah, not so brave without the big man, hey?' Clements' gaze was icy as he regarded the woman.

Keane shrugged, looked down at her phone and pressed at the screen. She then held it aloft. 'I've just sent an alert,' she announced smugly. 'In three minutes, I'll have an Army here. A fucking Army. Coppers too. You're all dead men. Nowhere will be safe for you. I've got people on the outside, and – when they put you away – I'll get to you on the inside too.' She smiled bitterly, trying desperately to recalibrate herself after the loss of her enforcer. 'I'm walking out of here.'

'Yeah, good luck with that,' Rivera said. 'Calling for help, I mean.'

'What are you talking about?' the gangster frowned.

'Check your phone,' Clarke suggested. 'It's worse than useless right now.' He paused. 'How many bars have you got?'

Keane frowned. She then looked at the face of her phone, panic in her eyes. She frantically pressed a few more times at the screen.

'Call it a gift from Lefty,' Rivera explained. 'Signal jammer. That phone of yours is redundant now.' He paused. 'This is how you wanted it, anyway – right? You and me. An arena finish. I mean – I don't know how you'll fare without Bullseye to back you up, but I'm willing to give you a try. I'm a modern man. I believe in equality. Anyway, you're a tough nut – or so they say.'

'What do you want?' Keane's tone was suddenly uneasy beneath her icy exterior.

'You call it.' Rivera licked his lips.

The gangster grinned. She withdrew the H&K pistol from inside her jacket and pointed it at Rivera.

'Clements. Clarke,' the ex-soldier called out, calmly. 'Kill her.' He put his hands in his pockets.

The other two men drew the Baikals Rivera had given them earlier. In the headlamp lights, they glittered menacingly. Each of them aimed at Keane. Their expressions were stony.

'Drop the gun,' Rivera instructed.

'Or what?' Keane blustered.

'We're not pissing about here, Keane,' Rivera snarled. 'You're going to do what you're bloody told for a change.'

'You're bluffing.' The woman's look was hateful.

The ex-soldier sighed, looked pointedly at the dead bulk of Bullseye in the boot of the car, and began counting. '3... 2...'

The woman flung the gun down angrily; it landed with a metallic thud.

'Right then,' Rivera announced, picking up the weapon. 'Showtime.'

Chapter 70.

Keane moved away swiftly, stepping back from the car. She turned, knowing she was hemmed in, but reasoning the two gunmen probably didn't want to fire. At least not yet. Rivera stood still, feet firmly planted on the ground.

'I'm sure we can come to an arrangement,' the woman blustered suddenly. 'Money makes the world go round, right? And I've got plenty of it.'

'No.' Rivera shook his head.

'What?'

'You live by the sword, you die by the sword.' The ex-soldier shrugged.

'I can pay you!' Keane insisted.

'That's not going to bring back Lefty's daughter. Or Fraser. Or any of the others,' the ex-soldier said, coldly.

'Collateral damage,' Keane spat.

'And what about all the others you've hooked in hock to your dealers? All that profit from poison – you've ruined their lives too,' the ex-soldier continued.

'So, what the fuck are you? Some kind of moral crusader? Jesus! You're starting to sound like a bloody preacher.'

'Big words,' Rivera sighed. 'No – this is a day of reckoning. I told you that already.'

Keane stared hard at her adversary. Rivera wasn't a huge man, but any conflict would be woefully mismatched. The boss had very rarely had to fight. Not since she was a teenager. She'd always paid men to settle conflicts for her. Or she'd relied on Bullseye. It was a lesson she'd learned early on – with a sharp tongue and back-up, there was little she couldn't achieve. She looked towards the deck. Clements and Clarke stared on impassively.

Suddenly, Keane rushed towards Rivera, swinging a hopeful punch as she did so. The ex-soldier moved his head slightly as the gangster's fist connected. The blow glanced off, smarting slightly, but doing no damage.

Rivera remained where he was, hands hanging down by his sides. 'That the best you can do?'

Keane stood, disconsolate.

'So, tell me - that little black book you have of names you want to get even with...' the ex-soldier began.

'I don't know what the fuck you're talking about,' the woman protested. 'I...'

'...of course you do,' Rivera interrupted. 'People like you always do.'

'Yeah – well, those names are in my head,' Keane shrugged. 'And you're top of the list - just ahead of that American prick.'

The ex-soldier laughed and removed the Walther P5 from his pocket. 'You know much about evolution?'

'What?' Keane stared back. Indignant.

'Yeah, I didn't think so.' He paused. 'Anyway, back in caveman times, the world was about strength. Fights would be won by the strongest man, and that was the end of it. But things don't work like that now. Especially not for you - you found a life hack somewhere along the line. A niche. You wormed your way in and manipulated people so they'd do what you wanted.'

'So?' Keane looked daggers at Rivera. 'That's how the world works.'

'So – I bet you never once got your hands dirty, did you?'

Keane bent down, pretending to tie her shoelace. As she did, she picked up a large stone from the gravelly ground. She began rising, ready to fling it.

The chance never came.

Rivera crashed the butt of his pistol into the side of the woman's head, sending her sprawling across the roadway.

* * *

'Funny how little she looks, stretched out like that,' Clements observed, almost pityingly.

'You feeling sorry for her?' Clarke asked, as if in amusement.

'No,' the other man shook his head. 'But she always seemed so invincible – I never thought the fight would be over so quickly.' He turned to Rivera. 'You alright then... caveman?'

Rivera nodded. He deftly plucked the mobile phone from Keane's pocket, conscious that the jammer's battery was probably waning. There was - he reasoned - no point leaving her with any hope of rescue.

'I didn't have you down as the type to hit women.' Clarke raised his eyebrows.

'Piss off.' The ex-soldier shook his head.

'I guess different rules apply with dykes, though, right?' Clements added. 'She was – wasn't she?'

Silence.

'Let's remember who're fucking avenging here, shall we?' Rivera's tone was cold; hard.

'Sorry,' Clements replied, admonished. 'I didn't mean... must be the adrenalin or something.'

Rivera nodded. 'I'm going to fetch Lefty,' he announced.

'You think he'll be down there?' Clarke asked.

'Yeah – bound to be,' Rivera answered. 'And it'll be Bourse guarding him. That's what I think.'

'You sure?' Clements enquired.

'I reckon,' Rivera said. 'Who else at the holiday park would she have used? I mean – I know she's got a long reach, but there's a limit to how many people she'd want to involve.'

The electrician shrugged.

'Right,' Rivera continued. 'Before I go - this basement. Tell me about it. I want to know what it looks like.' He paused. 'And whether Bourse is going to be dug in down there.'

Clements looked back, nodding earnestly. 'Well, when I dug it, I guess it was around twenty-feet square. The walls weren't completely true because it was done with hand tools. My theory is that Keane would have walled in any of her victims – it would make a good hiding place. Nobody knew it was there, after all. And no one does now – present company excepted.'

The ex-soldier nodded.

'Mind you – it depends how busy she's been. I mean, in terms of how big it might be now,' Clements continued. 'You never know with Bullseye doing her bidding. And the smaller it is...'

'Understood,' Rivera nodded. He picked up the stone Keane had tried to use against him and placed it into his pocket. Before clambering up onto the deck, he picked up the woman's discarded H&K P7 and handed it to Clarke. 'If she moves,' he announced, nodding down towards Keane, 'then shoot her. Got it?'

Clarke nodded, moving towards the prostrate woman. Standing guard.

Rivera stepped into the warehouse. As he walked towards the rear, he saw the exposed hatch. It was just over halfway back, towards the centre of the room. A dim light shone from it. He drew out the stone and held his pistol before him as he tip-toed forwards.

Approaching the lip of the hatch, he saw the flight of steps leading down. Peering over the edge, he noted they seemed to end in the middle of the hollowed-out space. Rivera turned and looked back towards the entrance of the warehouse, picturing the likely dimensions of the crypt in his mind's eye.

Looking at the set-up, he reasoned the bulk of the underground space was more likely to be beyond the staircase than behind it.

He decided to gamble.

Rivera stood in the darkness. He then lowered his arm, so it was almost at the same level as the hatch. Gently, he lobbed the stone in an arc. It landed on the stone floor beyond the foot of the stairs and bounced high. As it did, it made a loud, crashing noise that echoed throughout the subterranean chamber.

* * *

When the stone landed, Bourse had been in the act of placing the sawn-off on one of the surfaces that lined the wall of the cavern and was just approaching the workbench. He had the cattle prod in his hand and was set to administer another shock, as per Keane's orders. The holiday park owner was getting twitchy – it felt like a long time since Keane had departed. He wondered what was happening and why he wasn't privy to any of the plans.

As the stone hit, it startled him. His gaze was drawn involuntarily towards its progress as it scuttled across to the far concrete wall. It was only when its echoes receded that he became aware of another sound from the staircase; Rivera – taking the stairs three at a time, emerged into view a split-second later.

Bourse froze. He debated whether to go back for the firearm, but instead, raised the cattle prod.

'Drop it,' Rivera hissed.

Bourse remained in his pose; the weapon raised.

The ex-soldier pulled the trigger. Bourse's kneecap exploded. He fell to the floor, gripping the wound and screaming. The cattle prod skittered over into the corner as the report of the shot echoed massively in the confined space.

Rivera looked over at the workbench. Lefty was spread-eagled across its surface, cuffed to its corners.

'You alright?' the ex-soldier asked, raising his eyebrows.

'Never better,' the American replied groggily. 'You took your sweet fucking time, didn't you?'

'Just chewing the fat with Keane,' Rivera shrugged. 'She's a charmer.'

Chapter 71.

'Was Bourse down there then?' Clements enquired, frowning as Rivera and Lefty emerged. The American rubbed vigorously at his wrists.

'He was. *Is*. He won't be able to walk for a while, though,' the ex-soldier reported.

Lefty stepped out onto the deck. He still looked groggy as he shook his head and breathed the night air in deeply.

'I guess we were nearly fashionably late!' Clements grinned.

'Yeah, well – every party has to end sometime,' the freed man answered, flipping Clements the bird. 'So I think it's time for a clean-up. What's the plan?'

'Well,' Rivera began. 'We have two walk-in freezers – it's as you might imagine for an ice cream mogul.'

Lefty nodded. 'And?'

Clements outlined the set-up. 'One has a small crate filled with drugs, and the other freezer has some boxes stuffed with cash,' he explained. 'I'm surprised she didn't have a better way of washing her wealth; maybe she was more old school than we thought.'

Rivera nodded. 'And there I was hoping for a 99 Flake...'

Silence.

'Her company called itself *The Iceman*, right?' Lefty asked.

'Yeah,' Clarke nodded. 'There was a rumour went around that she froze the bodies of some of the people she'd whacked. That way the old bill couldn't tell when they'd been bumped off if they found them. Which – it seems – they never did.'

'Yeah, she admitted as much to me.' Lefty nodded.

'Unbelievable!' Clarke shook his head. 'I mean, Hobson was a prick, but he didn't deserve that. *Nobody* does.'

'Mind if I make a suggestion?' the American asked.

'Carrie was your daughter,' Rivera answered heavily. 'It's your call.'

Lefty nodded. 'Right, well – Rivera and I talked stuff through a while ago.' He turned to the ex-soldier. 'Want to put them in the picture about how things pan out from here?'

'Yes,' Rivera replied. 'First things first, we call Cobb.' He looked at Clarke and Clements as they opened their mouths to protest. The ex-soldier held up a hand. 'Don't worry,' he insisted. 'There's a reason. Here.' He handed the boss' confiscated phone to Clarke. 'See if you can get into it.' Rivera then turned to Clements. 'Root around and see if you can find Bullseye's.' He cleared his throat. 'And both of you have a look for Cobb's number. He probably won't be listed under his real name, but I doubt they'll be too imaginative with what they've decided to call him. I reckon if a call or text comes from either of them, then South Quay's finest will come running.'

Clarke nodded, a little flustered. 'Can I ask why we're calling Cobb, though? I mean, a bent copper's a bent copper - I know Keane's out of the way, but I still don't think we should be involving him. And...'

'...we're going to make him an offer he can't refuse,' Lefty explained.

'What?' Clarke frowned.

'Well, let's just say that a police officer with a gun in his mouth tends to be far less cocky than one who doesn't have a gun in his mouth.'

'Meaning what?' Clements pressed. 'You're going to shoot him?'

'No. Meaning that things are going to change around here,' Rivera said. 'Completely. And by the time we're done, there won't be any point in him calling for more back-up. First, we're going to film him as he makes a confession. We're going to make him outline every single misdemeanour he's been involved with over the years. Don't forget - you guys are all witnesses to what Keane said. We can use that as extra leverage if we really need to.'

'You think he'll go along with that?' Clarke enquired.

'He'll have no choice,' Lefty replied.

'And what are you going to do with the footage?' Clements asked.

'Nothing,' Rivera replied.

'Nothing!' Clements frowned, incredulous. 'Then why do it? You could stick it online or something, couldn't you?'

'No need,' Rivera said calmly. 'If we've got his confession, then there's nothing he can do without our say so. There are plenty of people we can show it to if necessary. He'd be looking at a ten-year stretch minimum.' The ex-soldier paused. 'You know how long an ex-Superintendent would survive in the joint?'

Silence.

'And then what?' Clarke asked.

'Then, if we can get into Keane's phone, we'll call up each and every one of her ice cream vendors. We'll make them drive up here one at a time. In strict secrecy – pain of death.'

'What then?' Clarke frowned.

'You'll see.' Rivera grinned as he spoke.

'And what if we can't get into her phone?' Clements asked.

'We'll ask her nicely.' Rivera shrugged.

'But what if she says no?' Clarke enquired.

'Then maybe we'll ask her again – only not so nicely,' the ex-soldier replied.

'I'll begin by breaking each of her fingers,' Lefty cut in. 'And then I'll start using my imagination. Anyway, I'm off to get us some coffee,' he announced. 'It's going to be a long night.' He paused. 'Can you gents carry the crate of pills down and stick it in the trunk of Bourse's car, please?'

'Why?' Clements asked.

'Part of the plan,' Rivera smiled.

'What about Bullseye?' Clarke demanded.

The ex-soldier paused. 'Well – why don't you two cart him out and stick him down the alleyway? We can decide what to do with him later.'

'I'm not doing it,' Clarke insisted. 'He'll weigh a bloody tonne.'

'Me neither,' Clements frowned. 'I'm an old man. Carrying that bastard would bugger my back.'

'Don't look at me!' Lefty exclaimed, shaking his head at the ex-soldier. 'I've just been electrocuted every fifteen minutes for God knows how long. I need to take it easy.'

Rivera sighed. 'Leave him then,' he said. He turned to the American. 'Looks like Bourse is going to be arrested for murder instead of drugs charges then?'

'I'm comfortable with that,' Lefty nodded. 'We can stick the drugs in Cobb's car instead if we need to – that should help make his mind up. It won't look very good – him in the frame for dealing pills to half of South Quay.'

'But won't he roll over and start informing?' Clarke began. 'Bourse, I mean.'

'I'll have a word,' Rivera answered. 'The thing is – he's only really got one option here. He'll pin it all on Keane. He'll have to. And with Cobb onside, the police will definitely go along with that. They won't have a choice. The other thing is that nobody's ever gone on record against Keane before – law enforcement will be positively salivating at the prospect. Especially the higher-ups.'

'But what are you going to do about her?' Clements enquired, looking down at Keane's unconscious figure. He prodded her with the toe of his boot.

'Chuck her in the empty freezer,' Lefty ordered. 'She called herself *The Iceman*, so let's see how well she lives up to the name.'

'It might kill her,' Clarke said.

'Yeah, that's pretty much the idea,' the American nodded.

Silence.

'What if she's still alive when we're done?' Clements asked.

'Then I'll put a bullet through her brain,' Lefty answered. His voice was cold, unwavering. 'She was never walking away from this. I think we all knew that, right?' He paused. 'She killed my daughter. The police will be only too happy to pin a whole host of other crimes on her. They don't need to have a body to do that. But I do – for my own peace of mind.'

The three other men nodded in grim silence.

Chapter 72.

Lefty returned on foot half an hour later. By then, Keane was in the freezer and Rivera had bound Bourse's broken and shattered knee. He'd not been gentle with him, but he'd ensured the patient was stable.

'Well?' the ex-soldier enquired, seeing the other man approach the loading dock.

'I guess it's time we call Cobb, no?' the American replied. He turned to Clarke. 'Did you manage to get his number?'

'I did,' the foreman nodded. 'He was listed in Bullseye's phone as PC Bacon – hardly the most imaginative name.'

'Hardly the most imaginative man,' Rivera sighed. 'That's if he had any imagination at all.' He turned to Clements. 'Think you can approximate his accent?'

'Can do,' the other man nodded. 'But won't the signal jammer stop the call?'

'It's unlikely to still be working,' Lefty replied. 'It has a limited battery life, remember? You may as well give it a go from here. We'll see what happens.'

'OK,' Clements shrugged. 'Stick it on speaker, then.'

Bullseye's phone worked; it showed two bars, and the call connected. The Superintendent answered after three rings. 'Yes,' the voice came from the other end of the line.

'Get yourself to the warehouse right now,' Clements ordered, growling. 'Alone. We've got a situation.'

'But...' Cobb's voice was panicked.

Rivera pressed the red icon to end the call.

'Think he'll come?' Clements enquired.

'Of course, he'll come,' the ex-soldier nodded. 'He knows who really keeps his bread buttered.'

'So, what now?' Clarke asked.

'We wait,' Rivera replied. 'There's nothing else we can do. Let's shift Clarke's car out of the way, shall we? We wouldn't want to make Cobb wary – not at first, anyway.'

Clements chortled. 'This is going to be great! That bastard's had it in for me ever since Keane came to town. He's picked me up for littering; loitering. Even public affray! I can't wait to see the fucker squirm.'

'Yeah,' Lefty replied. 'Well, just keep out of sight for the time being. We don't want to spook him. Yet. Remember – the signal jammer's stopped working now, so we need to get his phone off him, or at least shut him up, before he gets it into his head that he wants to raise some kind of alert.'

'You think he'll come alone?' Clarke enquired.

'Almost certainly,' Rivera nodded. 'He's a bent copper, so he's not going to want anyone thinking he's in bed with the enemy. But we'll keep our eyes peeled, just in case.'

* * *

Cobb arrived alone.

He was driving his own car. Rivera smiled. 'This is good, lads,' he announced, softly, before the Superintendent cut the engine. 'There's little chance he'll have any kind of tracking device on what he's driving. It certainly won't be the kind of thing they'll monitor at the station even if he does.'

As Cobb stepped out of the car, the four men pressed themselves back into the shadows, noticing the other man was still wearing his police uniform.

The Superintendent's footsteps sounded unnaturally loud as he crunched across the broken ground. Stepping into the yawning blackness of the warehouse, he whistled distractedly and removed a torch from his pocket.

Lefty pulled a lever, and the lights flashed on, blinding Cobb for a moment. He raised his hand, squinting in surprise.

'What the hell's going on here?' the officer demanded, looking around in confusion. 'Where's Keane?'

'Change of plan,' Rivera announced.

'What the fuck are you doing here?'

The ex-soldier nodded towards a chair that Clements was dragging into the centre of the floor. 'Sit.'

The Superintendent frowned, eying each of the four men in turn. 'Do I have a choice?' he asked.

'You do not,' Lefty answered.

Cobb sat down uncomfortably.

'Well?' the police officer demanded in annoyance.

Rivera cleared his throat. 'Do you see that crate?' He pointed towards a corner of the warehouse, just behind the concertina door.

Cobb nodded.

'It's what's inside it that's important.' He paused. 'But you know that already. Don't you?'

'I don't know what you're talking about,' the Superintendent replied haughtily.

'Oh, come on, Cobb!' Lefty cried angrily. 'Don't give us any babe-in-the-woods nonsense. You've been as thick as thieves – you and Keane. You've been taking her money for years. Why else would Bullseye have your number on his phone? And why would you come running here the moment he called if not?'

'I... er... don't know what you're talking about,' the Superintendent frowned. 'Where is he?'

'Here's how it's going to be.' Rivera ignored the other man's question. 'The contents of that crate have a street value of what we reckon to be about eight hundred grand.' He turned to Lefty. 'Is that correct?'

'Maybe even more,' Lefty nodded. He then indicated Clarke and Clements. 'And these two fine gentlemen are now going to carry it out and place it in the trunk of your car,' he continued.

'What?' Cobb's tone was incredulous.

'You heard,' Lefty growled.

'And if you don't do what we tell you to do,' Rivera went on, 'then we're going to call it in. The crate – *your* crate. After parking it on your driveway, of course. We'll make sure your fingerprints are all over it too, but that seems only fair.'

Clements and Clarke picked up the crate and made their way to the warehouse door, shuffling a little under its weight. 'While we're here,' Clements began, 'you're a prick, Cobb. Always were. Always will be.'

'Big words coming from a drunk!' the Superintendent scoffed.

'I'll strip you down and sling you in the same freezer as Keane if you don't shut the fuck up,' Clements growled.

'Alright. Enough.' Rivera held up his hand. Clements and Clarke exited the lock-up.

'That's a lot of dope,' Lefty said, turning to Cobb. 'Any way you look at it.'

'A lot of time,' Rivera nodded in agreement.

The American turned to face the ex-soldier. 'I'm guessing they don't like ex-law enforcement officials any better in the penitentiary here than they do Stateside, right?'

'Not the last time I checked.'

Silence.

'What do you want?' Cobb's tone was icy. 'You clearly haven't brought me here to fuck about, so cut to the chase.'

'A full confession,' Lefty announced.

The Superintendent chuckled.

'Maybe I didn't make myself clear, Cobb...' the American continued. 'My daughter died. And I believe you hushed it up.' He picked up the sawn-off shotgun Bourse had previously wielded. 'I have nothing to lose any more. So, if you want to play games, then you go ahead. But. I'd strongly suggest you don't.' His tone darkened. 'I've had a pretty damn shitty evening. I get a terribly itchy trigger finger late at night. And I'm pretty damn good at disappearing, too.'

'So...?' Cobb asked.

'So, you're going to make a full confession, and we're going to film you,' Rivera answered. 'We're not going to make it public. Unless...' He paused. 'You see, you – old son – are going to change your ways. You're going to become a pillar of the community; a force for good. Just think of us as being like the police watchdog or something. Understand?'

The Superintendent frowned.

'You know when a choice isn't really a choice?' Lefty announced.

Cobb shrugged.

'Well, this isn't really a choice,' the American went on. 'You either do this, or we hang you out to dry.'

* * *

'Satisfied?' Cobb sighed.

'It'll do.' Rivera nodded as he stopped the recording. 'So... how does it feel going straight?'

The Superintendent shrugged.

'You're going to need to promote Malone too – he's the only good man on the force so far as I can tell,' Rivera continued.

Cobb scowled.

Silence.

'What now then?' the Superintendent frowned, narrowing his eyes.

'Well, first, you'd better get used to the idea that you'll be arresting Bourse.'

'Why?' Cobb frowned.

'For Bullseye's murder,' Rivera replied. 'But...'

'What?' the Superintendent's eyes widened.

'That's right,' Lefty nodded. 'You need to encourage him to pin it on Keane. But I'm sure you have experience with – er – manipulating evidence.'

'Where's Keane?' Cobb demanded.

'Next,' Rivera continued, ignoring him once again, 'you're going to clean this town up.'

The Superintendent laughed. 'Do you have any idea how ridiculous that sounds?' Despite his combative words, his tone was one of defeat.

'I mean it,' the ex-soldier continued. 'It's time for you to do your civic duty. Your patriotic chore. Call it what you will.' He paused, his countenance hardening. 'I'm deadly serious.'

'So am I,' Cobb replied. 'You can't stop drugs from getting into a town. Especially not a town like this. Don't you know anything?'

'But you *can* clear out the dealers and stop supporting their trade,' Lefty argued. 'And whoever's been supplying Keane will have to look elsewhere then.'

'You're asking me to do something impossible.' Cobb shook his head.

'We're asking you to do your *job*,' Rivera insisted. 'And it starts now. A journey of redemption.'

'With what?' the Superintendent frowned.

'You'll see,' Lefty said. He raised his voice. 'Clarke!'

'What's up?' Clarke and Clements stepped inside from the deck where they'd been keeping a lookout.

'Have you still got Bullseye's phone there?'

Clarke nodded. 'He has.' He pointed to Clements.

'Anything useful?' Lefty asked.

'Yeah, he's surprisingly organised,' Clements reported.

'Most psychopaths are,' Lefty shrugged. 'And – by extension, their employees.' He paused. 'What makes you say that, anyway?'

'He's got all these groups in his contacts. None of the stuff's encoded – not really. There's even a group called *Ice Cream Vans*.'

'Good,' Rivera nodded, grinning broadly. 'That's going to make things easy.'

'How come?' Clarke asked.

'Because Cobb's gone straight,' Lefty announced. 'And now he's going to tell the world.' The American cleared his throat. 'He's going to start with his drivers.'

Chapter 73.

It was almost dawn when the final van crunched over the gravel and rolled to a halt in front of the warehouse. The driver stepped out and looked around, frowning a little. He yawned and sipped at a can of energy drink. It was still too early for any of the other units to be open; the industrial estate was deserted.

Just like all the others, he looked up in surprise as Clements and Clarke appeared, looming above him.

'What the hell are you doing here?' the driver demanded.

'Yeah, it's been a long time, Leon,' Clarke said. 'Anyway, there's been a change of plan – Keane, that is.'

The new arrival grinned and shook his head. 'Must be a hell of a change of plan if she's letting you two back on board.' He paused. 'Where is she?'

'Inside,' Clements replied.

As Leon stepped towards the door, Clarke moved into his path.

'What's going on?' the man asked. He gritted his teeth; his hackles were up.

'Your Uncle Ronnie passed, so I heard?' Clarke said, affecting an easier tone.

'Yeah.' Leon nodded. 'And the bastard's flat was given to someone else when he died. Whoever the last slag was that persuaded him to walk down the aisle got everything. I've got bugger all left now. I mean... without the – er – ice cream business. And you know what it's like trying to make rent in winter months.'

Clarke nodded. 'Don't worry – head on in. We'll sort you out.'

'What? What are you now – deputies or something? Have you been promoted or what?' Leon frowned.

'Something like that,' Clarke shrugged.

Leon stepped through the door.

* * *

The lights flicked on as the newcomer crossed the threshold. Leon froze. He saw Cobb standing beside one of the two chairs in the centre of the warehouse. Lefty was standing beside him, his arms folded.

'Sit down, Leon,' Cobb said quietly.

'What the fuck's going on?' the new arrival frowned.

'Change of leadership,' Lefty announced. 'Keane's gone.'

'What?'

'Yeah.' The Superintendent's expression was serious. 'I'm going to explain how things will work from now on,' he continued. 'So sit down and shut up.'

Leon shook his head. 'No,' he said, backing towards the door. 'I'm not interested. Not in coppers. Not in any of this shit. I'm leaving. I'm...'

'That would be very unwise,' Rivera broke in, holding up the sawn-off shotgun. 'This isn't a stage prop or a Christmas decoration.' He'd stood around the side of the door, unseen by the new arrival. He levelled the weapon. 'Now go and sit your arse down.'

Leon frowned and walked over to the chairs, muttering.

As he did, Rivera handed the shotgun to Clements, who'd stepped back inside the warehouse. Clarke, meanwhile, kept watch outside. All the ice cream vans had been parked in a space a few roads over from Keane's warehouse. By mid-morning, street corners would be stuffed full of anxious-eyed addicts yearning for the coming of vehicles that would never arrive. Rivera picked up a cardboard box and carried it over to the vacant chair.

'Sit down, Leon,' Cobb repeated.

The man did as he was told.

'Right then,' Lefty said, holding up his phone. 'Name?'

'You serious?' Leon frowned.

'Yeah – you see, here's the deal. That box there,' he pointed at the cardboard box, 'has fifty grand in it.' He paused. 'Keane killed my daughter. I blame her whole organisation for my Carrie's death. But, luckily for you, Rivera here had another plan. He's a little more liberal than me. If I'd have had my way, you'd have all been dead in a ditch by now. But he wants to do some good. To clean up this town. So I decided to humour him. We're going to give you that fifty grand,' he explained. 'But there's a tradeoff.'

'What?' Leon asked, his eyes wide.

'You leave town. And you never come back,' the American continued.

The other man laughed, uncertain. He then frowned as he realised the others were in earnest.

'He's right,' Rivera nodded. 'And now we're going to film your confession. Every single thing you've ever done wrong. All the things Keane had you doing. Everything. Clements here will prompt you – so, when he asks you a question, you damn well answer it truthfully.'

'And then?' Leon asked.

'And then you walk. With the money,' Lefty answered. 'The phone goes in a safe. Nobody will ever see that footage. Unless you come back to town. In which case – *everyone* will see it.' The American paused. 'Understand?'

Leon nodded. Then he sniffed. 'The person above Keane... I don't know who they are. But she cut them a deal once she got hold of all the pills. I know that, because one day – a while back – everything changed. And then she was in charge.'

'So?' Lefty replied.

'So – whoever they are, they're going to want their piece of the pie back, aren't they?' He looked sullen. 'I'll take your money, but there's still a big old organisation out there – you should understand that.' He paused. 'And somewhere out there, there's a shitload of pharmaceutical opioids. Nobody ever knew where she and Bullseye kept the good stuff... maybe nobody ever will know now.' Leon spat on the floor. 'And just because you've cut off the source, it doesn't mean you've got rid of the junkies. They're all going to need their pills soon enough.'

'Yeah, well – South Quay's cleaning itself up now,' Rivera replied. 'The entire fleet of *Iceman* vans is parked two roads over. They're going back to selling ice cream.' He paused. 'And Cobb here – he's going straight.'

'Bollocks!' Leon rasped, laughing in disbelief.

The Superintendent spoke with a heavy tone. 'Just... just do what these men tell you.'

Leon shrugged. 'You'll look well when the ones up from Keane come breathing down your neck wondering why their drug money's dried up,' he scoffed. 'The idea you can clean this place up is just fucking idiotic.'

'Then we'll deal with them using proper police procedure,' Cobb announced. 'And...'

'Let's get on with this,' Lefty interrupted. 'Simple choice. Money – or your life. I'm getting bored with waiting around, so what's it going to be?'

* * *

'So who are you?' Leon asked. 'Police guardian angels or something?'

'Yeah, something like that,' Rivera nodded, not interested in further conversation. He handed the box to Leon.

'You have until sundown to leave town,' Lefty announced. 'If you're seen around after that, your confession will be aired. Everywhere.'

Leon nodded.

'Oh. One more thing,' Rivera said.

'What?' the driver narrowed his eyes.

'Keys. To the van.'

Leon frowned 'But how will I get home?'

The ex-soldier shrugged. 'I don't know. Nor do I give a shit - not my problem.'

'Bloody walk, man,' Cobb said. 'Shank's Pony is more than good enough for the likes of you.'

Leon handed over the keys, grumbling as he made his way towards the door.

Chapter 74.

'So what now, then?' Clarke frowned.

Lefty glanced at Rivera and grinned. He looked back at Clarke and drew out the huge ring carrying the keys to each of the confiscated vans. 'Now you have a fleet of ice cream vans to use as ice cream vans.' He held them out and then drew his hand back. 'Nothing can bring back Carrie,' he began. 'But torching a whole fleet of vehicles in revenge seems pointless. Maybe you guys can do something good here now the dust has settled?'

Clements tilted his head, frowning. 'So we really get the keys?' he asked. He shook his head in disbelief. 'I never had you down as a fairy fucking godmother.'

The American nodded. 'Yeah, well – what can you do? First, though, you need to go downstairs and bring Bourse up.'

'Really?' Clarke asked. 'You don't want to leave him down there?'

'No,' Rivera cut in. 'Cobb's arresting him for murder, so put him in the back of his car. He can drive him down to the station later himself.'

Clarke nodded. 'What about The Diplomat? I mean – that's all built on bad money. And without Keane being around, then...'

'We've spoken to Cobb about that,' Lefty nodded. 'Production ceases – for now. All sorts of laws have been broken with zoning permissions. Not to mention all the payoffs. Cobb's already made the call – the gates have been locked up. No work today.'

'And then?' Clarke pressed.

'Those apartments will still get built,' the Superintendent answered. 'But these gentlemen want some kind of social housing commitment.' He paused. 'So that's what'll happen.'

'And Cobb thinks it's a great idea,' Rivera grinned. 'He's even agreed to set up a charitable commission – the staff down at Keane's call centre are going to be redeployed.'

'They'll refund all the money they've taken first, of course,' Lefty added. 'In full.'

The Superintendent nodded uneasily. He frowned. 'Can I – er...'

'What?' the American narrowed his eyes.

'Well, I'm not too comfortable having the best part of a million pounds' worth of narcotics in the trunk of my car.'

Rivera nodded, chewing his lip. He turned to Lefty. 'What do you think?'

'Well, I'm not thinking of becoming a drug dealer, if that's what you mean!' Lefty replied.

'No, no,' the ex-soldier shook his head. 'That's not what I meant. Shall we just ditch them?'

'How about decanting them all?' the American suggested. 'We can pour them off the end of the pier.'

Rivera sighed. 'You're going to have a whole load of fish getting high!' he grinned.

Lefty shrugged. 'Yeah. I don't care what Leon said. I still reckon if you dry up the supply, then it's the first step to solving the problem.'

The ex-soldier nodded and removed his phone from his pocket. 'Let's just film Cobb tasking us with disposing of the narcotics. I'd hate to think he'd have a change of heart and become too rigorous in executing his duties before the dope's in the drink.' He paused. 'It wouldn't do to be discovered with that many pills. Would it?'

The American nodded.

Clements and Clarke carried the catatonic Bourse past the other men and out onto the loading dock. As he'd been conveyed up the steps, the holiday camp owner's wig had fallen off. The blotchy surface of his bald head glinted palely in the early morning sun.

'Will he be alright?' Clements asked, pausing for a moment. He glanced at Bourse's knee. 'He's a dead weight, and his bandages are covered in blood.'

'He'll live,' Rivera answered bluntly. 'The wound's clean and the bleeding's stopped. I gave him something for the pain. That's why he's out of it. Just leave him out there – move him into the sun.'

Clements nodded.

'What's the story?' Cobb demanded, frowning. 'I mean, when I book him?'

The ex-soldier looked hard at him. 'I'm pleased you're coming round to the idea of the new you,' he nodded.

'Yeah, but what's the story?' the Superintendent sighed.

'Gangland shootout at The Diplomat,' Rivera replied. 'The site's empty, so it's a good fit.' He paused. 'He'd been lying injured for a while when you found him. So book him and then check him in to the hospital. Here,' he said, reaching into his pocket. He withdrew Bullseye's pistol, emptied it of bullets, cleaned it thoroughly, and handed it over. 'If your forensics lads want to roll up their sleeves, they'll see this weapon's been recently fired. And the bullet calibre will be consistent with Bourse's injuries.'

The Superintendent nodded. 'And his car?' he asked.

'It's parked at the far end of the mall car park – the one just off the expressway. Behind the drive-through coffee place.'

Cobb nodded.

'I'm sure you can concoct a story about how Keane tried to frame Bourse and then had one of her goons try to whack him,' Rivera continued. 'It won't be the first time you've had to cover things up.'

The Superintendent frowned as the ex-soldier's comment hung in the air. 'You've bloody thought this through, haven't you, you pair?' He grimaced in begrudging admiration.

'Of course,' Lefty smiled thinly. 'And this is the point when your journey of redemption begins. I mean *properly* begins. Remember – we'll be watching. So fucking behave yourself.'

Rivera yawned. 'You can carry that useless sack of shit Bourse yourself.'

'Yeah,' Lefty nodded, throwing Cobb his car keys. 'Drive safe, asshole.'

Chapter 75.

'Well, that's the last of it,' Lefty announced. He and Rivera had taken the best part of two hours emptying out each of the opioid pills from the blister packs and pouring them into buckets. Throughout, there had been a parade of ice cream vans being driven down the road and out of the industrial estate. Clements and Cobb had called upon a litany of family members to move them. Second and third cousins had been drafted in until the whole fleet had been removed. The pair had vowed that the new legitimate business – *Carrie's American Ice Creams* – would be operational by the end of the week.

Rivera placed a lid upon the final bucket.

As he did, the last two vans pulled up in front of the warehouse. One was driven by Clements; the other by Clarke. The two men climbed out.

The situation was an odd one. The four men weren't given to displaying much in the way of emotions; they were at a loss regarding how to do it.

'I wanted to thank you,' Clarke began. 'Working for Bourse has been like having one hand tied behind my back all this time.'

'And because of Keane, the bastard's had me doing the worst of the worst,' Clements nodded. 'So here's to a fresh start, I guess?'

Silence.

'What'll become of the Golden Sands?' Clarke asked.

Rivera shrugged. 'Depends how good the lawyers are that Bourse hires, I suppose. I'd imagine it'll carry on. There's no shortage of people wanting the kind of holiday it offers.' He paused. 'What's the story with the rest of your work crew, though? They might be out of a job, I'm afraid.'

'Seasonal labour,' Clarke shrugged. 'They're pretty much done now, anyway.'

The ex-soldier nodded. He held up an envelope. 'This is the last of the cash.' He grinned. 'I guess we were a little stingy paying off Keane's lot. I should think there's enough in here to give the Golden Sands crew a bonus. Or severance pay. Whatever you want to call it.'

'Appreciate it,' Clarke said, taking the envelope. 'The rest of the set-up there will work pretty well without him for the rest of the summer – he always was a lazy bastard who delegated everything, anyway. I guess they'll bring in some suits and ties who'll get things to run smoothly again.'

Rivera nodded.

'And this is a little more seed money for the vans,' Lefty announced. 'He held up another envelope.'

'Use it to buy some flakes or something,' Rivera joked. 'But also - give those vans a new look.'

An awkward silence then descended.

'I'm sorry about Carrie.' Clarke spoke first.

Lefty nodded.

'What about Keane?' Clements asked. 'Is she dead?'

Rivera shrugged. 'Maybe. Probably. Hopefully. Let's go and take a look, shall we?'

* * *

The industrial freezer could only be opened from the outside. Rivera wrenched at its handle and the thick door swung open with a screech.

Arranged on the loading dock, the four men peered inside.

Keane lay upon the ground of the empty room. She'd rolled slightly, and her face was visible. The woman was pale, with a blueish tinge around her lips. Frost had begun to form on her eyebrows and at the end of her nose.

'Well?' Clements enquired. 'Think she's cooled off?' He chuckled to himself.

'Yeah – she looks pretty fucking dead to me,' Clarke announced.

'You want to do the honours?' Lefty asked, turning to Rivera.

'Can do,' the ex-soldier shrugged. He stepped into the freezer and held a hand against the neck of Keane's corpse, searching for a pulse. 'Yeah,' he nodded when he felt nothing. 'Pretty conclusive I'd say.'

Silence.

'So...' Lefty began. 'This might seem like an obvious question, but we've got a body here, and it's broad daylight.' He paused. 'Any ideas?'

'Nobody knows about the crypt,' Clements announced. 'I have no doubt Keane's walled in a bunch of stiffs down there. I had a look – I know memory can be a funny thing, but the room's definitely smaller now than it was. I swear.' He shrugged. 'So why not stick her down there with the others?' He paused. 'If you call it in, then you'll have a whole host of forensics here – they'll exhume the whole thing. It'll be grisly shit, but most of them were grisly people. It's all gangland stuff.'

'So, what are you saying?' Lefty asked. 'Let sleeping dogs lie?'

'Something like that,' Clements nodded.

'Sounds logical,' Rivera nodded. 'Bourse will keep his mouth shut about what went on here, if he has any sense. Once Cobb pins everything on Keane, it's not going to be in his interests to encourage anyone to dig up any bodies, anyway. His best bet is having the police think that Keane's still out there somewhere – at large. The less he's implicated in things, the better. That's how he'll see it.'

Lefty nodded. 'But we've still got a great big hole down there. And one of these days, someone's going to take over that warehouse space. Remember, Laramie Holdings will be wound up now. Liquidated. So the lease on the lock-up will expire.'

'And you're sure nobody else knew about this place?' Rivera asked Clements.

'Positive,' he replied. 'It was only Hobson that was supposed to know. And it was only by chance that I had any knowledge – it was always supposed to be Keane's dirty little secret.'

Silence.

'I think we should just fill it in,' Clarke announced bluntly.

'Yeah?' Lefty asked.

'Why not?' Clements shrugged.

'Do you happen to have a few truckloads of earth lying around then?' Rivera frowned.

'No,' Clements shook his head, 'but The Diplomat Hotel site does. And since no work's taking place there currently, nobody's going to kick up a fuss if we borrow some.'

Lefty nodded. 'Good thinking. And then concrete over the top?'

'Yeah,' Clarke nodded. 'There's a whole load of concrete and cement left over in the tool shed at the Sands – we were using it to build the abseiling wall, but Bourse ordered too much. No surprise there...'

'And you know how to do it properly?' the American enquired. 'I mean – we don't want anyone redoing the damp course in a few years and finding a whole load of bones, right?'

'I know how to sort it,' Clements said. 'Thanks to Keane making me a pariah, I've done just about every kind of construction job going. On the quiet, of course. Cash in hand. But I know how to lay a floor: hard-core; sand-blinding; damp-proof membrane; pouring concrete; letting it cure. Trust me.'

Rivera nodded. 'So, can we leave that to you?' he asked. 'I mean – South Quay is a nice town and all. But...'

'...you want to get the hell out of Dodge, right?' Clarke nodded. 'Yeah – no worries. We'll see to it that this place scrubs up perfect. And then we'll screw it up so that it looks torn and frayed.' He looked towards Clements. 'I'm thinking we might even take on the lease here – it's big enough to store most of the vans over the winter, right?'

'Yeah, I like your thinking,' Clarke nodded. 'Keep things on the QT.'

The sun was now climbing in the sky. It peered above the jagged outlines of the pine trees on the ridge above the industrial estate, suddenly flooding the cul-de-sac with daylight.

'So, this is us then,' Lefty announced.

The four men shook hands, wearing serious expressions.

'Where are you staying?' Clements asked.

'I'm at the campsite up near Brushton,' Rivera replied.

'And I'm heading back to Heathrow,' Lefty explained. 'I'll take a train to the airport.'

'Want a lift?' Clements asked.

'That would be kind,' the American nodded. 'Drop me at Rivera's campsite first, though.' He sighed. 'He has a few of Carrie's things for me to collect.'

The men stood for a moment, uncomfortable once again.

'We need to swing by the pier first anyway,' Rivera announced, attempting to lighten the mood. 'Those drugs need ditching – the fish won't know what's hit them!'

'Right you are,' Clements nodded. He turned to Clarke. 'Coming?'

'No – I'm going to see a man about a dog.'

'What?' Clements frowned.

'Cobb. And some truckloads of earth.' Clarke smiled. 'I strongly suspect he might be requisitioning a vehicle for me. I think it'll be best to hit him up while he's still keen and eager.'

Chapter 76.

'Stay out of trouble then boys!' Clements' grin was wide; genuine. He looked over towards where Iris was parked on Rivera's campsite pitch. 'She yours?' he asked the ex-soldier. The campsite was relatively quiet. Occasional wafts of barbecue smoke drifted on the air.

'Yeah,' Rivera nodded. Rosie was in his arms, and he stroked her as he spoke.

'Nice!' the other man beamed. 'So – where to now?'

'I don't know,' Rivera answered. 'I might have to flip a coin. There's a hot woman up north who's gone cold on me. Or...' he turned to Lefty. 'Carrie told me about her Uncle Jesus...'

The American grinned. 'Yeah – he's a character. You'd like him.'

'Amsterdam, right?' Rivera asked as Rosie jumped down onto the floor.

Lefty nodded. 'Affirmative. What – you think you might head over there?'

The ex-soldier shrugged. 'I thought it might be nice this time of year. I'm done with Devon for now – I've only been here twice and both times it's ended up being like downtown Kabul... but with more fighting.'

'I'll give you his number – Jesus,' the American said. 'He's a good person to hit up for work. He always knows someone who knows someone. He's one of those types.'

'Sounds like my kind of guy.' Rivera nodded, grinning.

'Yeah, he would be.' Lefty paused. 'Do you not want to try and patch things up with that woman of yours?' he asked.

'It's complicated.'

'It always is,' Clarke chuckled. 'Anyway, I'll leave you two ladies to it.' He gave a theatrical wave and walked off towards his vehicle.

* * *

As Clarke drove away, the sun crawled out from behind a cloud that had obscured it momentarily. Light shone down in great shafts that made the sky appear dramatic; foreboding. Both men looked hard at the vista.

'Impressive!' Lefty remarked. 'If I was a painter, I'd be setting up an easel about now.' He turned to Rivera. 'So... Carrie's things?'

'Yeah – there's a cardboard box in the campervan. There's not much, but I thought you'd want them.'

'Appreciate it,' the American nodded.

Silence.

'You want a coffee or something?' the ex-soldier asked. 'The kettle's just boiled.'

'Why not?' Lefty nodded.

Rivera stood two folding chairs on the ground beside the T2. He pulled across the canopy, securing it with a couple of poles. As Lefty looked through the contents of the box, the ex-soldier stirred two cups of instant coffee.

'Pretty sweet set-up you have here,' the American remarked. As he sat down, Rosie jumped up and settled into his lap, purring. 'I mean – must feel pretty free.'

Rivera nodded and then looked pensive. 'Yeah – free to go wherever I want.' He smiled. 'But there's some things you can't ever get free from. You ever think about the military? Things you've done, I mean?'

'All the time.' Lefty paused. 'In dreams... and sometimes when I'm wide awake.'

'You think it affects you? I mean – badly?'

He shrugged. 'I thought I'd made peace with my past a long time ago. But it has a habit of jumping up and biting me in the ass from time to time.' He turned to the other man. 'You?'

Rivera sighed. 'I guess it's guilt. Guilt for what I did. Guilt for what other people did. Guilt at the way I didn't stop them. That kind of thing.'

'Is that why you do what you do now?' Lefty asked.

'What do you mean?' Rivera frowned.

'Oh, come on man!' the American sighed. 'You acting like you do. Like a vigilante and all.'

'I'm not a vigilante!' the ex-soldier protested.

'No,' Lefty replied. 'I didn't say you *were* a vigilante. I said you were *like* a vigilante.'

'So?'

'So – you could just drive around the country with your cat; read your books; work a little here or there.' He paused. 'But you do more than that, don't you?'

Silence.

Rivera stepped back into the van and placed the kettle on the hob again.

Lefty chuckled. 'What I mean is - it didn't take you more than a heartbeat to agree to join me on my little quest here, did it?'

'Yeah, well – you looked like you could use a hand...'

'I'm glad you came along for the ride. But, from what I hear, this isn't the first time you've been sucked into something like this.' Lefty nodded to himself. 'I get it. We all have crosses to bear. And – I know it's none of my business, but I've done my time. I've served. I've met guys like you before.' He paused. 'You're trying to make amends. Trying to balance the books.' He rose from his chair and patted the other man affectionately on the shoulder. 'And from where I'm standing, you're doing a pretty damn good job of it. So don't stop. You couldn't bring Carrie back,' he announced heavily, 'but you got justice.' He cleared his throat. 'I appreciate that. And if you're ever Stateside, then give me a call. I'll owe you a beer or three.'

Lefty held out his hand. Rivera shook it. The two men looked hard at each other for a moment and then broke into smiles.

'Safe trip,' the ex-soldier said.

'You too,' the American nodded. 'Wherever the hell it might be that you're going. But do look up my brother Jesus, if you're over his way. Carrie was always his favourite – I guess he'd like to hear about her from you.'

Lefty began walking away. He turned. 'Don't let him get you on the weed, though! He smokes so much of the stuff I'm amazed he can even pilot boats sometimes. I guess he's lucky the canals are pretty much straight.' He paused. 'He'll still drive up and down them in zig-zags, though!'

Rivera laughed. He turned and folded up Lefty's chair. Rosie rubbed against his leg and the whistle of his kettle sounded once more.

He didn't see the figure step silently around the side of Iris.

Chapter 77.

Rivera looked up from where he was folding the chair and smiled in recognition as Malone stepped towards him. 'Nice day for it,' he grinned.

'I'm sorry,' Malone announced.

'What for?' the ex-soldier asked. Something about the Constable's tone didn't seem quite right. He straightened up by the side of the campervan and registered Malone's expression; it was drawn; haggard. He wasn't wearing his uniform – it was the first time the ex-soldier had seen the other man dressed casually.

'This is Keane – not me,' the Constable said, bluntly.

'What is?'

'This.'

Rivera's reflexes had always been lightning fast; he threw himself towards the hand that emerged from Malone's pocket. It was holding a pistol. The Constable's honesty had wrong-footed the other man. He hadn't been on his guard – it gave the policeman an extra split-second to fire.

That was all he needed.

What happened next felt like a blur; slow-motion. Rivera didn't feel the shot that struck him. He was aware of a feeling of pressure on his right shoulder joint. He then watched his hand. It felt almost disembodied as it floated towards Malone's trigger finger. It was a dive that seemed to last for minutes. Throughout it, Rivera never seemed to get any closer to the pistol. His vision kept falling; resetting itself, and then falling again, like the blurred lines on a broken television.

When he finally hit the ground, everything accelerated – it was as if time was rushing; suddenly trying to catch up with itself; making amends for holding him in suspension. He crashed, rolling on the dry grass, and glanced down at his shoulder. A dark burgundy stain was already swelling through the fabric of his shirt.

Chapter 78.

Lefty was almost at the gate of the campsite when the shot rang out.

He turned slowly and took in the scene. Then he started sprinting towards the campervan. The shooter ducked around the back of the vehicle and was gone. Lefty ignored him and reached for his phone instead.

The American reached Rivera and turned him over, examining the injury and grimacing at the blood loss. 'You're OK,' he spoke softly. 'You're fine.' He hauled the ex-soldier up and half carried him towards the vehicle. He then leaned him against Iris' wheel hub. 'Stay with me now, buddy,' he whispered as he stood.

Moments later, Lefty emerged from the cab of the campervan with a pile of freshly-laundered t-shirts. He bundled one of them up and then tucked it against Rivera's wound. 'Pressure,' he ordered calmly, but with authority. He grabbed the other man's free hand and made him press hard against the pad of wadded material.

Rivera groaned.

'I know. I know,' the American cooed, softly. His emergency call connected.

'Which service do you require?' the operator's voice through the speaker sounded metallic; grating.

'Ambulance,' the American said. 'I'm at the Brushton campsite outside South Quay. Male casualty. Mid-forties. Bullet wound. You need to get your medics here now.' He glanced down anxiously at how Rivera's wound had already bled through and was coating the hand positioned against his shoulder. 'I mean it.' The tone of his voice took on an increased urgency as he turned away from the injured man. 'Massive blood loss already,' he announced.

'How bad is it?' Rivera asked groggily.

Lefty slapped his cheek. 'Hey!' he hissed angrily. 'Stay with me.' A crowd of concerned holidaymakers was starting to gather, gawking at the scene before them. 'It's a flesh wound – that's all. Stop milking it – just stay with me.' He paused. 'It'll start stinging in a minute, once the shock wears off.'

'Anything we can do?' a man asked, stepping forward.

'Are you a doctor?' the American asked.

'No.' The man shook his head.

'Doesn't matter. Get on over here and put some pressure on the wound for me, please,' Lefty instructed. 'I'm going to see if we can bandage this better.'

A sudden stillness descended.

'I can hear the waves,' Rivera rasped. He sat up suddenly, frowning.

'Yeah?' Lefty nodded. 'Well, I can hear the ambulance, so hang in there. They'll be here any minute.' He patted the casualty's arm once more.

Rivera leaned back and closed his eyes. He laughed for a moment. 'It was bloody Malone!' he announced. 'The one I trusted. I never saw it coming. I must be losing my touch.' He shook his head. 'Keane must have had something on him – something *big*. He wouldn't have heard about anything we've done. He wouldn't have known we got them...'

'OK,' Lefty nodded. He pinched the quicks of Rivera's nails. 'You stay with us now,' he ordered.

On the breeze, the sound of an ambulance siren began drifting closer.

'Is that soda can cold, kid?' Lefty called out to a nearby child.

The boy nodded, wide-eyed. Innocent.

'Bring it here, please.'

The child did as instructed, approaching uncertainly. The American took it and held it hard against Rivera's forehead. With a gasp, the ex-soldier sat up and opened his eyes. He then sank back and coughed deeply.

'He wouldn't have known we got them...' Rivera repeated.

'I know – it doesn't matter now,' Lefty replied. He looked over at the crowd. A couple of people were waving frantically, directing the ambulance as it approached. The American reached down. Rivera felt cold and clammy to the touch. His voice now was little more than a sandpapered croak. His eyes rolled in their sockets, wildly dilated.

'...we got them...' he whispered.

Chapter 79.

Thank you so much for reading this novel. I hope you have enjoyed it. Should you have a spare 5 minutes and would like to leave a short review, I would be hugely grateful.

Please enjoy the first chapter of FIVE OF CLUBS over the next pages.

Very best wishes.
Blake Valentine

Chapter 80.

The First Chapter of *FIVE OF CLUBS* – the next novel in the TRENT RIVERA SERIES.

Lancashire, UK.

Precisely seventeen minutes after the Talbot Express departed the Foulmile camp, it appeared on the large screen which dominated the basement office of LD Chopper Tours. An instant later, a pre-programmed alert pinged loudly, drawing Sanderson's attention to the moving vehicle. The man had been dozing in a gamer's chair, but sprang into wakefulness.

'Trout!' he called out, gruffly, his voice echoing through the basement office.

'What?' an irritated voice from the adjacent room enquired.

'Get in here!' Sanderson called out more urgently. 'I think we've got a bogie.'

As the other man stepped into the office, he squinted at the same screen as the other man. The grainy outline of an old RV was crawling slowly up the steep slope towards Black Fell Beacon on the road towards Brynworth. The image was wide-angled and jumped slightly; it was fuzzy at the edges where the headlights danced across the uneven tarmac. 'Is it one of theirs? The fucking crusties?' Trout enquired.

'We'll know in a minute.' Sanderson tapped at his keyboard. 'If it is then it's in the right zone.' He paused. 'And there's no other traffic – not by the look of things – no headlights for miles.'

Silence.

'You think it might be a Sierra Bravo job then?' The other man spoke a little hesitantly, raising his eyebrows.

'Maybe. We'll have to see what her ladyship says, won't we?'

'Shit!' Trout sighed, the hint of a smile appearing on his face. 'Fucking death from the skies or what!'

Sanderson scoffed, but couldn't help smiling himself.

Fifty thousand feet above, Big Bird - the military-grade drone procured for the two men - responded to the string of numbers Sanderson inputted on his keyboard. It turned sharply and angled its nose downwards, its focus now firmly on the moving vehicle. At that altitude, the temperature was below minus fifty degrees Celsius; the two laser-guided Hellfire missiles the drone carried were coated with a delicate frosting of ice. It was – as the men knew – invisible to anyone on the ground; the darkness cloaked its vapour trails.

Such weapons were highly illegal in almost all countries. The reason was simple: a drone manufactured to such specifications had no place outside a combat zone. And there was no way a craft of such deadly potential had any reason to be in the location it was – high above northern England.

Especially not when it was being piloted by civilians.

But the drone didn't belong to Trout or Sanderson. Their role was simple: in return for close to twenty grand a month each, they launched the fully-loaded craft when they were instructed. They flew it in a holding pattern within the confines of very specific coordinates. And they waited. Orders came from a faceless source – Sierra Bravo. A well-spoken woman who'd made them her operatives. They'd never met her – they'd only ever heard her voice. Any business conducted with the pair was done through Foxtrot Delta – a man their mistress described as being a handler.

Neither Trout nor Sanderson ever questioned the legality of what they were doing. It wasn't that they were unintelligent – rather the way it was sold to them made the righteousness of what they were doing irrefutable. They didn't ponder the connection between illegal drones; devastating weaponry, and a list of civilian targets. And, anyway, the money blinded them to any moral worries they may have had.

When it came down to it, they believed they were doing good. They believed the few they were sacrificing in would save many more in the long term.

On the rare occasions Sierra Bravo addressed them, she described them as being assets. They were under her protection. And, under the tutelage of Foxtrot Delta, Trout and Sanderson were no longer simply tourist pilots.

They were agents.

***

Earlier, Mohawk and Nomad had punched the air in celebration. The diesel engine of the bruised and battered Talbot Express spluttered into life at the first time of asking. It was a minor miracle: a plume of dark blue smoke emanated from the exhaust and the vehicle's side panels rattled vigorously as Mohawk revved its engine. The RV was thirty-five years old – older than either of them.

Gently slipping the Talbot into gear, Mohawk depressed the clutch and eased the RV over the boggy, broken ground at the edge of the Foulmile Protest Camp. The camp – an ever-growing collection of tents; yurts; cabins, and campervans, clung to the edge of a hillside in rural Lancashire. Its inhabitants were a loosely organised collective led by the shady figure of Daltrey – a veteran of such environs. Their cause was an environmental one: experimental fracking had been started by what was rumoured to be an international conglomerate. Permission had been granted with the understanding that drilling was being done on a trial basis. But Daltrey and his acolytes knew what that meant: the moment Westminster approved it as being safe, the operation would be entrenched. And fracking would spread to the dozen or so other sites earmarked for further experimentation.

Deep down, the protestors knew that once the money began rolling in, there would be no way back for them.

The hillside opposite Black Fell had been ravaged. Though the fracking organisation claimed its work would be done underground, the scarred landscape was clear evidence of the truth. Verdant greenery had been stripped back, and heavy drilling and pumping equipment littered the incline. At all times of day and night, the earth reverberated as high-pressure jets of water and sand were used to drive valuable shale gas out from the broken bedrock where it had remained undisturbed for millions of years. What had once been a spot deemed an area of outstanding natural beauty now looked like a giant industrial wasteland. Beyond the barbed wire of the perimeter fence, hard-hatted men in fluorescent uniforms continually moved vehicles back and forth, and laid mile after mile of thick piping and cabling. It didn't take a qualified environmentalist to appreciate the damage being done; the Foulmile protestors had significant support among naturalists and ecological action groups. And a petition launched on social media had gathered close to three million signatures in support of its cause.

But Westminster wasn't listening. At least that was how it felt. The protest group had sent three delegations to present its petition.

Three times they'd been turned away. But – thanks to a groundswell of support – they'd become a thorn in the side of the fracking efforts. A nuisance. Operations were continuing near Brynworth, but drilling had been stalled at the other proposed sites. And the movement was being kept afloat by regular donations.

***

'Is it on the list?' Trout enquired.

'It is,' Sanderson nodded. With each tap of the keyboard, the drone camera zoomed in. For a split-second the image was blurred; pixelated. Then, its focus sharpened. Once the registration plate was visible, Sanderson checked it against the numbers he'd been provided with. 'Yeah. Fucking bingo! It's one of them. One of the crusties,' he nodded.

Trout sighed and leaned back against the wall. The basement office was built with bare brick surfaces, but it had been modified; it bore the kind of shabby-chic fashion one might expect to find in a converted wharf warehouse in a well-to-do former industrial town. Their office space was located twenty feet below the ground in rural Lancashire. It was a location few people ever saw, but it was decked out with the type of toys one might expect to find in the offices of a profitable software start-up.

The two men had come into a great deal of money. And they had to spend it on something – it wasn't as if they could bank the cash that Foxtrot Delta regularly provided. A full-size snooker table; a collection of pinball machines, and an indoor golf range were among their purchases.

Operating the drone hadn't been their idea when they'd first arrived just outside of Brynworth. They'd purchased the Goreton Hall site cheaply. During World War Two, the RAF had begun building a runway there. Construction had commenced in early 1943, but had ceased shortly afterwards; the course of the conflict had altered by then, and there was no need for a Bomber Command squadron to be stationed so far north.

So the ageing concrete had been left to crack and deteriorate. Nature had reclaimed much of the cleared surface, and the hangars had fallen into disrepair. The foundations, though, remained solid. It was a simple enough job for Trout and Sanderson to freshly concrete a small section of the runway; their helicopter didn't require a huge space to take off or land. And although the hangars weren't worth saving, a new, inexpensive one was quickly erected on the existing site.

And then they were in business.

It was nearly a year later when the call had come. The deal was simple – the drone would be able to operate from the LD Chopper Tours site. It would be stored in the hangar alongside the helicopter. They were to become deep cover operatives and would be extremely well-paid for their trouble.

And that was that.

***

The Foulmile site was located close to Brynworth – the Lancashire county seat centuries before. On a map it was simply a dot between Blackpool and Preston; a name etched against a wash of green. It was a place that – prior to the fracking operation propelling its name into the media – few people had ever heard of.

It was Brynworth to which Mohawk and Nomad were heading. The collective pooled resources like food and fuel; people paid into a central budget, and responsibilities for cleaning and cooking were divided accordingly. The rota meant that it was the pair's turn to visit the supermarket on the edge of the nearby town. Such excursions always took place in the evening – it increased the chances of securing purchases whose prices had been slashed at the end of the day. The protest camp had a vegetarian policy – that way the stews and soups cooked up in giant vats could cater for everyone.

The more the merrier.

Mohawk had a shaved head and a thick beard. Once upon a time, as a dedicated punk rocker, he'd sported the haircut that had give him his nickname. An array of home-grown tattoos with the logos of various bands of yesteryear covered his arms, attesting to his years in the counter culture. He was a dedicated revolutionary: he'd been arrested on numerous occasions; had been evicted from protest sites; had been forcibly removed from forests to whose trees he'd chained himself; had been dragged down from buildings while dressed as a variety of superheroes; had been dug out of underground tunnels where he'd railed against the building of bypasses, and he'd marched more miles holding banners and bullhorns than he cared to remember. Mohawk had never had what would have classed as a regular job. Instead, he'd crossed the country moving from one protest camp to another, fitting in with whoever lived there and hooking up with the loosely affiliated groups of people who trod a similar path. Along the way, he'd fathered several children – some of them he saw occasionally, but most he didn't. The traveller's brother worked in the city. He was a senior partner in an investment firm, and made a salary so large it resembled a telephone number. He was Mohawk's antithesis. The two only met occasionally; usually while attending family funerals. Mohawk believed himself to be a free spirit. His brother thought he was a loser.

Nomad had a PhD in Geological Sciences and a further degree in Ecology. As a career student, he'd only recently strayed from his white tower of academia. Where Mohawk was sharp, streetwise, and gregarious, Nomad was quiet, withdrawn, and naïve about matters of the world. He spoke with a soft lisp and wore his long hair in dreadlocks. The experienced traveller had taken him under his wing upon his arrival. There was a mutual respect between the two men: Nomad admired the other man's survival knowledge – it was from him that he'd learned about how life in the camp operated. Mohawk, meanwhile, used the other man's scientific knowledge to to bolster any arguments he was making. If he was the voice, then Nomad was becoming the brains. Before his arrival at the camp, he'd been known to the world as Barnabus Hoffman-Gates. It had been Mohawk who'd renamed him. It had been Mohawk – too – who'd engineered him getting laid for the first time in his life. After three celibate decades, the academic had finally lost his cherry to an ageing earth mother called Alice who had extremely low standards when it came to members of the opposite sex. Nomad's new friend didn't mention the twenty pound note and bottle of vodka he'd proffered to sweeten the deal. Instead, he'd seen it as a worthy way of securing the other man's undying loyalty.

'Have you got the list?' Nomad asked, looking at the driver.

'All up here,' Mohawk tapped at his forehead. 'I could make veggie shepherd's pie in my sleep, mate!

Nomad nodded. As the pair drove along the perimeter of the fracking site, he looked out at the stationary diggers, JCBs, and pumping trucks. Under the garish glow of security lights, the area was eerily silent – at night, the crew were housed in hotels on the Brynworth industrial estate, or further afield in Preston. At one point, Daltrey had planned night raids on the site where the protestors might damage the fracking equipment. But shortly after drilling had commenced, the perimeter fence had been strengthened, and a private security firm had been brought in. Nomad perceived the pinprick lights of some of the night-watchmen's torches high up on the hill. In recent weeks, they'd brought in further reinforcements.

'Bastards!' Mohawk hissed, angrily grinding the Talbot's gears as the incline increased. The pale beams of the RVs headlights raked across the edge of the industrial wasteland before them as the vehicle swung round onto the steep road that led up to Black Fell Beacon.

'You think we'll be able to stop them?' Nomad asked the other man, for what felt like the thousandth time, nodding at the space beyond the wire.

'Yeah,' Mohawk nodded. 'They might win a battle here and there, but we'll win the war.' He paused. 'Don't worry. We've got the people on our side. You can't buy that.' He narrowed his eyes and stared fixedly ahead as the RV began to climb.

***

'So – do we do this?' Trout looked hard at the other man. 'Call it in, I mean?'

Sanderson nodded. His jacket was a Vietnam War-era replica. It had been purchased from a boutique seller online and had arrived in a state of fashionable distress. He had a large pair of mirrored Aviator sunglasses perched on the black hair that was swept back from his forehead. Trout was similarly attired; both men wore jeans and motorcycle boots. Each of them was the wrong side of fifty. They'd managed to keep most of the spread of their middle-aged paunches at bay, but they still looked heavy. Slow. Their jowls and pock-marked complexions spoke of too much time indoors. And a propensity for booze.

The pair had founded LD Chopper Tours when they reunited a decade after they'd last seen one another. Sanderson had worked for years in Arizona where he'd spent his days flying tourists over the Grand Canyon. Trout had been employed by various different companies in Dubai. Sometimes he'd flown guests on chartered flights, acting as a rich person's taxi service. At other times he'd given tours, flying high over the city's rapidly ascending skyline.

But then Covid had struck. And, suddenly, neither man's services were required.

After successive lockdowns, they'd both wound their ways back to Lancashire, moving like homing pigeons. They'd run into each other on the first evening restrictions were lifted. Standing in line in the pub they used to drink in, they'd renewed their acquaintance. The idea for LD Choppers was simple: people liked the Lake District, and what better way was there to see it than from the air? Founding the company had been a formality, and securing funding for the lease of a helicopter had been relatively easy. Within three months they were turning a profit, and – after two years – they were ready to expand. That's when they brought in Granger, an ex-Navy helicopter pilot who'd fallen on hard times. He'd drunk his way through three divorces in under a decade, and was desperate for any kind of job that would keep him on the straight and narrow. His estranged family had all but given up on him. LD was his last chance.

Granger had fitted in fine. He'd been more than happy to go along with the demands of Sierra Bravo's deputation that had arrived at the Goreton Hall site too. The instructions they gave were easy to follow. They simply had to fly the drone within specific coordinates; the film footage it captured would them be conveyed to Upavon where British Military Intelligence would scrutinise it – at least that's what they were told. The deputation had described the fly-zone as an aeronautical blind-spot; as long as the controllers kept the craft within it, they would be able to ensure it remained invisible and able to do its vital work.

'Why the need for weapons?' Sanderson had pressed.

His question had been met with a cold, hard stare. 'National Security,' Foxtrot Delta had shrugged. 'When we need you to strike, you strike.' He'd paused. 'Otherwise we could have another 9/11 on our hands.' The man had let his statement hang in the air.

In the silence, Sanderson had nodded, grimacing. He'd puffed out his chest feeling a strange tingle of patriotic pride.

'You men have no idea how important the work is that you're doing here,' Foxtrot Delta went on. 'The country will owe you an enormous debt of gratitude. And I mean the entire country. We're talking medals, gentlemen. I mean it – that's exactly what Sierra Bravo would be telling you if she was able to be here in person.'

Buoyed by a sense of responsibility, the men had approached their task with gusto. The only issue was that, one night when he was supposed to be monitoring the drone, Granger had started drinking. And, once he started, he was the kind of man who didn't stop until he fell off his chair.

By the time Granger woke up, Foxtrot Delta had arrived at LD with three other armed agents. They were polite; pleasant even, and Trout, Sanderson and Granger answered their questions truthfully.

Once they'd ascertained who was to blame, Trout and Sanderson were asked to wait in another room.

Twenty minutes later, they were marshalled out onto the tarmac where Granger was positioned. He had been made to kneel down – a brown hessian sack covering his head. His hands were bound behind his back. Two men pointed pistols at him, while another held up a phone, filming proceedings.

'What the fuck's this?' Sanderson demanded, bullishly, rolling his shoulders as he strode forwards, attempting to portray a confidence he didn't feel.

'Heads or tails?' Foxtrot Delta asked, ignoring his question.

'What?' Trout frowned.

'Call it,' the handler pressed, flipping a coin.

'Heads,' Trout shrugged.

'Tails it is,' Foxtrot Delta announced, peering down at where the coin had landed.

'So fucking what?' Sanderson growled.

'So, this is what happens when grubby little drunks fuck up matters of national security,' Foxtrot Delta replied. He spoke in a clipped, unemotional tone. 'We can't take such chances.' He withdrew a handgun and slid out its magazine. Then, using his thumb, he flipped out the bullets one-by-one until there was only one left. Sliding the bolt, he then chambered the final round. Before handing the gun to Sanderson, he removed another gun from his pocket and levelled it at him.

Sanderson frowned. 'What...?' His voice had lost its earlier bravado.

'It's graduation day,' Foxtrot Delta announced, holding out the handgun for the other man to take. 'We take your commitment to our cause as a given. We didn't make you swear an oath - your flying of the drone made it unnecessary. But this is a step up.' He paused and spoke heavily. 'Sometimes just monitoring threats isn't enough.'

Sometimes we have to eliminate them. It's as simple as that – for the greater good.'

Sanderson nodded.

Silence.

'It's time for you to grow a set of balls,' Foxtrot Delta announced. 'Anyone not with us is against us. Understand?'

Sanderson nodded once more, his jaw set firm.

***

'Dangerous bit of road this,' Mohawk announced. He was rolling a cigarette one-handed as he rested his other hand on the wheel. 'If you don't know what you're doing I mean!' He grinned, and turned the wheel slightly. The Talbot wasn't going quickly enough to swerve, but Nomad gripped at the dashboard nonetheless. Mohawk laughed. 'Nearly had you there!' he grinned.

'Is it, though...?' Nomad asked. 'Dangerous, I mean?'

'Maybe,' Mohawk shrugged, yawning. 'Although you're probably in as much danger from sheep and bloody potholes as anything else. The fluffy little bastards just come wandering out like they don't give a shit.' He laughed. 'Here. Hold the wheel a minute will you?'

Nomad reached across and took control, holding the vehicle on its juddering course as Mohawk lit his cigarette.

'Cheers,' the driver said as he grabbed the steering wheel once again. He exhaled a lungful of smoke and then squinted into the pools of yellow cast by the headlights. 'Now this bit *is* more dangerous,' he explained, his tone growing more serious. 'Black Fell Beacon – it's a bit bloody precipitous for the next couple of miles.'

Silence.

'Yeah,' Mohawk nodded to himself. 'I've driven it in the snow before and it was fucking lethal – you leave the road and you *really* leave it. Know what I mean?'

'Long way down, huh?' Nomad said, trying to affect a tone of nonchalance.

'Damn right!' Mohawk replied.

Both men jumped slightly as the ancient hulk rattled over the bars of a cattle grid. The vibrations made the sun visor above Mohawk fall down. The shredded remains of a long-forgotten spliff cascaded into his lap as it did. He laughed as he pushed the visor back up and brushed the mess of tobacco strands, buds, and yellowed cigarette papers onto the floor. 'Not sure we're going to need the sun blinds tonight – we're going to Brynworth, not fucking Bikini Atoll!'

Nomad chuckled.

'Anyway – how about you and that Alice?' Mohawk continued. 'Fancy going in there again? She'd be up for it, I reckon...'

Nomad blushed.

'What?' Mohawk laughed. 'You're a man of the world now, mate! Might as well start putting some notches on the bedposts of that doctoral thesis of yours, right?'

'I thought this was a serious business – protesting,' Nomad replied, changing the subject.

'It is mate. It is. But every soldier has to have a little rest and recuperation from time to time, don't they?' The man paused. 'Even God had a day off, right? I bet even Elvis put his feet up once in a while!'

Nomad laughed. The two men stared ahead as the insipid yellow headlights of the Talbot cut through the pitch blackness towards Black Fell Beacon.

***

The drone's lithium-ion battery meant that it could remain airborne for almost all the hours of darkness. Sierra Bravo had informed them that its main purpose was data collection, but she'd also warned them there would come a time when the missiles might need to be deployed in order to save giant swathes of the population. So, night after night, Trout and Sanderson had launched it, piloting it in concentric circles miles above Brynworth. And, after each flight, they'd dutifully disarmed its ordnance. Once uncoupled, they'd wheeled it to a makeshift silo in a hangar that looked – to all the world- as though it hadn't been touched since the 1950s. As ever, they'd ensured the Hellfires were armed prior to the drone taking off. Deploying the weapons had always been an abstract concept, though; something that would possibly happen somewhere in the distant future.

Until it wasn't.

'Well?' Trout enquired, looking up. 'What do we do?' His expression was slightly drawn.

'It's go-time,' Sanderson answered.

'Yeah?'

'Yeah,' Sanderson nodded, forcibly. 'It's going to have to be – we don't want to risk her ladyship pulling the purse strings back up. Make the fucking call.' He clicked a couple of keys; white crosshairs appeared on-screen. A further couple of clicks turned them into a green roundel.

'What does that mean?' Trout asked, squinting as he waited for his call to connect.

'We're locked and fucking loaded!' the man at the keyboard replied, turning to face his colleague. He theatrically lowered his sunglasses over his eyes, and grinned broadly. 'I...'

'Lima,' Trout announced into the phone's receiver, holding up his hand to silence his colleague. 'Fifty-three point seven eight seven five North. Two point eight nine five three West.' He frowned, listening intently to the voice on the other end of the line. 'You're sure?' he pressed. 'Do I have confirmation?'

Sanderson stared at him, raising his eyebrows.

'Can you confirm th-that I have confirmation?' Trout stuttered. He turned and shrugged, lowering the receiver. Then, he gave Sanderson the thumbs up.

***

'Well, fuck me!' Sanderson announced under his breath. 'I wasn't expecting that – whoever it is in that van must be a proper big shot. Who's driving it – Bin-fucking-Laden?'

Trout's brow furrowed. 'Yeah... How the hell are they going to square this? I mean – it's going to blow a hole in half of fucking Lancashire, isn't it?' He shook his head in bewilderment. 'And this order is straight from Sierra Bravo, right?'

'Yeah – I mean, it must be, mustn't it?' Sanderson nodded. 'She's the only one with the authority. Right?'

Trout puffed out his cheeks and exhaled slowly. He looked hard at the other man. 'So, how do we do it?'

'We press the button,' the other man shrugged. 'Ready?' Despite his usual bullishness, a slight hint of doubt had entered his voice.

'I guess,' Sanderson replied, unconvinced. He hesitated again. The vehicle on the screen hit a point where the road rose and turned to closely follow the contour of a ridge. It slowed; a steep fall bordered each side of the asphalt. 'Fuck it!' The man hit the button, slamming the keyboard several times harder than was necessary.

The green crosshairs turned red.

***

Fifty thousand feet above Brynworth, an electronic pulse bounced off the underside of the drone. The sensors built into its operating systems triggered, setting into motion a chain reaction. Within the space of half a second, the two Hellfire missiles – already locked onto their target – were launched. The drone rose in the air slightly as it was relieved of its two-hundred-pound payload.

An instant later, the missiles' burners ignited in fabulous fingers of flame that spat and streaked across the blackboard of the dark. Had anyone been looking upwards, they would have seen something akin to the wrathful arc of an amphetamine-fuelled comet.

But nobody was watching.

Indeed, the only indication anyone had on the ground of anything untoward was the sonic boom as the missiles broke the sound barrier. From then on, it was a simple case of mathematics: each missile accelerated to its top speed of just under a thousand miles an hour. They were locked onto their slow target, closing the distance with every passing heartbeat.

It was only a matter of seconds before the path of the vehicle and the trajectory of the missiles would intersect.

***

'Have you met Geordie?' Mohawk enquired, scratching at the stubble on his neck.

'No – I don't think so,' Nomad replied.

'Nice guy,' the other man explained. 'You'd like him – he's an intellectual. Just like you.'

'Yeah?'

'Yeah – he's done all these studies on badger habitats. And some nights he goes out and catches bats – the mad bastard! He counts them and studies their populations – shit like that.' Mohawk paused. 'Anyway, I was thinking he could be useful. The pair of you could write a paper or some shit. You know – figure out how much fracking is fucking up the local wildlife.' He grinned. 'The public loves stuff like that. Science and the like. You never know, you could get Attenborough involved. And...'

***

'Wow!' Sanderson slammed the palm of his hand onto the desk. 'Did you fucking see that?'

In response Trout laughed in exhilaration like an over-excited school boy.

Once the crosshairs had turned red, the onscreen picture had juddered a little. For a moment after the launch, the display had turned blinding white as the burners ignited.

After that, the pair lost sight of the missiles; they simply kept their eyes fixed on the Talbot as the red roundel in the centre of the screen remained locked upon it, pulsing.

The room was silent. Both men were conscious of the sound of their breathing; aware of the thudding of their heartbeats.

And then the missiles impacted.

One moment the vehicle was there, and the next it wasn't. The night vision of the drone's camera showed the scene to be nothing more than a giant smoking cloud of dust, debris and destruction.

'Sierra Bravo's going to be fucking delighted!' Sanderson grinned.

'Yeah – I'll take a CBE,' Trout smiled. 'I might even settle for an OBE.'

'You'll be lucky! It was me that hit the button. So, I reckon I'll be outranking you any day of the week.' He paused. 'You'll have to salute me and call me sir, I reckon.' He laughed. 'Beer?'

'Abso-fucking-lutely!' Trout nodded. 'Actually – sod that! Let's land Big Bird and crack out the champagne, no?'

About the Author

Blake Valentine is the author of the TRENT RIVERA MYSTERY SERIES. Prior to becoming a writer, he worked in the music industry as both performer and producer before moving into various roles in education. He has lived in Osaka, Japan and San Diego, California, and now resides on the south coast of England with his wife, 2 children, and a cat.

All books featuring Trent Rivera are available on Amazon and can be read for free on Kindle Unlimited. Please take a look at Blake's website for more information. News, updates and competitions are also featured on Facebook (www.facebook.com/blakevalentineauthor).

If you've enjoyed reading any of Blake's books and have 5 minutes to spare, then do please leave a short review online.

Read more at https://www.blakevalentine.com.

Printed in Great Britain
by Amazon